WE HAVE DEMONS™

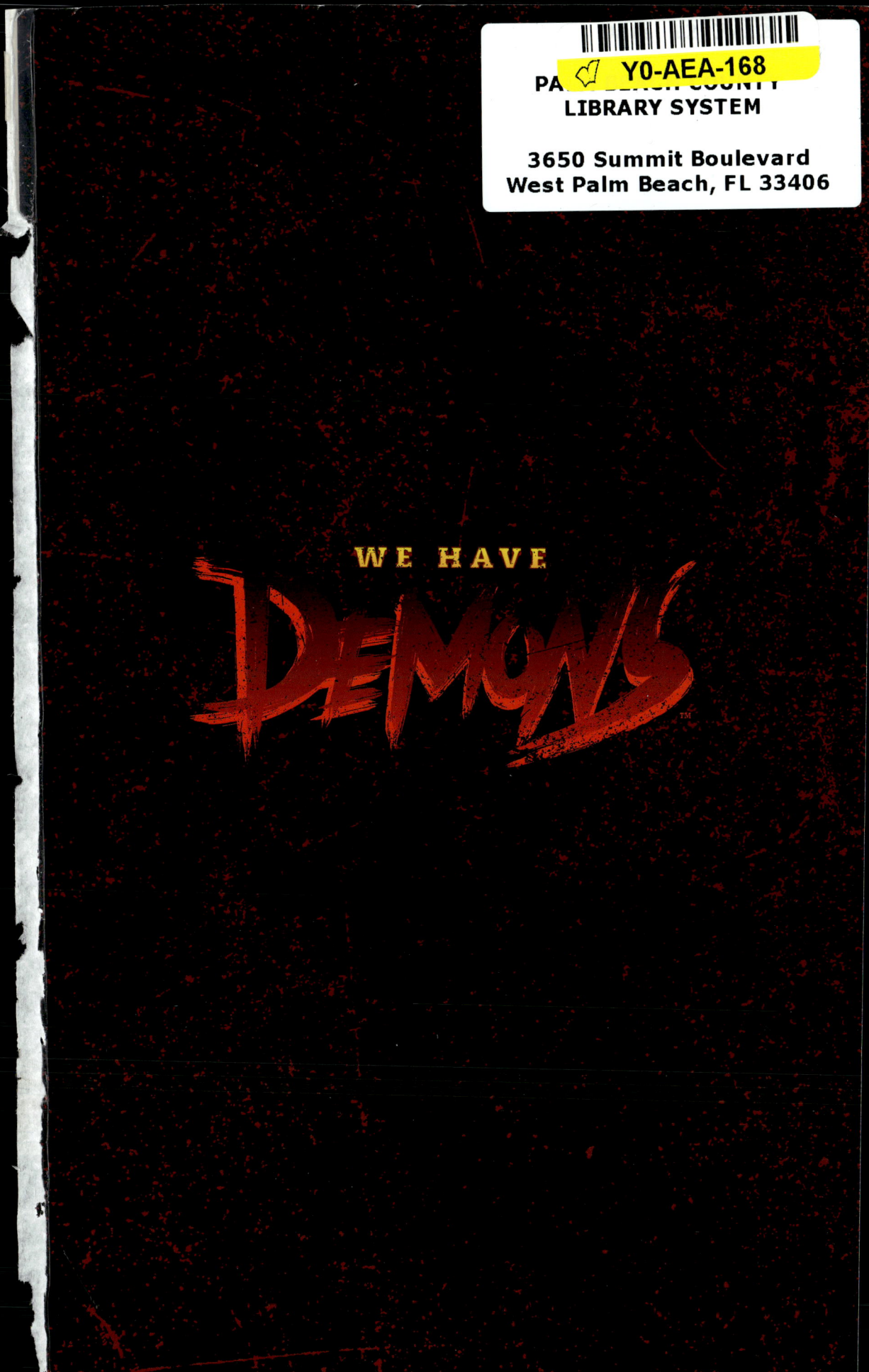

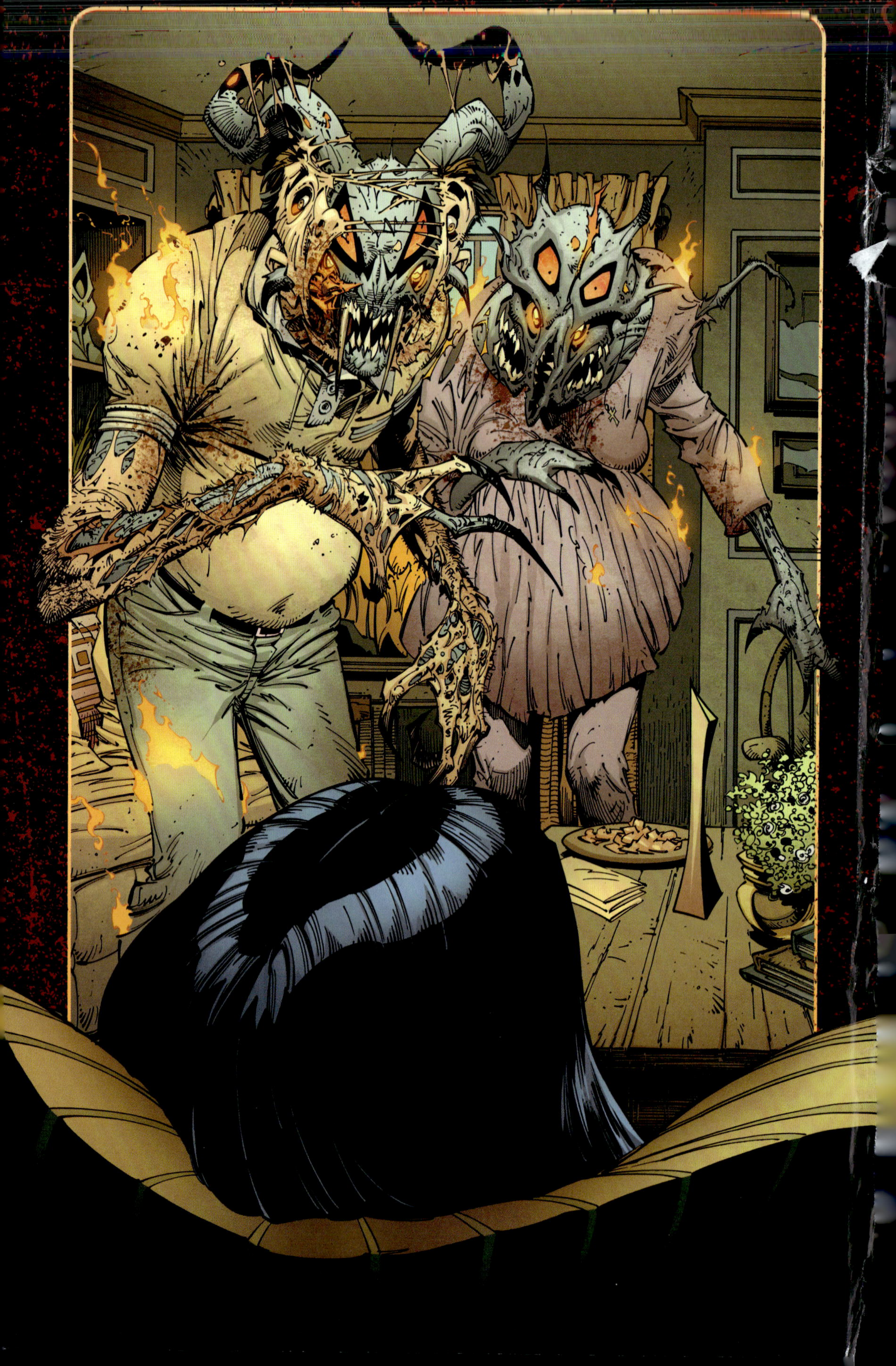

WE HAVE DEMONS

Scott Snyder — WRITER
Greg Capullo — PENCILS
Jonathan Glapion — INKS
Dave McCaig — COLORS
Tom Napolitano — LETTERS

Cover and Chapter Breaks by **Greg Capullo**, **Jonathan Glapion**, and **Dave McCaig**

WE HAVE DEMONS
created by **Scott Snyder** and **Greg Capullo**

DARK HORSE BOOKS

PRESIDENT AND PUBLISHER **Mike Richardson**

BEST JACKETT PRESS TEAM

EDITOR
Will Dennis

ASSISTANT EDITOR
Tyler Jennes

GRAPHIC DESIGN
Emma Price

DARK HORSE TEAM

EDITOR
Daniel Chabon

ASSISTANT EDITORS
Chuck Howitt and **Misha Gehr**

DESIGNER
Kathleen Barnett

DIGITAL ART TECHNICIANS
Josie Christensen and **Jason Rickerd**

Special thanks to **David Steinberger**, **Chip Mosher**, and **Bryce Gold**.

WE HAVE DEMONS

We Have Demons™ © 2021, 2022 Scott Snyder and Greg Capullo. "Comixology" and the Comixology logos are registered trademarks of Comixology. All rights reserved. Dark Horse Books® and the Dark Horse logo are registered trademarks of Dark Horse Comics LLC. All rights reserved. No portion of this publication may be reproduced or transmitted, in any form or by any means, without the express written permission of Scott Snyder and Greg Capullo, Comixology, or Dark Horse Comics LLC. Names, characters, places, and incidents featured in this publication either are the product of the author's imagination or are used fictitiously. Any resemblance to actual persons (living or dead), events, institutions, or locales, without satiric intent, is coincidental.

Collects issues #1–#3 of the comics series *We Have Demons*.

Neil Hankerson Executive Vice President / **Tom Weddle** Chief Financial Officer / **Dale LaFountain** Chief Information Officer / **Tim Wiesch** Vice President of Licensing / **Matt Parkinson** Vice President of Marketing / **Vanessa Todd-Holmes** Vice President of Production and Scheduling / **Mark Bernardi** Vice President of Book Trade and Digital Sales / **Randy Lahrman** Vice President of Product Development / **Ken Lizzi** General Counsel / **Dave Marshall** Editor in Chief / **Davey Estrada** Editorial Director / **Chris Warner** Senior Books Editor / **Cary Grazzini** Director of Specialty Projects / **Lia Ribacchi** Art Director / **Matt Dryer** Director of Digital Art and Prepress / **Michael Gombos** Senior Director of Licensed Publications / **Kari Yadro** Director of Custom Programs / **Kari Torson** Director of International Licensing

Published by
Dark Horse Books
A division of Dark Horse Comics LLC
10956 SE Main Street
Milwaukie, OR 97222

DarkHorse.com

To find a comics shop in your area, visit comicshoplocator.com
First edition: August 2022
Trade Paperback ISBN 978-1-50672-833-9

Library of Congress Cataloging-in-Publication Data

Names: Snyder, Scott, writer. | Capullo, Greg, penciller. | Glapion, Jonathan, inker. | McCaig, Dave, colourist. | Napolitano, Tom, letterer..
Title: We have demons / Scott Snyder, writer ; Greg Capullo, pencils ; Jonathan Glapion, inks ; Dave McCaig, colors ; Tom Napolitano, letters.
Description: First edition. | Milwaukie, OR : Dark Horse Books, 2022. | "Collects issues #1-#3 of the comics series We Have Demons." | Summary: "Since the very dawn of man, legends have been told of the conflict between angel and demon-kind. Lam Lyle, a woman of science, dismissed these stories as just that--fiction. But when the loss of a loved one leads to the discovery of a hulking, benevolent demon named Hellvis, Lam realizes that her life is about to undergo a dire new direction. With a newfound partner and awesome powers now at her disposal, our hero suddenly finds herself thrust into a climactic war of good and evil with no less than the fate of the world hanging in the balance."-- Provided by publisher.
Identifiers: LCCN 2022003208 | ISBN 9781506728339 (trade paperback)
Subjects: LCGFT: Fantasy comics. | Horror comics.
Classification: LCC PN6728.W3986 S69 2022 | DDC 741.5/973--dc23/eng/20220224
LC record available at https://lccn.loc.gov/2022003208

1 3 5 7 9 10 8 6 4 2
Printed in China

CHAPTER 1

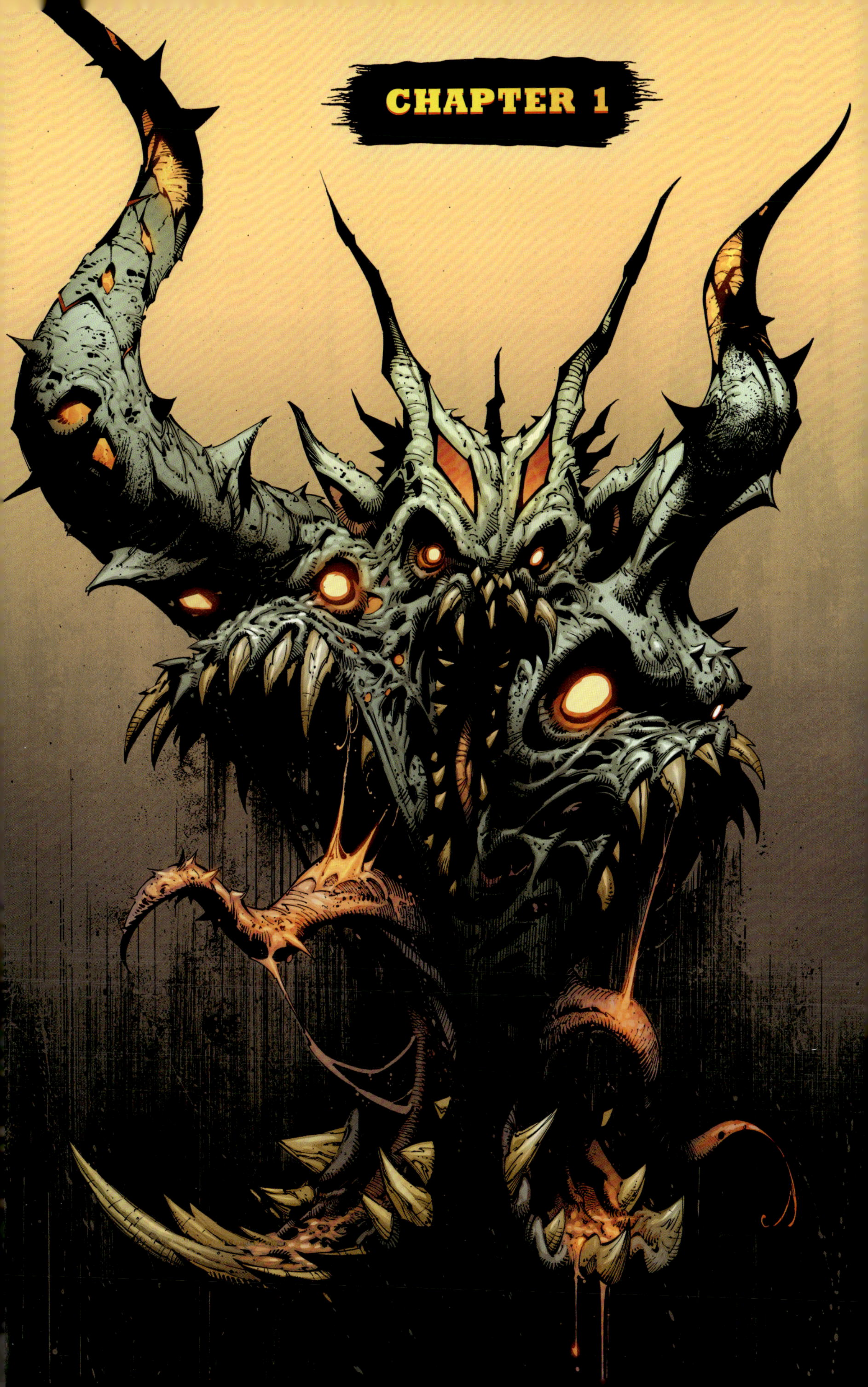

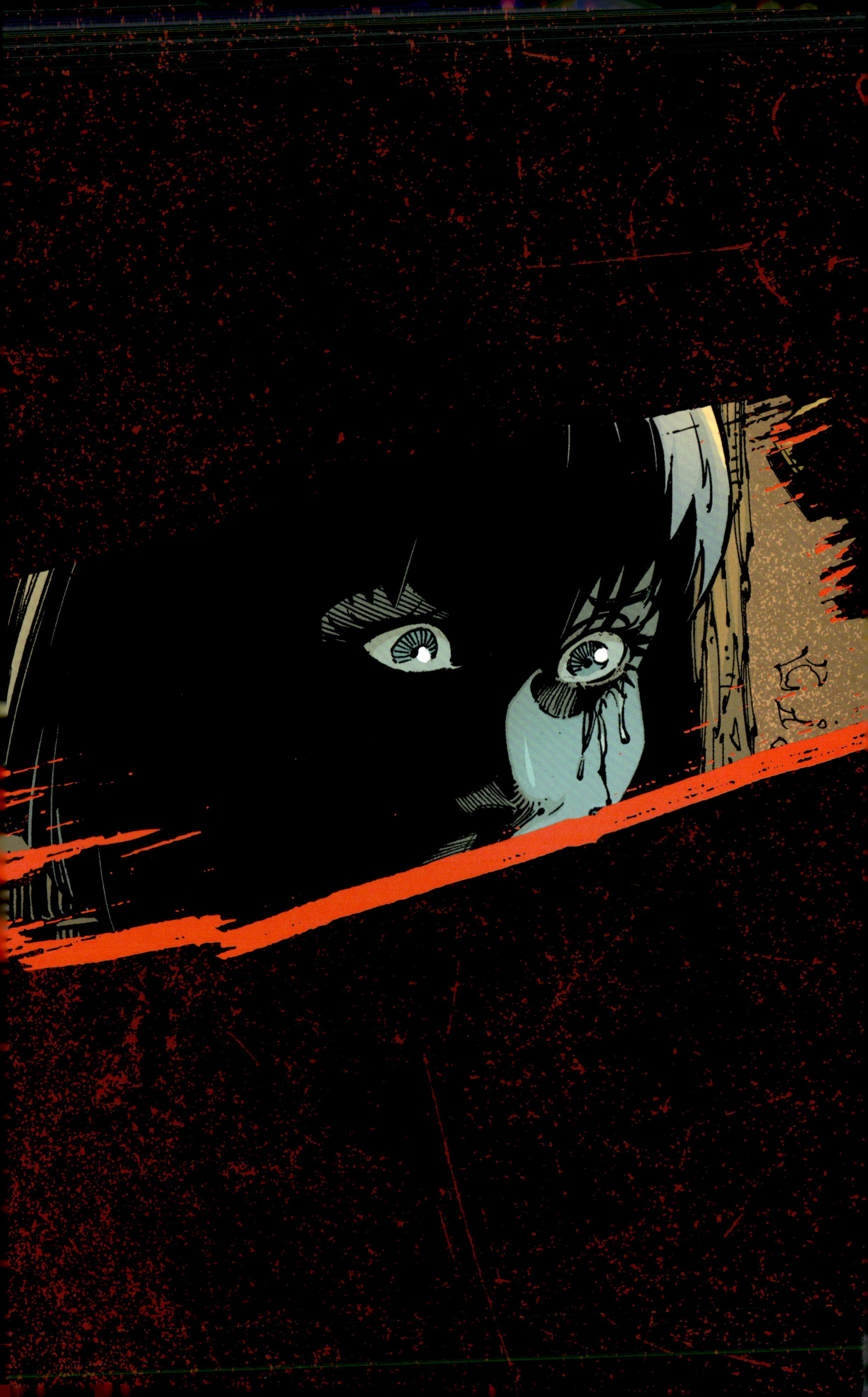

HARK!

Before we start, a WARNING for the squeamish.

This is a story about the Fall of Mankind.
The big FOM. Not in a poetic sense, though.

More in a faces-ripped-off-skulls-and-eaten sense.

Or like in the sense that it has actual DEMONS reaching up and pulling people's GUTS out through their BUTTHOLES while ALL around them the earth CRACKS open and the sky CRASHES down in white-hot chunks that turn their friends and family and everyone they love into clouds of blood splatter and burnt-hair smell. Like in that sense.

BUT... it's also about FAITH.

THAT'S the trigger-warning part. Because for some people (like me), faith makes them queasy. So I felt I needed to just put it out there.
You've been warned.

Now. Where to start?

Maybe with

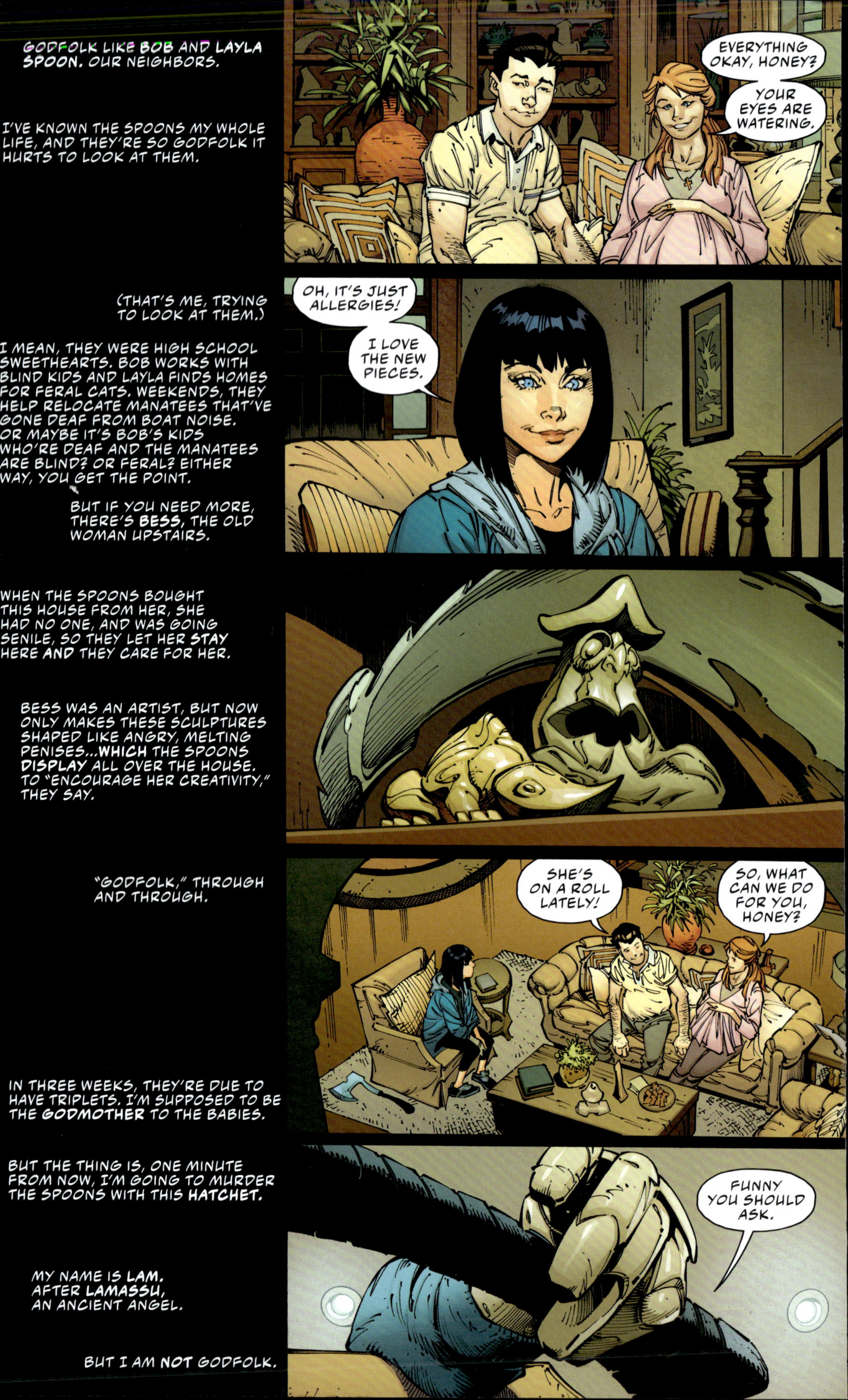
GODFOLK LIKE BOB AND LAYLA SPOON. OUR NEIGHBORS.
EVERYTHING OKAY, HONEY?
YOUR EYES ARE WATERING.
I'VE KNOWN THE SPOONS MY WHOLE LIFE, AND THEY'RE SO GODFOLK IT HURTS TO LOOK AT THEM.
(THAT'S ME, TRYING TO LOOK AT THEM.)
OH, IT'S JUST ALLERGIES!
I LOVE THE NEW PIECES.
I MEAN, THEY WERE HIGH SCHOOL SWEETHEARTS. BOB WORKS WITH BLIND KIDS AND LAYLA FINDS HOMES FOR FERAL CATS. WEEKENDS, THEY HELP RELOCATE MANATEES THAT'VE GONE DEAF FROM BOAT NOISE. OR MAYBE IT'S BOB'S KIDS WHO'RE DEAF AND THE MANATEES ARE BLIND? OR FERAL? EITHER WAY, YOU GET THE POINT.
BUT IF YOU NEED MORE, THERE'S BESS, THE OLD WOMAN UPSTAIRS.
WHEN THE SPOONS BOUGHT THIS HOUSE FROM HER, SHE HAD NO ONE, AND WAS GOING SENILE, SO THEY LET HER STAY HERE AND THEY CARE FOR HER.
BESS WAS AN ARTIST, BUT NOW ONLY MAKES THESE SCULPTURES SHAPED LIKE ANGRY, MELTING PENISES...WHICH THE SPOONS DISPLAY ALL OVER THE HOUSE. TO "ENCOURAGE HER CREATIVITY," THEY SAY.
"GODFOLK," THROUGH AND THROUGH.
SHE'S ON A ROLL LATELY!
SO, WHAT CAN WE DO FOR YOU, HONEY?
IN THREE WEEKS, THEY'RE DUE TO HAVE TRIPLETS. I'M SUPPOSED TO BE THE GODMOTHER TO THE BABIES.
BUT THE THING IS, ONE MINUTE FROM NOW, I'M GOING TO MURDER THE SPOONS WITH THIS HATCHET.
FUNNY YOU SHOULD ASK.
MY NAME IS LAM. AFTER LAMASSU, AN ANCIENT ANGEL.
BUT I AM NOT GODFOLK.

CHAPTER ONE: "THE NYECLOPS"

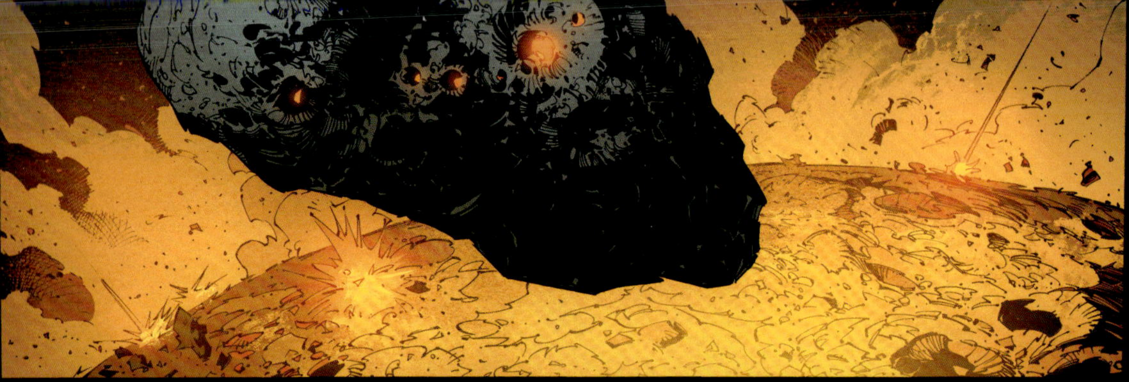

BUT IT'S POSSIBLE I'M
GETTING AHEAD OF MYSELF.

MAYBE I SHOULD START THIS **FALL OF MAN STORY** FARTHER BACK. BUT WHERE? SHOULD I START **THREE BILLION** YEARS AGO? WITH THE ARRIVAL OF THE **PRIME SERAPHIM STONE?**

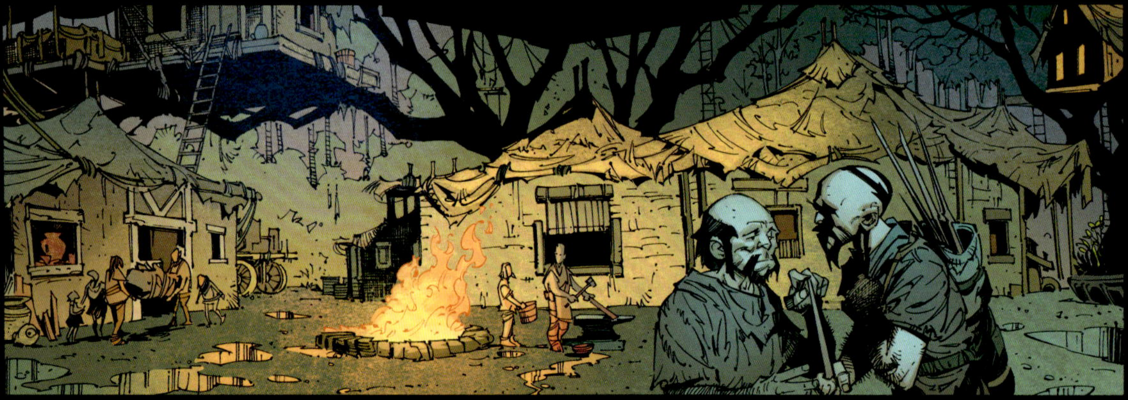

OR **ONE HUNDRED THOUSAND** YEARS AGO, WITH THE **SECRET SPECIES** OF MAN NO ONE KNOWS ABOUT?

OR FIVE **THOUSAND YEARS** AGO WITH THE FORGING OF THE **THOUSAND BLADES?**

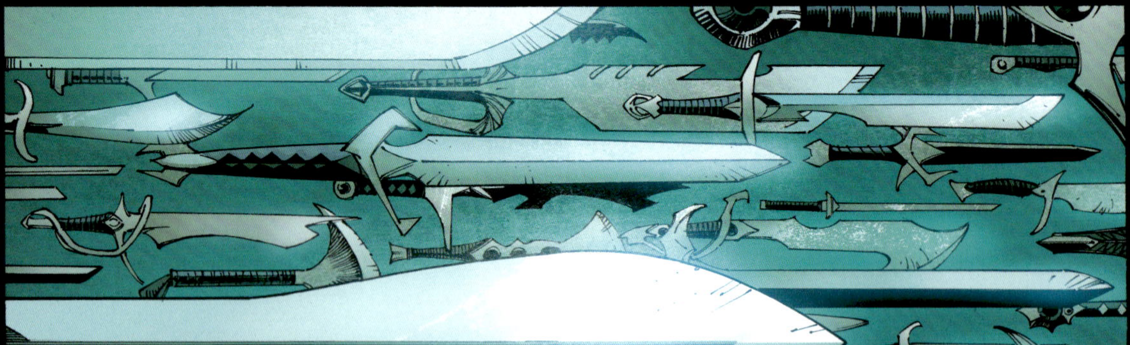

MAYBE WITH **THIS** F.O.M. STORY, I SHOULD JUST START WHERE IT FEELS MOST NATURAL...

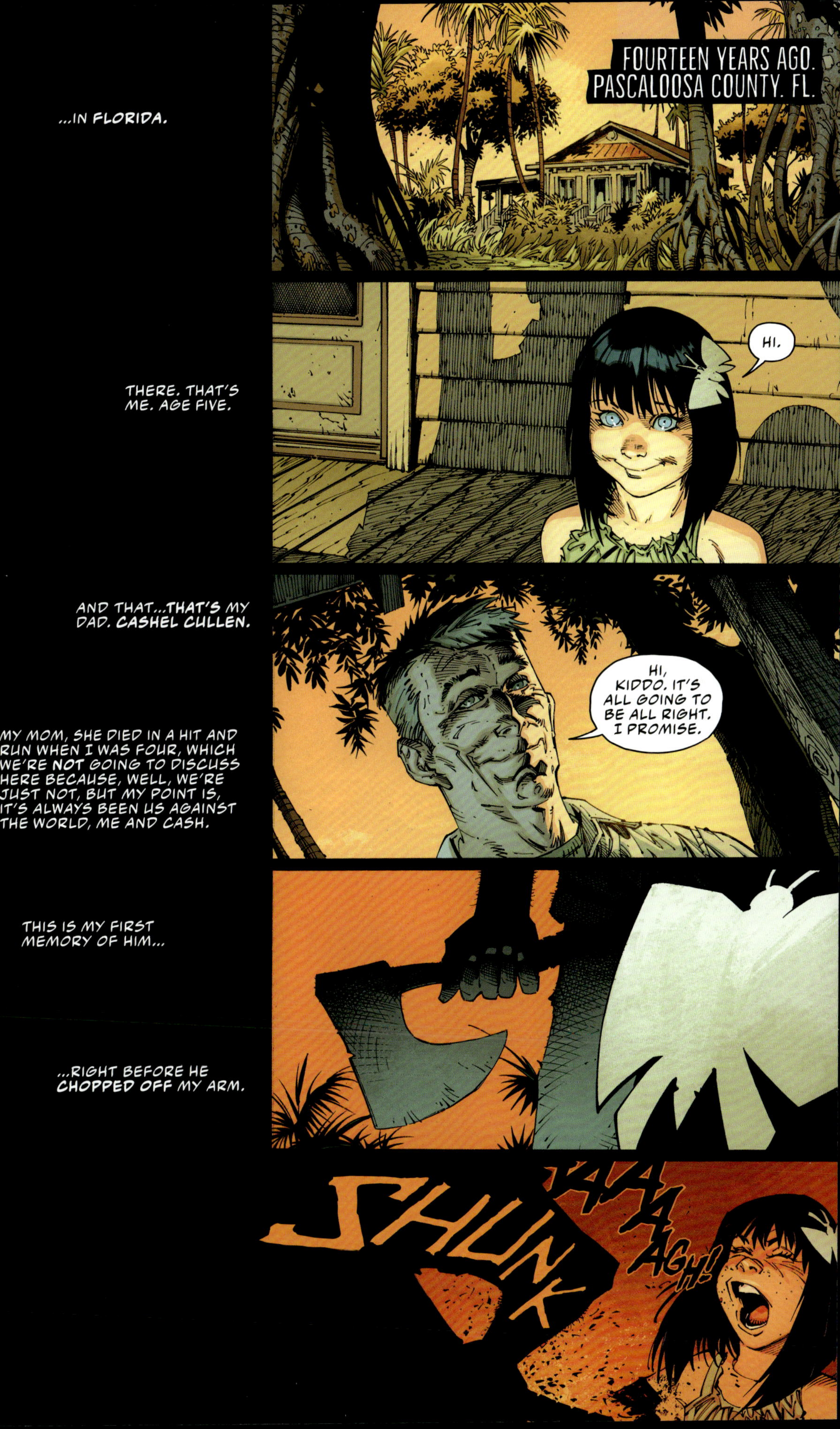

...IN FLORIDA.
FOURTEEN YEARS AGO. PASCALOOSA COUNTY, FL.
THERE. THAT'S ME. AGE FIVE.
HI.
AND THAT...THAT'S MY DAD. CASHEL CULLEN.
HI, KIDDO. IT'S ALL GOING TO BE ALL RIGHT. I PROMISE.
MY MOM, SHE DIED IN A HIT AND RUN WHEN I WAS FOUR, WHICH WE'RE NOT GOING TO DISCUSS HERE BECAUSE, WELL, WE'RE JUST NOT, BUT MY POINT IS, IT'S ALWAYS BEEN US AGAINST THE WORLD, ME AND CASH.
THIS IS MY FIRST MEMORY OF HIM...
...RIGHT BEFORE HE CHOPPED OFF MY ARM.
SHUNK
AGH!

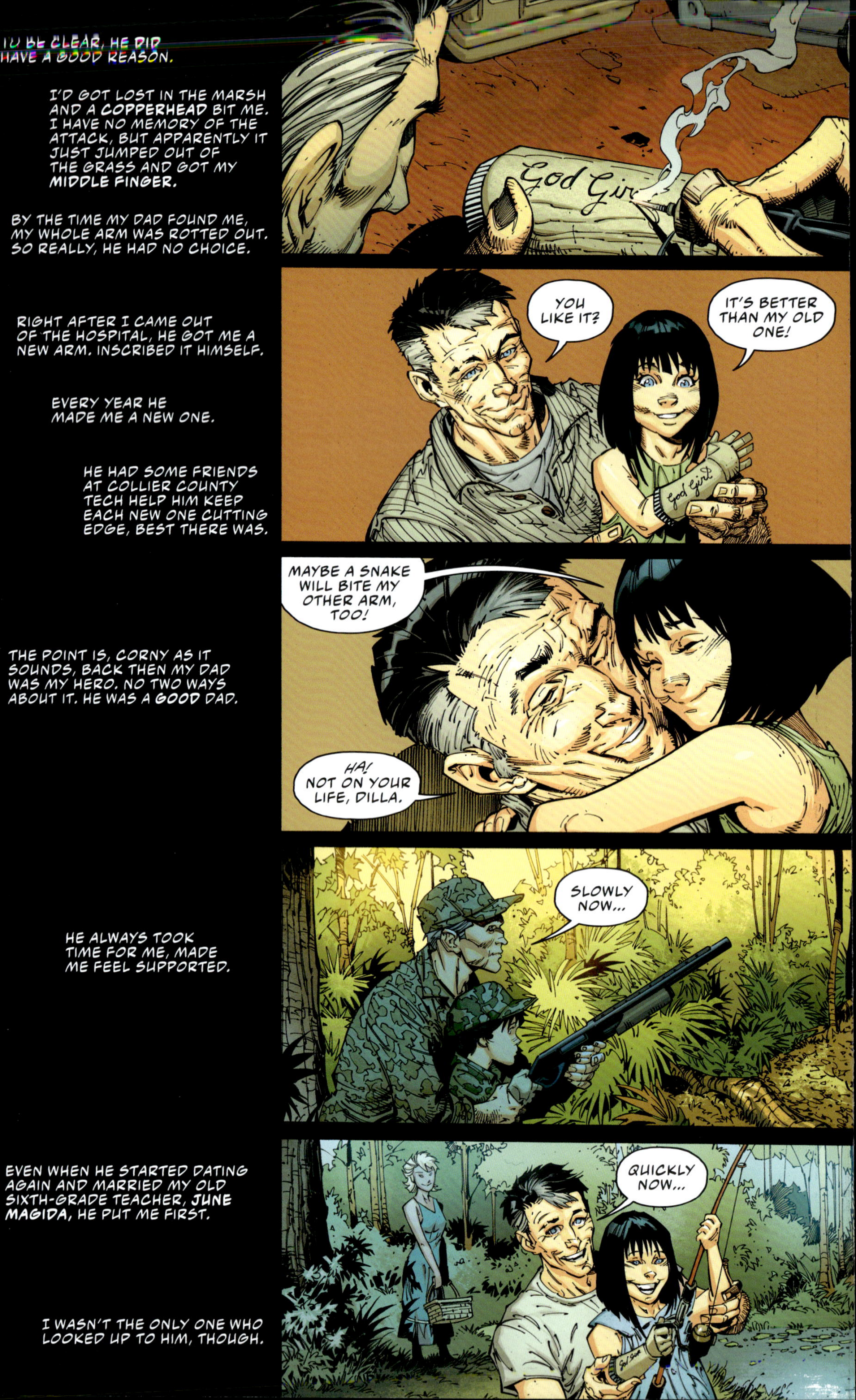
TO BE CLEAR, HE DID HAVE A GOOD REASON.
I'D GOT LOST IN THE MARSH AND A COPPERHEAD BIT ME. I HAVE NO MEMORY OF THE ATTACK, BUT APPARENTLY IT JUST JUMPED OUT OF THE GRASS AND GOT MY MIDDLE FINGER.
BY THE TIME MY DAD FOUND ME, MY WHOLE ARM WAS ROTTED OUT. SO REALLY, HE HAD NO CHOICE.
God Girl
RIGHT AFTER I CAME OUT OF THE HOSPITAL, HE GOT ME A NEW ARM. INSCRIBED IT HIMSELF.
YOU LIKE IT?
IT'S BETTER THAN MY OLD ONE!
EVERY YEAR HE MADE ME A NEW ONE.
HE HAD SOME FRIENDS AT COLLIER COUNTY TECH HELP HIM KEEP EACH NEW ONE CUTTING EDGE, BEST THERE WAS.
MAYBE A SNAKE WILL BITE MY OTHER ARM, TOO!
THE POINT IS, CORNY AS IT SOUNDS, BACK THEN MY DAD WAS MY HERO. NO TWO WAYS ABOUT IT. HE WAS A GOOD DAD.
HA! NOT ON YOUR LIFE, DILLA.
HE ALWAYS TOOK TIME FOR ME, MADE ME FEEL SUPPORTED.
SLOWLY NOW...
EVEN WHEN HE STARTED DATING AGAIN AND MARRIED MY OLD SIXTH-GRADE TEACHER, JUNE MAGIDA, HE PUT ME FIRST.
QUICKLY NOW...
I WASN'T THE ONLY ONE WHO LOOKED UP TO HIM, THOUGH.

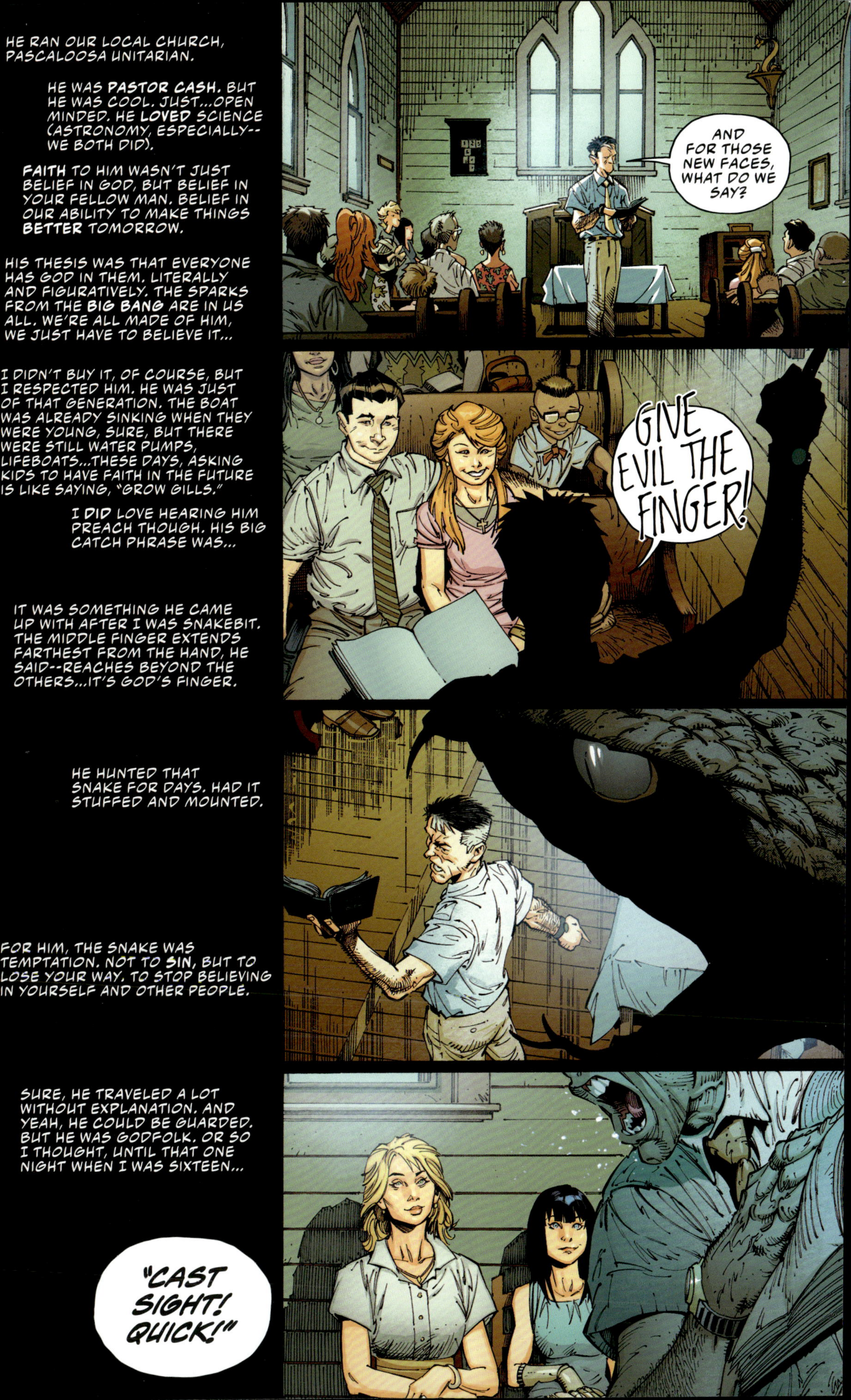
HE RAN OUR LOCAL CHURCH, PASCALOOSA UNITARIAN.
HE WAS PASTOR CASH. BUT HE WAS COOL. JUST...OPEN MINDED. HE LOVED SCIENCE (ASTRONOMY, ESPECIALLY--WE BOTH DID).
FAITH TO HIM WASN'T JUST BELIEF IN GOD, BUT BELIEF IN YOUR FELLOW MAN. BELIEF IN OUR ABILITY TO MAKE THINGS BETTER TOMORROW.
HIS THESIS WAS THAT EVERYONE HAS GOD IN THEM, LITERALLY AND FIGURATIVELY. THE SPARKS FROM THE BIG BANG ARE IN US ALL. WE'RE ALL MADE OF HIM, WE JUST HAVE TO BELIEVE IT...
AND FOR THOSE NEW FACES, WHAT DO WE SAY?
I DIDN'T BUY IT, OF COURSE, BUT I RESPECTED HIM. HE WAS JUST OF THAT GENERATION. THE BOAT WAS ALREADY SINKING WHEN THEY WERE YOUNG, SURE, BUT THERE WERE STILL WATER PUMPS, LIFEBOATS...THESE DAYS, ASKING KIDS TO HAVE FAITH IN THE FUTURE IS LIKE SAYING, "GROW GILLS."
I DID LOVE HEARING HIM PREACH THOUGH. HIS BIG CATCH PHRASE WAS...
GIVE EVIL THE FINGER!
IT WAS SOMETHING HE CAME UP WITH AFTER I WAS SNAKEBIT. THE MIDDLE FINGER EXTENDS FARTHEST FROM THE HAND, HE SAID--REACHES BEYOND THE OTHERS...IT'S GOD'S FINGER.
HE HUNTED THAT SNAKE FOR DAYS. HAD IT STUFFED AND MOUNTED.
FOR HIM, THE SNAKE WAS TEMPTATION. NOT TO SIN, BUT TO LOSE YOUR WAY. TO STOP BELIEVING IN YOURSELF AND OTHER PEOPLE.
SURE, HE TRAVELED A LOT WITHOUT EXPLANATION. AND YEAH, HE COULD BE GUARDED. BUT HE WAS GODFOLK. OR SO I THOUGHT, UNTIL THAT ONE NIGHT WHEN I WAS SIXTEEN...
"CAST SIGHT! QUICK!"

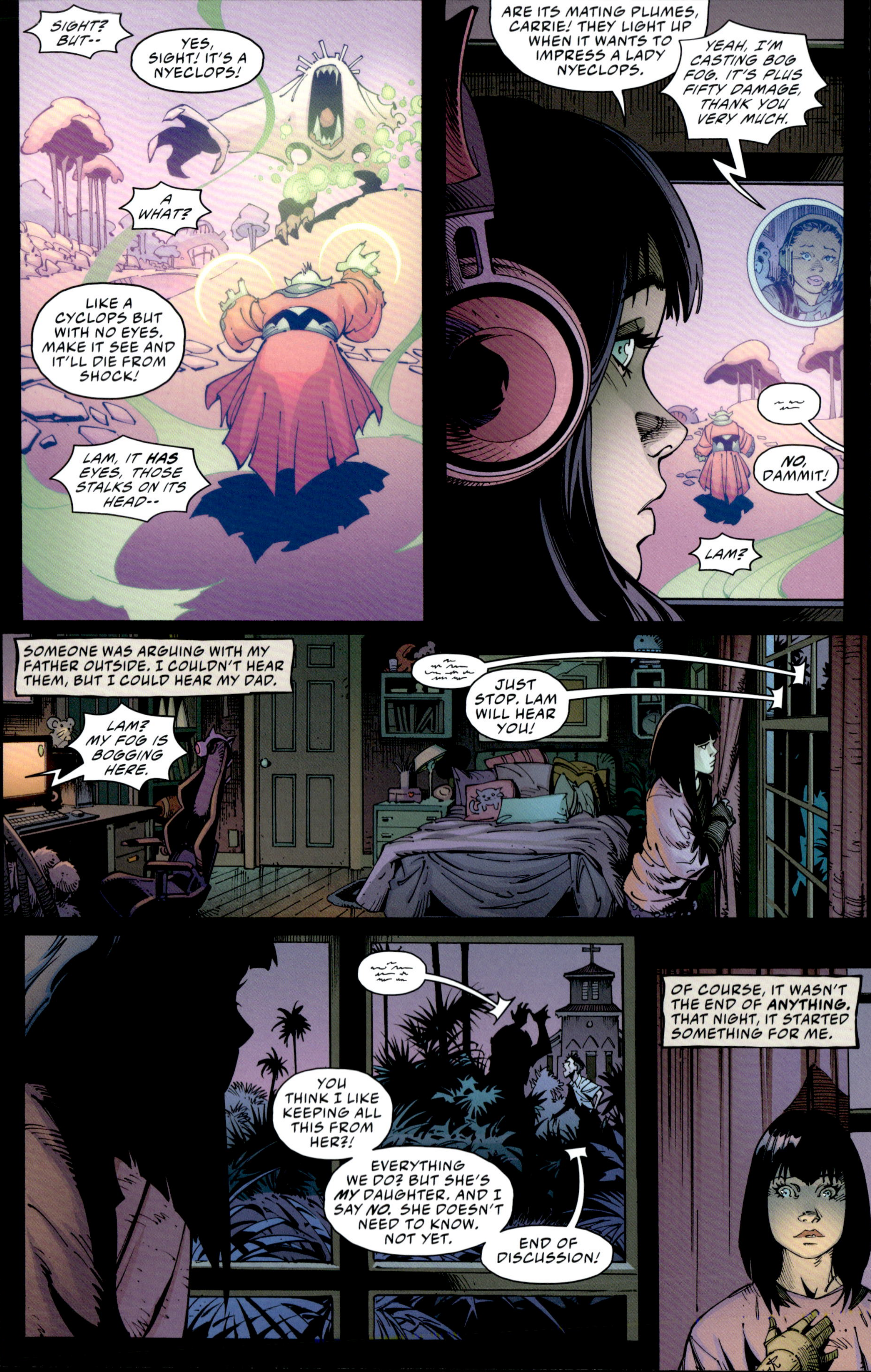
SIGHT? BUT--
YES, SIGHT! IT'S A NYECLOPS!
A WHAT?
LIKE A CYCLOPS BUT WITH NO EYES. MAKE IT SEE AND IT'LL DIE FROM SHOCK!
LAM, IT HAS EYES, THOSE STALKS ON ITS HEAD--
ARE ITS MATING PLUMES, CARRIE! THEY LIGHT UP WHEN IT WANTS TO IMPRESS A LADY NYECLOPS.
YEAH, I'M CASTING BOG FOG. IT'S PLUS FIFTY DAMAGE, THANK YOU VERY MUCH.
NO, DAMMIT!
LAM?
SOMEONE WAS ARGUING WITH MY FATHER OUTSIDE. I COULDN'T HEAR THEM, BUT I COULD HEAR MY DAD.
LAM? MY FOG IS BOGGING HERE.
JUST STOP. LAM WILL HEAR YOU!
YOU THINK I LIKE KEEPING ALL THIS FROM HER?!
EVERYTHING WE DO? BUT SHE'S MY DAUGHTER, AND I SAY NO. SHE DOESN'T NEED TO KNOW. NOT YET.
END OF DISCUSSION!
OF COURSE, IT WASN'T THE END OF ANYTHING. THAT NIGHT, IT STARTED SOMETHING FOR ME.

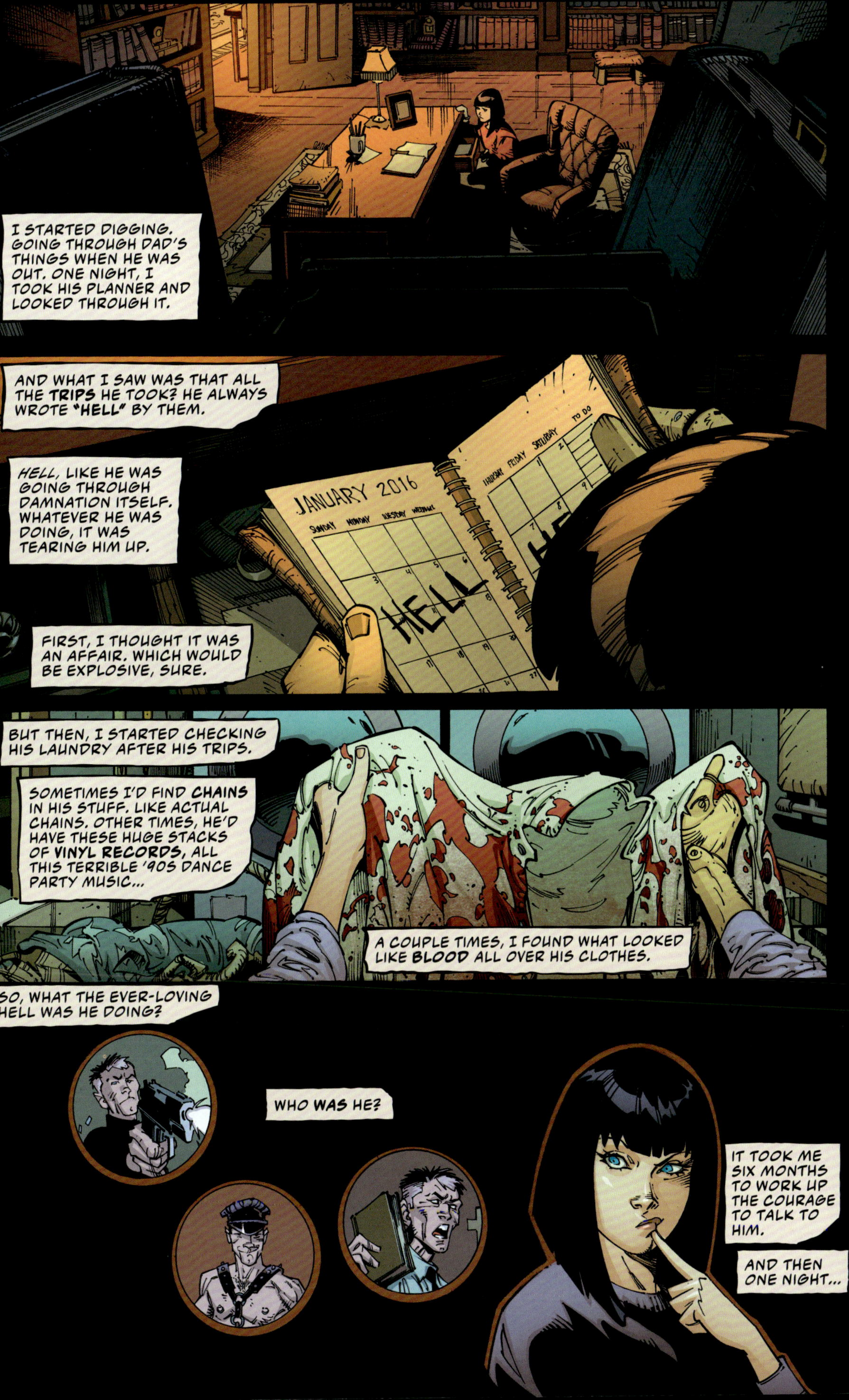
I STARTED DIGGING. GOING THROUGH DAD'S THINGS WHEN HE WAS OUT. ONE NIGHT, I TOOK HIS PLANNER AND LOOKED THROUGH IT.
AND WHAT I SAW WAS THAT ALL THE TRIPS HE TOOK? HE ALWAYS WROTE "HELL" BY THEM.
JANUARY 2016
SUNDAY MONDAY TUESDAY WEDNES
THURSDAY FRIDAY SATURDAY
TO DO
HELL
HELL, LIKE HE WAS GOING THROUGH DAMNATION ITSELF. WHATEVER HE WAS DOING, IT WAS TEARING HIM UP.
FIRST, I THOUGHT IT WAS AN AFFAIR. WHICH WOULD BE EXPLOSIVE, SURE.
BUT THEN, I STARTED CHECKING HIS LAUNDRY AFTER HIS TRIPS.
SOMETIMES I'D FIND CHAINS IN HIS STUFF. LIKE ACTUAL CHAINS. OTHER TIMES, HE'D HAVE THESE HUGE STACKS OF VINYL RECORDS, ALL THIS TERRIBLE '90S DANCE PARTY MUSIC...
A COUPLE TIMES, I FOUND WHAT LOOKED LIKE BLOOD ALL OVER HIS CLOTHES.
SO, WHAT THE EVER-LOVING HELL WAS HE DOING?
WHO WAS HE?
IT TOOK ME SIX MONTHS TO WORK UP THE COURAGE TO TALK TO HIM.
AND THEN ONE NIGHT...

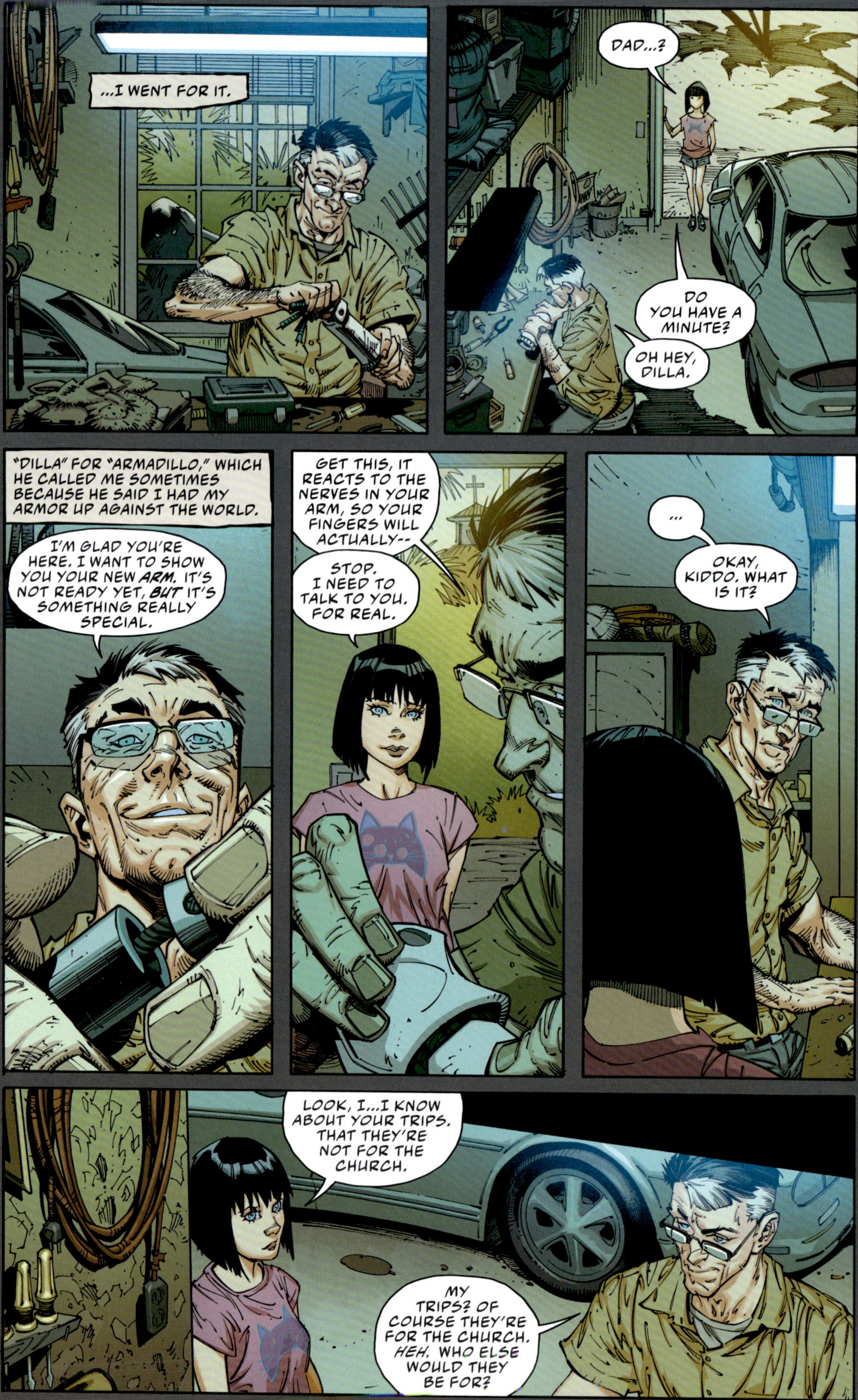
...I WENT FOR IT.
DAD...?
DO YOU HAVE A MINUTE?
OH HEY, DILLA.
"DILLA" FOR "ARMADILLO," WHICH HE CALLED ME SOMETIMES BECAUSE HE SAID I HAD MY ARMOR UP AGAINST THE WORLD.
I'M GLAD YOU'RE HERE. I WANT TO SHOW YOU YOUR NEW *ARM*. IT'S NOT READY YET, *BUT* IT'S SOMETHING REALLY SPECIAL.
GET THIS, IT REACTS TO THE NERVES IN YOUR ARM, SO YOUR FINGERS WILL ACTUALLY--
STOP. I NEED TO TALK TO YOU. FOR REAL.
...
OKAY, KIDDO. WHAT IS IT?
LOOK, I...I KNOW ABOUT YOUR TRIPS. THAT THEY'RE NOT FOR THE CHURCH.
MY TRIPS? OF COURSE THEY'RE FOR THE CHURCH. *HEH.* WHO ELSE WOULD THEY BE FOR?

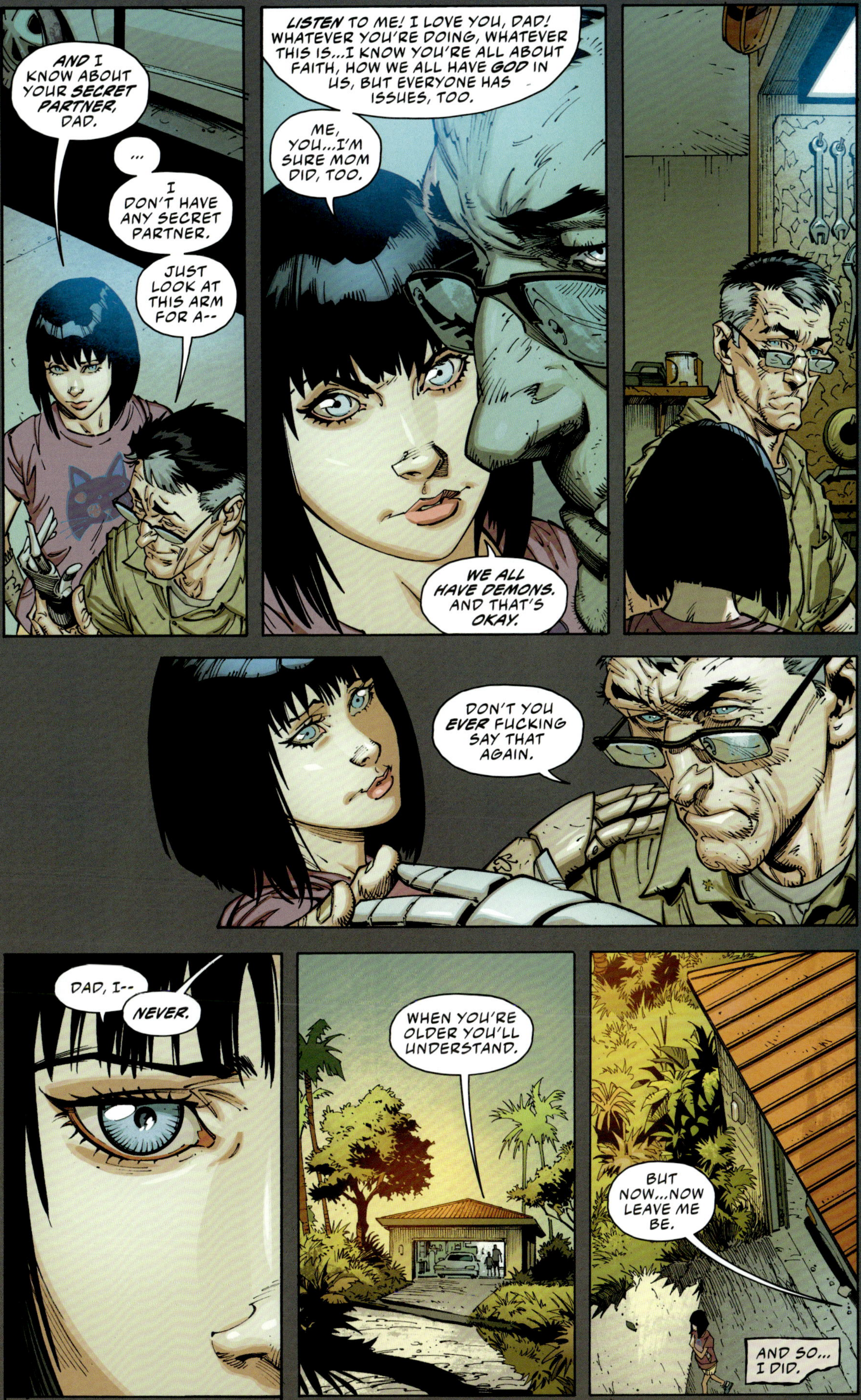
AND I KNOW ABOUT YOUR SECRET PARTNER, DAD.
...
I DON'T HAVE ANY SECRET PARTNER.
JUST LOOK AT THIS ARM FOR A--
LISTEN TO ME! I LOVE YOU, DAD! WHATEVER YOU'RE DOING, WHATEVER THIS IS...I KNOW YOU'RE ALL ABOUT FAITH, HOW WE ALL HAVE GOD IN US, BUT EVERYONE HAS ISSUES, TOO.
ME, YOU...I'M SURE MOM DID, TOO.
WE ALL HAVE DEMONS. AND THAT'S OKAY.
DON'T YOU EVER FUCKING SAY THAT AGAIN.
DAD, I--
NEVER.
WHEN YOU'RE OLDER YOU'LL UNDERSTAND.
BUT NOW...NOW LEAVE ME BE.
AND SO... I DID.

CHAPTER TWO:
"PASSAGE"

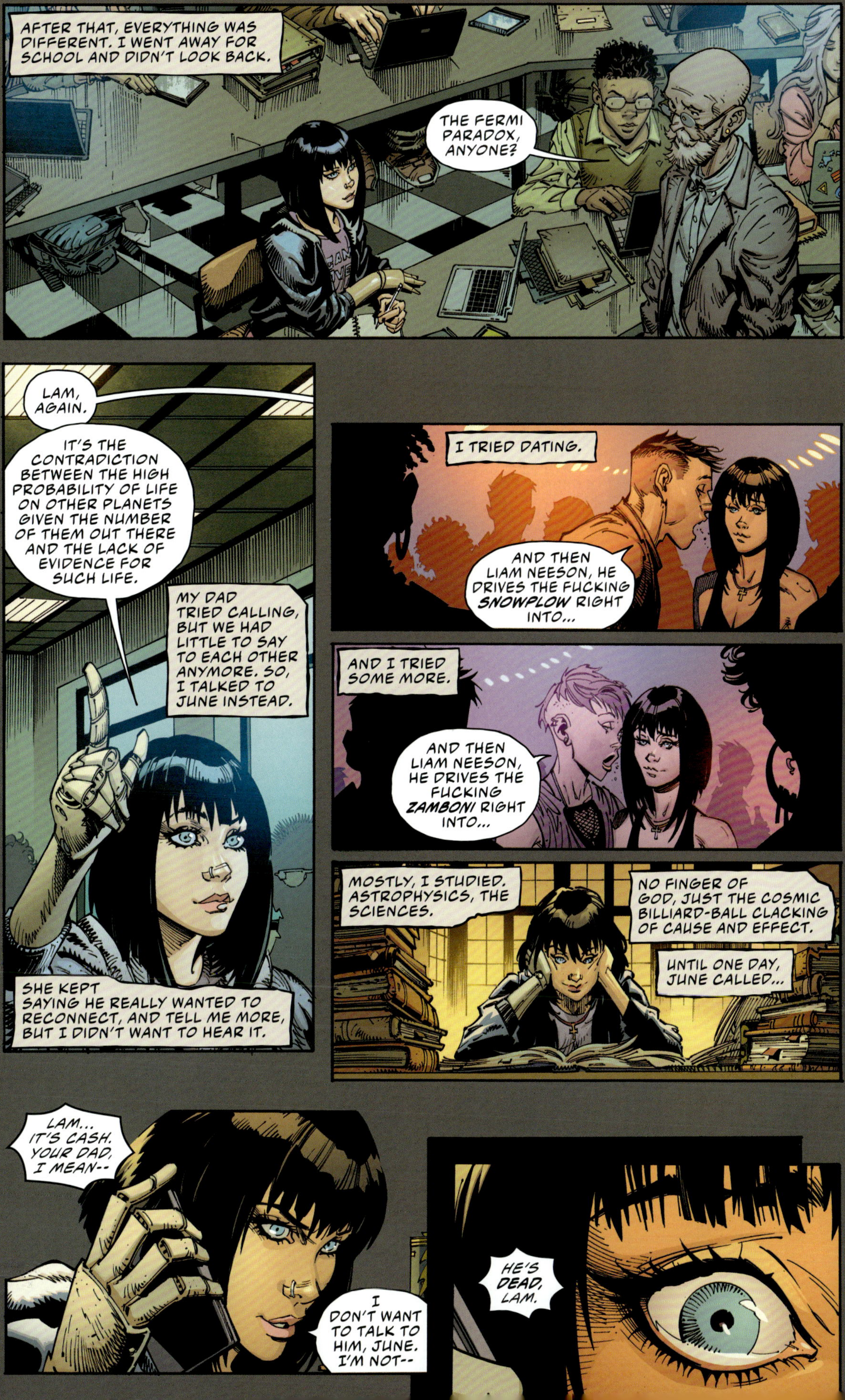
AFTER THAT, EVERYTHING WAS DIFFERENT. I WENT AWAY FOR SCHOOL AND DIDN'T LOOK BACK.
THE FERMI PARADOX, ANYONE?
LAM, AGAIN.
IT'S THE CONTRADICTION BETWEEN THE HIGH PROBABILITY OF LIFE ON OTHER PLANETS GIVEN THE NUMBER OF THEM OUT THERE AND THE LACK OF EVIDENCE FOR SUCH LIFE.
MY DAD TRIED CALLING, BUT WE HAD LITTLE TO SAY TO EACH OTHER ANYMORE. SO, I TALKED TO JUNE INSTEAD.
SHE KEPT SAYING HE REALLY WANTED TO RECONNECT, AND TELL ME MORE, BUT I DIDN'T WANT TO HEAR IT.
I TRIED DATING.
AND THEN LIAM NEESON, HE DRIVES THE FUCKING SNOWPLOW RIGHT INTO...
AND I TRIED SOME MORE.
AND THEN LIAM NEESON, HE DRIVES THE FUCKING ZAMBONI RIGHT INTO...
MOSTLY, I STUDIED. ASTROPHYSICS, THE SCIENCES.
NO FINGER OF GOD, JUST THE COSMIC BILLIARD-BALL CLACKING OF CAUSE AND EFFECT.
UNTIL ONE DAY, JUNE CALLED...
LAM... IT'S CASH. YOUR DAD, I MEAN--
I DON'T WANT TO TALK TO HIM, JUNE. I'M NOT--
HE'S DEAD, LAM.

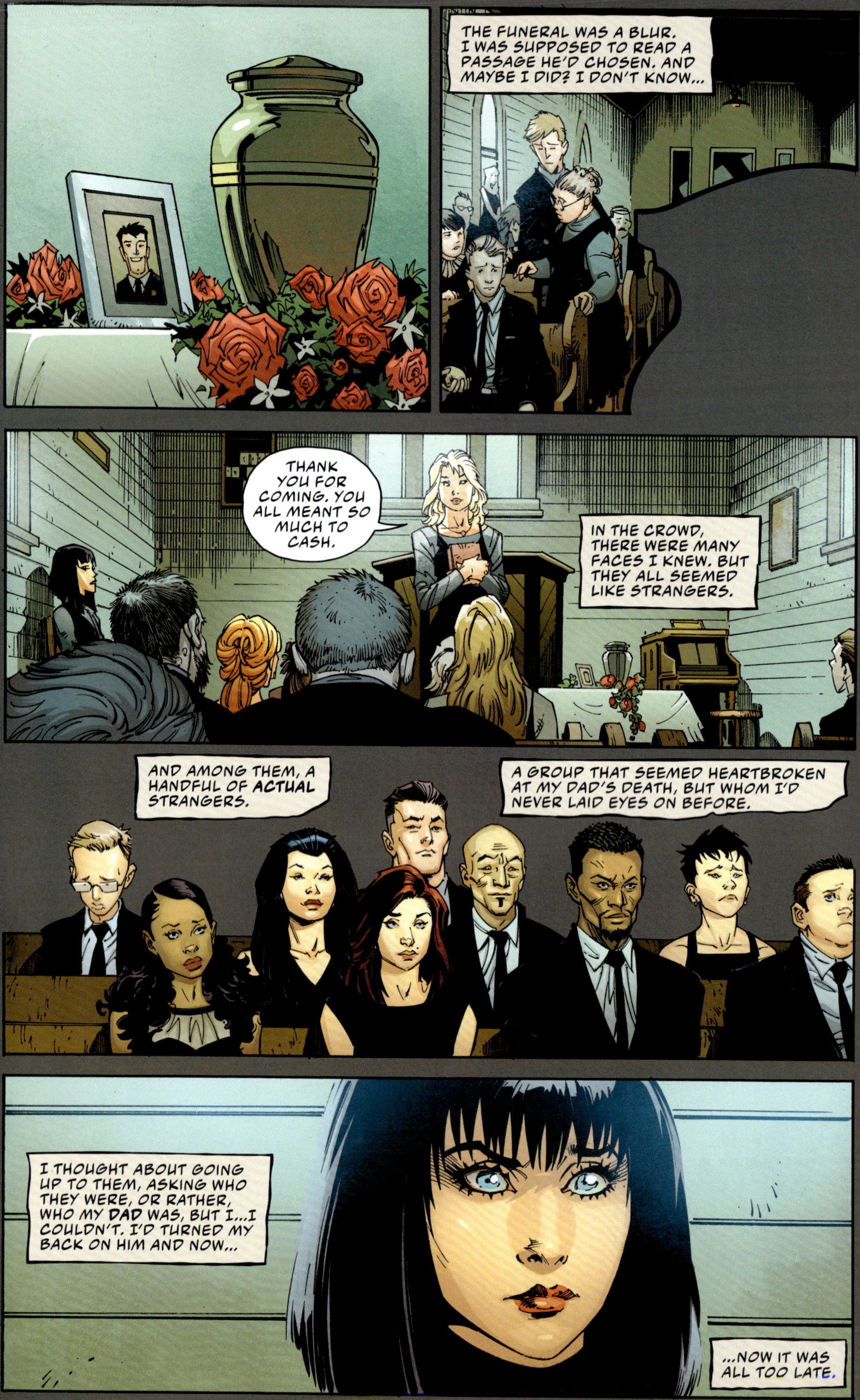
THE FUNERAL WAS A BLUR. I WAS SUPPOSED TO READ A PASSAGE HE'D CHOSEN. AND MAYBE I DID? I DON'T KNOW...
THANK YOU FOR COMING. YOU ALL MEANT SO MUCH TO CASH.
IN THE CROWD, THERE WERE MANY FACES I KNEW. BUT THEY ALL SEEMED LIKE STRANGERS.
AND AMONG THEM, A HANDFUL OF ACTUAL STRANGERS.
A GROUP THAT SEEMED HEARTBROKEN AT MY DAD'S DEATH, BUT WHOM I'D NEVER LAID EYES ON BEFORE.
I THOUGHT ABOUT GOING UP TO THEM, ASKING WHO THEY WERE, OR RATHER, WHO MY DAD WAS, BUT I...I COULDN'T. I'D TURNED MY BACK ON HIM AND NOW...
...NOW IT WAS ALL TOO LATE.

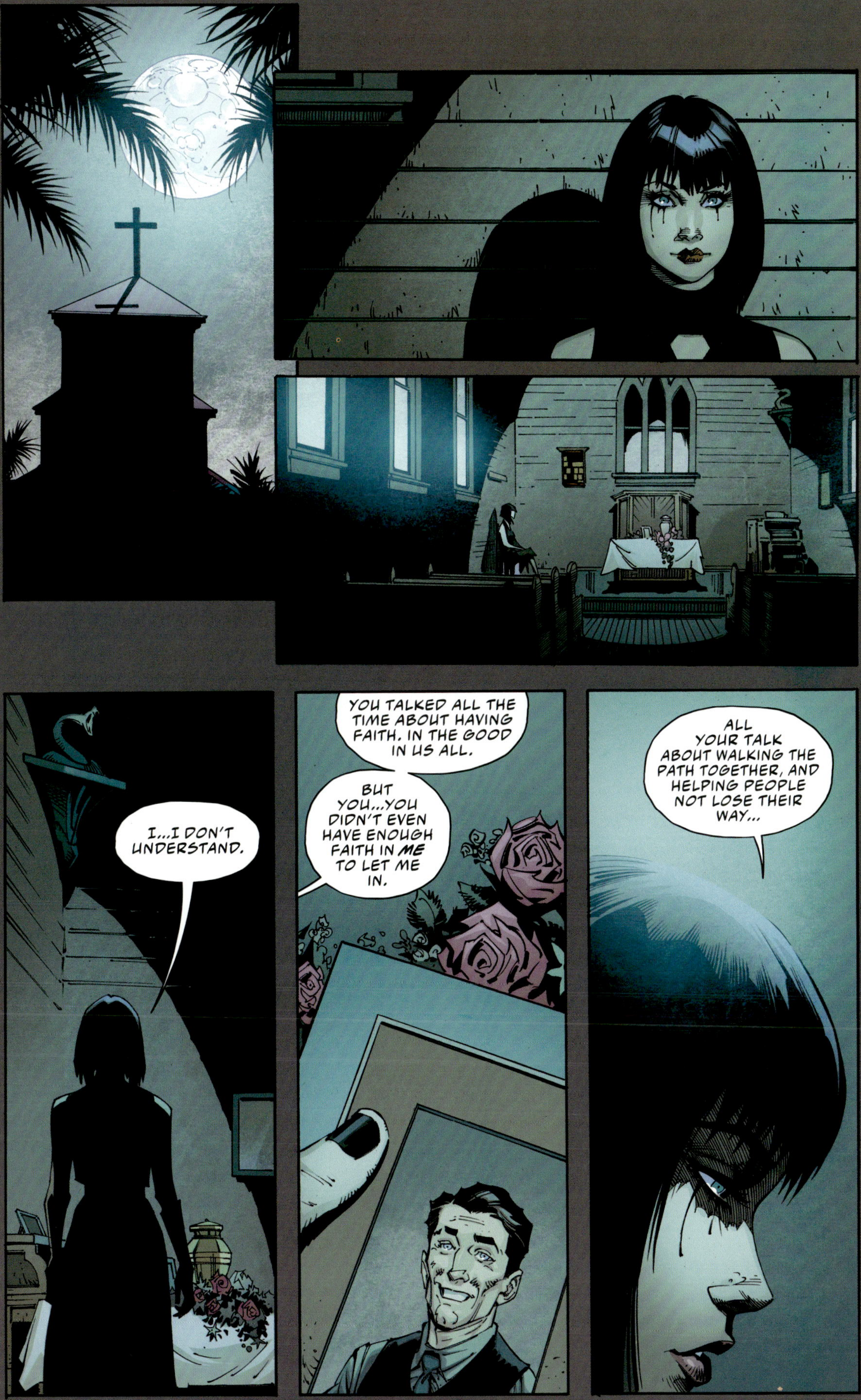
I...I DON'T UNDERSTAND.
YOU TALKED ALL THE TIME ABOUT HAVING FAITH. IN THE GOOD IN US ALL.
BUT YOU...YOU DIDN'T EVEN HAVE ENOUGH FAITH IN *ME* TO LET ME IN.
ALL YOUR TALK ABOUT WALKING THE PATH TOGETHER, AND HELPING PEOPLE NOT LOSE THEIR WAY...

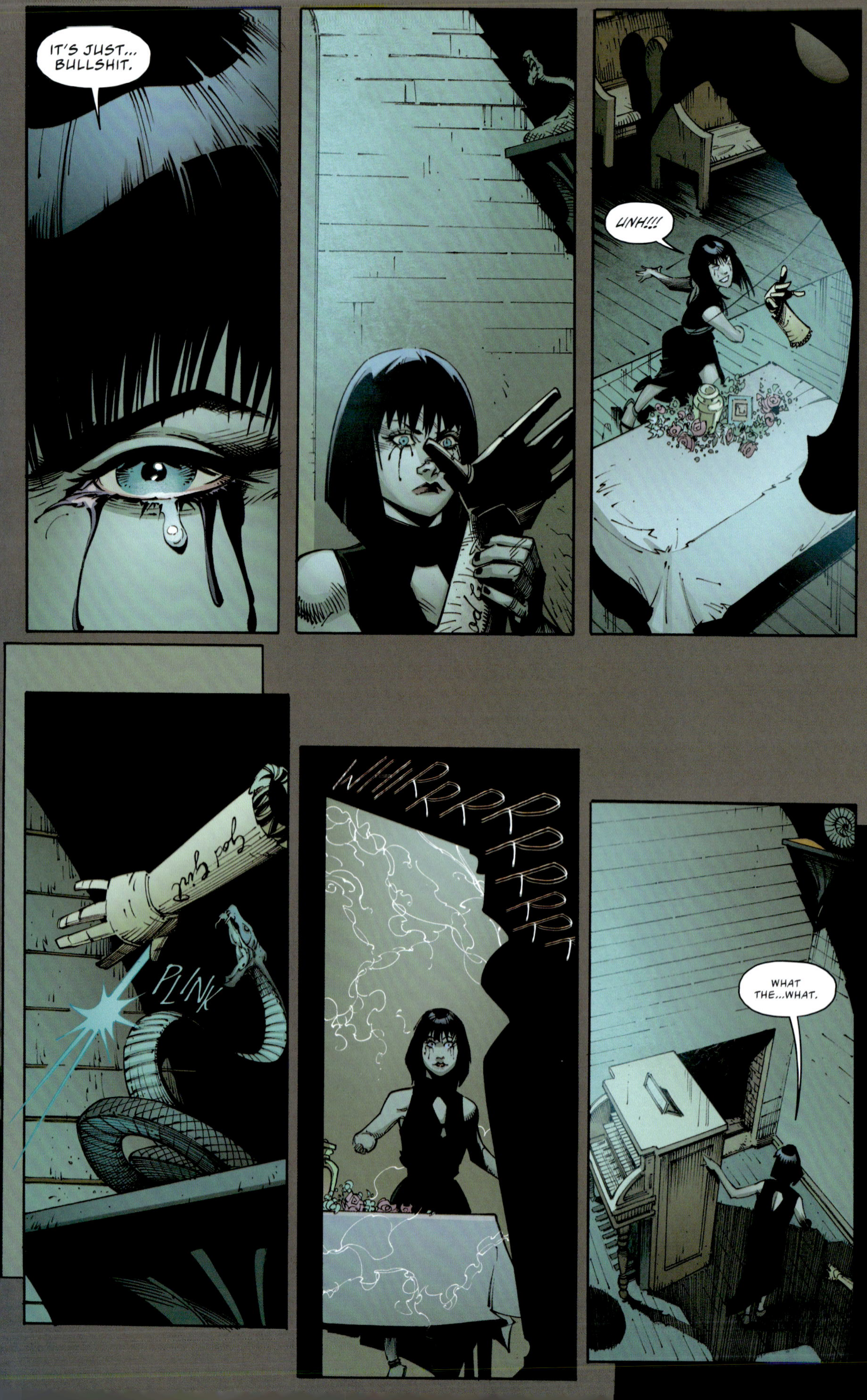
IT'S JUST... BULLSHIT.
UNH!!!
PLINK
WHIRRRRRRRRRRRT
WHAT THE...WHAT.

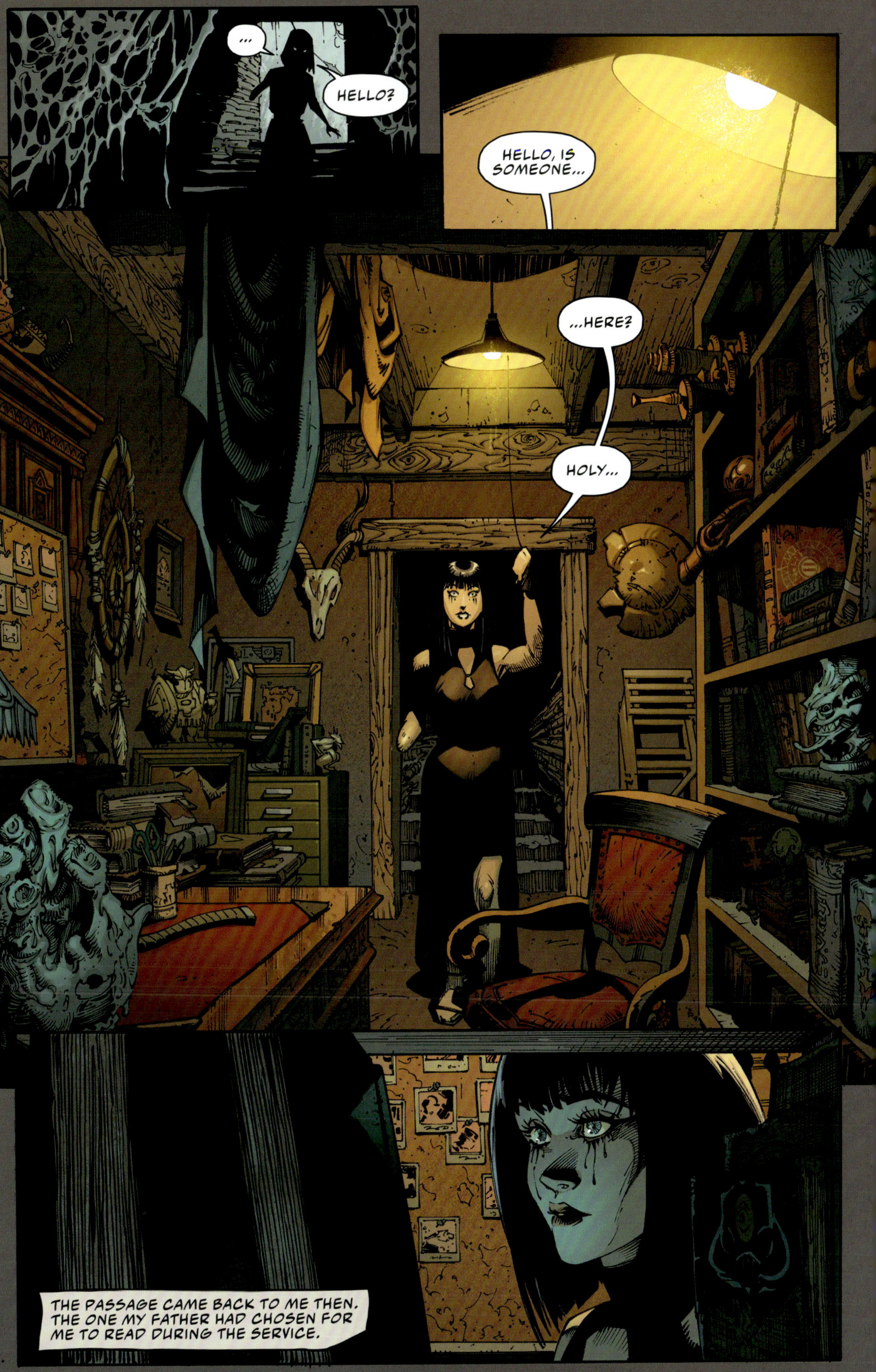
...
HELLO?
HELLO, IS SOMEONE...
...HERE?
HOLY...
THE PASSAGE CAME BACK TO ME THEN. THE ONE MY FATHER HAD CHOSEN FOR ME TO READ DURING THE SERVICE.

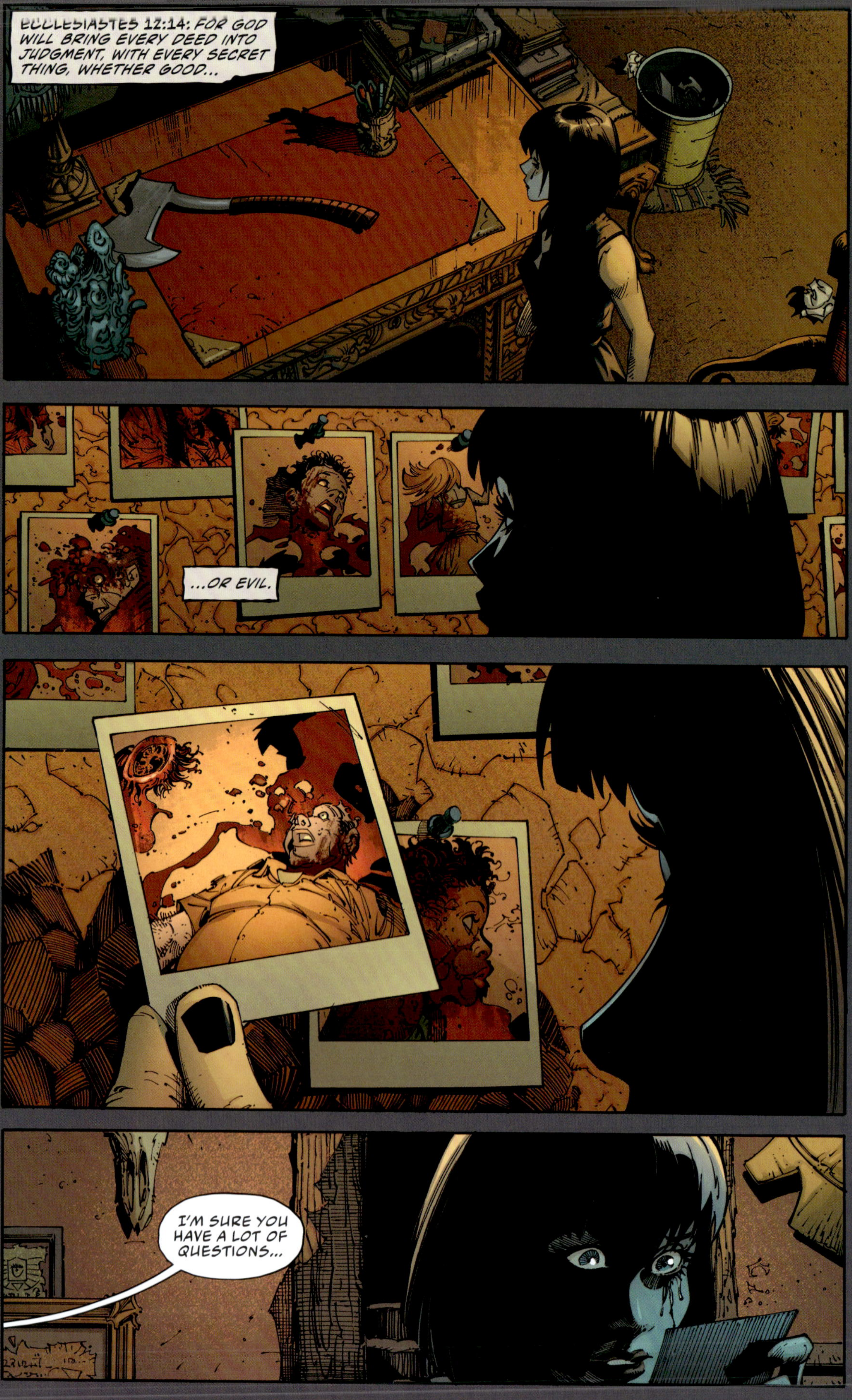
ECCLESIASTES 12:14: FOR GOD WILL BRING EVERY DEED INTO JUDGMENT, WITH EVERY SECRET THING, WHETHER GOOD...
...OR EVIL.
I'M SURE YOU HAVE A LOT OF QUESTIONS...

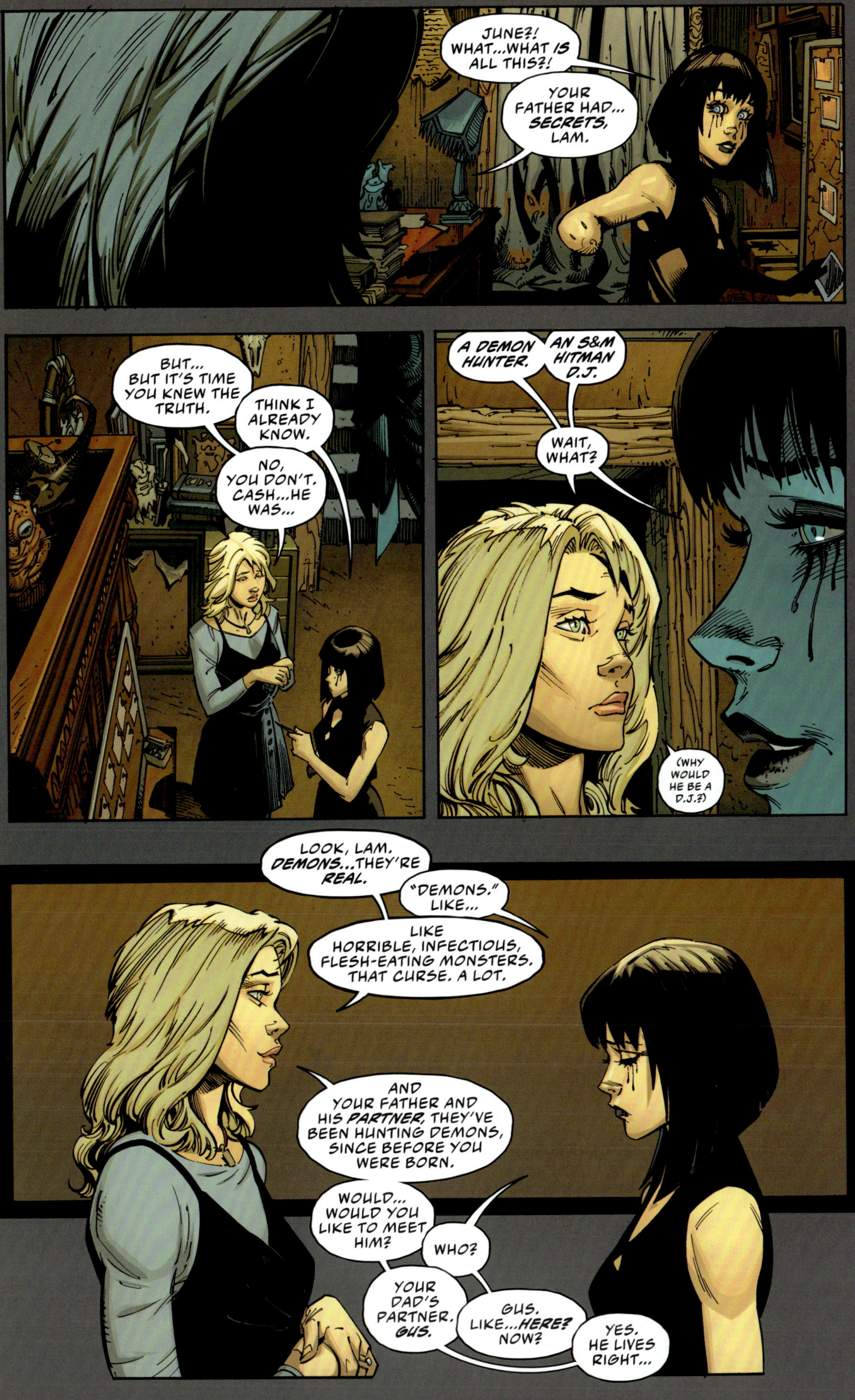

JUNE?! WHAT...WHAT IS ALL THIS?!
YOUR FATHER HAD... SECRETS, LAM.
BUT... BUT IT'S TIME YOU KNEW THE TRUTH.
THINK I ALREADY KNOW.
NO, YOU DON'T. CASH...HE WAS...
A DEMON HUNTER.
AN S&M HITMAN D.J.
WAIT, WHAT?
(WHY WOULD HE BE A D.J.?)
LOOK, LAM. DEMONS...THEY'RE REAL.
"DEMONS." LIKE...
LIKE HORRIBLE, INFECTIOUS, FLESH-EATING MONSTERS. THAT CURSE. A LOT.
AND YOUR FATHER AND HIS PARTNER, THEY'VE BEEN HUNTING DEMONS, SINCE BEFORE YOU WERE BORN.
WOULD... WOULD YOU LIKE TO MEET HIM?
WHO?
YOUR DAD'S PARTNER. GUS.
GUS. LIKE...HERE? NOW?
YES. HE LIVES RIGHT...

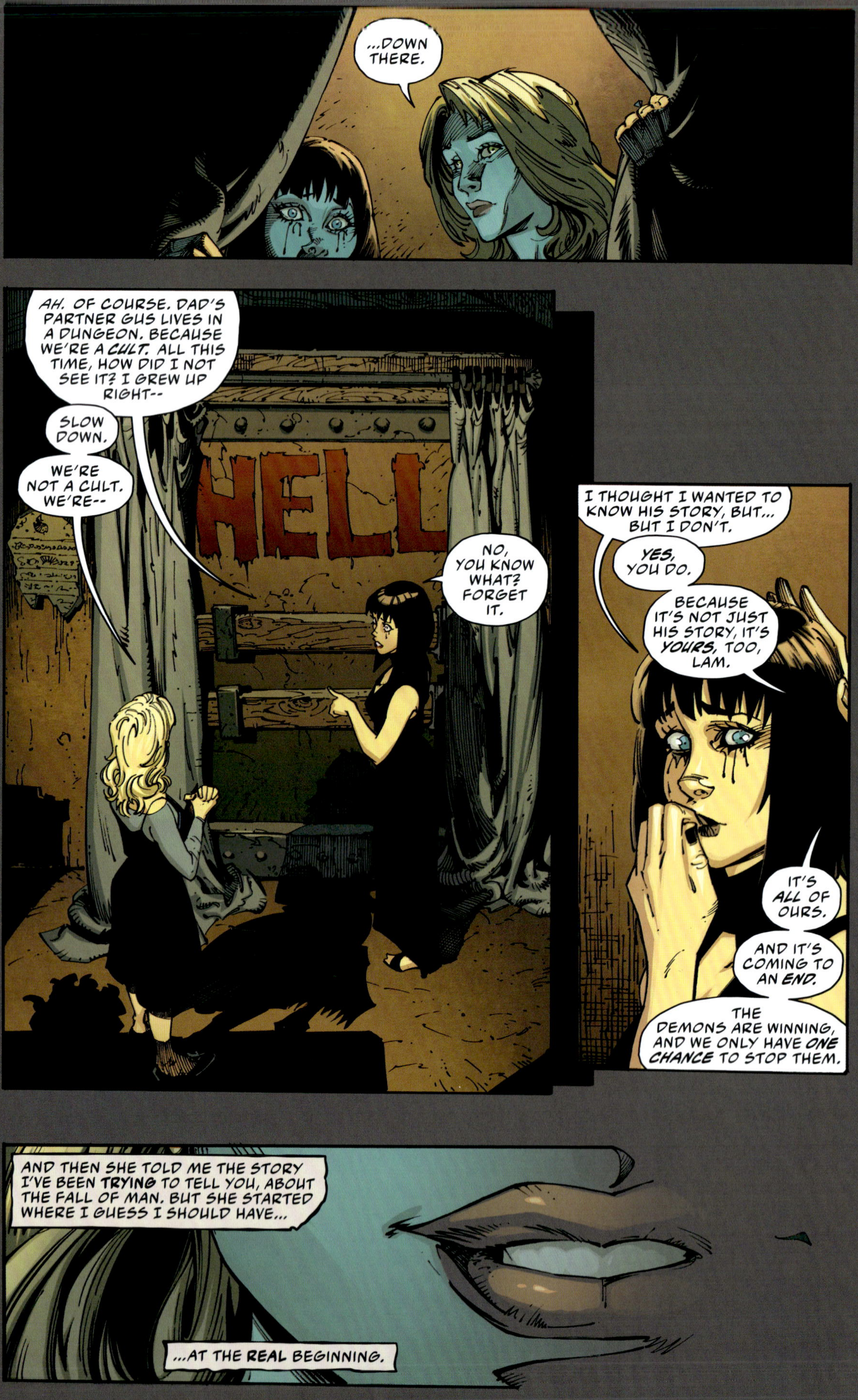
...DOWN THERE.
AH. OF COURSE. DAD'S PARTNER GUS LIVES IN A DUNGEON. BECAUSE WE'RE A CULT. ALL THIS TIME, HOW DID I NOT SEE IT? I GREW UP RIGHT--
SLOW DOWN.
WE'RE NOT A CULT. WE'RE--
HELL
NO, YOU KNOW WHAT? FORGET IT.
I THOUGHT I WANTED TO KNOW HIS STORY, BUT... BUT I DON'T.
YES, YOU DO.
BECAUSE IT'S NOT JUST HIS STORY, IT'S YOURS, TOO, LAM.
IT'S ALL OF OURS.
AND IT'S COMING TO AN END.
THE DEMONS ARE WINNING, AND WE ONLY HAVE ONE CHANCE TO STOP THEM.
AND THEN SHE TOLD ME THE STORY I'VE BEEN TRYING TO TELL YOU, ABOUT THE FALL OF MAN. BUT SHE STARTED WHERE I GUESS I SHOULD HAVE...
...AT THE REAL BEGINNING.

CHAPTER THREE: "THE DEVIL'S FINGER"

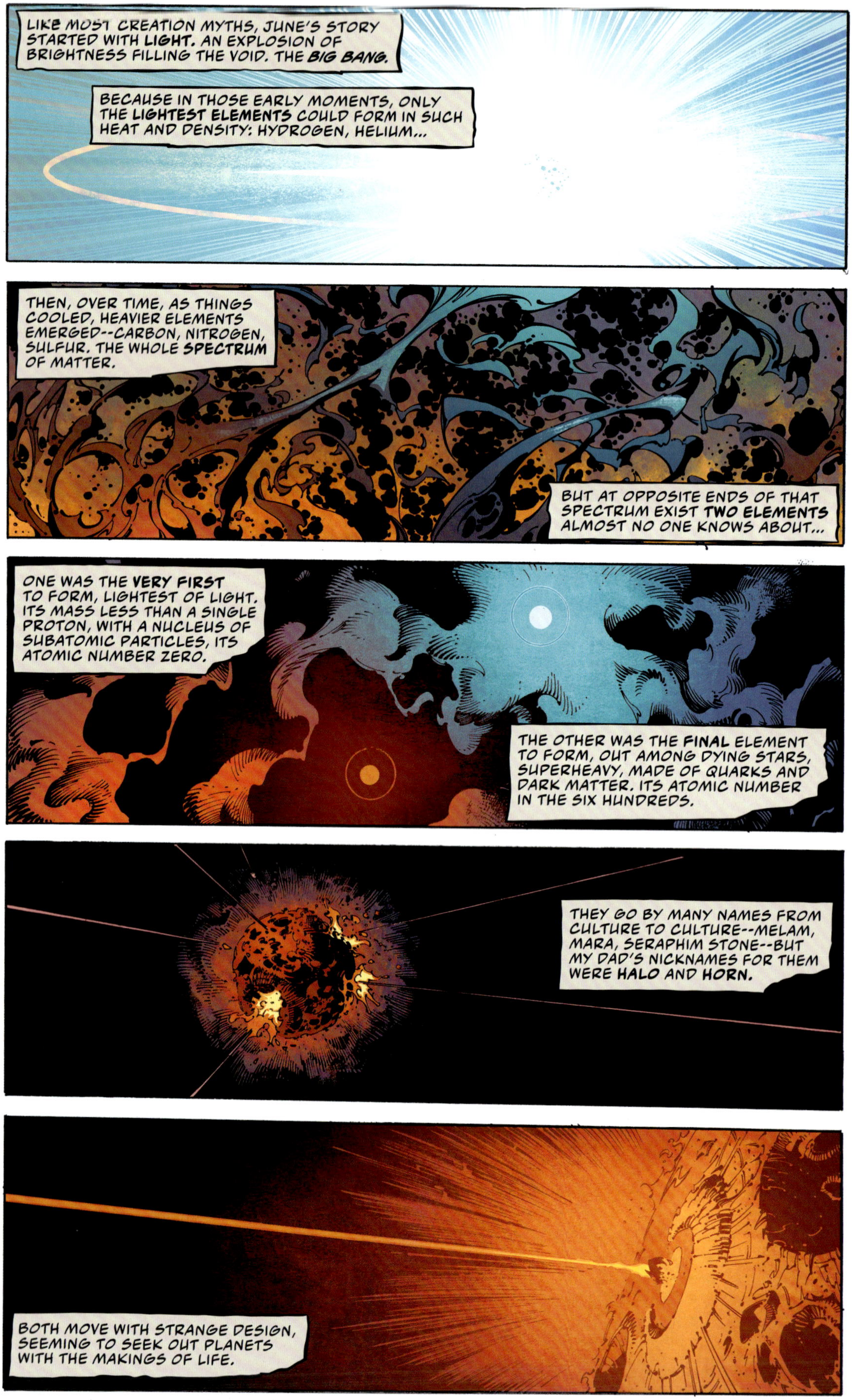

LIKE MOST CREATION MYTHS, JUNE'S STORY STARTED WITH LIGHT. AN EXPLOSION OF BRIGHTNESS FILLING THE VOID. THE BIG BANG.
BECAUSE IN THOSE EARLY MOMENTS, ONLY THE LIGHTEST ELEMENTS COULD FORM IN SUCH HEAT AND DENSITY: HYDROGEN, HELIUM...
THEN, OVER TIME, AS THINGS COOLED, HEAVIER ELEMENTS EMERGED--CARBON, NITROGEN, SULFUR. THE WHOLE SPECTRUM OF MATTER.
BUT AT OPPOSITE ENDS OF THAT SPECTRUM EXIST TWO ELEMENTS ALMOST NO ONE KNOWS ABOUT...
ONE WAS THE VERY FIRST TO FORM, LIGHTEST OF LIGHT. ITS MASS LESS THAN A SINGLE PROTON, WITH A NUCLEUS OF SUBATOMIC PARTICLES, ITS ATOMIC NUMBER ZERO.
THE OTHER WAS THE FINAL ELEMENT TO FORM, OUT AMONG DYING STARS, SUPERHEAVY, MADE OF QUARKS AND DARK MATTER. ITS ATOMIC NUMBER IN THE SIX HUNDREDS.
THEY GO BY MANY NAMES FROM CULTURE TO CULTURE--MELAM, MARA, SERAPHIM STONE--BUT MY DAD'S NICKNAMES FOR THEM WERE HALO AND HORN.
BOTH MOVE WITH STRANGE DESIGN, SEEMING TO SEEK OUT PLANETS WITH THE MAKINGS OF LIFE.

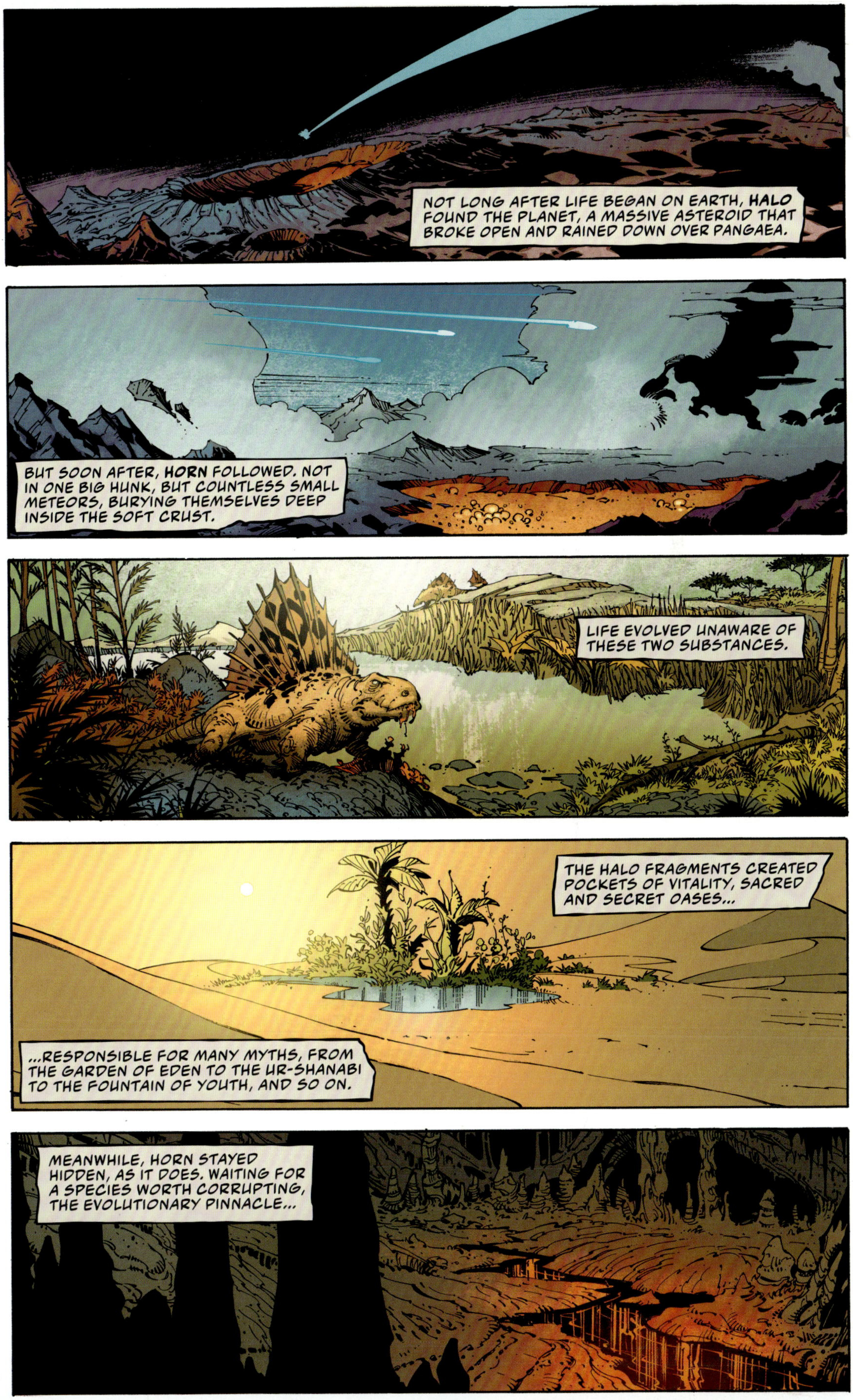
NOT LONG AFTER LIFE BEGAN ON EARTH, HALO FOUND THE PLANET, A MASSIVE ASTEROID THAT BROKE OPEN AND RAINED DOWN OVER PANGAEA.
BUT SOON AFTER, HORN FOLLOWED. NOT IN ONE BIG HUNK, BUT COUNTLESS SMALL METEORS, BURYING THEMSELVES DEEP INSIDE THE SOFT CRUST.
LIFE EVOLVED UNAWARE OF THESE TWO SUBSTANCES.
THE HALO FRAGMENTS CREATED POCKETS OF VITALITY, SACRED AND SECRET OASES...
...RESPONSIBLE FOR MANY MYTHS, FROM THE GARDEN OF EDEN TO THE UR-SHANABI TO THE FOUNTAIN OF YOUTH, AND SO ON.
MEANWHILE, HORN STAYED HIDDEN, AS IT DOES. WAITING FOR A SPECIES WORTH CORRUPTING, THE EVOLUTIONARY PINNACLE...

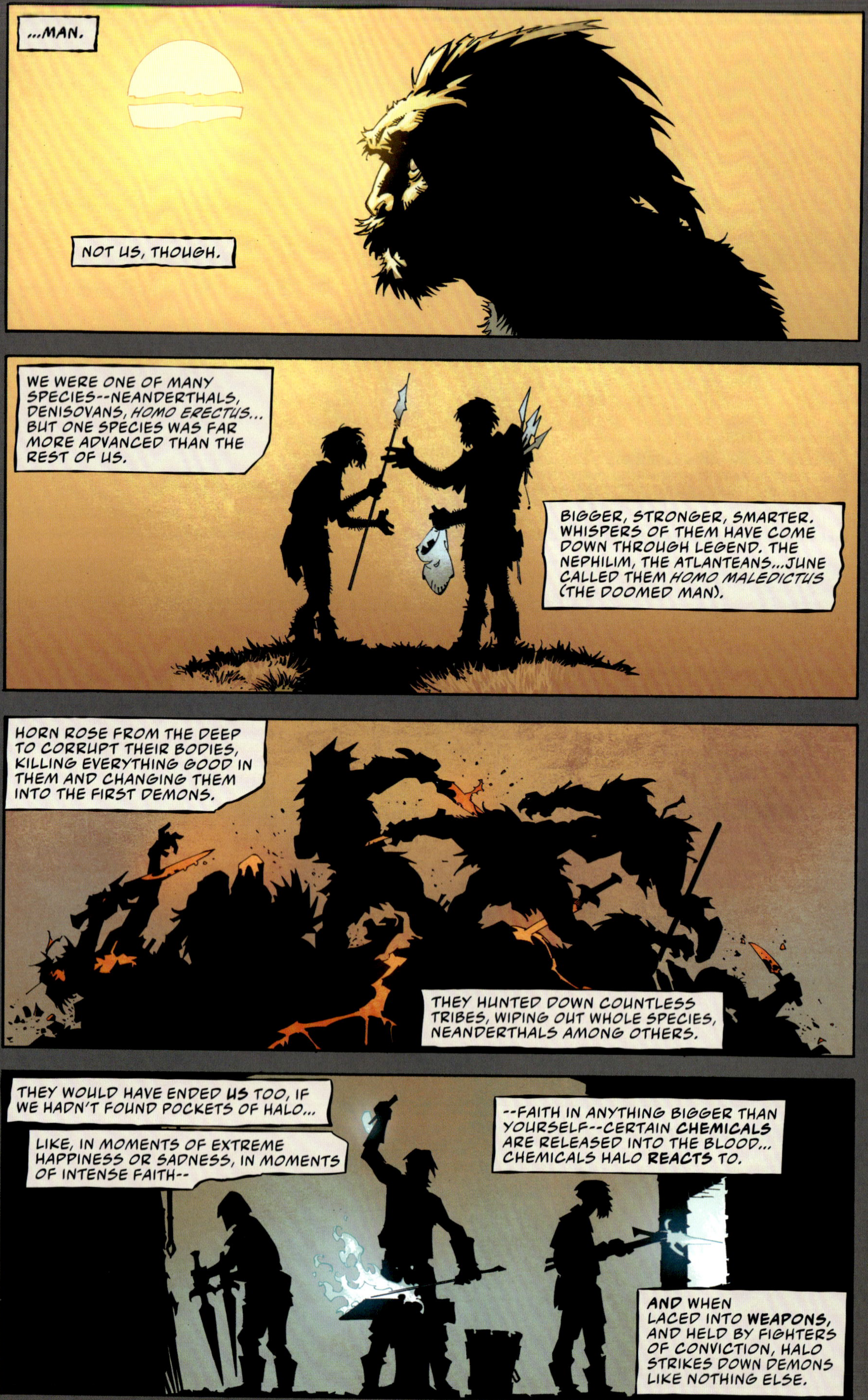
...MAN.
NOT US, THOUGH.
WE WERE ONE OF MANY SPECIES--NEANDERTHALS, DENISOVANS, *HOMO ERECTUS*... BUT ONE SPECIES WAS FAR MORE ADVANCED THAN THE REST OF US.
BIGGER, STRONGER, SMARTER. WHISPERS OF THEM HAVE COME DOWN THROUGH LEGEND. THE NEPHILIM, THE ATLANTEANS...JUNE CALLED THEM *HOMO MALEDICTUS* (THE DOOMED MAN).
HORN ROSE FROM THE DEEP TO CORRUPT THEIR BODIES, KILLING EVERYTHING GOOD IN THEM AND CHANGING THEM INTO THE FIRST DEMONS.
THEY HUNTED DOWN COUNTLESS TRIBES, WIPING OUT WHOLE SPECIES, NEANDERTHALS AMONG OTHERS.
THEY WOULD HAVE ENDED **US** TOO, IF WE HADN'T FOUND POCKETS OF HALO...
LIKE, IN MOMENTS OF EXTREME HAPPINESS OR SADNESS, IN MOMENTS OF INTENSE FAITH--
--FAITH IN ANYTHING BIGGER THAN YOURSELF--CERTAIN **CHEMICALS** ARE RELEASED INTO THE BLOOD... CHEMICALS HALO **REACTS** TO.
AND WHEN LACED INTO **WEAPONS**, AND HELD BY FIGHTERS OF CONVICTION, HALO STRIKES DOWN DEMONS LIKE NOTHING ELSE.

THE LEGEND IS A THOUSAND BLADES WERE FORGED AND GIVEN TO WARRIORS ACROSS THE LAND, AND IN TIME, THE DEMON SPECIES WERE DESTROYED.

OVER THE CENTURIES, THESE BLADES HAVE BEEN PASSED DOWN TO WARRIORS OF EVERY FAITH. OFTEN THE SOURCE OF LEGENDS AROUND MYSTICAL SWORDS, AXES, SPEARS, THEY'VE BEEN USED TO BEAT BACK RESURGENCES OF HORN.

AND HORN, IT NEVER STOPPED HITTING THE EARTH. HELL, ALL THOSE VIDEOS YOU SEE LATELY OF U.F.O.'S? OBJECTS ZIPPING AROUND BEFORE DISAPPEARING INTO THE HILLS? HORN.

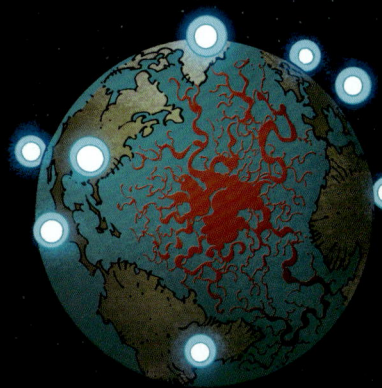

BY NOW, IT'S EVERYWHERE. JUNE SAID IT'S ALREADY LIKELY INFECTED PEOPLE ALL OVER. MAYBE IT'S WHY THINGS HAVE BEEN SO CRAZY.

MEANWHILE, HALO? AFTER THAT FIRST CHUNK, NO MORE HAS EVER HIT THE EARTH. NONE.

SO NOW, OUT OF THOSE THOUSAND BLADES?

ONLY NINE ARE LEFT. THAT'S RIGHT.

NINE BLADES, ENTRUSTED TO BEARERS AROUND THE GLOBE. THEY WEAR ITS SYMBOL ON THEIR CHESTS, THE ATOMIC NUMBER ZERO, THE RING. THEY CALL THEMSELVES THE GLORIES. IF THEY'RE ANGELS, THEIR HALOS ARE IN THEIR BLADES.

AND ACCORDING TO JUNE, MY DAD, PASTOR CASH, WAS ONE OF THEM. HE WAS LIKE THE LIAM NEESON OF THEM ALL. HE AND HIS PARTNER, GUS.

MY DAD BELIEVED ANOTHER CHUNK OF HALO WAS DUE TO HIT THE EARTH SOON. HE EVEN HAD A THEORY AS TO WHEN AND WHERE.

SHE SAID THAT'S WHY HE DIED. PEOPLE INFECTED BY HORN GOT TO HIM. DEMONS HIDING RIGHT HERE, IN FLORIDA. IN FACT...

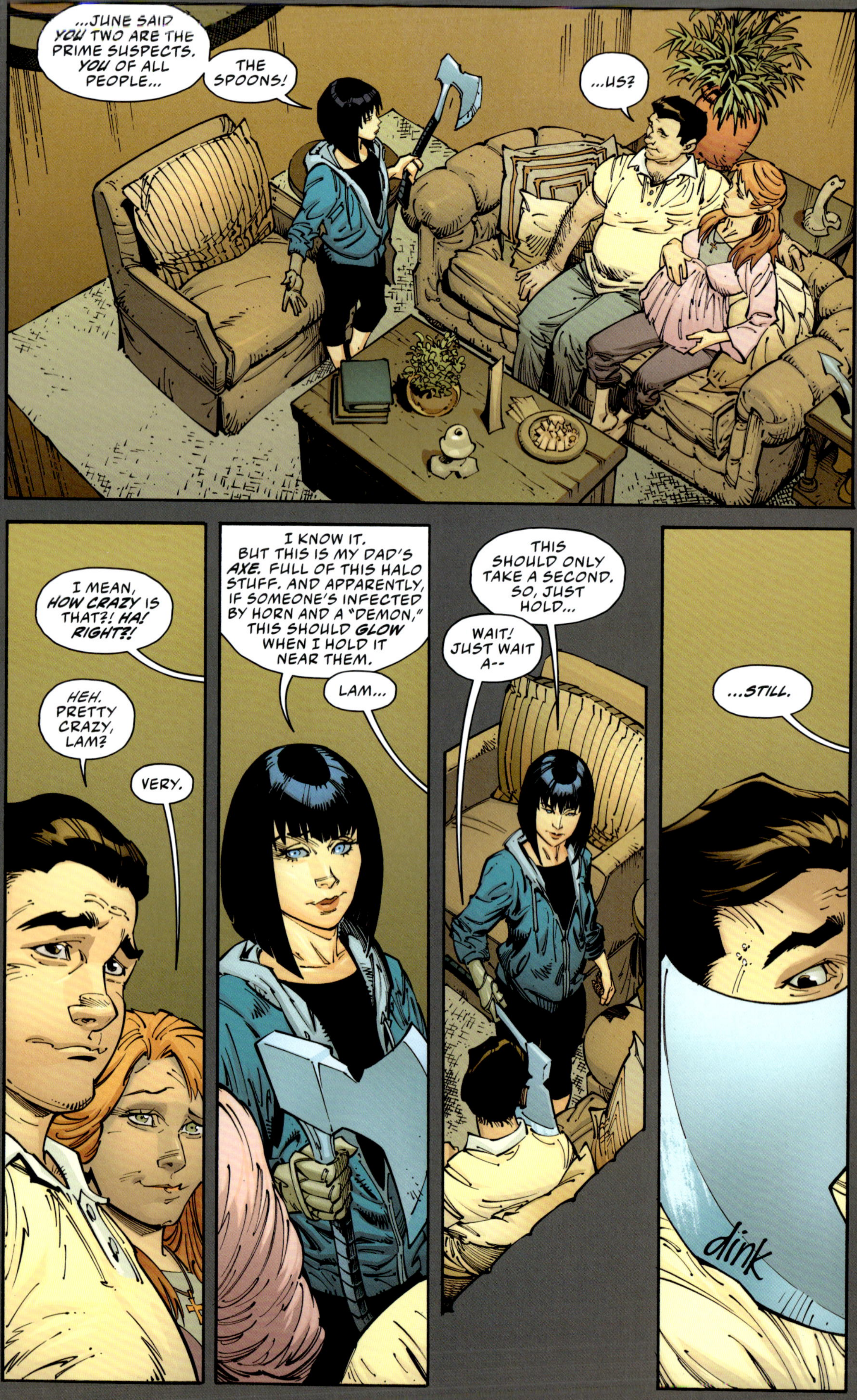
...JUNE SAID YOU TWO ARE THE PRIME SUSPECTS. YOU OF ALL PEOPLE...
THE SPOONS!
...US?
I MEAN, HOW CRAZY IS THAT?! HA! RIGHT?!
HEH. PRETTY CRAZY, LAM?
VERY.
I KNOW IT. BUT THIS IS MY DAD'S AXE. FULL OF THIS HALO STUFF. AND APPARENTLY, IF SOMEONE'S INFECTED BY HORN AND A "DEMON," THIS SHOULD GLOW WHEN I HOLD IT NEAR THEM.
LAM...
THIS SHOULD ONLY TAKE A SECOND. SO, JUST HOLD...
WAIT! JUST WAIT A--
...STILL.
dink

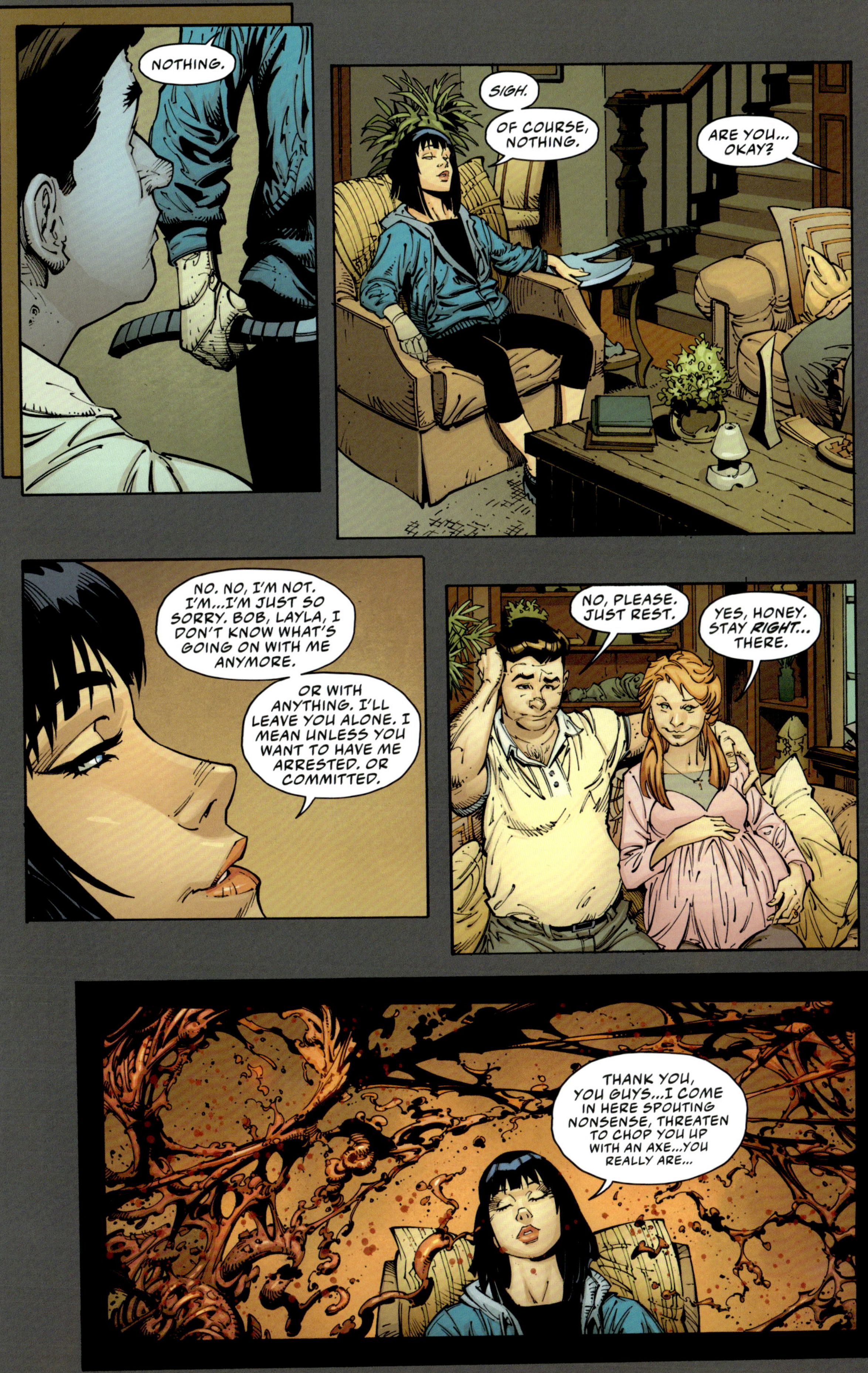
NOTHING.
SIGH.
OF COURSE, NOTHING.
ARE YOU... OKAY?
NO. NO, I'M NOT. I'M...I'M JUST SO SORRY. BOB, LAYLA, I DON'T KNOW WHAT'S GOING ON WITH ME ANYMORE.
OR WITH ANYTHING. I'LL LEAVE YOU ALONE. I MEAN UNLESS YOU WANT TO HAVE ME ARRESTED. OR COMMITTED.
NO, PLEASE. JUST REST.
YES, HONEY. STAY *RIGHT*... THERE.
THANK YOU, YOU GUYS...I COME IN HERE SPOUTING NONSENSE, THREATEN TO CHOP YOU UP WITH AN AXE...YOU REALLY ARE...

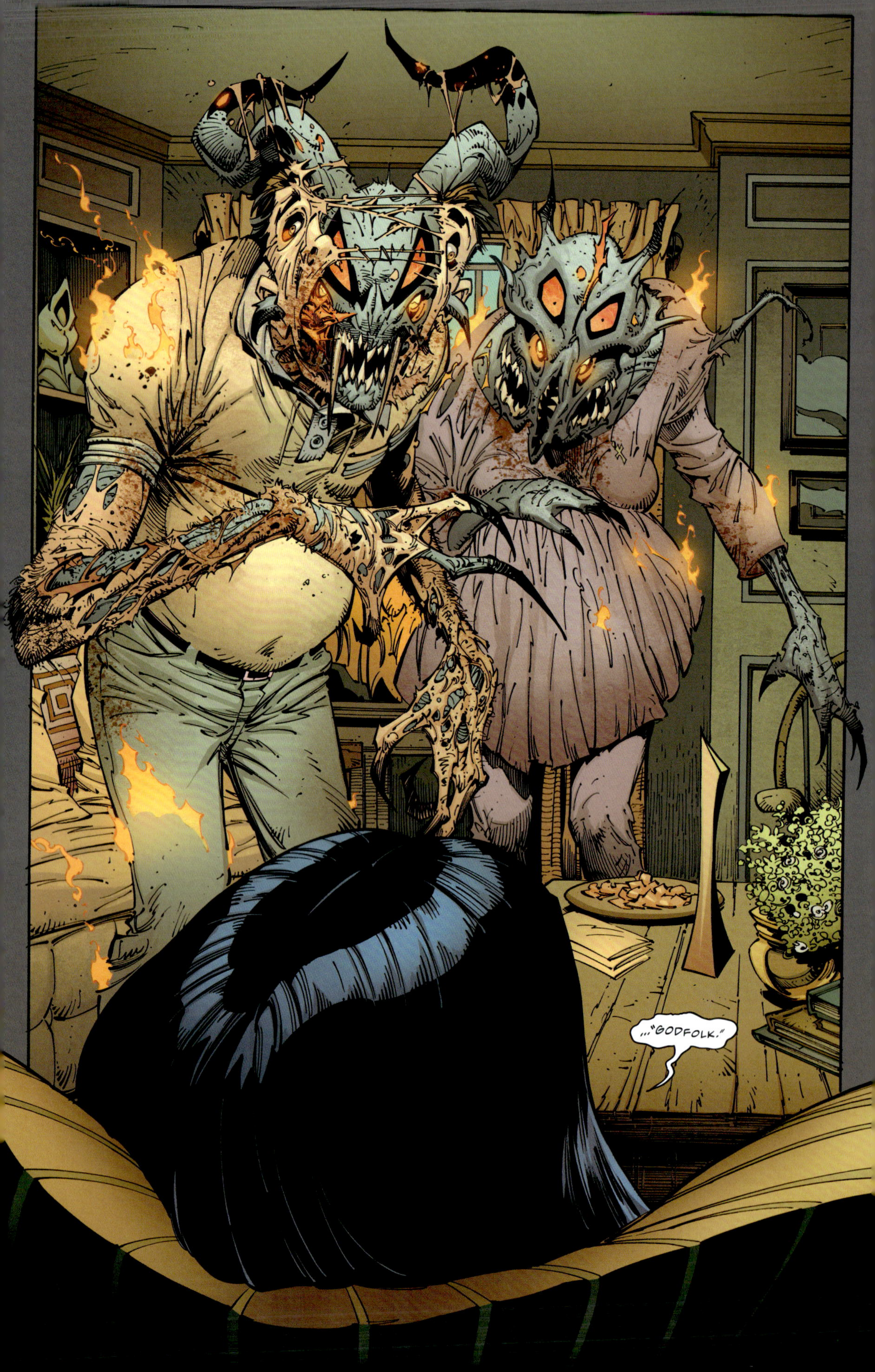
..."GODFOLK."

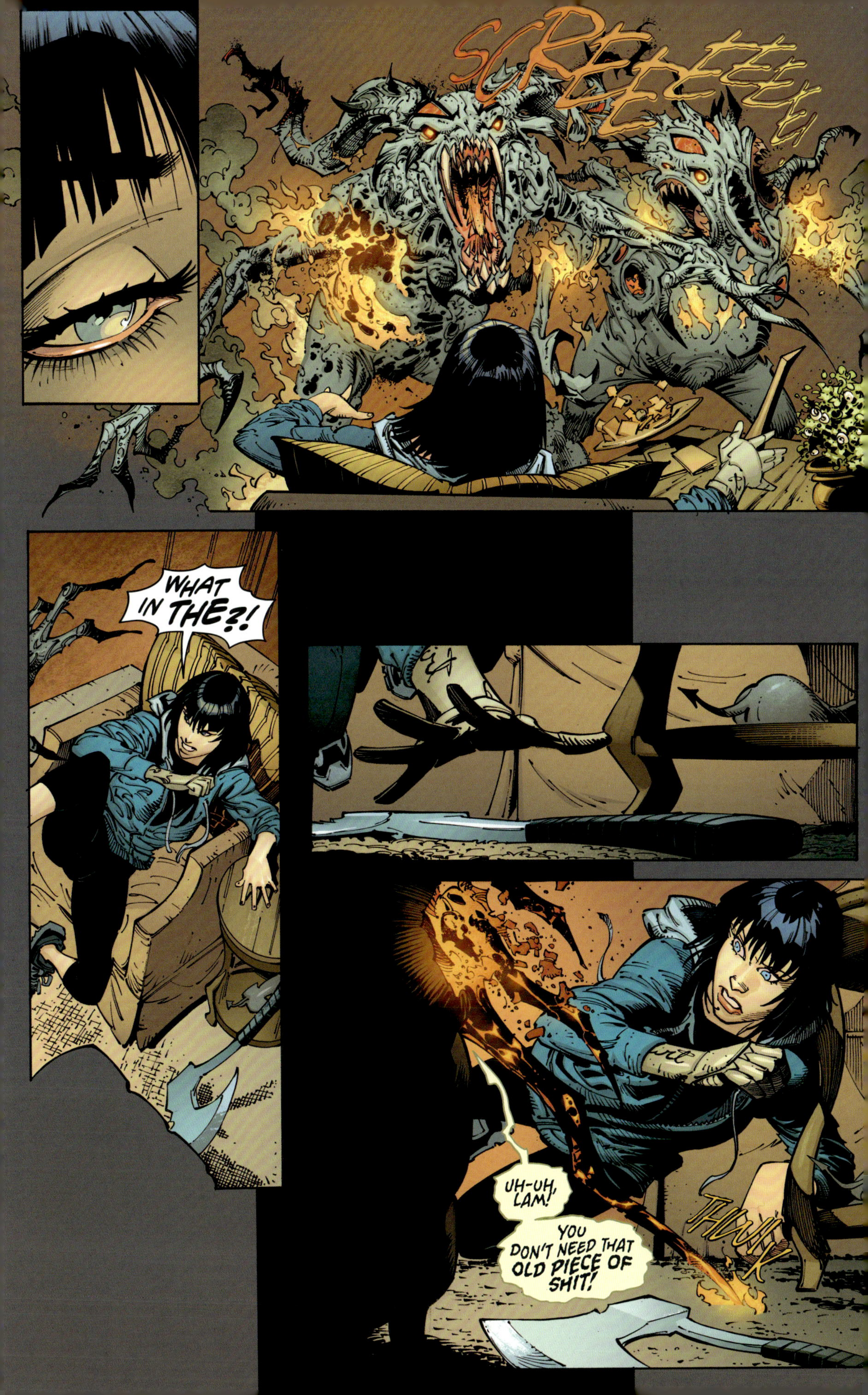
SCREEEEEE!!
WHAT IN THE?!
UH-UH, LAM!
YOU DON'T NEED THAT OLD PIECE OF SHIT!
THUNK!

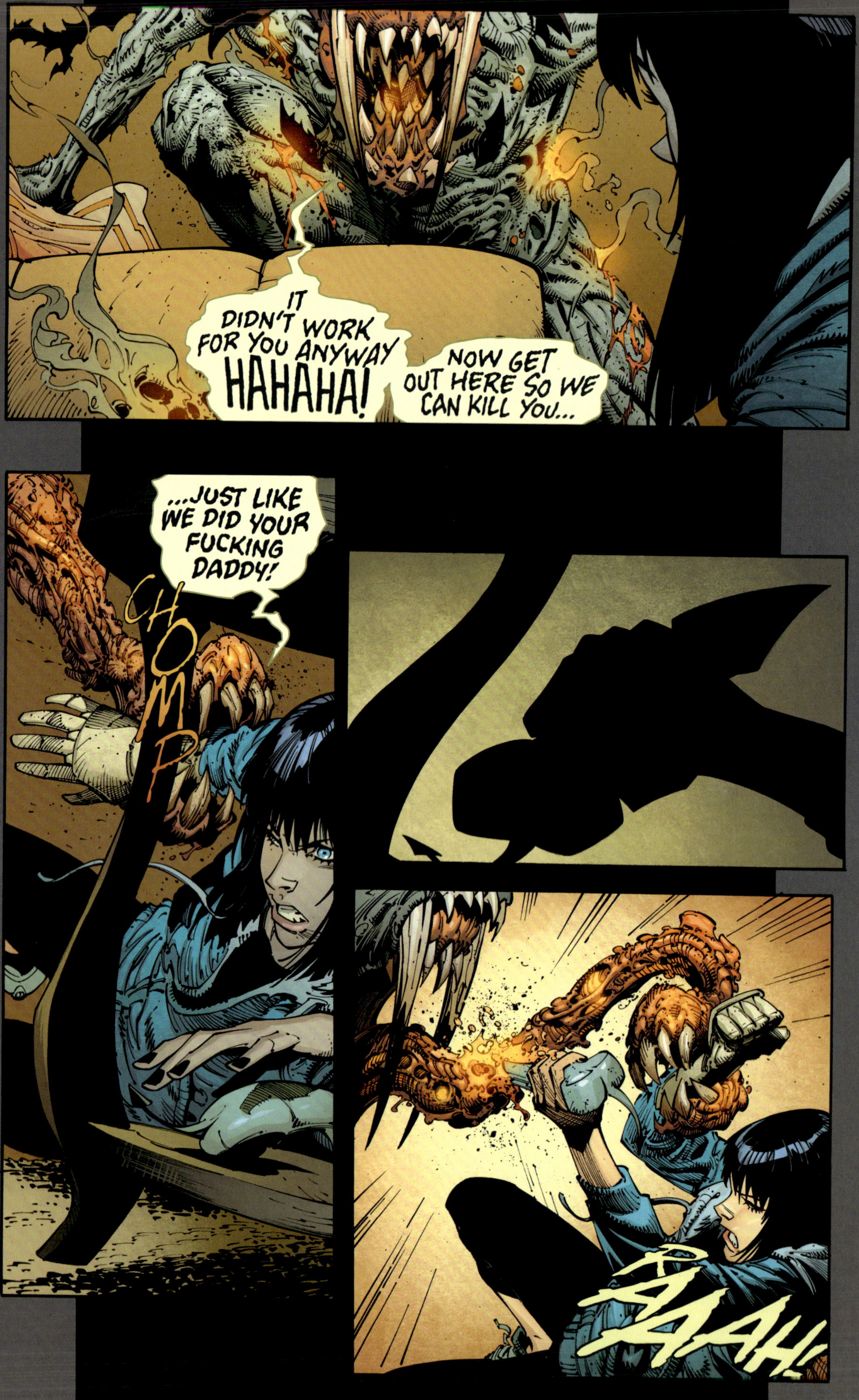
IT DIDN'T WORK FOR YOU ANYWAY HAHAHA!
NOW GET OUT HERE SO WE CAN KILL YOU...
...JUST LIKE WE DID YOUR FUCKING DADDY!
CHOMP
RAAAH!

AW, DON'T RUN, SWEETIE!
...YOU'RE STILL THE GODMOTHER TO OUR BABIES!
AREN'T THEY CUTE?!
SHIT
FUCK
BALLS
NOW, BEFORE WE EAT YOU, HANDS AND FEET FIRST, I WANT YOU TO KNOW THAT YOUR DAD, HE DIED SCREAMING ABOUT YOU...
...HOW YOU'D COME BACK AND SHOW US. HOW YOU'D BE THE BEST THERE WAS.
BUT LOOK AT YOU. YOU COULDN'T EVEN GET HIS "WIDDLE AXE" TO LIGHT UP.
HE DIDN'T TEACH YOU JUMPING JACK SHIT, DID HE?

HE TAUGHT ME THIS.
THEY RUSHED AT ME THEN AND I KNEW IT WAS OVER.
SO I CLOSED MY EYES AND GOT READY FOR IT. I SWORE I WOULDN'T SCREAM, BUT SOON AS IT STARTED, THE SCREAMS CAME.
THEY SHOOK THE HOUSE.
SO LOUD IT TOOK ME A SECOND TO REALIZE...
THEY WEREN'T COMING FROM ME.
EEEEEEEEEE

FOR A MOMENT, THERE WERE OTHER NOISES. SOUNDS LIKE I'VE NEVER HEARD. BABIES SWEARING AND MEAT BEING CLEAVED FROM BONE, FLESH SEARED. AND THEN...

IT'S OKAY. YOU CAN LOOK NOW.

WHAT THE...

WHO... WHO ARE YOU?!

MY NAME IS **GUS.**
AND I WAS YOUR FATHER'S PARTNER, LAM.
IT'S NICE TO FINALLY MEET YOU.

ARE YOU HURT?
NO...NO, I'M ALL RIGHT.
THANK YOU. FOR SAVING ME.
HERE. YOUR DAD WANTED YOU TO HAVE IT.
HE WORKED ON IT A LONG TIME, LAM. MAYBE IT'S TIME TO PUT IT ON.
YOU...
...MOTHER-FUCKING COCK-GOBBLING PIECES OF ANAL--
NOW THAT PART I TOLD YOU ABOUT, WHERE DEMONS PULL SOMEONE'S GUTS OUT OF THEIR BUTTHOLE? WELL, GUS IS THE DEMON. AND BESS...
...THIS IS WHERE "HER CREATIVITY" STOPS GETTING ENCOURAGED. FOREVER.
BUT COME TO THINK OF IT, MAYBE THE BEST START TO THIS STORY WASN'T THREE BILLION YEARS AGO, OR EVEN AT THE BIG BANG.
GO ON.
YOU KNOW WHAT TO DO.
MAYBE THE BEST START IS HERE. NOW, AT THE MOMENT I REALIZED THAT NO...
...I MIGHT NOT BE GODFOLK...

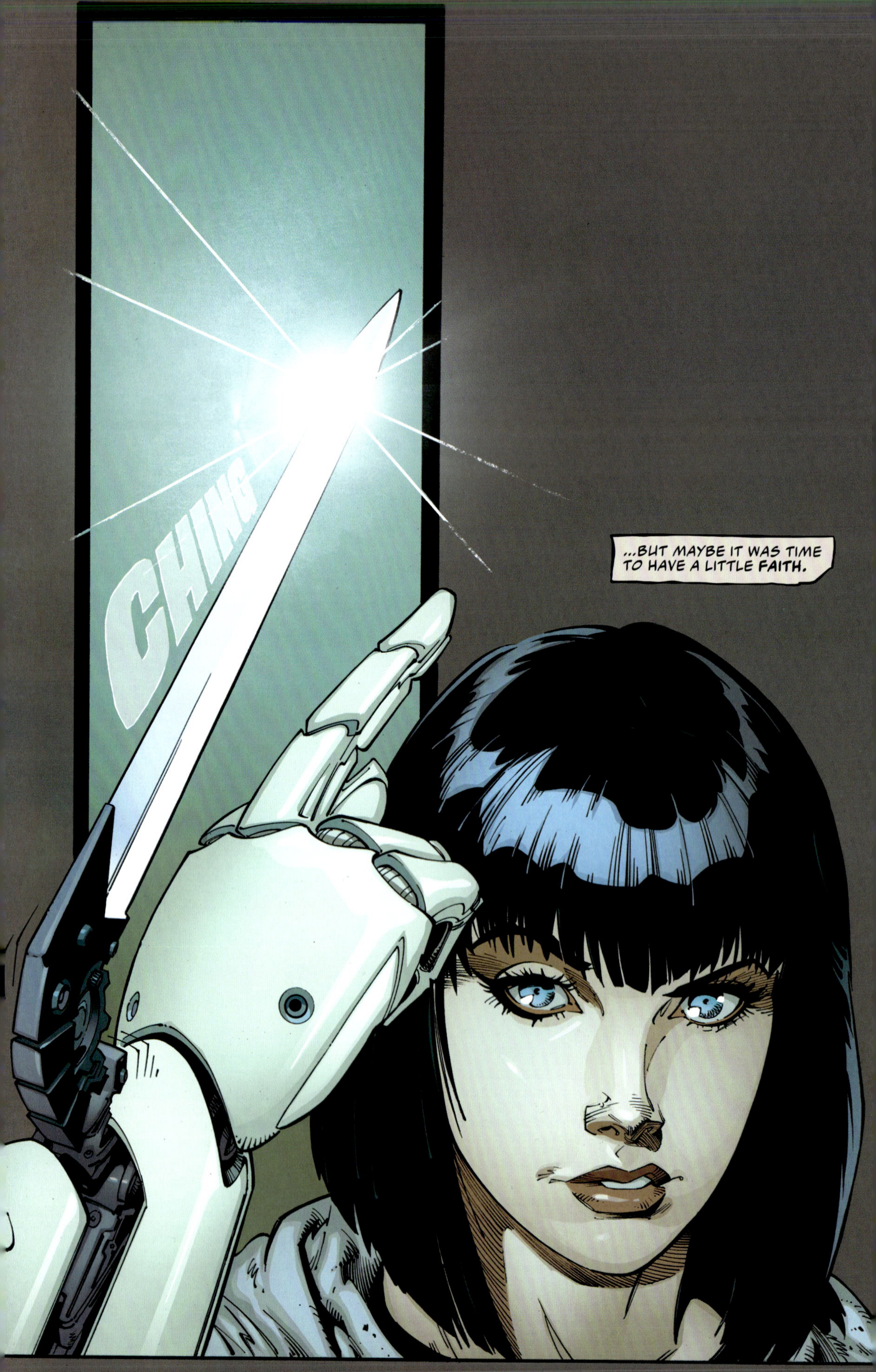
CHING
...BUT MAYBE IT WAS TIME TO HAVE A LITTLE FAITH.

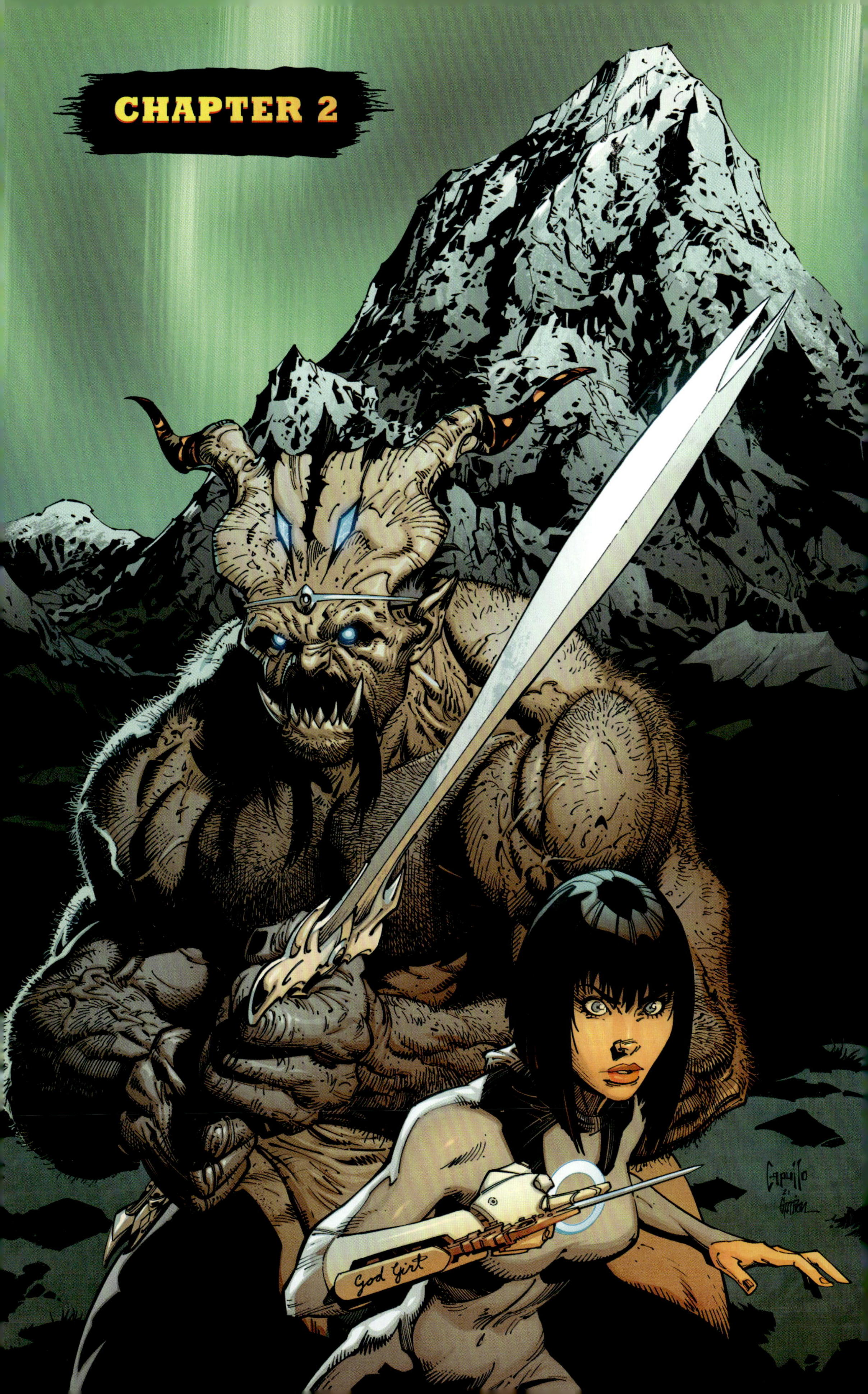
CHAPTER 2
God Girl

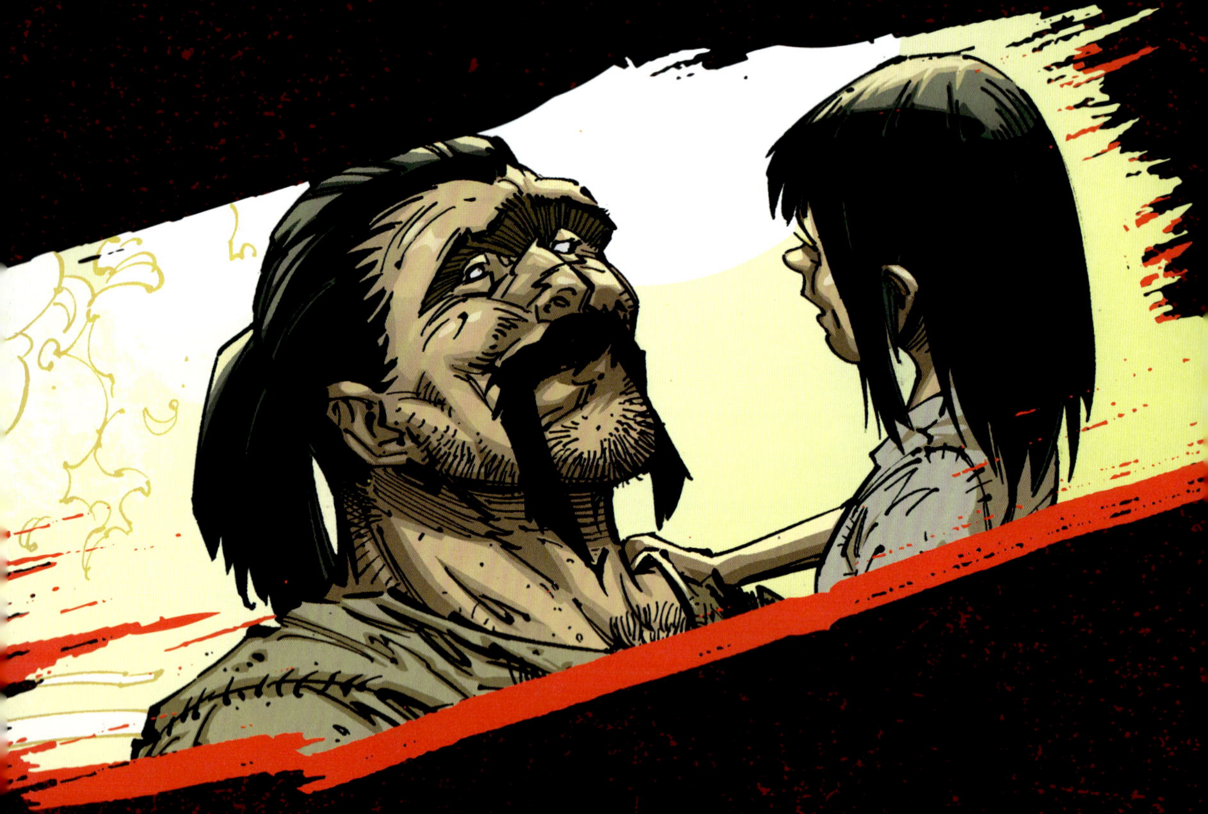

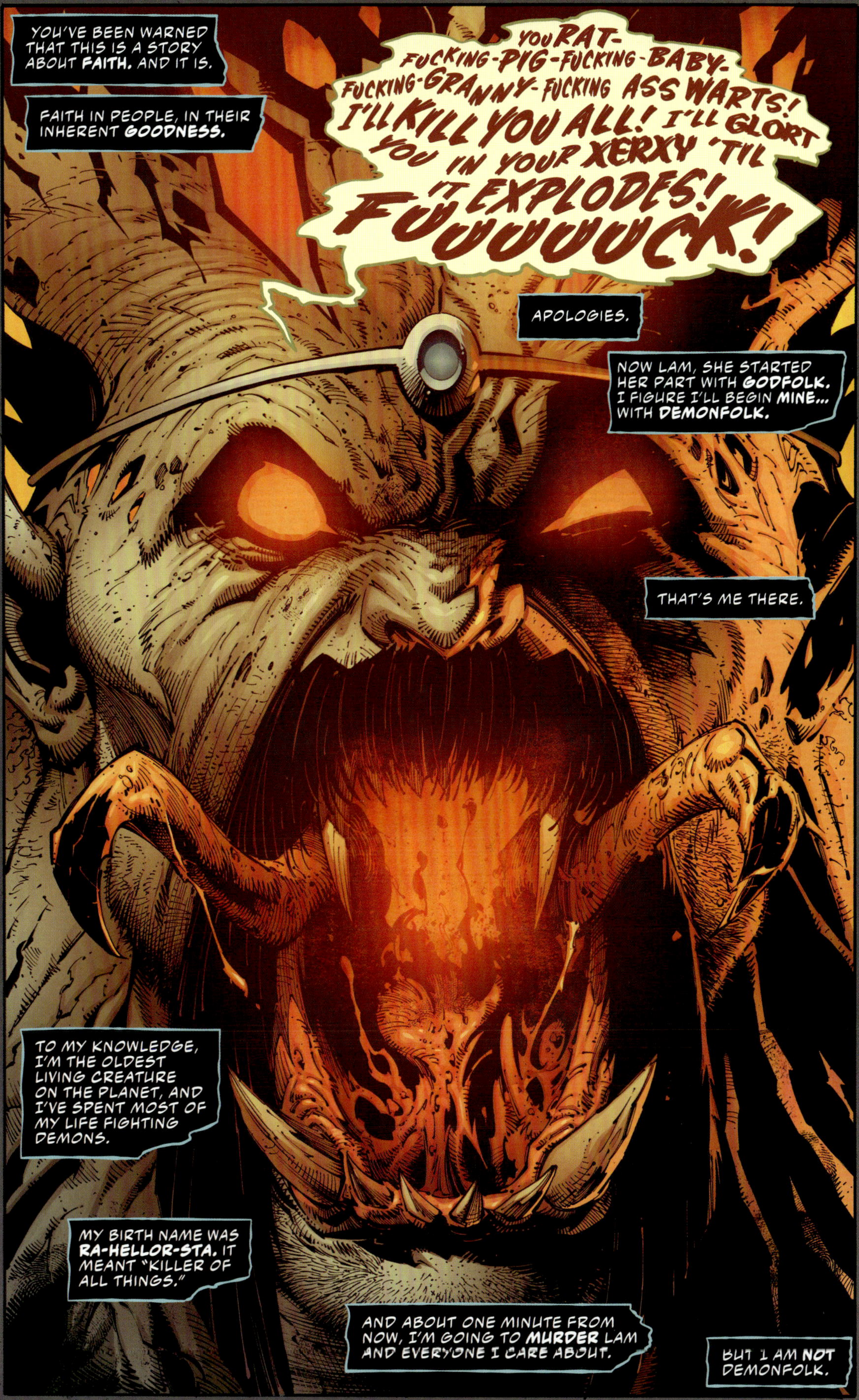

YOU'VE BEEN WARNED THAT THIS IS A STORY ABOUT FAITH. AND IT IS.
FAITH IN PEOPLE, IN THEIR INHERENT GOODNESS.
YOU RAT-FUCKING-PIG-FUCKING-BABY-FUCKING-GRANNY-FUCKING ASS WARTS! I'LL KILL YOU ALL! I'LL GLORT YOU IN YOUR XERXY 'TIL IT EXPLODES! FUUUUUUCK!
APOLOGIES.
NOW LAM, SHE STARTED HER PART WITH GODFOLK. I FIGURE I'LL BEGIN MINE... WITH DEMONFOLK.
THAT'S ME THERE.
TO MY KNOWLEDGE, I'M THE OLDEST LIVING CREATURE ON THE PLANET, AND I'VE SPENT MOST OF MY LIFE FIGHTING DEMONS.
MY BIRTH NAME WAS RA-HELLOR-STA. IT MEANT "KILLER OF ALL THINGS."
AND ABOUT ONE MINUTE FROM NOW, I'M GOING TO MURDER LAM AND EVERYONE I CARE ABOUT.
BUT I AM NOT DEMONFOLK.

CHAPTER FOUR: "TOUGH MOTHERS"

LAM BEGAN IN THE PAST.

I'LL START IN THE PRESENT. AFTER ALL, WHEN IT COMES TO DEMONS, THERE'S NOWHERE BETTER, BECAUSE **THESE** DAYS, THEY'RE EVERYWHERE. IN JUST THE LAST TEN YEARS MORE HORN HAS HIT THE EARTH THAN IN THE PREVIOUS FIFTY.

SO, YOU BETTER BELIEVE THAT NOWADAYS **ANYONE** CAN BE DEMONFOLK...

...ANYONE AT ALL.

YOU'RE SHITTING ME, RIGHT?

LANGUAGE, KID.

AH. SORRY. "YOU'RE *FUCKING* SHITTING ME, RIGHT?"

LAM, YOUR FATHER, HE BELIEVED THAT *ONE WEEK* FROM NOW, AN *ASTEROID OF HALO* IS GOING TO HIT EARTH.

FOR THE FIRST TIME IN MILLENNIA, A LAST HOPE FOR US.

YES, IT'S TRUE THAT TWICE BEFORE IN THE LAST DECADE HE'D BEEN WRONG ABOUT POSSIBLE IMPACTS. THIS TIME, THOUGH, HE SEEMED MORE CONFIDENT THAN I'D EVER SEEN HIM.

BUT, HE'D *JUST* FINISHED HIS CALCULATIONS AS TO *WHERE*, WHEN THE SPOONS KILLED HIM. THE POINT IS, THE WHOLE JOURNEY WE'RE ABOUT TO TAKE TO THE IMPACT POINT...IT COULD BE A *TRAP*.

NOW YOUR *BLADE* DIDN'T IGNITE WHEN YOU FOUGHT BESS. TO BE A PART OF THIS, YOU NEED--

TO HAVE FAITH. I GET IT.
"IN SOMETHING BIGGER THAN MYSELF."
REMEMBER, IT DOESN'T HAVE TO BE IN A GOD. IT'S JUST FAITH IN--
YEAH, WHAT ABOUT LIKE...GRAVITY? OR GOOD DENTAL HYGIENE??
HISSSSSSSS
OR BASEBALL! BUT THAT OLD-TIMEY BASEBALL. IN A CORNFIELD?
BEHIND YOU.
HOW ABOUT FAITH IN FUCKING DYING TODAY, RUNT?! HOW ABOUT THAT?

FAITH ACTIVATE!
SHUNK
GO GO FAITH!
COME ON!
YOU CAN DO IT, KID! CONCENTRATE!
THINK OF THINGS LIKE LOVE! LIKE FAMILY!
LOVE AND...
...AND FAMILY...
SHUNK
SHUNK
...LOVE AND...
SHUNK
THINGS YOU BELIEVE IN, LAM! FAST!
...IT'S NOT FUCKING WORKING!
TAXING THE RICH!
SHUNK
BEYONCÉ!
SHUNK
COFFEE?!
SHUNK
COME ON!
SHUNK
SHUNK

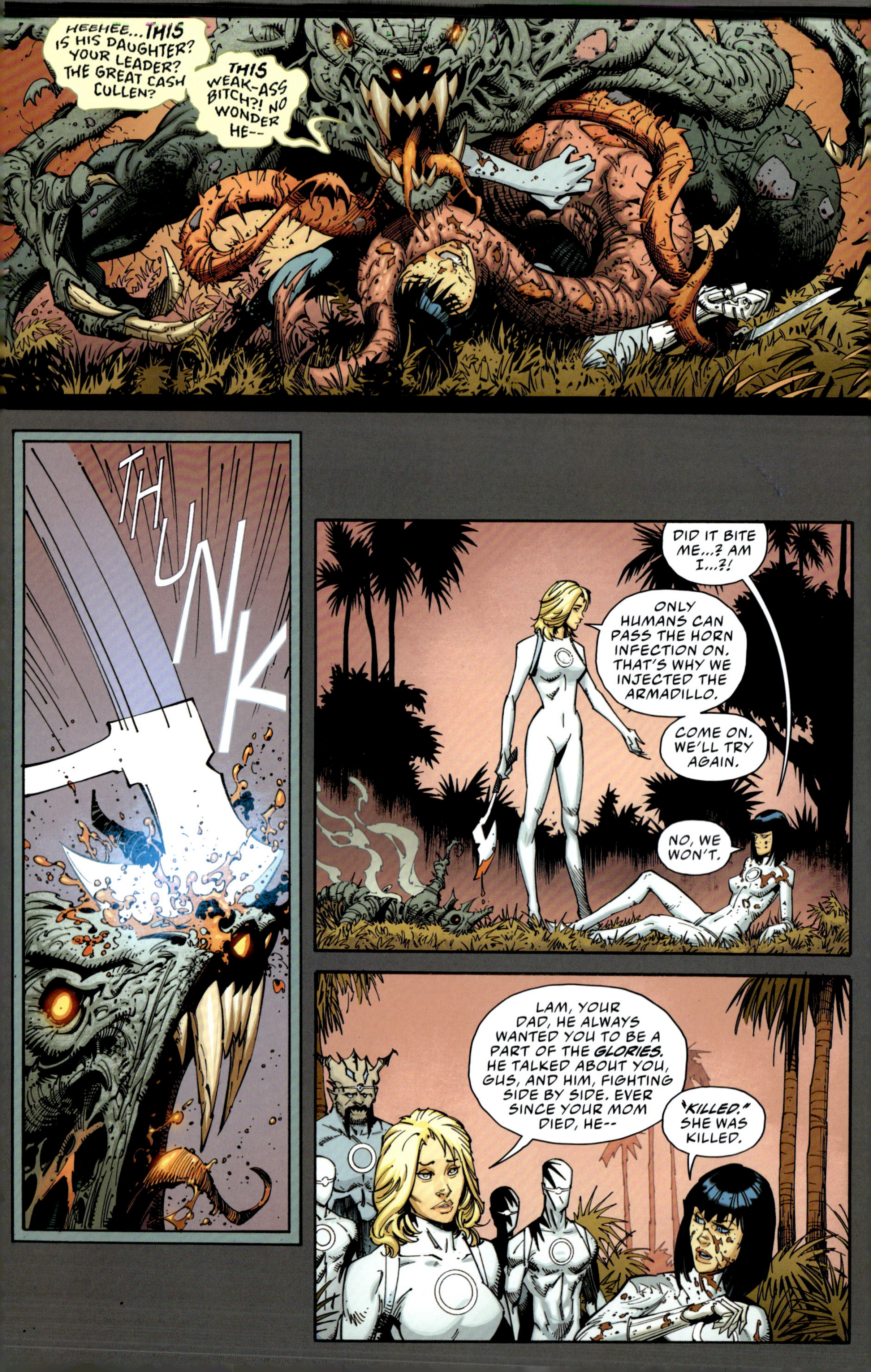
HEEHEE...THIS IS HIS DAUGHTER? YOUR LEADER? THE GREAT CASH CULLEN?
THIS WEAK-ASS BITCH?! NO WONDER HE--
THUNK
DID IT BITE ME...? AM I...?!
ONLY HUMANS CAN PASS THE HORN INFECTION ON. THAT'S WHY WE INJECTED THE ARMADILLO.
COME ON. WE'LL TRY AGAIN.
NO, WE WON'T.
LAM, YOUR DAD, HE ALWAYS WANTED YOU TO BE A PART OF THE GLORIES. HE TALKED ABOUT YOU, GUS, AND HIM, FIGHTING SIDE BY SIDE. EVER SINCE YOUR MOM DIED, HE--
"KILLED." SHE WAS KILLED.

Panel 1
"I'M SORRY. ...COME ON, JUST TRY ONE MORE--"

"NO. I DIDN'T CHOOSE ANY OF THIS. I DON'T WANT IT. NOW PLEASE..."

"...LEAVE ME ALONE."

Panel 4
"THAT BLADE, IT WAS YOUR MOTHER'S, YOU KNOW."

"AND DID IT WORK FOR HER? LOOK. 'GUS.'"

"I GET THAT YOU AND MY PARENTS WERE MONSTER-SLAYING BUDDIES AND MY DAD HAD SOME VISION OF ME ENDING UP LIKE YOU GUYS..."

KLUNK

Panel 5
"...BUT THIS...IT'S *NOT* WHO I AM. HE WAS WRONG, OKAY, I'M NOT ONE OF YOU...'GLORIES' OR WHATEVER."

"YOUR DAD WAS MY BEST FRIEND, LAM. MY BROTHER. BUT HE DIDN'T THINK YOU'D BECOME ONE OF US."

"HE DIDN'T?"

NO, HE THOUGHT YOU'D BECOME SOMETHING BETTER.
HAVING FAITH IN THINGS, IT'S NEVER EASY. AND IT DOESN'T GET ANY EASIER. IF ANYTHING, IT GETS HARDER.
BUT YOUR FATHER BELIEVED IN ME WHEN THERE WAS NO REASON TO. HE BELIEVED IN ALL OF THIS. AND HE BELIEVED IN YOU.
I DO TOO. I ALWAYS HAVE. YOU'LL FIND YOUR OWN WAY, WITH US OR WITHOUT.
IT WAS HIS NICKNAME FOR ME, YOU KNOW.
"DILLA" FOR "ARMADILLO."
BECAUSE THEY'RE "TOUGH LITTLE MOTHERS."
ACTUALLY... I MADE THAT ONE UP.
SHUT UP.
IT'S TRUE. I'VE BEEN WATCHING OVER YOU YOUR WHOLE LIFE, LAM. I CALLED YOU THAT ONCE TO CASH, AND HE LIKED IT. OF COURSE, I DID IT BECAUSE DILLAS SLEEP OVER SIXTEEN HOURS A DAY AND SMELL GOD AWFUL AND ARE MEAN AS ALL GET OUT.
HEY!
HEH. I'M JUST TEASING YOU. I DID IT BECAUSE THEY'RE TOUGH MOTHERS.
SIGH FINE, I'LL COME ON THIS MISSION.
BUT JUST TO...TO LAY HIM TO REST. TO LAY ALL OF IT TO REST.
WELCOME TO THE GLORIES, LAMASSU CULLEN! GET IN HERE!
OH, FUCK RIGHT OFF.
LANGUAGE, KID. LANGUAGE.

CHAPTER FIVE: "ICEBERGS"

BUT WHAT IS **FAITH**? I MEAN WHEN YOU GET DOWN TO IT.

IS IT A BELIEF SYSTEM? A LEAP?

WHAT CAUSES THE CHEMICAL REACTION THAT MAKES **HALO** LIGHT UP?

CASH AND I DISCUSSED IT MANY TIMES OVER THE YEARS. OFTEN OVER A GLASS OF WINE, MORE OFTEN, WHILE WIPING OFF DEMON BLOOD.

HE BELIEVED IT WAS A CONVICTION. FOR ME, THOUGH...IT WAS ALWAYS MORE OF A **FEELING.**

IT'S THE SENSATION I HAD BEING WITH MY TRIBE. MY FRIENDS. SPEAKING A LANGUAGE LONG VANISHED FROM THE EARTH.

100,000 YEARS AGO.

HOLDING MY WIFE, REN-HELLOT.

LIFTING MY DAUGHTER, PIL-ARIE, INTO THE AIR.

IT WAS FEELING AGLOW.

AND SOMEHOW... CONNECTED.

A TINY POINT IN A CONSTELLATION TOO BIG TO MAP ON ANY PARCHMENT.

I SUPPOSE IT'S FEELING LIKE **HALO** ITSELF--LIGHT REACHING FOR LIGHT.

AND IT WAS EASY, BACK THEN.

UNTIL THAT DAY...

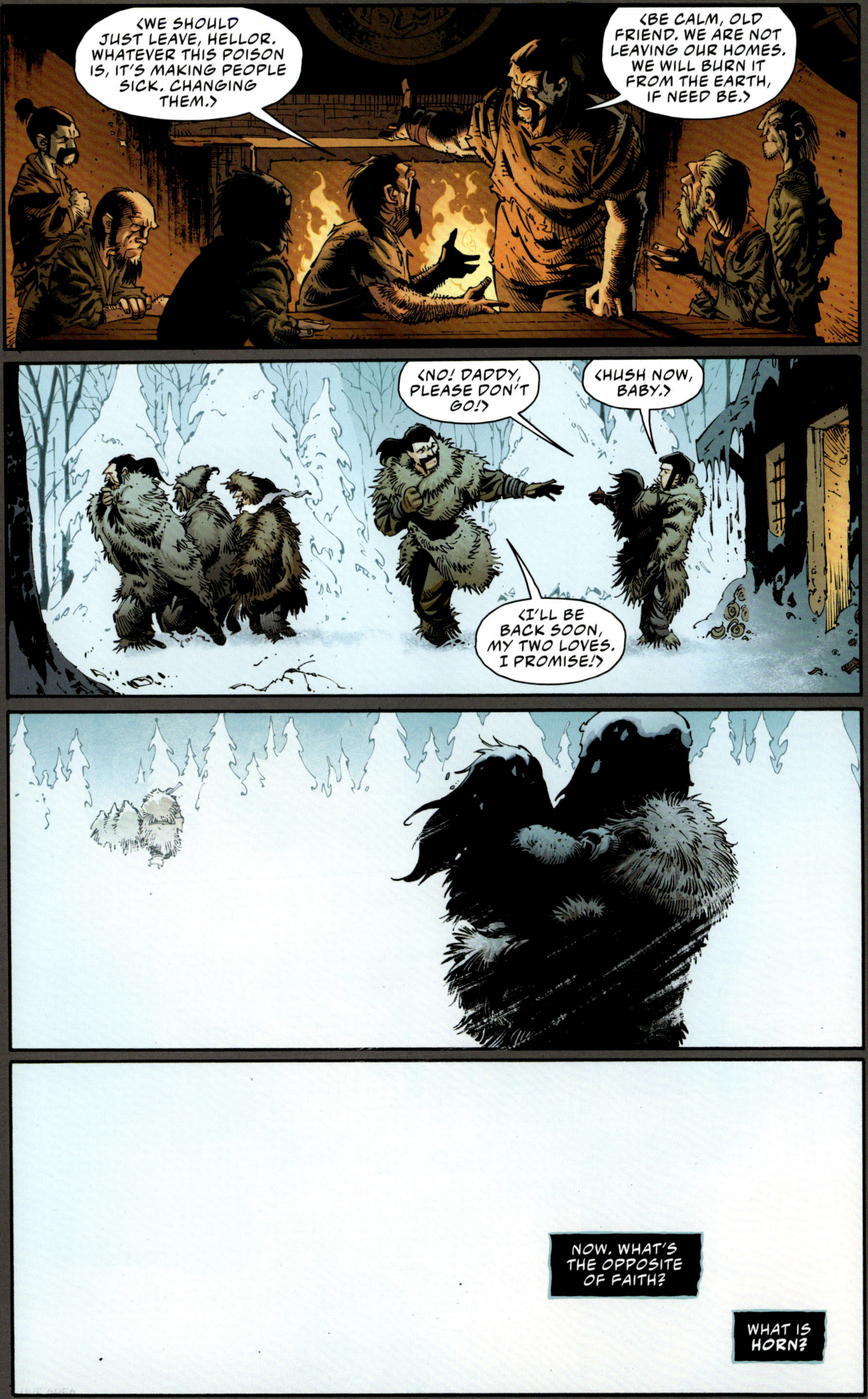

<WE SHOULD JUST LEAVE, HELLOR. WHATEVER THIS POISON IS, IT'S MAKING PEOPLE SICK. CHANGING THEM.>
<BE CALM, OLD FRIEND. WE ARE NOT LEAVING OUR HOMES. WE WILL BURN IT FROM THE EARTH, IF NEED BE.>
<NO! DADDY, PLEASE DON'T GO!>
<HUSH NOW, BABY.>
<I'LL BE BACK SOON, MY TWO LOVES. I PROMISE!>
NOW. WHAT'S THE OPPOSITE OF FAITH?
WHAT IS HORN?

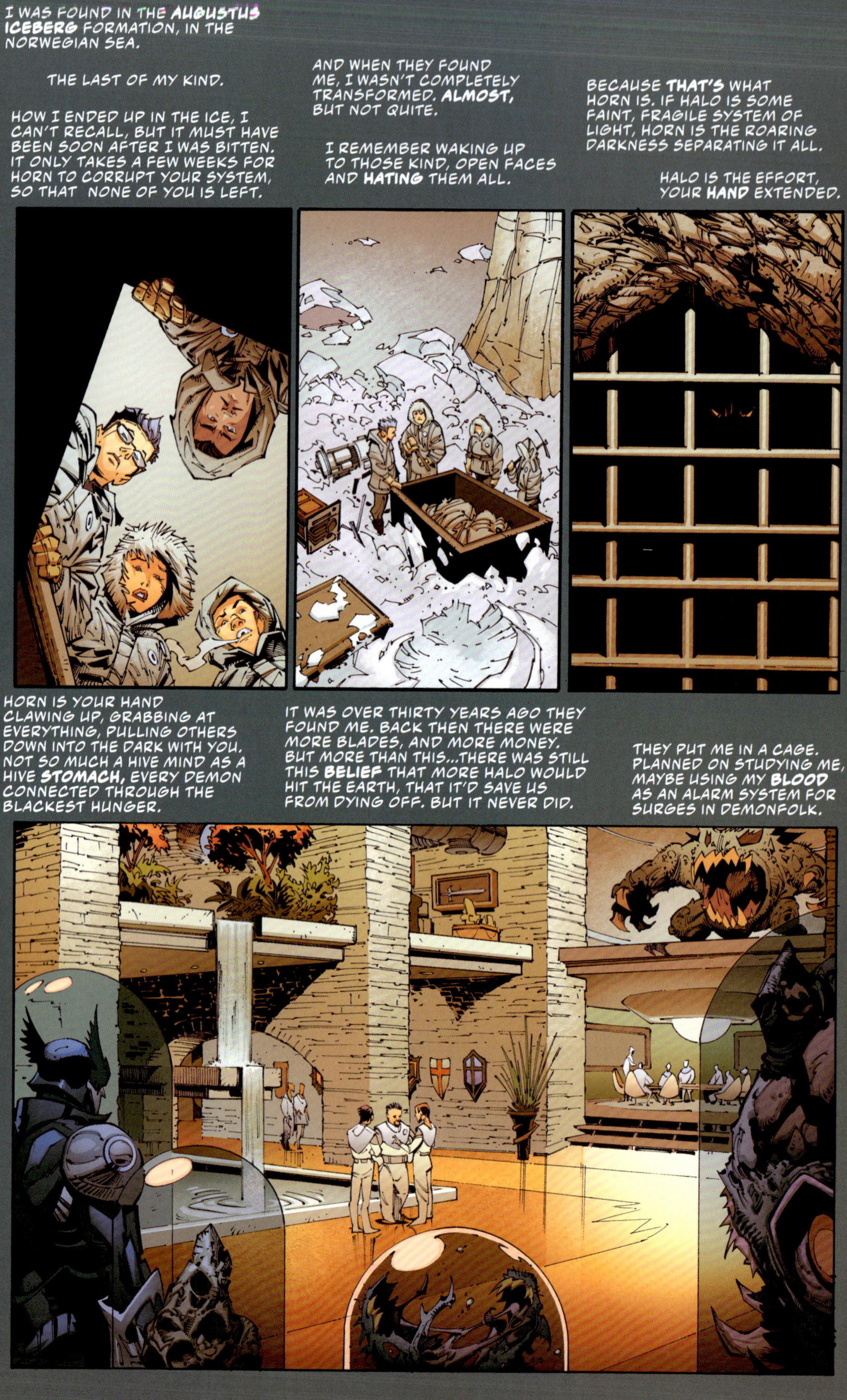
I WAS FOUND IN THE AUGUSTUS ICEBERG FORMATION, IN THE NORWEGIAN SEA.
THE LAST OF MY KIND.
HOW I ENDED UP IN THE ICE, I CAN'T RECALL, BUT IT MUST HAVE BEEN SOON AFTER I WAS BITTEN. IT ONLY TAKES A FEW WEEKS FOR HORN TO CORRUPT YOUR SYSTEM, SO THAT NONE OF YOU IS LEFT.
AND WHEN THEY FOUND ME, I WASN'T COMPLETELY TRANSFORMED. ALMOST, BUT NOT QUITE.
I REMEMBER WAKING UP TO THOSE KIND, OPEN FACES AND HATING THEM ALL.
BECAUSE THAT'S WHAT HORN IS. IF HALO IS SOME FAINT, FRAGILE SYSTEM OF LIGHT, HORN IS THE ROARING DARKNESS SEPARATING IT ALL.
HALO IS THE EFFORT, YOUR HAND EXTENDED.
HORN IS YOUR HAND CLAWING UP, GRABBING AT EVERYTHING, PULLING OTHERS DOWN INTO THE DARK WITH YOU. NOT SO MUCH A HIVE MIND AS A HIVE STOMACH, EVERY DEMON CONNECTED THROUGH THE BLACKEST HUNGER.
IT WAS OVER THIRTY YEARS AGO THEY FOUND ME. BACK THEN THERE WERE MORE BLADES, AND MORE MONEY. BUT MORE THAN THIS...THERE WAS STILL THIS BELIEF THAT MORE HALO WOULD HIT THE EARTH, THAT IT'D SAVE US FROM DYING OFF. BUT IT NEVER DID.
THEY PUT ME IN A CAGE. PLANNED ON STUDYING ME, MAYBE USING MY BLOOD AS AN ALARM SYSTEM FOR SURGES IN DEMONFOLK.

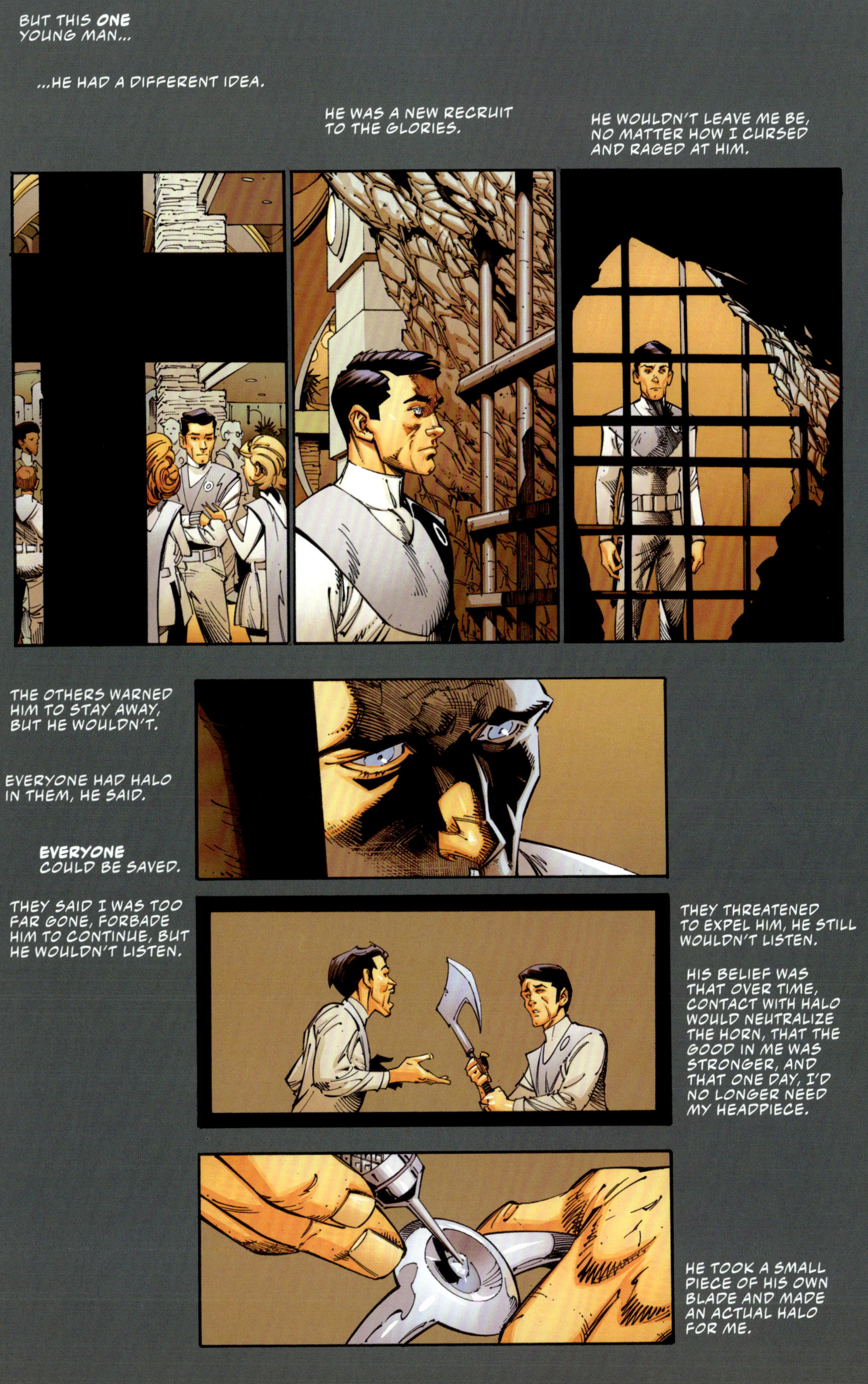
BUT THIS ONE YOUNG MAN...
...HE HAD A DIFFERENT IDEA.
HE WAS A NEW RECRUIT TO THE GLORIES.
HE WOULDN'T LEAVE ME BE, NO MATTER HOW I CURSED AND RAGED AT HIM.
THE OTHERS WARNED HIM TO STAY AWAY, BUT HE WOULDN'T.
EVERYONE HAD HALO IN THEM, HE SAID.
EVERYONE COULD BE SAVED.
THEY SAID I WAS TOO FAR GONE, FORBADE HIM TO CONTINUE, BUT HE WOULDN'T LISTEN.
THEY THREATENED TO EXPEL HIM, HE STILL WOULDN'T LISTEN.
HIS BELIEF WAS THAT OVER TIME, CONTACT WITH HALO WOULD NEUTRALIZE THE HORN, THAT THE GOOD IN ME WAS STRONGER, AND THAT ONE DAY, I'D NO LONGER NEED MY HEADPIECE.
HE TOOK A SMALL PIECE OF HIS OWN BLADE AND MADE AN ACTUAL HALO FOR ME.

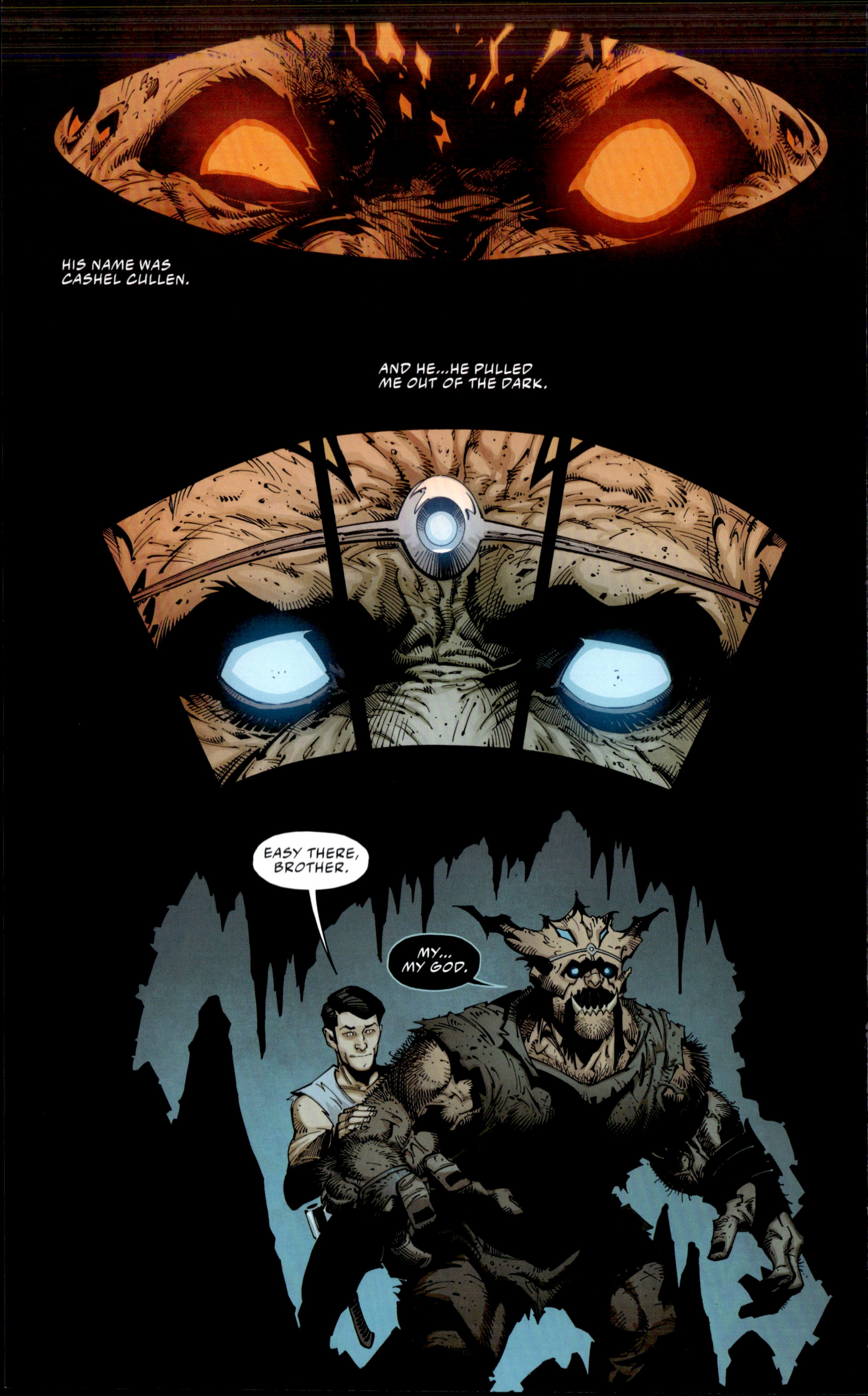
HIS NAME WAS
CASHEL CULLEN.
AND HE...HE PULLED
ME OUT OF THE DARK.
EASY THERE,
BROTHER.
MY...
MY GOD.

WE FOUGHT TOGETHER FOR MANY YEARS.
IN THE ATTACK OF '91.
THE RESURGENCE OF 2003.
EVEN AS MORE HORN HIT THE EARTH, AND MORE BLADES BROKE, AND MORE GLORIES FELL...
...WE KEPT ON.
THROUGH IT ALL, CASH NEVER LOST FAITH. HUMANS WERE CREATURES OF HALO. AND MORE HALO WOULD COME ONE DAY.
ENOUGH TO MAKE NEW BLADES...
HE FELL IN LOVE WITH KATHERINE, GOT MARRIED.
WHAT GREATER SIGN OF FAITH IS THERE THAN HAVING A CHILD?
WHAT BETTER WAY TO GIVE EVIL THE FINGER...THAN GIVING THE WORLD LAM?
CASH CULLEN.
I MISS YOU, OLD BUDDY.

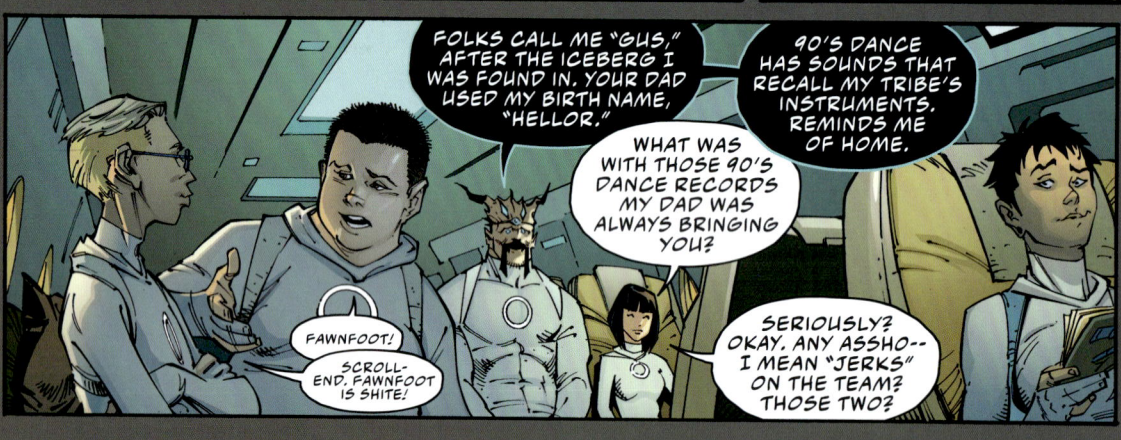

THERE'S SO MUCH I WISH I COULD SAY TO YOU. FOR YEARS, YOU WERE MY SAVIOR.

I PROMISE TO DO RIGHT BY YOU NOW.

NO...STAY THE FUCK... AWAY...

LANGUAGE, KID.

HUH? ≶YAWN≶ WHY DO YOU KEEP SAYING THAT?

CURSING. IT'S THE NATURAL SPEECH OF DEMONFOLK. THEY WORK TO HIDE IT.

AH. ANY OTHER FUN GLORY HANDBOOK FACTS I SHOULD KNOW?

ASK AWAY.

WHY THE TIGHTS?

THEY'RE WOVEN WITH SILVER TO HELP HALO CONDUCTION.

WHY DID MY DAD REFER TO YOU AS "HELL" IN HIS BOOK AND ON THE DOOR?

FOLKS CALL ME "GUS," AFTER THE ICEBERG I WAS FOUND IN. YOUR DAD USED MY BIRTH NAME, "HELLOR."

WHAT WAS WITH THOSE 90'S DANCE RECORDS MY DAD WAS ALWAYS BRINGING YOU?

90'S DANCE HAS SOUNDS THAT RECALL MY TRIBE'S INSTRUMENTS. REMINDS ME OF HOME.

FAWNFOOT!

SCROLL-END. FAWNFOOT IS SHITE!

SERIOUSLY? OKAY. ANY ASSHO-- I MEAN "JERKS" ON THE TEAM? THOSE TWO?

THE ONES ARGUING OVER BLADE HANDLES ARE KETCH AND KELLAN.

THEY WORK AS A TEAM IN BRITAIN. "CATCH AND KILL 'EM."

CHARMING. HOW ABOUT THEM?

"MARK MANAGES WESTERN CANADIAN TERRITORIES. KANJI WORKS OUT OF HONSHŪ, JAPAN. AND TIRO IS GAUTENG PROVINCE, SOUTH AFRICA, I THINK?"

BUT WHY *THESE* FORTS ON *THIS* NITE?

"MANU AND AVA ARE GERMANY AND IRAN. TOUGH AS NAILS."

TRY BLOCKING WITH YOUR LEFT AND--

THEN COMING UP WITH THE KNEE.

GOT IT.

"THE PLANE IS JOAO'S. HE WORKS OUT OF BRAZIL. HE'S A GOOD ONE. A TRUE LEADER. ONLY ONE OF US WITH MONEY, TOO."

"AND THAT'S EVERYONE? *ALL* THE GLORIES?"

THERE ARE MORE, BUT WITHOUT BLADES, THEY JUST OFFER WHATEVER SUPPORT THEY CAN.

THOSE COUPLE TIMES THAT CASH THOUGHT HALO HAD HIT...AND WE WENT TO SEE IF IT HAD AND FOUND *NOTHING*...

...IT HURT ALL OF US. HURT HIM.

I'M JUST SAYING...HE'D BE HAPPY TO SEE EVERYONE HERE, TAKING A LEAP TOGETHER ONE MORE TIME, LAM.

AH, THERE YOU ARE. I HEARD YOU ASK ABOUT THE JERK ON THE TEAM, AND WELL, IT'S ME. BECAUSE I HAVE TO INTERRUPT.

LISTEN UP, EVERYONE!

WE'RE ALMOST THERE. SO LET'S TALK WHAT WE'RE IN FOR.

CASH'S CALCULATIONS HAD THE HALO METEOR HITTING IN TWO DAYS. RIGHT HERE. IN RURAL NORWAY. HE'D RENTED A CABIN NEAR THE SITE AND CONDUCTED TESTS. IT'S WHERE WE'LL BE STAYING.
LIKE I SAID, CASH BELIEVED IN THIS MISSION. SO MUCH SO THAT HE ASKED TO BE LAID TO REST NEAR THE IMPACT SITE. HALO TO HALO.
AND IF CASHEL WAS CORRECT THIS TIME, WHAT'S THE PLAN ONCE THE METEOR LANDS?
UH...HOW ABOUT WE PARTY?
SECONDED, MATE.
IF CASH WAS RIGHT, THIS CHUNK OF HALO WILL BE ENOUGH TO MAKE A THOUSAND BLADES. MORE.
SO WHAT DO WE DO WHEN WE GET IT?
"GIVE EVIL ALL THE FINGERS."
WHAT IN...
"I KNOW IT'S A LONG SHOT..."
...BUT I HAVE FAITH. AND I KNOW YOU DO, TOO.

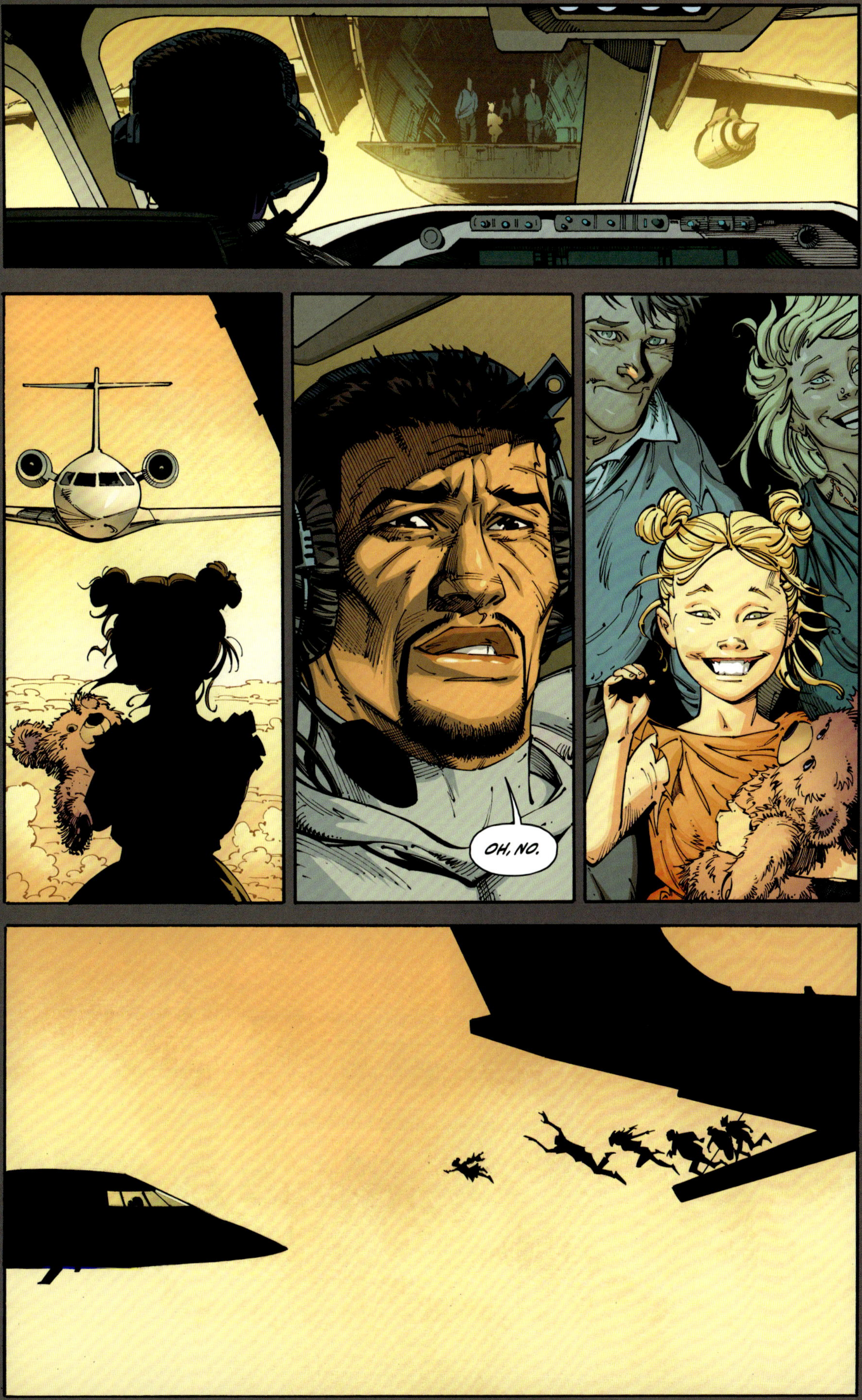
OH, NO.

SCREE—

DEMONFOLK... THEY'RE ONBOARD THE PLANE!!

BLADES!

NOW!

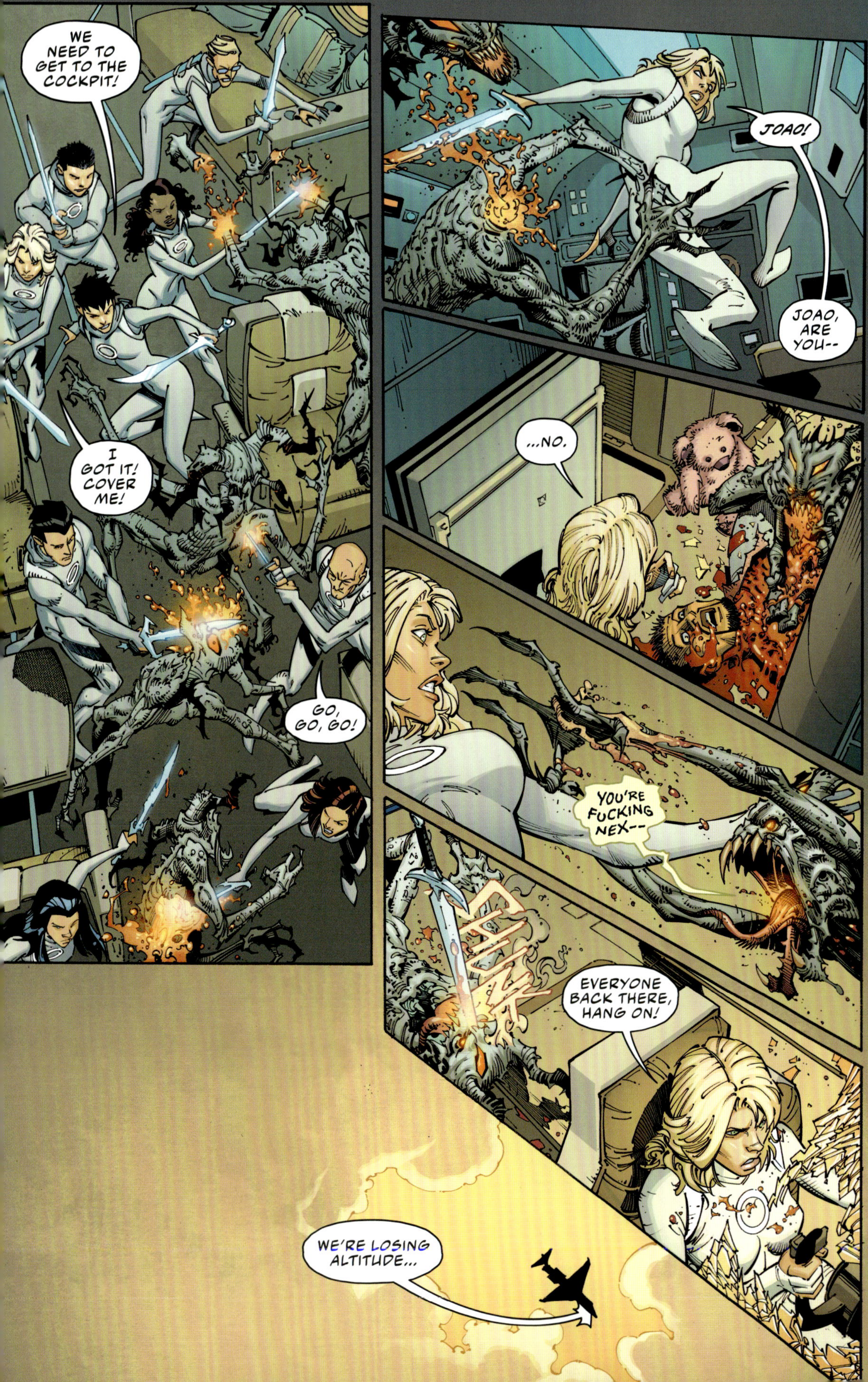

"...AND FAST!"
ON YOUR RIGHT!
GOT HIM!
LAM! YOUR BLADE!
SCRUNCH
IT'S WORKING! I THOUGHT OF MY DAD AND... AND...
good girl
...SHI-- SHOOT.
flicker
SCREEEE

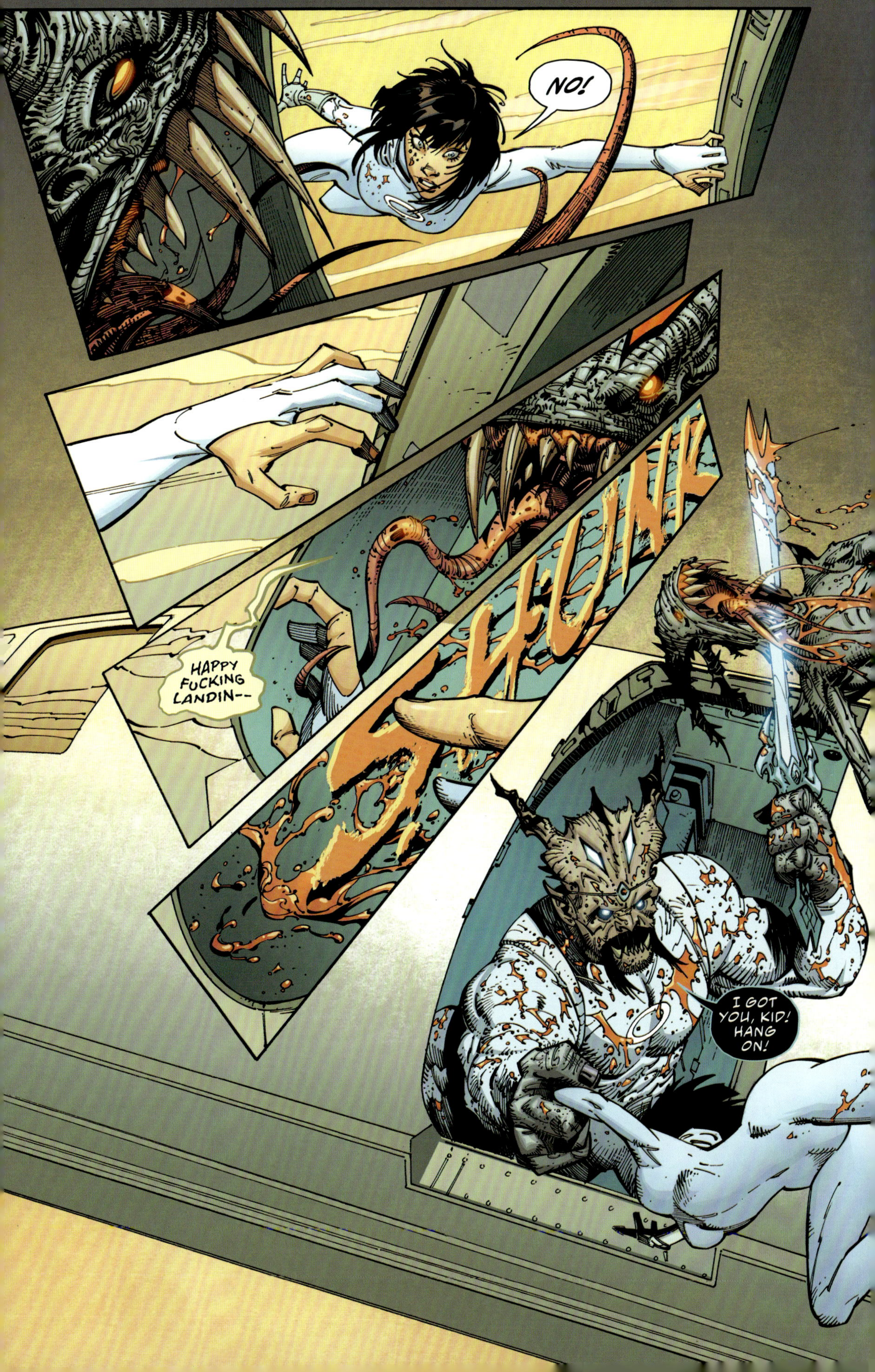
NO!
HAPPY FUCKING LANDIN--
SHUNK
I GOT YOU, KID! HANG ON!

GUS! BEHIND YOU!
ARGH!
CHOMP
GUS! YOU...WATCH OUT! DON'T LET THEM TAKE YOUR...
...HALO.
NO! I LOST TOO MUCH FAMILY ALREADY! I WON'T...
...WON'T...
...LET FUCKING GO!

UH... GUS?
Stay... aWay from me...LaM.
WHOAAA!
RRAAAAHH!
YES! JOIN US, BROTH-- AGH!
GUS! FIGHT IT! DON'T LET IT--UNH!
...WIN.

GUS, IT'S US. YOUR FRIENDS.
TELL US YOU RECOGNIZE US!
I...i dO... aNd...
...And...
...I HATE YOU ALL!
YOU SHITHEELS PRETEND TO BE MY GODDAMNED FAMILY...BUT MY FAMILY IS FUCKING DEAD. YOU...

YOU WANTED TO PUT ME IN A SHITTY LITTLE CAGE. DIDN'T YOU?!
EVERYONE! I...I CAN'T HOLD IT! WE'RE GOING DOWN!
YOU RAT-FUCKING-PIG-FUCKING-BABY-FUCKING-GRANNY-FUCKING ASS WARTS! I'LL KILL YOU ALL! I'LL GLORT YOU IN YOUR XËRXY 'TIL IT EXPLODES! FUUUUUCK!
GLORIES! BRACE FOR IMPACT!
I'LL... I'LL...
EVERYONE HANG O--
THOOM

CHAPTER SIX:
"COMPLETELY GLORTED"

=GASP=

SHH. IT'S OKAY.

LAM, I... I DIDN'T HURT YOU, DID I?

JUST MY DELICATE SENSIBILITIES. KANJI TOLD ME WHAT "GLORT" MEANS IN YOUR LANGUAGE. YEAH, HOW IS THAT EVEN ANATOMICALLY POSSIBLE?

MY...MY SPECIES HAS WIDER HIPS THAN--

IT DOESN'T MATTER.

GUS, CAN I ASK YOU SOMETHING?

OF COURSE.

IT WASN'T SOME *SNAKE* THAT BIT MY ARM WHEN I WAS LITTLE, WAS IT?

IT WAS YOU.

YES.

YOUR MOTHER, KATHERINE. SHE WAS KILLED SO SENSELESSLY.
AFTER BATTLING EVIL WITH US FOR YEARS... TO BE RUN DOWN AND LEFT FOR--
I GET IT.
KATHERINE HAD ALWAYS HAD FAITH IN MY TRANSFORMATION. AND SO...SO, TO HONOR HER, YOUR FATHER WANTED TO TRY...
REMOVING YOUR HALO.
BUT I... I COULDN'T HOLD ON. YOU REACHED OUT TO ME, SMILING, WIDE EYED.
YOU WERE ONLY FIVE AND I...*SIGH* YOUR FATHER, HE USED HIS BLADE TO STOP THE INFECTION IN TIME.
BUT YOU'RE SAYING THAT AFTER THIS... MY DAD, HE STILL DIDN'T...
LOSE FAITH? NO. NEVER.
HE FORGAVE ME AND TOLD ME SOON ENOUGH I'D OVERCOME IT. BUT THAT...*PULL*. IT'S SO DEEP. IT FEELS SO GOOD, TOO.
YOUR FATHER NEVER WANTED TO ADMIT IT, BUT MUCH AS WE ALL HAVE HALO IN US, I FIGURE--
WE ALL HAVE HORN IN US, TOO.
THAT NIGHT, AFTER THE POLICE LEFT, I REMEMBER HEARING DAD CURSE AS HE GOT HIS COAT ON. HE YELLED *DAMN*. JUST ONCE BUT LIKE A WAIL.
AFTER HE LEFT I SAID IT OVER AND OVER INTO MY PILLOW, AND IT DID FEEL...SO GOOD.
KNOCK KNOCK. COME ON...

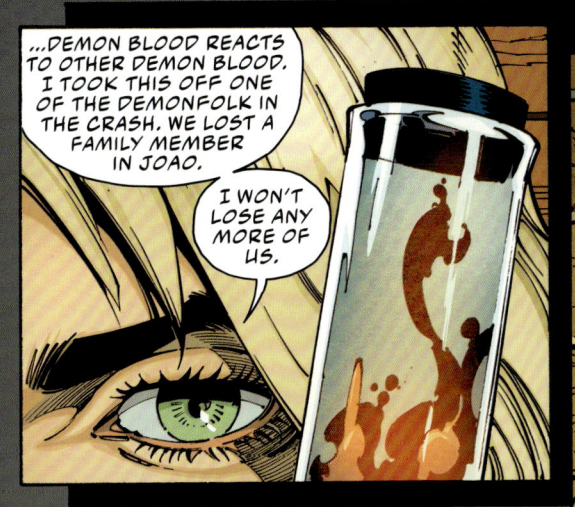

"...MEETING TIME."

GUS, IT'S GOOD TO HAVE YOU BACK.

BUT THAT ATTACK UP THERE...IT PROVED SOMETHING TO ME.

THERE'S A *TRAITOR* AMONG US.

JUNE...

THAT PLANE COULD'VE FOLLOWED US.

YEAH, MAYBE--

NO ONE KNEW ABOUT THE PLANE, OR OUR FLIGHT PATH, EXCEPT *US*. NO ONE.

WE NEED TO DO THE *TEST*.

LAM, BECAUSE YOU'RE NEW, JUST LIKE HALO REACTS TO OTHER HALO...

...DEMON BLOOD REACTS TO OTHER DEMON BLOOD. I TOOK THIS OFF ONE OF THE DEMONFOLK IN THE CRASH. WE LOST A FAMILY MEMBER IN JOAO.

I WON'T LOSE ANY MORE OF US.

REALLY NOW, JUNE. YOU CAN'T THINK--

EVERYONE STEP AWAY FROM ONE ANOTHER...

...NOW.

MARK, YOU'RE CLEAR.

TIRO.

KANJI.

THIS IS A SAD DAY, ALL.

AVA, MANU. YOU'RE GOOD.

KELLAN.

THIS IS BLOODY RIDICULOUS. WE'RE A TEAM, NO ONE HERE WOULD...

SCREE

... NO. NO, I--

WAIT. IT'S NOT REACTING TO KELLAN. IT'S REACTING TO SOMETHING...

...BEHIND HIM?

LAM? WHAT ARE YOU DOING, HONEY?
YEAH, KIDDO, COME ON. LET'S--
SCREEE
NO.
NO, NO, NO...
IT CAN'T BE.

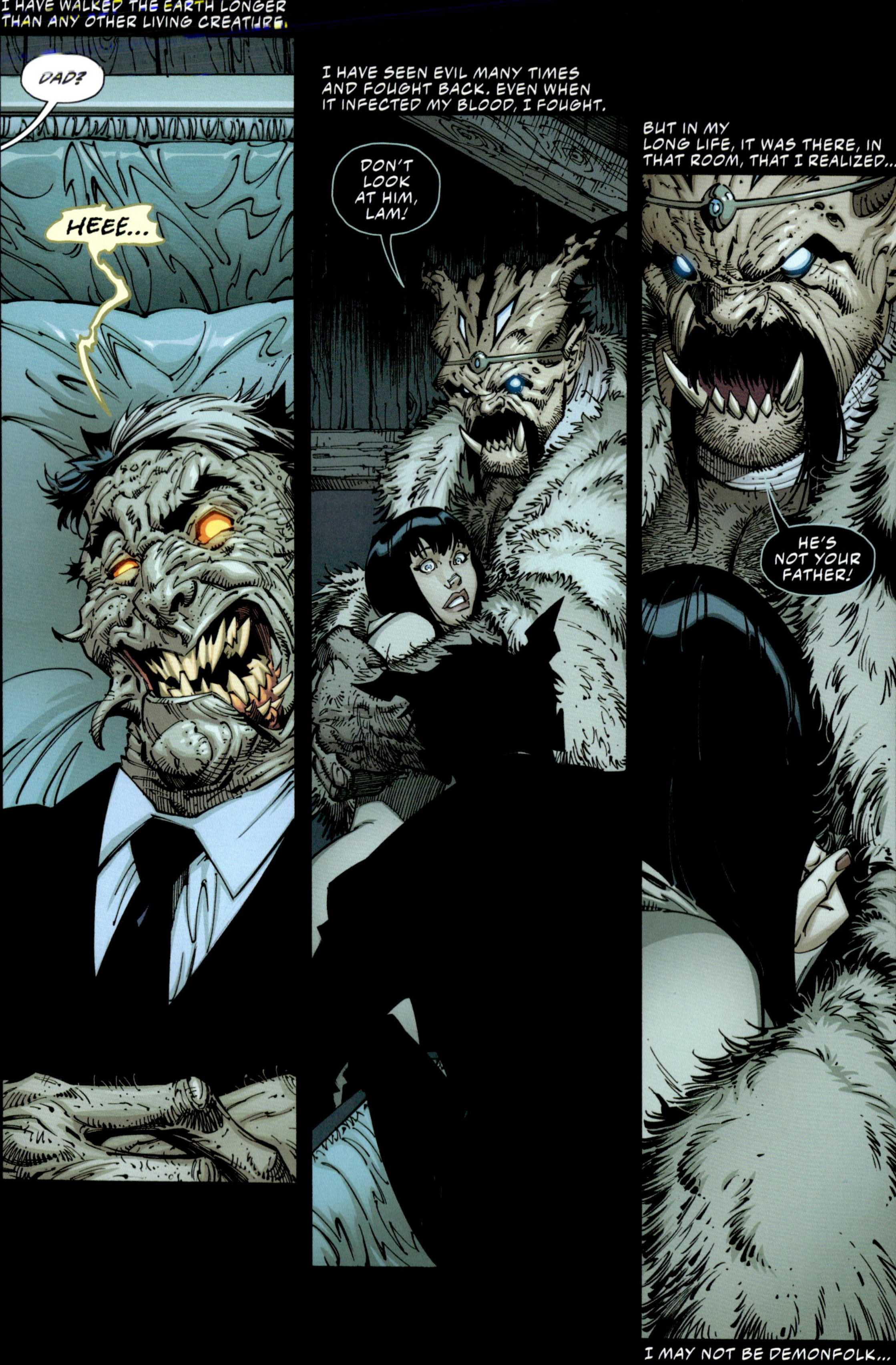

I HAVE WALKED THE EARTH LONGER THAN ANY OTHER LIVING CREATURE.
DAD?
HEEE...
I HAVE SEEN EVIL MANY TIMES AND FOUGHT BACK. EVEN WHEN IT INFECTED MY BLOOD, I FOUGHT.
DON'T LOOK AT HIM, LAM!
BUT IN MY LONG LIFE, IT WAS THERE, IN THAT ROOM, THAT I REALIZED...
HE'S NOT YOUR FATHER!
I MAY NOT BE DEMONFOLK...

...BUT MAYBE IT WAS TIME TO FINALLY GIVE UP FAITH.
HELLO, GUS. DILLA, HONEY...SO FUCKING GOOD TO SEE YOU AGAIN!

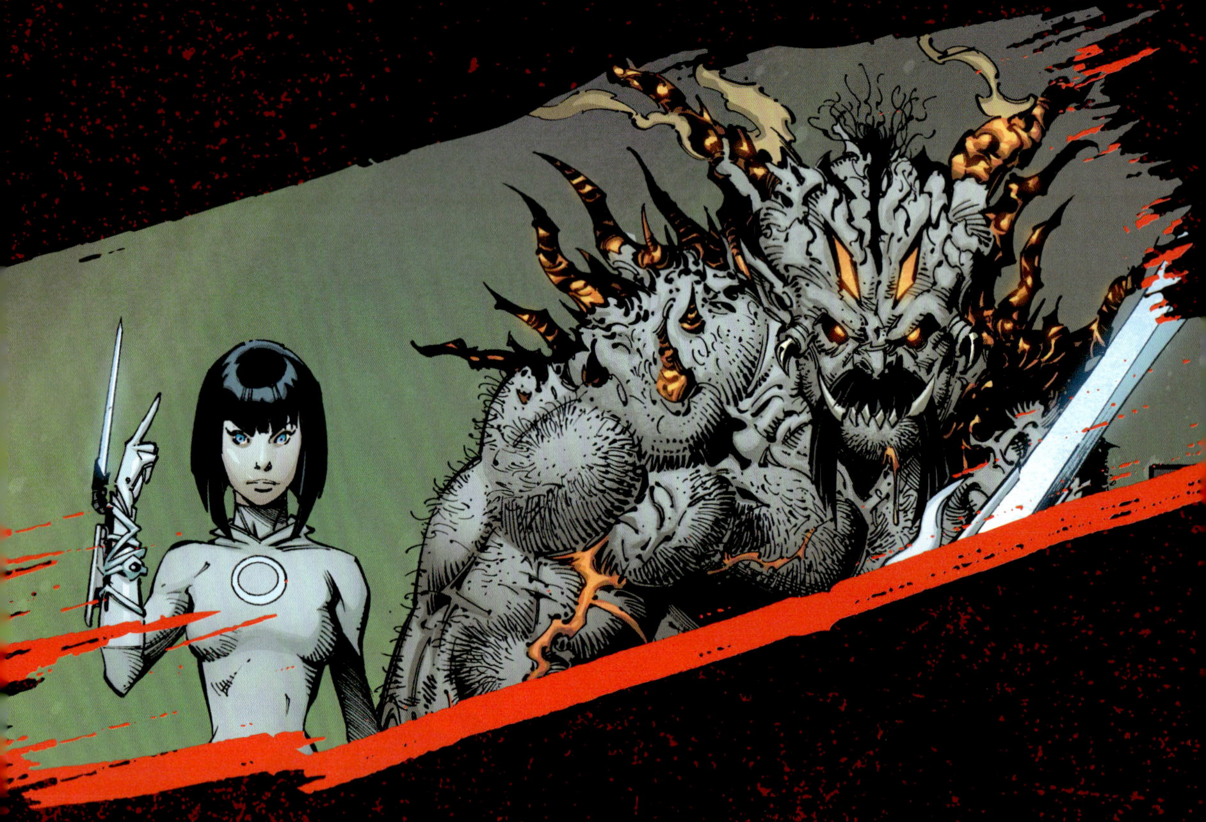

CHAPTER 3

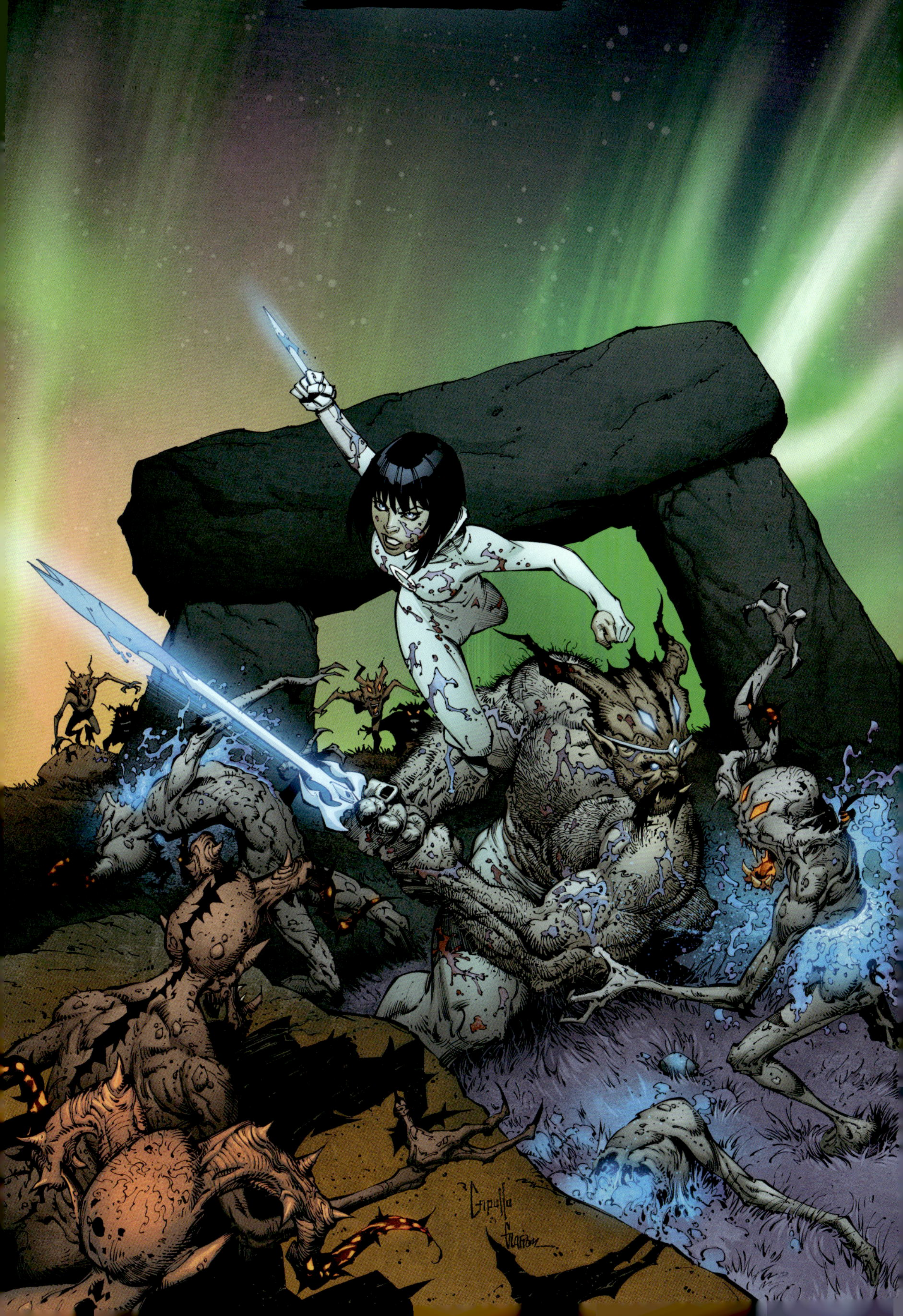

CHAPTER SEVEN: "BURN IT DOWN"

MY NAME IS LAMASSU "LAM" CULLEN, DAUGHTER OF CASHEL CULLEN, AND I STARTED MY PART OF THIS STORY WITH **GODFOLK**.

AND MY NAME IS **GUS** OF LINE *HOMO MALEDICTUS*, TRIBE OF THE DOOMED MAN, AND I BEGAN MY PART WITH **DEMONFOLK**. NOW YOU KNOW EVERYTHING, FROM THIRTEEN BILLION YEARS AGO TO RIGHT NOW...EXCEPT WHICH SIDE **WINS**.

BUT I WARNED YOU WHEN WE STARTED THAT THIS IS A STORY ABOUT THE **FALL OF MAN**, SO YOUR ANSWER IS RIGHT THERE. BECAUSE AN F.O.M. STORY? IT NEVER, **EVER**...

...HAS A HAPPY ENDING.
SCREEEEEE
DAD!
NO!
LAM, GET BACK!
I KNOW HE'S IN THERE!
DAD, IT'S ME!
YOUR DAUGHTER, LAM!
... L-Lam? Is that... you?
YES! YES, I'M RIGHT HERE, DAD! COME BACK TO US! PLEASE!
I HAVE FAITH IN YOU!
I'm trying, but it's so...so dark in here. I can't... can't find you!
Maybe if you just come a little...

...CLOSER!
splurk
NO!
LAM, LOOK OUT!
FOOM
GUS!
K-KRACK
HA! ALMOST HAD YOU, DILLA!
BANG BANG
LAM! LAM, LET US IN!
THAT'S BETTER.
WE HAVEN'T HAD ANY REAL GODDAMN FATHER-DAUGHTER TIME IN A WHILE, HAVE WE? HEH.

AGH!

CRASH

YOU'RE... YOU'RE *NOT* MY FATHER!

SHHICK

AW, MOM'S BLADE *STILL* NOT LIGHTING UP FOR YOU, DILLA? YOU KNOW I ENHANCED IT BEFORE I GAVE IT TO YOU? PUT *EXTRA* HALO IN IT. AND YOU? YOU *STILL* CAN'T MUSTER THE *FUCKING* FAITH TO MAKE IT GLOW.

HOW ASHAMED YOUR POOR MOTHER KATHERINE WOULD BE RIGHT NOW.

DON'T YOU SAY HER *NAME!*

WHAM

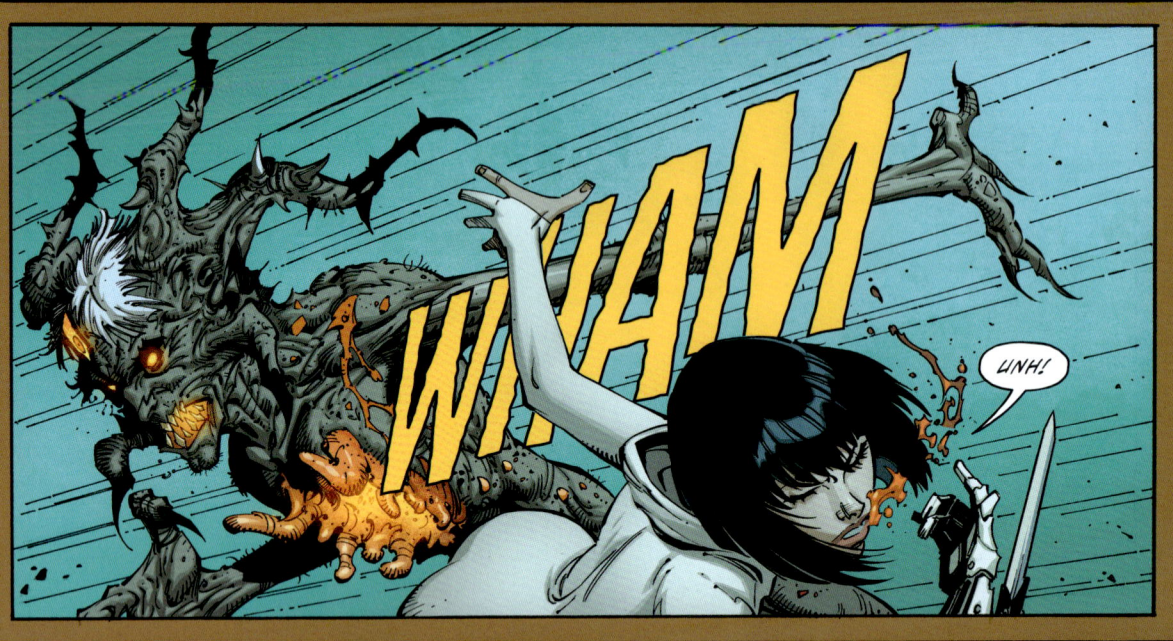

UNH!

SEE, KATHERINE TRIED TO DENY IT, BUT I ALWAYS KNEW YOU'D FAIL US. AND AFTER SHE WENT FUCKING SPLAT, WELL, IT WAS DONE.

STILL, I TRIED. OH LORD HOW I TRIED TO GET YOU TO HAVE FAITH, TO SEE THAT PEOPLE ARE MORE GOOD THAN BAD. BUT YOU...

DO YOU REMEMBER WHAT YOU SAID TO ME IN THE GARAGE THAT DAY, WHEN I WAS MAKING THAT ARM FOR YOU?

"WE ALL HAVE DEMONS."

THAT WAS THE MOMENT I KNEW YOU'D ALWAYS BELIEVE PEOPLE ARE MADE MORE OF HORN THAN HALO.

THAT'S WHEN I GAVE IN. YOU DID THIS TO ME, LAM. YOU.

NO! YOU'RE LYING!!!

YOU'RE LYING!

SHUNK SHUNK SHUNK

YOU'RE LYING!

YOU'RE FUCKING LYING!!!

SHUNK SHUNK
SHUNK
:SOB:... YOU'RE... :SOB:
SHHH NOW. IT'S OKAY, LAM. I'M GRATEFUL.
SEE, YOU WERE **RIGHT** ALL ALONG. YOU SHOWED **ME** THE WAY.
NOW, IT'S TIME TO FULFILL YOUR DESTINY, WHICH WAS NEVER TO **RENEW** THE GLORIES, BUT TO **END** THEM.
ORIGINALLY, YOU **WERE** SUPPOSED TO LEAD THEM OUT THERE, INTO MY TRAP. BUT **THIS** WAY IS SO MUCH BETTER. I'LL TURN YOU AND WE'LL KILL THEM TOGETHER, HERE AND NOW, A **TEAM.**
DON'T WORRY, DILLA, IT'LL ONLY HURT FOR A MOMENT!
NO!
SCREEEEEE
TSSSSSS
DID I...?
MY BLADE...?

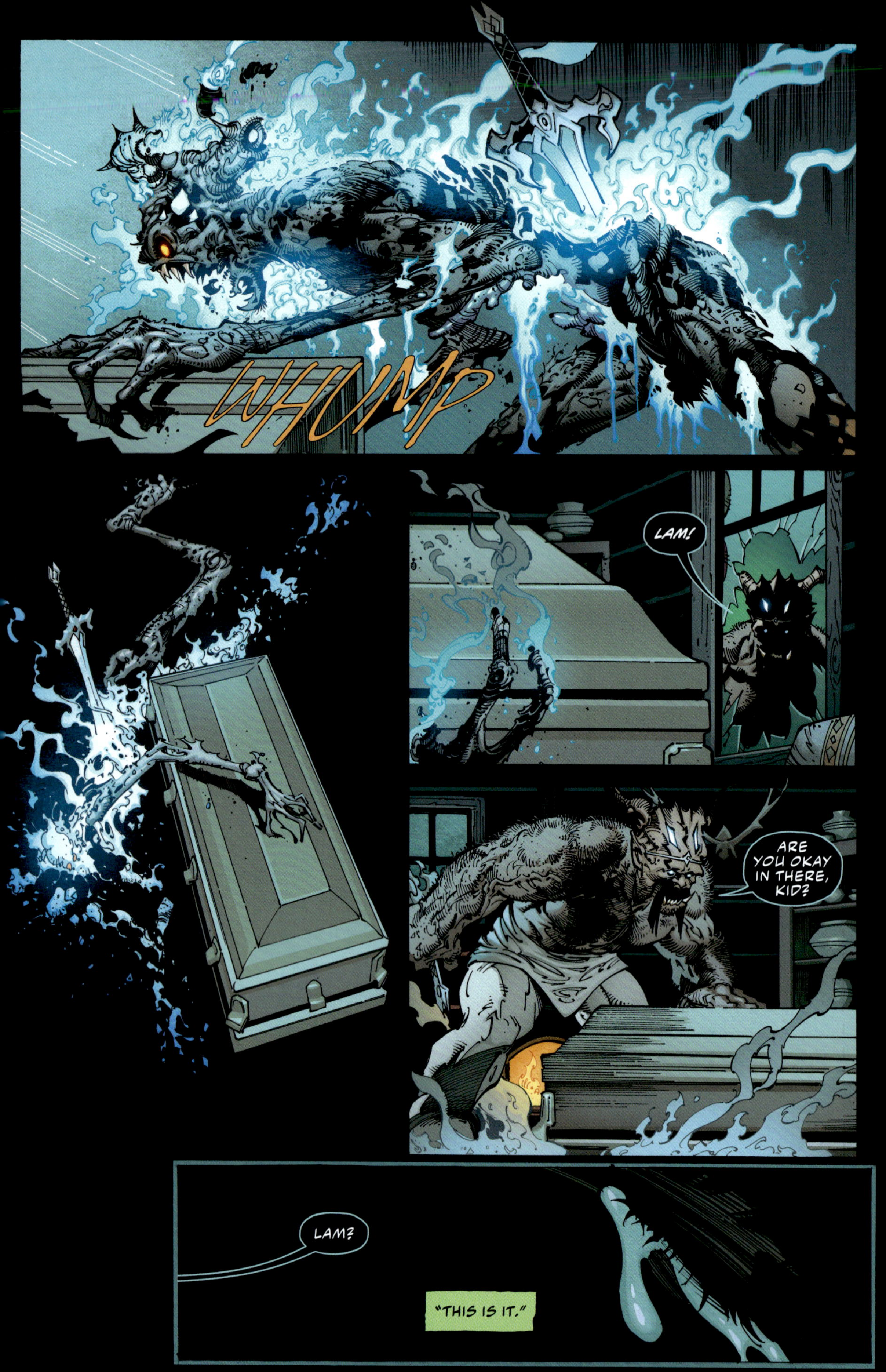
WHUMP
LAM!
ARE YOU OKAY IN THERE, KID?
LAM?
"THIS IS IT."

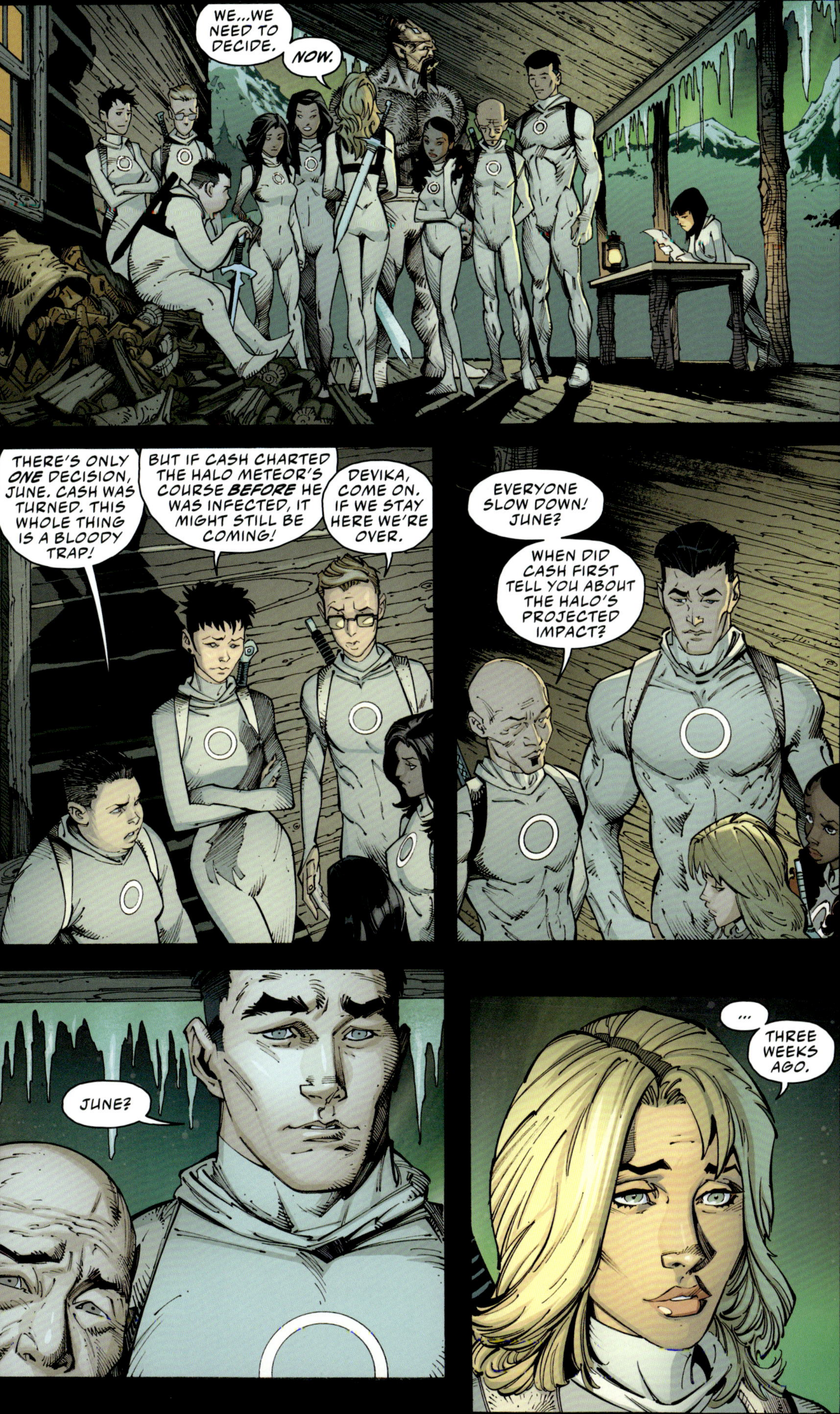
WE...WE NEED TO DECIDE.
NOW.
THERE'S ONLY ONE DECISION, JUNE. CASH WAS TURNED. THIS WHOLE THING IS A BLOODY TRAP!
BUT IF CASH CHARTED THE HALO METEOR'S COURSE BEFORE HE WAS INFECTED, IT MIGHT STILL BE COMING!
DEVIKA, COME ON. IF WE STAY HERE WE'RE OVER.
EVERYONE SLOW DOWN! JUNE?
WHEN DID CASH FIRST TELL YOU ABOUT THE HALO'S PROJECTED IMPACT?
JUNE?
...
THREE WEEKS AGO.

THERE YOU GO! NOT EVEN ONE MONTH. YOU SAW THAT DEMON. HE WAS FULL HORN. IT TAKES WHAT, AT LEAST A MONTH FOR THE INFECTION TO DO THAT TO YOU...
...
FINE, BUT LET'S SPEAK THE TRUTH. WITHOUT MORE HALO, THE GLORIES ARE DONE. WE ALL KNOW IT.
THAT DOESN'T CHANGE THE FACT THAT CASH GOT INFECTED BY HIS NEIGHBORS AND LIED TO US ABOUT THE SERAPHIM STONE COMING HERE SO HIS DEMON MATES COULD WIPE US OUT.
HE BETRAYED US.
SHUT YOUR DAMNED MOUTH, KETCH.
CASHEL CULLEN DIDN'T BETRAY US. WHATEVER THAT THING WAS, IT WASN'T HIM.
WHAT DOES IT MATTER, GUS? JAYSUS. A PIECE OF HALO HASN'T HIT THE EARTH IN FIVE THOUSAND YEARS!
BUT HE DISCOVERS ONE COMING HERE RIGHT BEFORE HE'S INFECTED?
COME ON.
MANU, YOU HAD A CONTACT. A BOAT. I SAY WE TAKE IT. NOW. WE ALL LOVED CASHEL, BUT--
YES, WE DID ALL LOVE HIM.
SO MAYBE WE GIVE HIM THE BENEFIT OF THE FUCKING DOUBT AND DON'T YOU DARE SAY "LANGUAGE" TO ME, ANY OF YOU.

THE VIAL, JUNE. THE DEMON BLOOD. DO YOU STILL HAVE IT?
MANU'S RIGHT. WE CAN STILL USE IT. A DEMON'S BLOOD REACTS TO OTHER DEMONS.
IF THERE'S AN AMBUSH WAITING DOWN THERE IN THE CLEARING, THAT VIAL WILL TELL US ONCE AND FOR ALL.
...
LAM?
GO ON.
DO IT.
SCREE
SCREEE
NO...

MANU?
DONE. THE BOAT WILL BE HERE IN AN HOUR.
AND THIS PLACE?
YOU KNOW THE PROTOCOL, KANJI. WE BURN IT DOWN.
NO ONE'S BURNING ANYTHING.
WHAT?
THUNK
I SAID, NO ONE IS BURNING ANYTHING, KELLAN.
NOW, THAT DEMON, HE TOLD ME I'D NEVER HAVE FAITH.
DEMONS, THERE'S NO TRUTH TO WHAT THEY SAY, LAM, ONLY CRUELTY.
YOU KNOW, MY MOTHER... SHE WAS FOUND OFF TO THE SIDE OF THE ROAD, IN THIS...FIELD. THE THING IS, WHEN SHE WAS HIT WALKING, HER ARMS AND LEGS WERE ALL BROKEN ON IMPACT.
WHICH MEANS WHOEVER HIT HER...MOVED HER TO THE SIDE OF THE ROAD SO HER BODY WOULDN'T BLOCK THEIR CAR AS THEY DROVE AWAY TO LET HER DIE.
MY DAD FOUND FAITH BY BELIEVING THAT PEOPLE ARE MORE GOOD THAN BAD. BUT THAT DEMON WAS RIGHT. I DO BELIEVE WE'RE MORE HORN THAN HALO. I ALWAYS HAVE.
BUT MEETING YOU ALL, ESPECIALLY YOU, GUS, I...
...I ALSO BELIEVE THAT WHAT MAKES US SPECIAL, HOLY EVEN, IS HOW WE KEEP REACHING, FIGHTING TO BE BETTER THAN WE'RE SUPPOSED TO BE.
SO NO, I DON'T HAVE MY FATHER'S FAITH. I HAVE MY OWN. AND IT'S NO LESS POWERFUL.

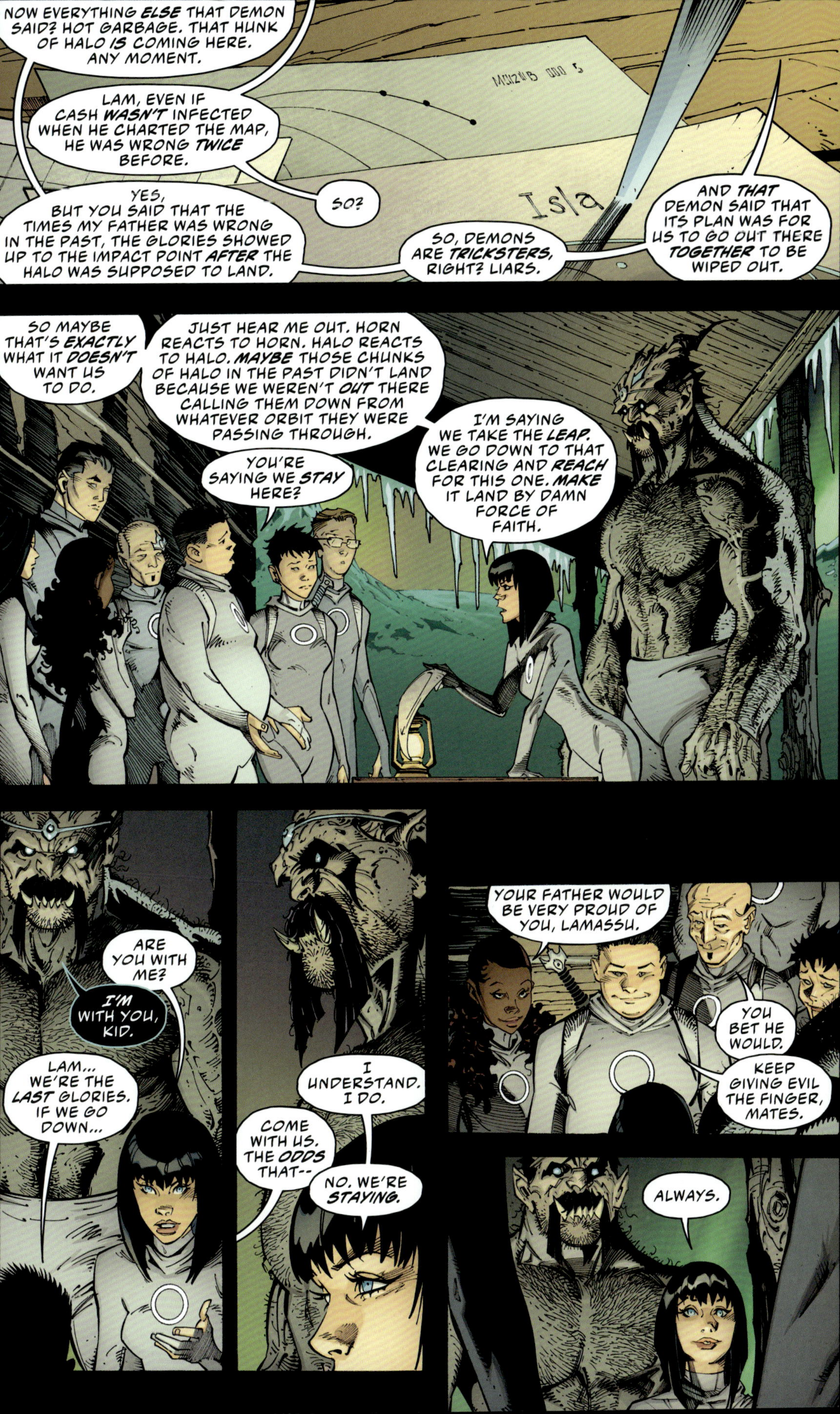
NOW EVERYTHING ELSE THAT DEMON SAID? HOT GARBAGE. THAT HUNK OF HALO IS COMING HERE. ANY MOMENT.
LAM, EVEN IF CASH WASN'T INFECTED WHEN HE CHARTED THE MAP, HE WAS WRONG TWICE BEFORE.
SO?
YES, BUT YOU SAID THAT THE TIMES MY FATHER WAS WRONG IN THE PAST, THE GLORIES SHOWED UP TO THE IMPACT POINT AFTER THE HALO WAS SUPPOSED TO LAND.
Isla
SO, DEMONS ARE TRICKSTERS, RIGHT? LIARS.
AND THAT DEMON SAID THAT ITS PLAN WAS FOR US TO GO OUT THERE TOGETHER TO BE WIPED OUT.
SO MAYBE THAT'S EXACTLY WHAT IT DOESN'T WANT US TO DO.
JUST HEAR ME OUT. HORN REACTS TO HORN. HALO REACTS TO HALO. MAYBE THOSE CHUNKS OF HALO IN THE PAST DIDN'T LAND BECAUSE WE WEREN'T OUT THERE CALLING THEM DOWN FROM WHATEVER ORBIT THEY WERE PASSING THROUGH.
YOU'RE SAYING WE STAY HERE?
I'M SAYING WE TAKE THE LEAP. WE GO DOWN TO THAT CLEARING AND REACH FOR THIS ONE. MAKE IT LAND BY DAMN FORCE OF FAITH.
ARE YOU WITH ME?
I'M WITH YOU, KID.
LAM... WE'RE THE LAST GLORIES. IF WE GO DOWN...
I UNDERSTAND. I DO.
COME WITH US. THE ODDS THAT--
NO. WE'RE STAYING.
YOUR FATHER WOULD BE VERY PROUD OF YOU, LAMASSU.
YOU BET HE WOULD.
KEEP GIVING EVIL THE FINGER, MATES.
ALWAYS.

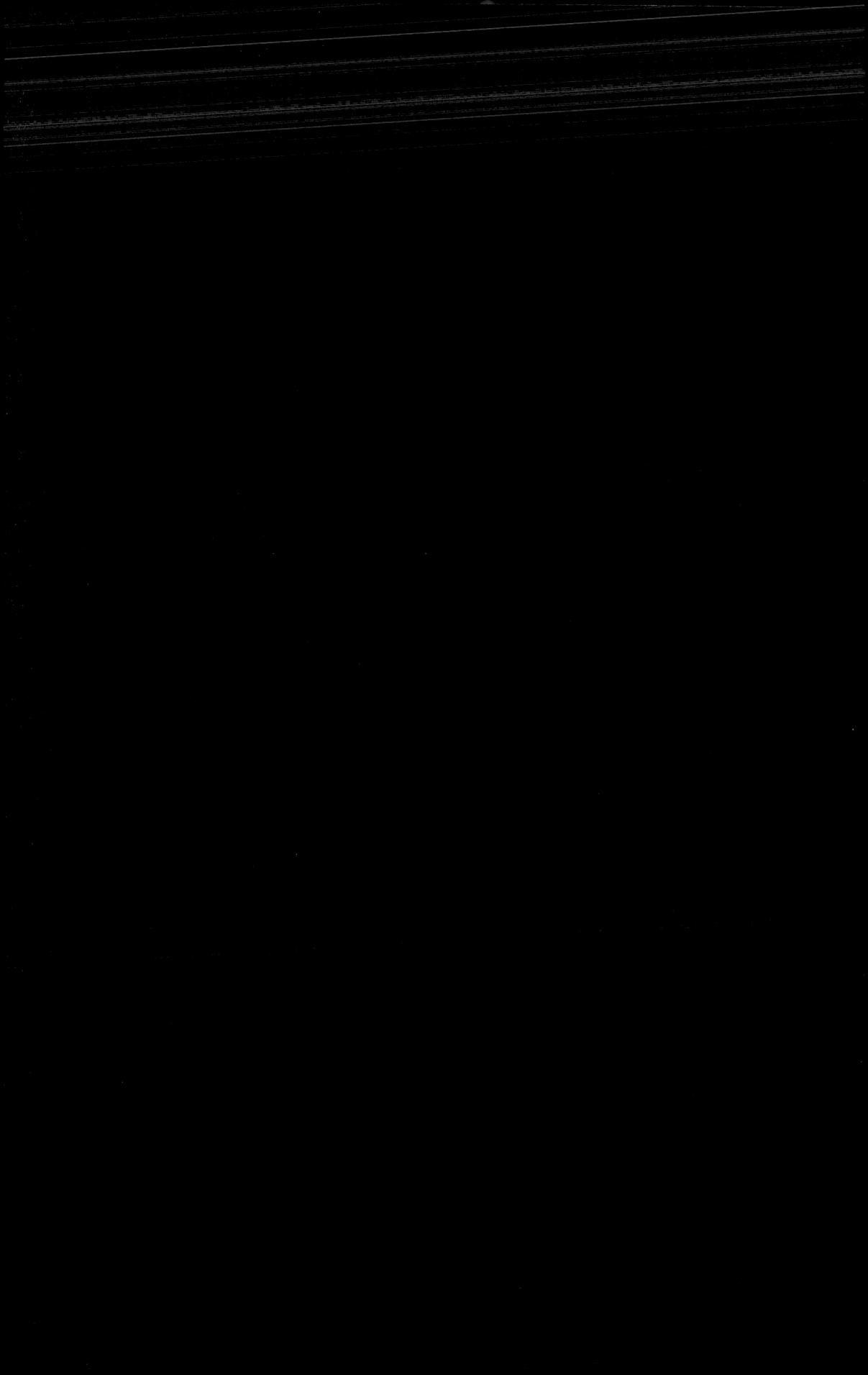

CHAPTER EIGHT: "THE CLEARING"

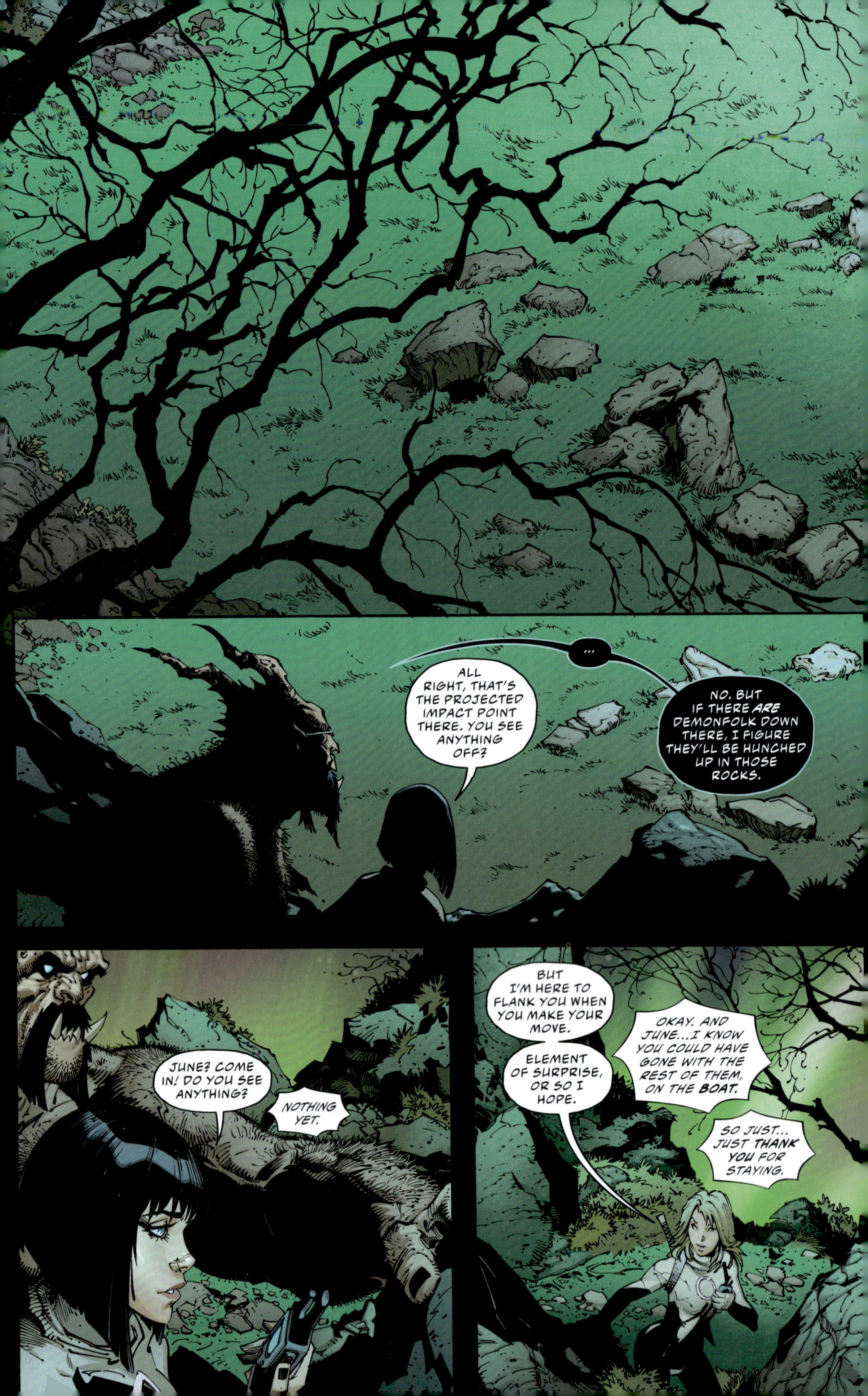
ALL RIGHT, THAT'S THE PROJECTED IMPACT POINT THERE. YOU SEE ANYTHING OFF?
...
NO. BUT IF THERE *ARE* DEMONFOLK DOWN THERE, I FIGURE THEY'LL BE HUNCHED UP IN THOSE ROCKS.
JUNE? COME IN! DO YOU SEE ANYTHING?
NOTHING YET.
BUT I'M HERE TO FLANK YOU WHEN YOU MAKE YOUR MOVE.
ELEMENT OF SURPRISE, OR SO I HOPE.
OKAY. AND JUNE...I KNOW YOU COULD HAVE GONE WITH THE REST OF THEM, ON THE **BOAT**.
SO JUST... JUST **THANK YOU** FOR STAYING.

"WHAT ABOUT THE BLOOD?"

"GOING *CRAZY*, BUT...A STRANGE KIND OF CRAZY? WHATEVER IS DOWN THERE ISN'T ANY RUN-OF-THE-MILL DEMONFOLK."

"WE'RE *FAMILY*, LAM. HOWEVER THIS GOES, WE'RE IN IT TOGETHER..."

"...EVEN IF WE'RE ON OUR OWN."

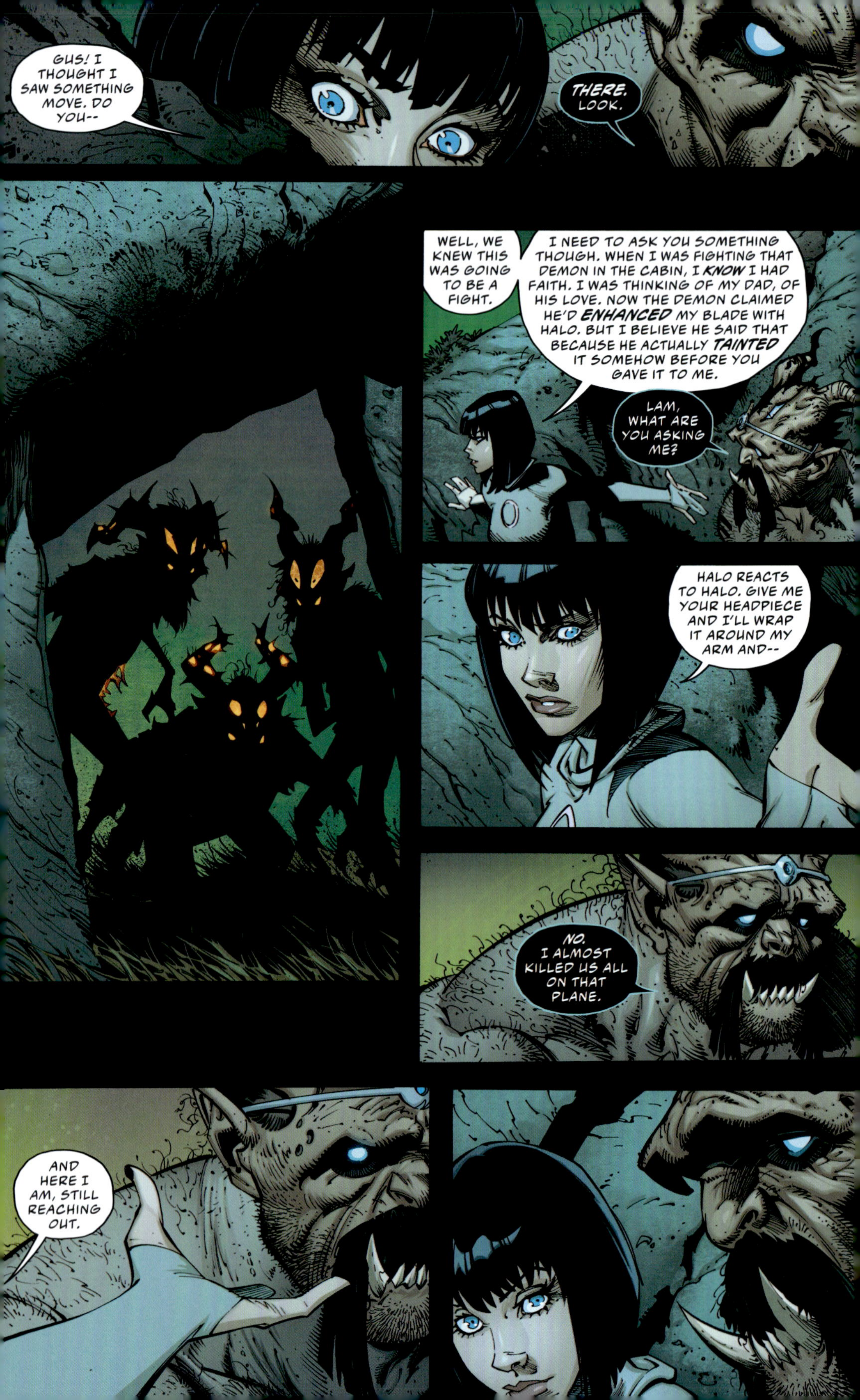
GUS! I THOUGHT I SAW SOMETHING MOVE. DO YOU--
THERE. LOOK.
WELL, WE KNEW THIS WAS GOING TO BE A FIGHT.
I NEED TO ASK YOU SOMETHING THOUGH. WHEN I WAS FIGHTING THAT DEMON IN THE CABIN, I KNOW I HAD FAITH. I WAS THINKING OF MY DAD, OF HIS LOVE. NOW THE DEMON CLAIMED HE'D ENHANCED MY BLADE WITH HALO. BUT I BELIEVE HE SAID THAT BECAUSE HE ACTUALLY TAINTED IT SOMEHOW BEFORE YOU GAVE IT TO ME.
LAM, WHAT ARE YOU ASKING ME?
HALO REACTS TO HALO. GIVE ME YOUR HEADPIECE AND I'LL WRAP IT AROUND MY ARM AND--
NO. I ALMOST KILLED US ALL ON THAT PLANE.
AND HERE I AM, STILL REACHING OUT.

I BELIEVE IN YOU, GUS.
SO DID YOUR FATHER. AND I BIT OFF YOUR ARM.
I HAVE TOO MUCH HORN IN ME, KID.
WE ALL HAVE TOO MUCH HORN IN US.
BUT THERE'S HALO IN YOU TOO. I MEAN THAT PART OF YOU WAY DOWN DEEP THAT'S INCORRUPTIBLE. PURE.

THE LIGHT IN THE DARK. WHAT IS IT?
THE EVENING BEFORE MY TRIBE FOUND HORN IN THE GROUND, I WAS WITH MY WIFE, MY DAUGHTER. WE HAD A *KORVA*, A DINNER PICNIC JUST US THREE. WE SAT IN THE SUNSET AND ATE THIS FRUIT WE CALLED *YEE*. PINK WITH RED STRIPES.
IT'S EXTINCT NOW, BUT IT TASTED LIKE CHERRIES, BUT SWEETER, RICHER. MY DAUGHTER ATE SO MUCH SHE FELL ASLEEP ON MY CHEST... AND THE STARS...
HERE.
THANK YOU.
NOW HOW DO YOU FEEL?
I...I FEEL...
...LIKE GOING DOWN THERE AND GETTING OUR DAMN *HALO*.

ATTENTION, DEMONFOLK! MY NAME IS LAM CULLEN, AND THIS IS MY PARTNER, GUS. AND WE'RE HERE TO TAKE WHAT HALO FALLS FROM THE SKY AND KILL YOU ALL.
SO SHOW YOUR ROTTEN FUCKING HELL-SCORCHED ASSES!
WHOA. LANGUAGE.
SORRY.
YOU HEARD HIM!
COME OUT AND...
...SHOW YOURSELVES.
WITH PLEASURE, LAMASSU.
WHAT THE...
OH NO, NONONO... THIS CAN'T BE HAPPENING.
<WHAT'S THE MATTER, HELLOR?>

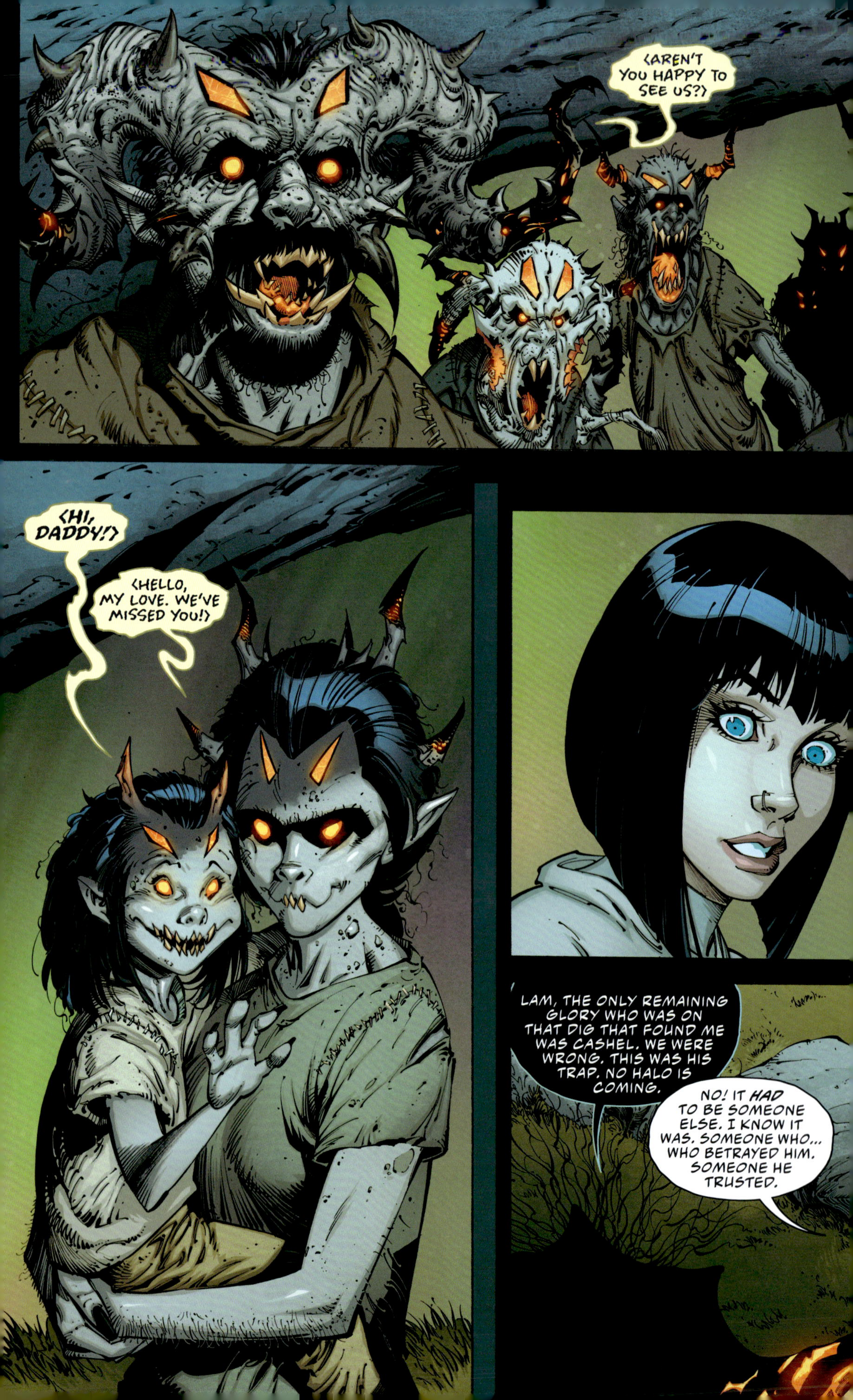

<AREN'T YOU HAPPY TO SEE US?>
<HI, DADDY!>
<HELLO, MY LOVE. WE'VE MISSED YOU!>
LAM, THE ONLY REMAINING GLORY WHO WAS ON THAT DIG THAT FOUND ME WAS CASHEL. WE WERE WRONG. THIS WAS HIS TRAP. NO HALO IS COMING.
NO! IT *HAD* TO BE SOMEONE ELSE. I KNOW IT WAS. SOMEONE WHO... WHO BETRAYED HIM. SOMEONE HE TRUSTED.

"GUS... IS THAT..."

"MY... MY TRIBE."

"SOMEONE..."

"...HE LOVED."

JUNE?!
I'M SORRY, GUS.
BUT WHY?! WHY WOULD YOU DO THIS?
NOT LONG AGO, CASH GOT WORD THAT SOME OF YOUR TRIBE HAD BEEN FOUND. BUT HE DIDN'T WANT TO TELL YOU UNTIL HE SAW WHETHER OR NOT THEY COULD STILL BE SAVED.
SO HE BROUGHT ME ALONG TO HELP HIM FIND THE ANSWER. SADLY, IT WAS TOO LATE FOR THEM, GUS.
CASH, HE WAS GOING TO DESTROY THEM.
BUT I STOPPED HIM...
...BY MAKING HIM A DEMON.
JUST LIKE ME.
BUT...HOW? YOU AND MY DAD. YOU...
OH, LAM.
AFTER YOUR MOMMY DIED, YOUR DADDY WAS JUST SO CRUSHED! HE WASN'T AS CAREFUL AS HE SHOULD'VE BEEN.
TO BE FAIR THOUGH, I AM A HARD ONE TO DETECT.
I'VE WALKED THE EARTH LONGER THAN I CARE TO SAY. I'M ONE OF THE OLDEST. AND IN MY YEARS, I'VE BEEN WOUNDED BY PLENTY OF GLORY BLADES--
--ENOUGH THAT THE HALO RESIDUE IN MY BLOOD KEEPS ME IN CONSTANT FUCKING PAIN. BUT IT ALSO LETS ME HIDE FROM YOUR SHITTY LITTLE GLOW TEST.
SO YES, THIS IS MY TRAP. AND YOU ALL FELL FOR IT. EVEN THE OTHERS. BECAUSE THAT BOAT? RIGHT NOW THE BOMBS IN THE HULL ARE GOING OFF. I'LL BET IF WE LISTEN CLOSELY, WE CAN EVEN HEAR THE SCREAMS...

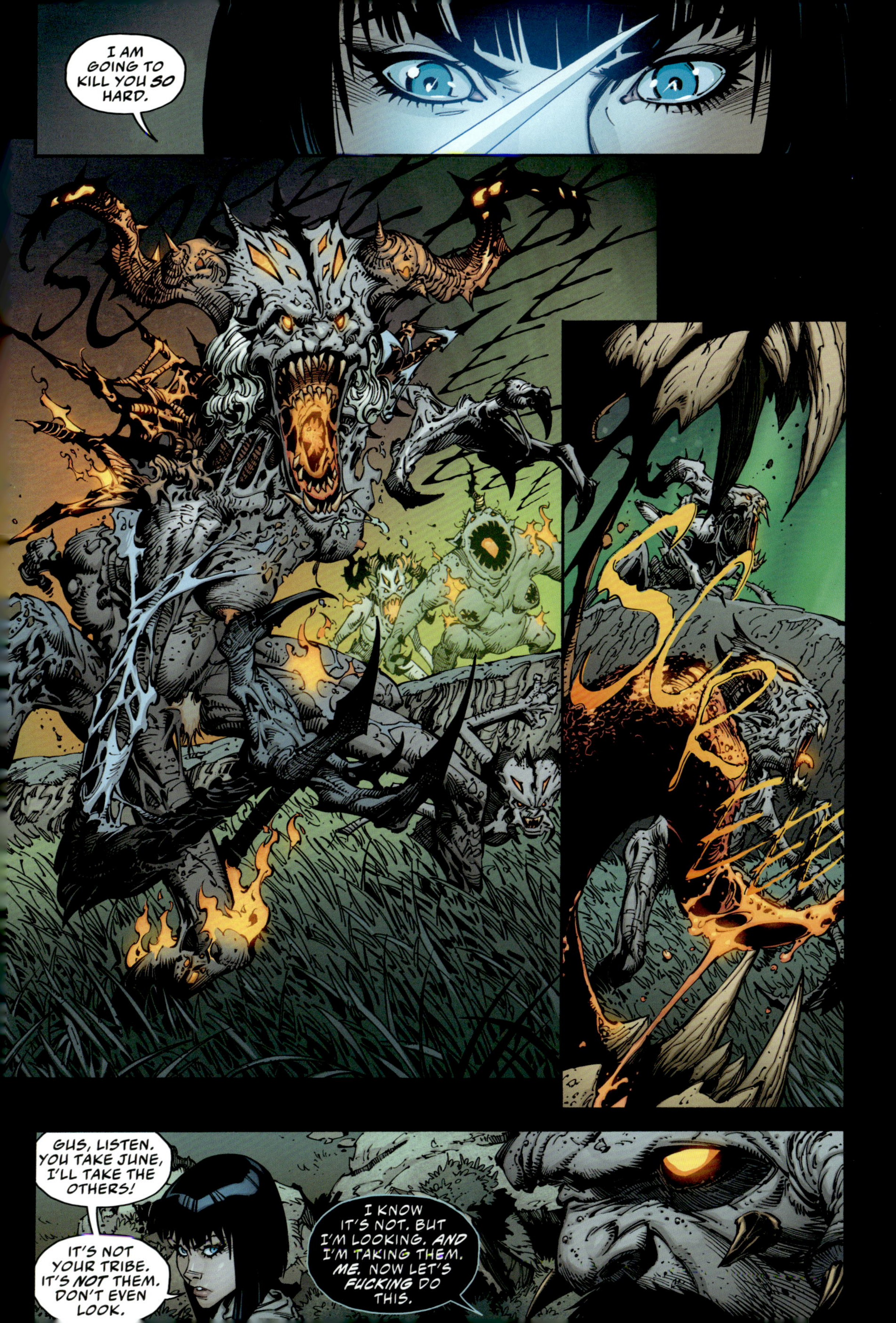
I AM GOING TO KILL YOU SO HARD.
GUS, LISTEN. YOU TAKE JUNE, I'LL TAKE THE OTHERS!
IT'S NOT YOUR TRIBE. IT'S NOT THEM. DON'T EVEN LOOK.
I KNOW IT'S NOT. BUT I'M LOOKING. AND I'M TAKING THEM. ME. NOW LET'S FUCKING DO THIS.

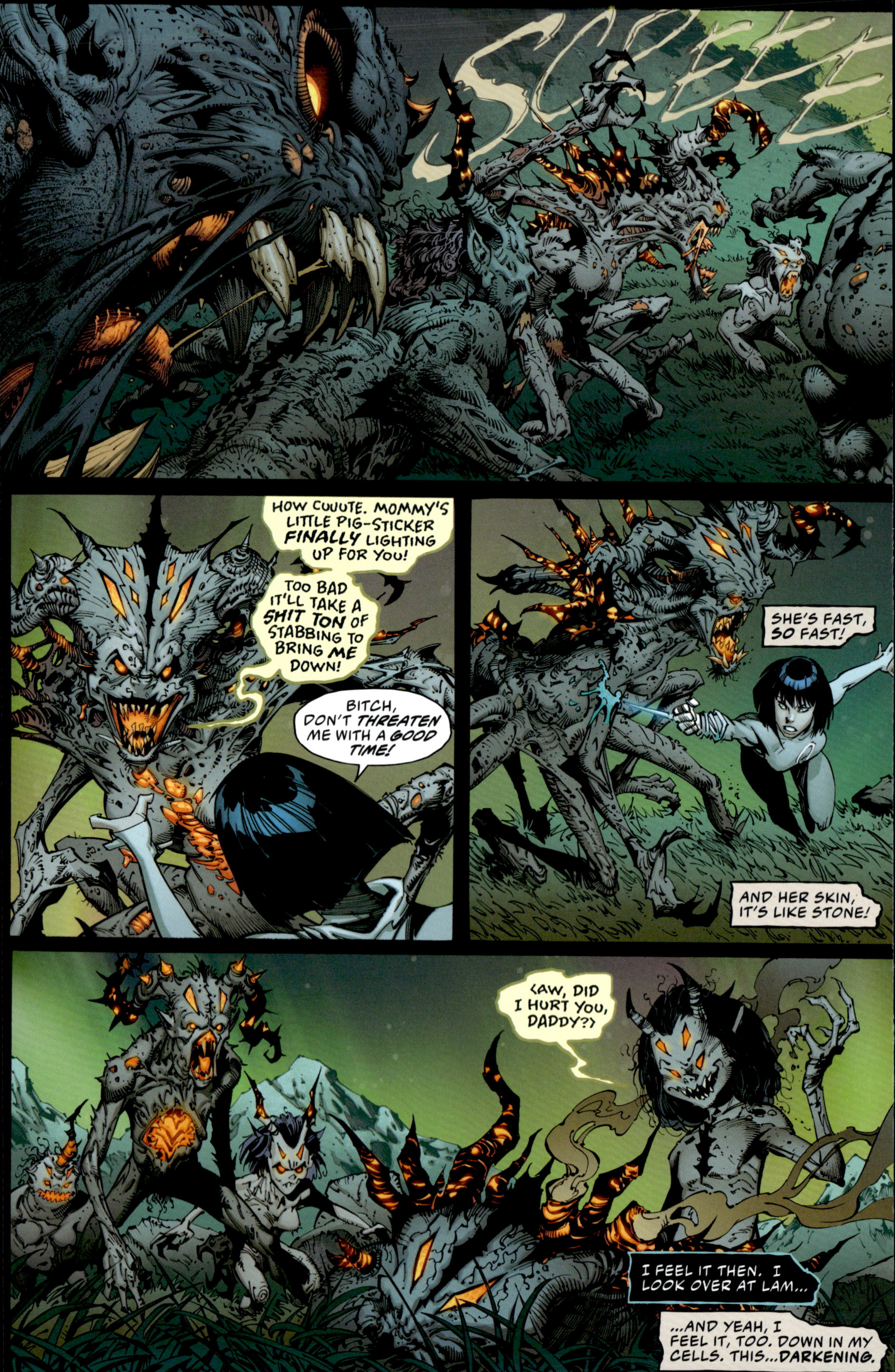
SCREEE
HOW CUUUTE. MOMMY'S LITTLE PIG-STICKER FINALLY LIGHTING UP FOR YOU!
TOO BAD IT'LL TAKE A SHIT TON OF STABBING TO BRING ME DOWN!
BITCH, DON'T THREATEN ME WITH A GOOD TIME!
SHE'S FAST, SO FAST!
AND HER SKIN, IT'S LIKE STONE!
<AW, DID I HURT YOU, DADDY?>
I FEEL IT THEN. I LOOK OVER AT LAM...
...AND YEAH, I FEEL IT, TOO. DOWN IN MY CELLS. THIS...DARKENING.

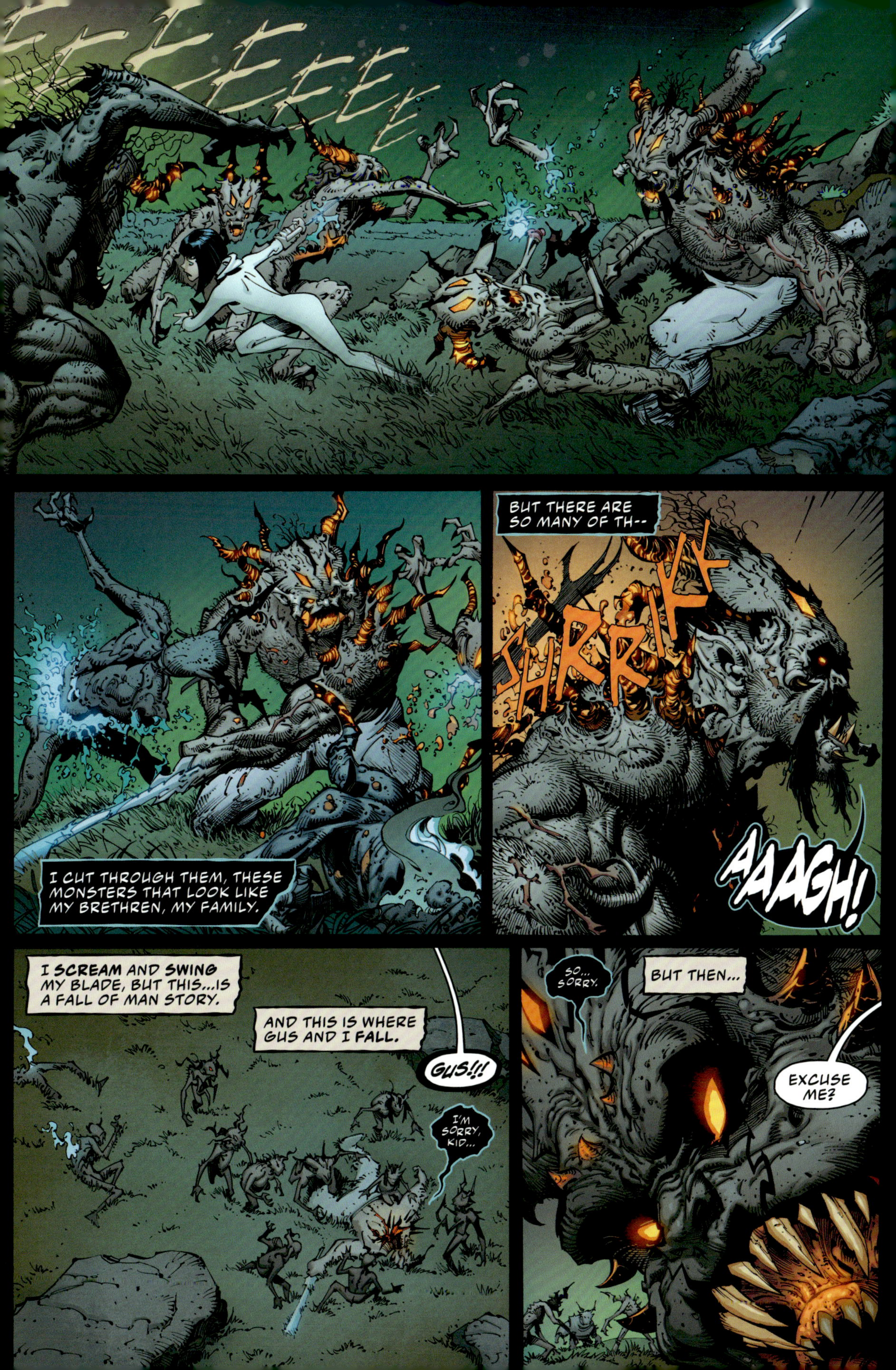
EEEEEEE
BUT THERE ARE SO MANY OF TH--
SHRRIKK
AAAGH!
I CUT THROUGH THEM, THESE MONSTERS THAT LOOK LIKE MY BRETHREN, MY FAMILY.
I SCREAM AND SWING MY BLADE, BUT THIS...IS A FALL OF MAN STORY.
AND THIS IS WHERE GUS AND I FALL.
GUS!!!
I'M SORRY, KID...
SO... SORRY.
BUT THEN...
EXCUSE ME?

WE'RE HERE FOR THE END-OF-THE-WORLD PARTY.
IS THIS THE RIGHT PLACE?
SORRY WE'RE LATE, MATES!
WE WANTED TO FIND JUST THE RIGHT OUTFITS!
SO, HOW DO WE LOOK?
HEAVENLY.
NOW...

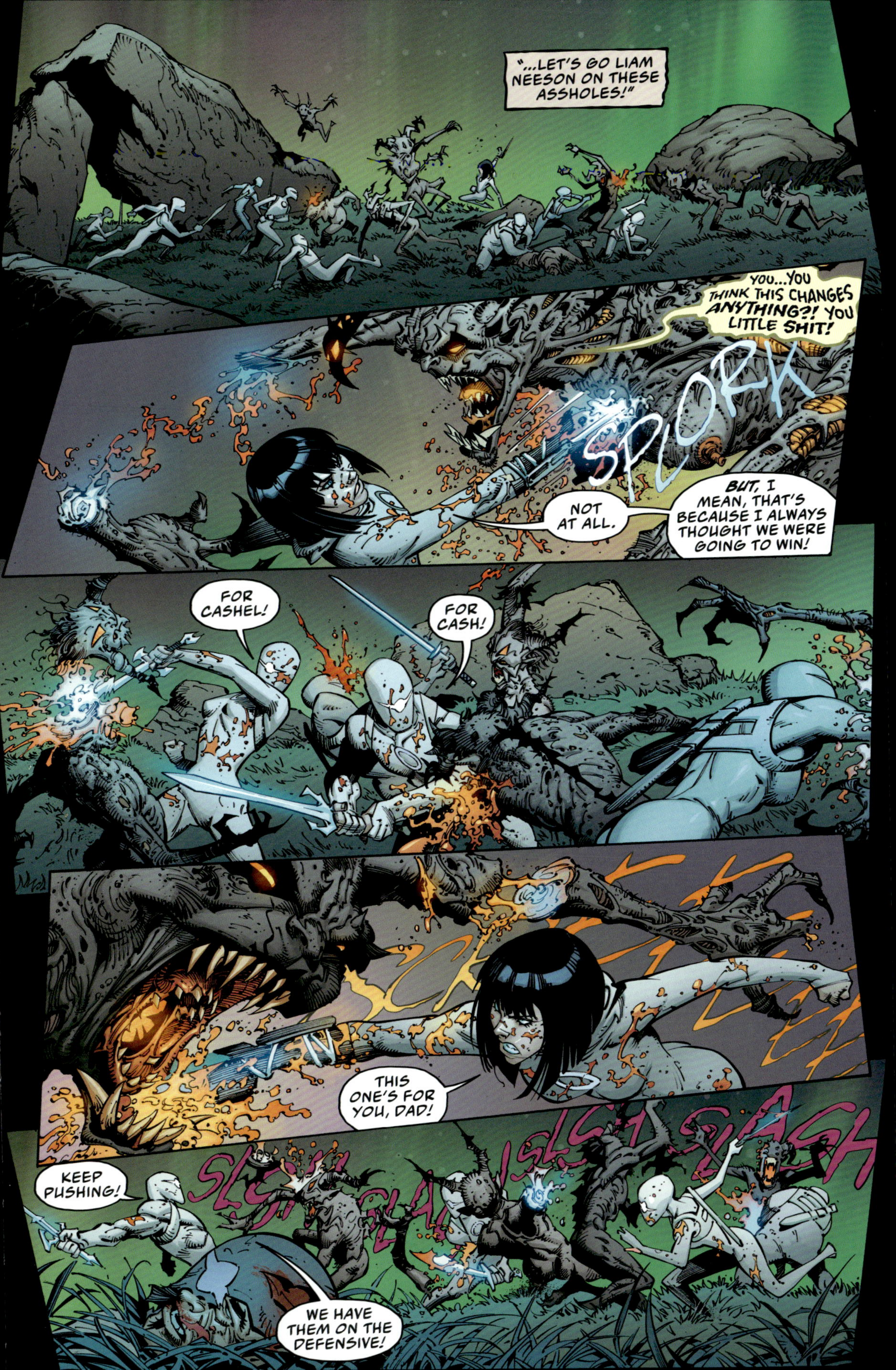

"...LET'S GO LIAM NEESON ON THESE ASSHOLES!"
YOU...YOU THINK THIS CHANGES ANYTHING?! YOU LITTLE SHIT!
SPLORK
NOT AT ALL.
BUT, I MEAN, THAT'S BECAUSE I ALWAYS THOUGHT WE WERE GOING TO WIN!
FOR CASHEL!
FOR CASH!
THIS ONE'S FOR YOU, DAD!
KEEP PUSHING!
SLASH
WE HAVE THEM ON THE DEFENSIVE!

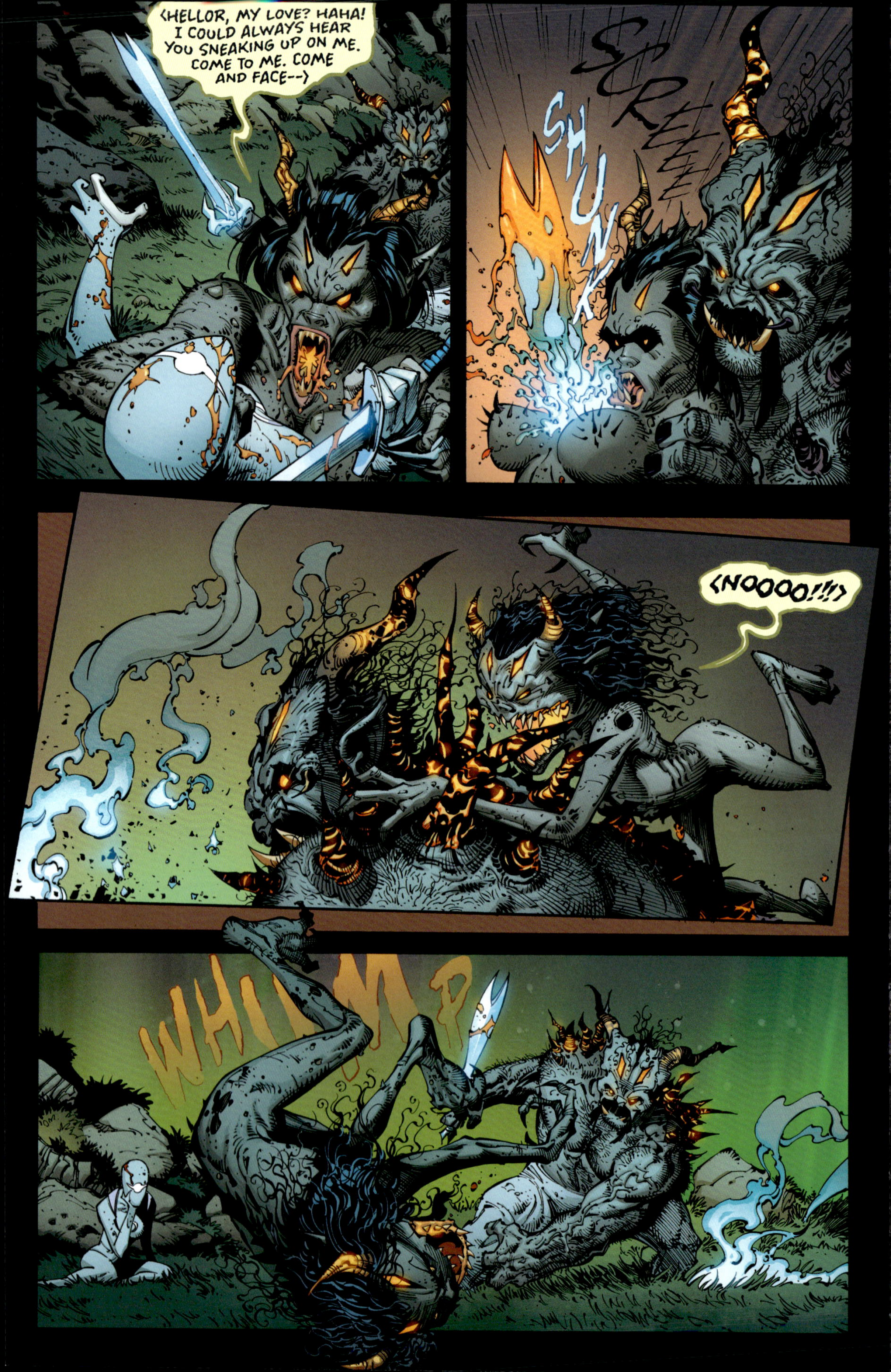

‹HELLOR, MY LOVE? HAHA! I COULD ALWAYS HEAR YOU SNEAKING UP ON ME. COME TO ME. COME AND FACE--›
SCREEEE
SHUNK
‹NOOOO!!!›
WHUMP

<DADDY? DADDY, PLEASE. IT'S ME, PIL-ARIE.>
<I...I LOVE YOU.>
GUS--
DON'T.
...
I MISS YOU, SWEETHEART. I MISS YOU EVERY MOMENT OF EVERY DAY. AND I'M SO SORRY.
BUT YOU? YOU'RE NOT PIL. SO GO ON. MAKE YOUR MOVE.
<YOU MAMMOTH-FUCKING, PISS-DRINKING-->
SHRIK
"IS...IS IT OVER?"

DID WE ACTUALLY WIN?
IS EVERYONE ACCOUNTED FOR? WHERE'S LAM?
IS SHE ALL RIGHT?
SHE'S JUST FINE.
HEY, KID! NEED ANY HELP?
HUFF HUFF I... I THINK I GOT IT.

YOU...YOU THINK THIS IS OVER?!
NO, WE DON'T. BUT WE'RE HERE. AND WE'RE READY.
"READY"? HA!
YOU'RE SO FUCKING STUPID, ALL OF YOU!
YOU HAVE NO IDEA WHAT YOU'RE UP AGAINST!
NO CLUE WHAT'S COMIN--

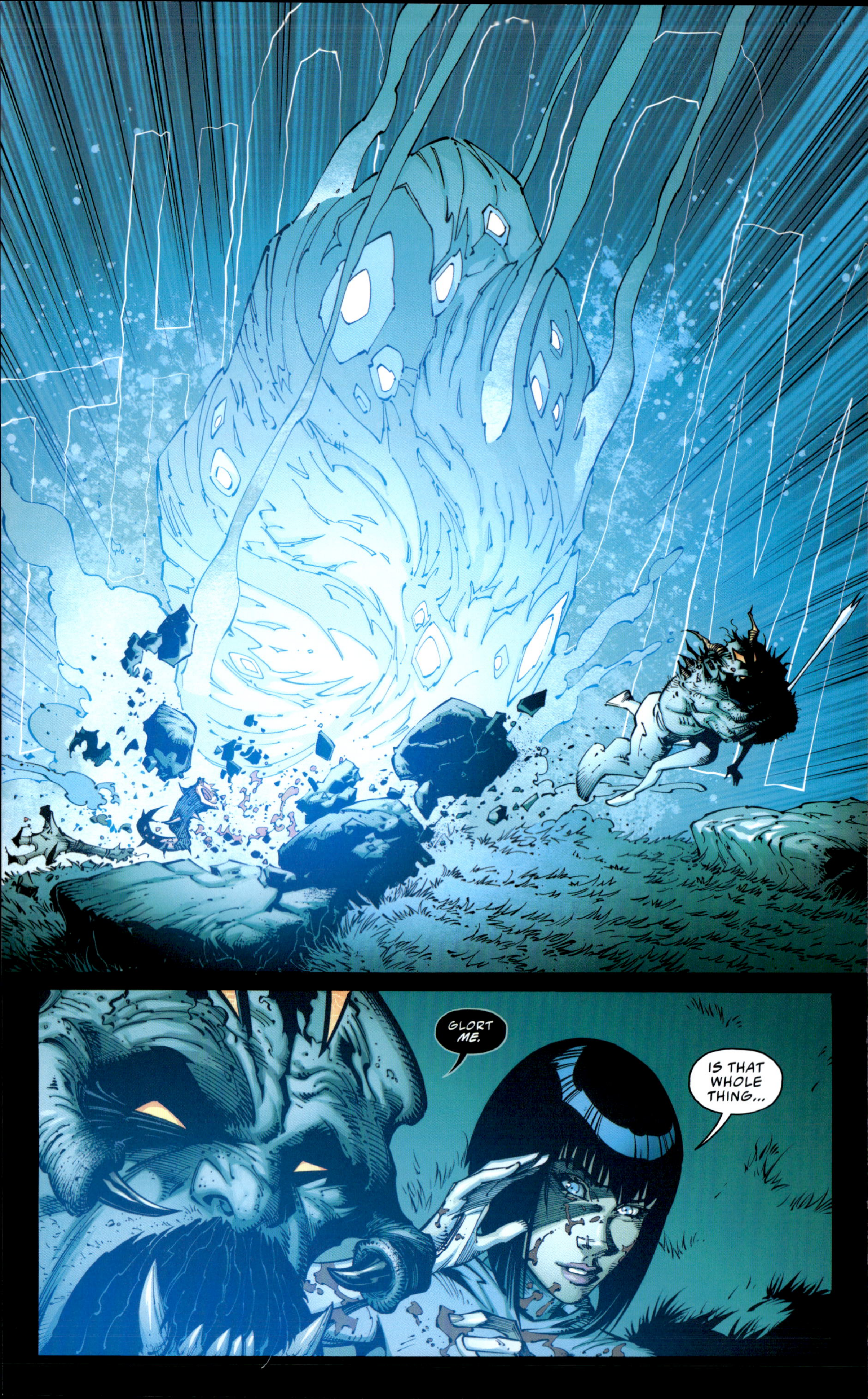
GLORT ME.
IS THAT WHOLE THING...

HALO!
MY GOD.
IT'S ENOUGH TO... TO MAKE A THOUSAND BLADES!
MAYBE MORE!
HEY.
NO.
I'M...OKAY.
WELL I'M OKAY, TOO.
HEH. I THINK WE'RE ALL OKAY TODAY.
AND WE GOT YOU TWO TO THANK.
NO. NOT US.
SOMEONE ELSE...

CHAPTER NINE: "HALO"

I MEAN, I DID WARN YOU.

SHE DID.

I EVEN SAID "HARK." BECAUSE THIS WAS, IS, AND ALWAYS WILL BE A STORY ABOUT THE FALL OF MAN. THE BIG F.O.M. SO THE THING IS, THERE CAN'T BE A HAPPY ENDING. NOT REALLY.

NO WAY.

SO, HOW TO END IT THEN, GUS?

HUH. HOW ABOUT RIGHT BACK WHERE IT STARTED, KID...

IN FLORIDA.
IN FLORIDA.
ONE YEAR LATER.

YEAH, THIS FEELS RIGHT.

FULL CIRCLE.

BECAUSE THAT'S THE THING, ISN'T IT? IT'S ALL CIRCLES AND RINGS. THIS IS A STORY ABOUT THE FALL OF MAN.

EVERY DAY MORE AND MORE HORN HITS THE EARTH. WHY? BECAUSE WE *DRAW* IT HERE. IT'S IN US, AND WE WANT MORE. YOU FEEL IT, WE KNOW YOU DO. BECAUSE THE TRUTH IS, WE *ALL* HAVE DEMONS.

BUT WE ALL HAVE HALO IN US, TOO. NOT AS MUCH AS HORN, NO, BUT IT'S THERE. AND WE KNOW YOU FEEL *THAT*, TOO.

NOW IT'S EASY TO GIVE IN TO YOUR DEMONS. ESPECIALLY **THESE** DAYS.
I MEAN FACE IT, THE WHOLE PLANET'S A FOUR-ALARM FIRE. EVERYONE IS READY FOR HIGH NOON. HORN IS EVERYWHERE.
AND IT'S HARDER THAN *EVER* TO FIND YOUR BETTER ANGELS. BUT WE'RE ASKING YOU TO. BECAUSE YES, THIS IS A STORY ABOUT THE FALL OF MAN. BUT IT'S ALSO A STORY ABOUT THE **RISE OF MAN.**
AN R.O.M. STORY. BECAUSE LOTS OF US ARE GIVING IN, SURE.
BUT EVERY DAY NOW, MORE AND MORE OF US ARE FIGHTING BACK, TOO.

IT'S TRUE THAT IN JUST ONE YEAR THERE ARE WAY MORE DEMONS OUT THERE, AND WHAT WE'VE LEARNED ABOUT THEM...

...WHAT THEY DID TO OTHER PLANETS, WHERE THEY CAME FROM, ALL THE SPECIES... IT COULD FILL A LIBRARY. (WHICH IT ACTUALLY DOES, OUR NEW ONE.)

BUT WE'VE GROWN A LOT TOO, THE GLORIES. WE HAVE MORE MEMBERS, IN MORE COUNTRIES.

AND YEP, MORE MONEY TOO. LOTS MORE.

SO THE TIME IS NOW.

IT IS. BECAUSE THERE ARE NO HAPPY ENDINGS. THERE'S ONLY THE CIRCLE. THE FALL AND THE RISE. IT HAS GONE ON FOREVER AND WILL GO ON FOREVER, BUT IT'S ALL THERE IS.

FIND SOMETHING TO HAVE FAITH IN.

HORRIBLE '90S DANCE MUSIC. COMIC BOOKS.

I AM...

SOMETHING BIGGER THAN YOURSELF. BECAUSE THIS IS THE MOMENT. THE BEGINNING OF EVERYTHING, AND WE NEED YOU.

SO WHAT DO YOU SAY?

YOU IN?

THEN WELCOME TO THE GLORIES, KID.
NOW PICK YOUR BLADE.
AND LET'S GIVE EVIL THE *FINGER.*
END OF BOOK ONE

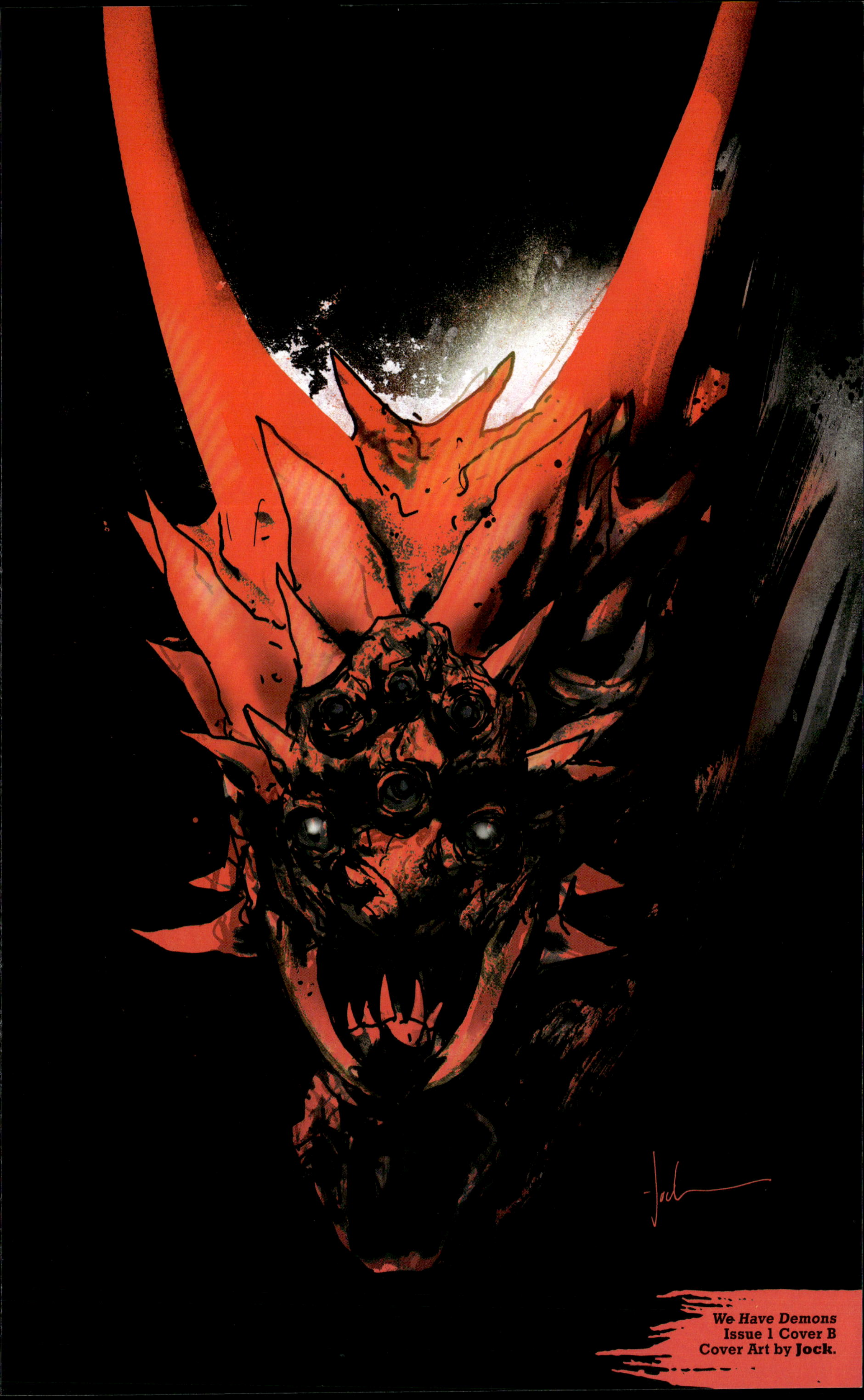

We Have Demons
Issue 1 Cover B
Cover Art by **Jock**.

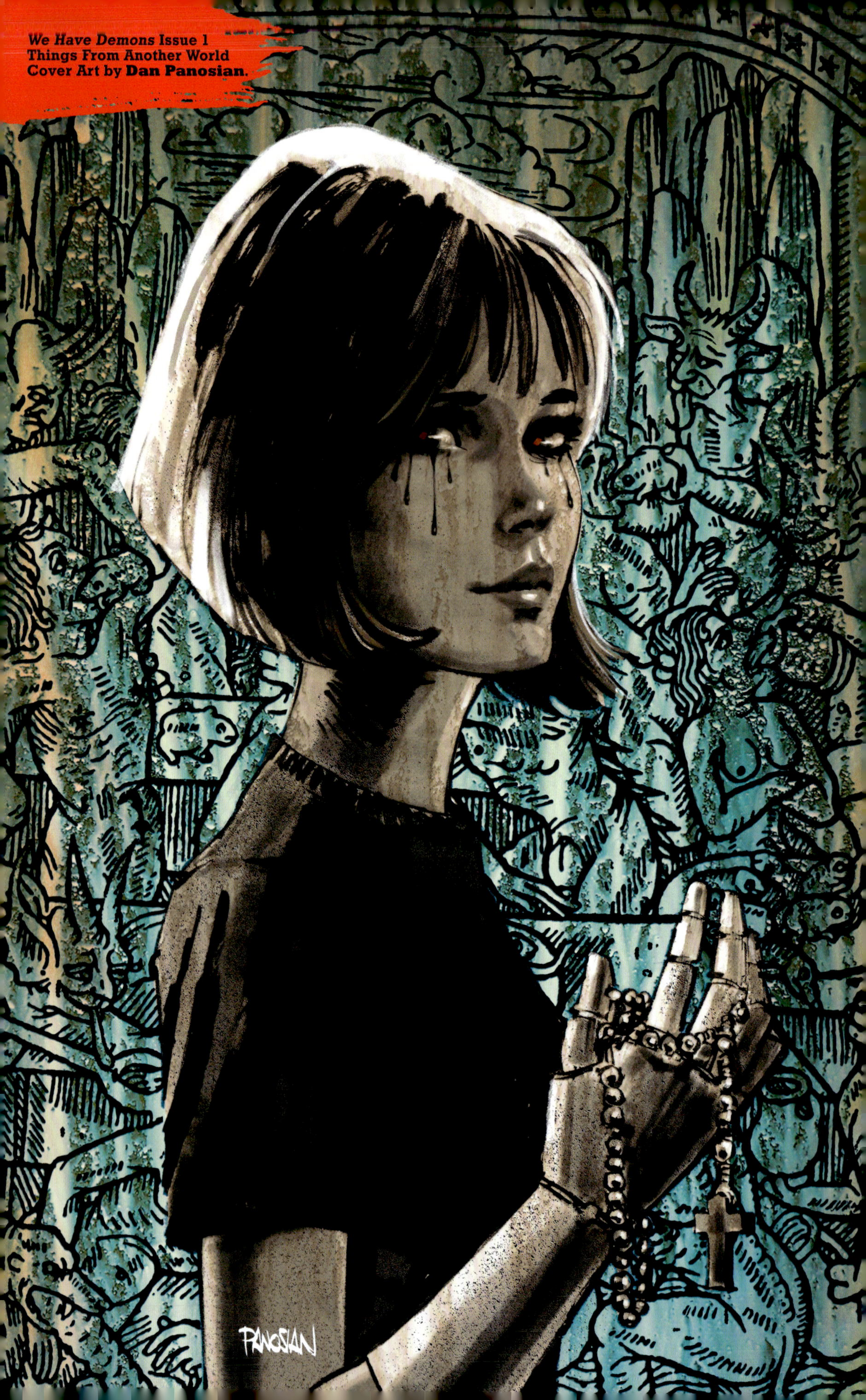
PANOSIAN

We Have Demons Issue 1
Things From Another World
Cover Art by **Dan Panosian**.

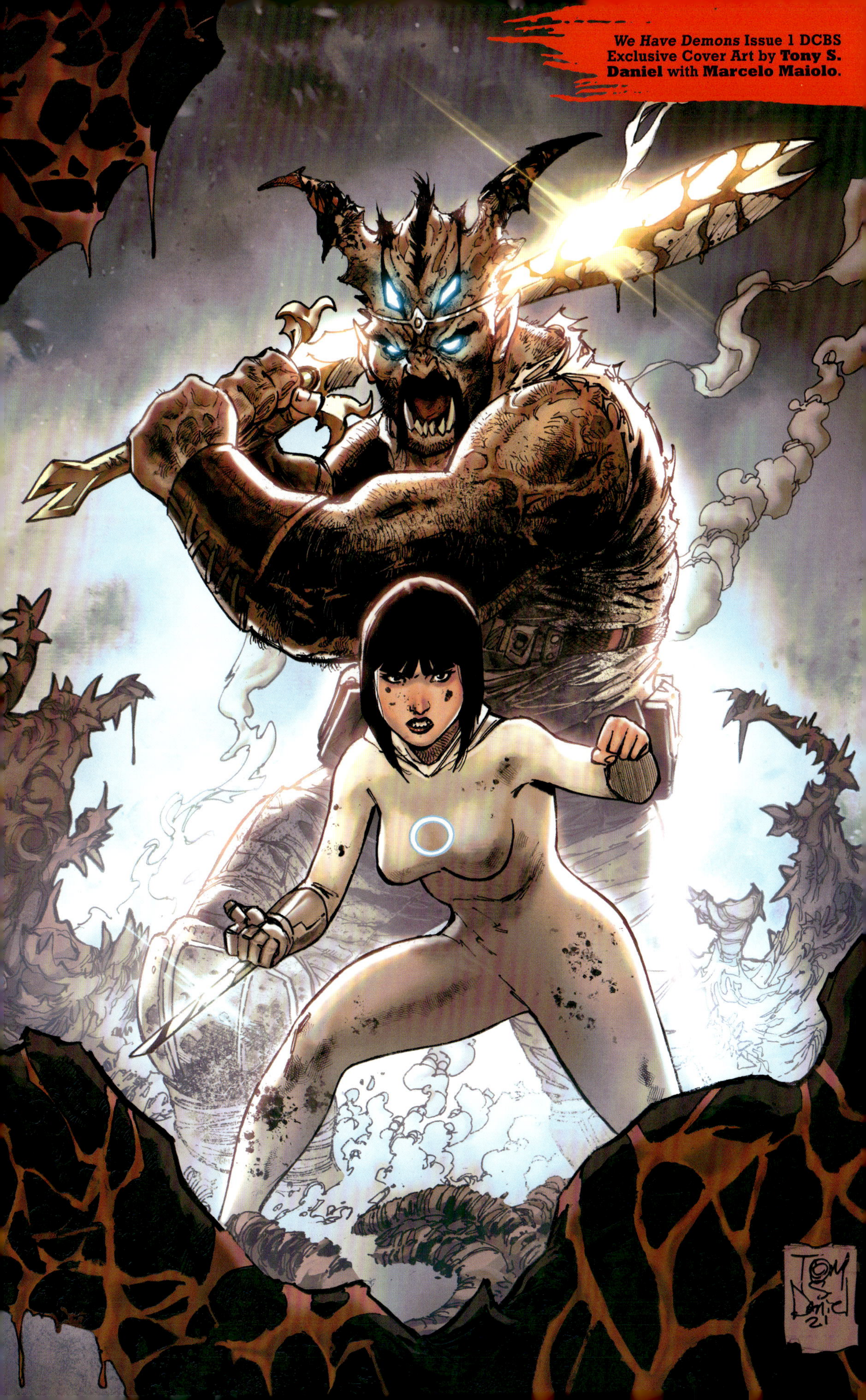

We Have Demons Issue 1 DCBS Exclusive Cover Art by **Tony S. Daniel** with **Marcelo Maiolo.**

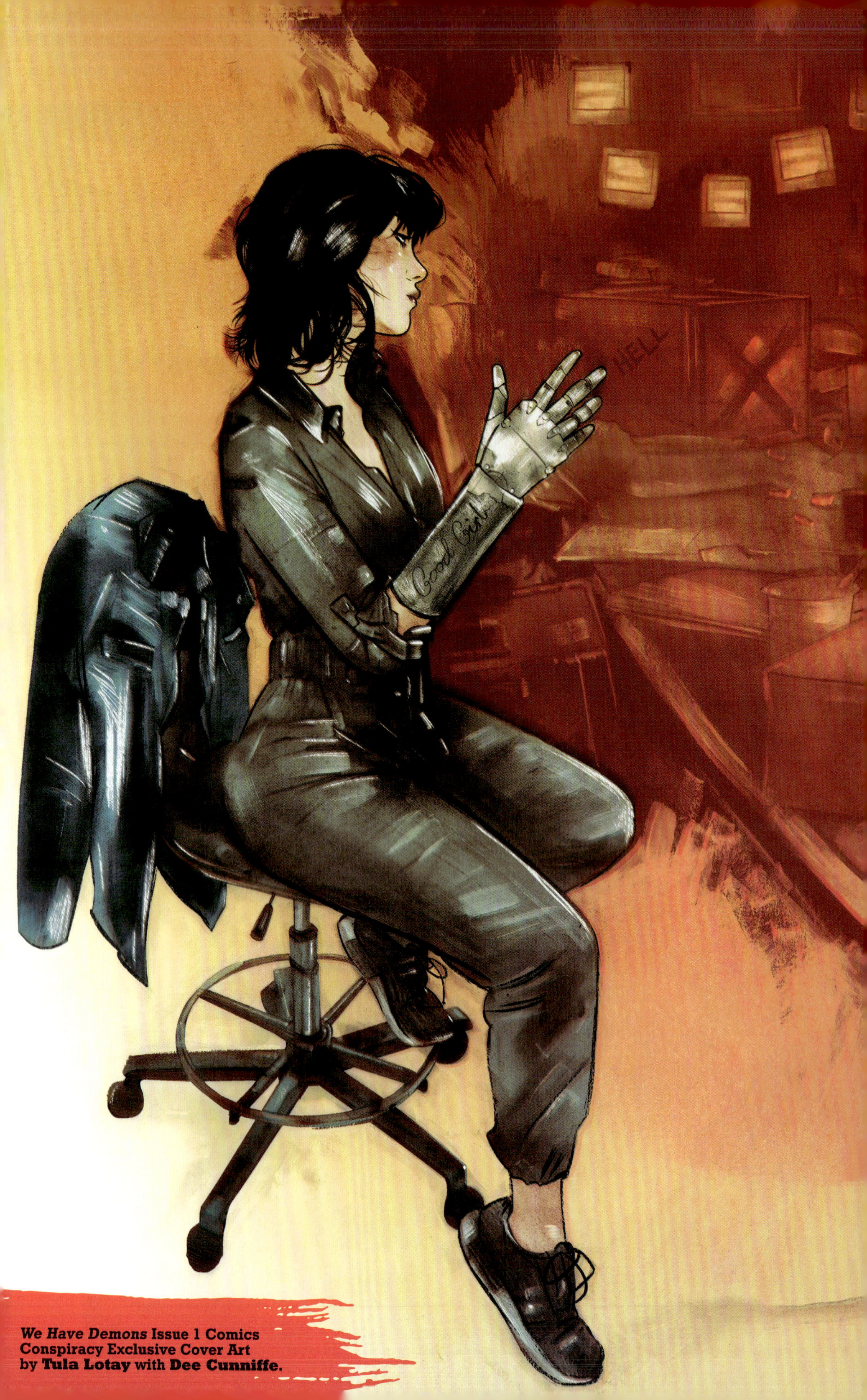
HELL

We Have Demons Issue 1 Comics Conspiracy Exclusive Cover Art by **Tula Lotay** with **Dee Cunniffe.**

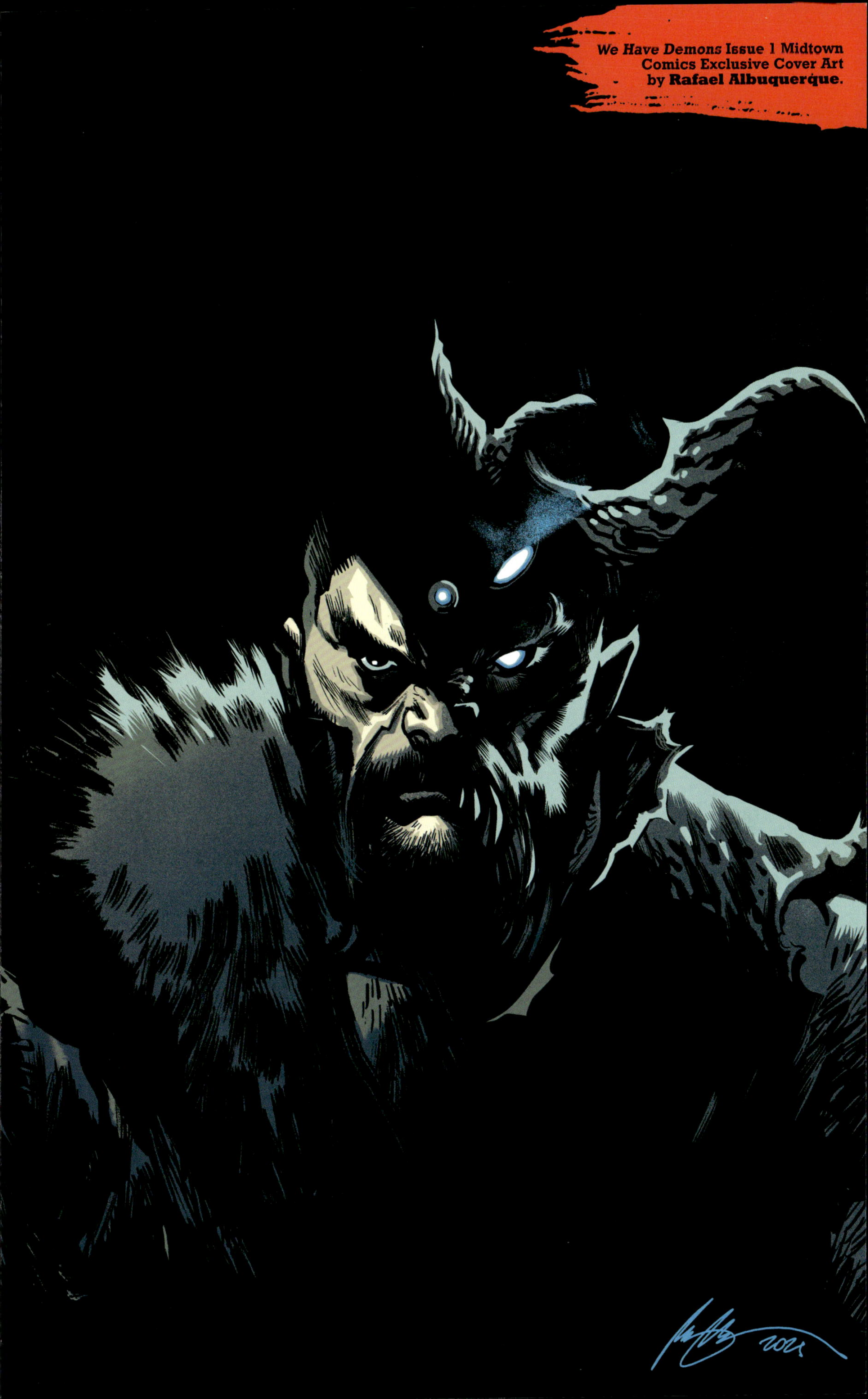

We Have Demons Issue 1 Midtown Comics Exclusive Cover Art by **Rafael Albuquerque**.

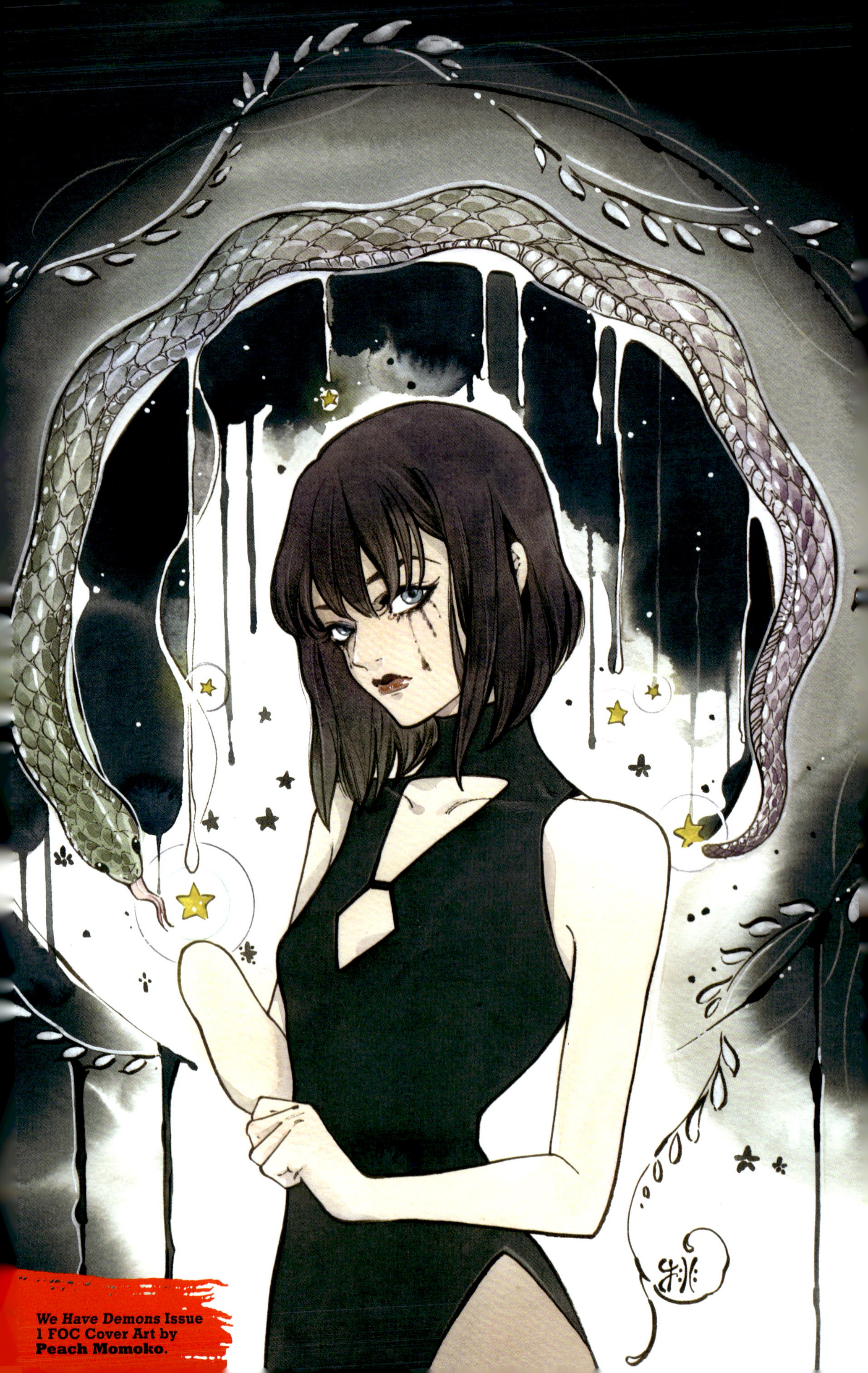

We Have *Demons* Issue 1 FOC Cover Art by **Peach Momoko.**

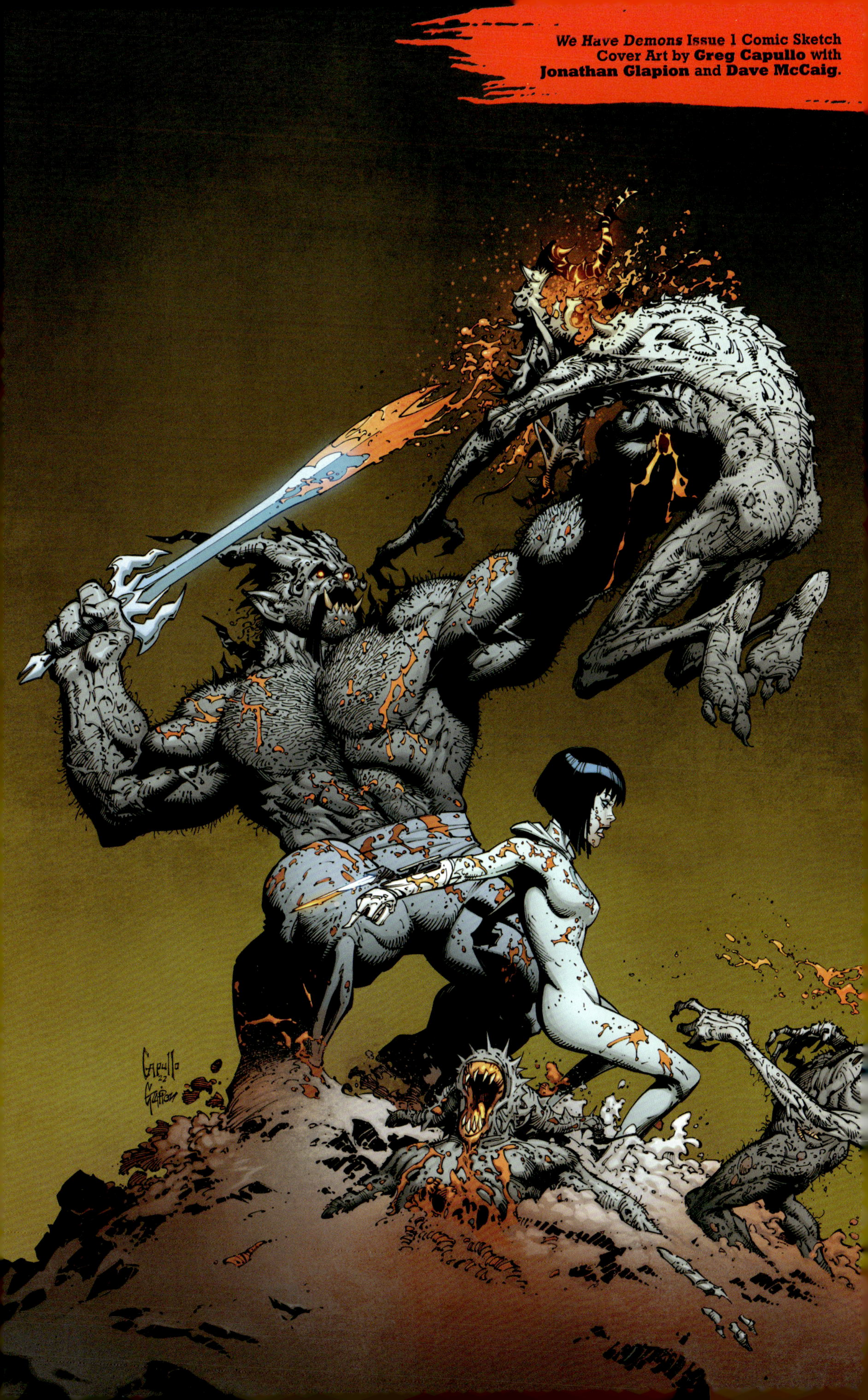

We Have Demons Issue 1 Comic Sketch Cover Art by **Greg Capullo** with **Jonathan Glapion** and **Dave McCaig**.

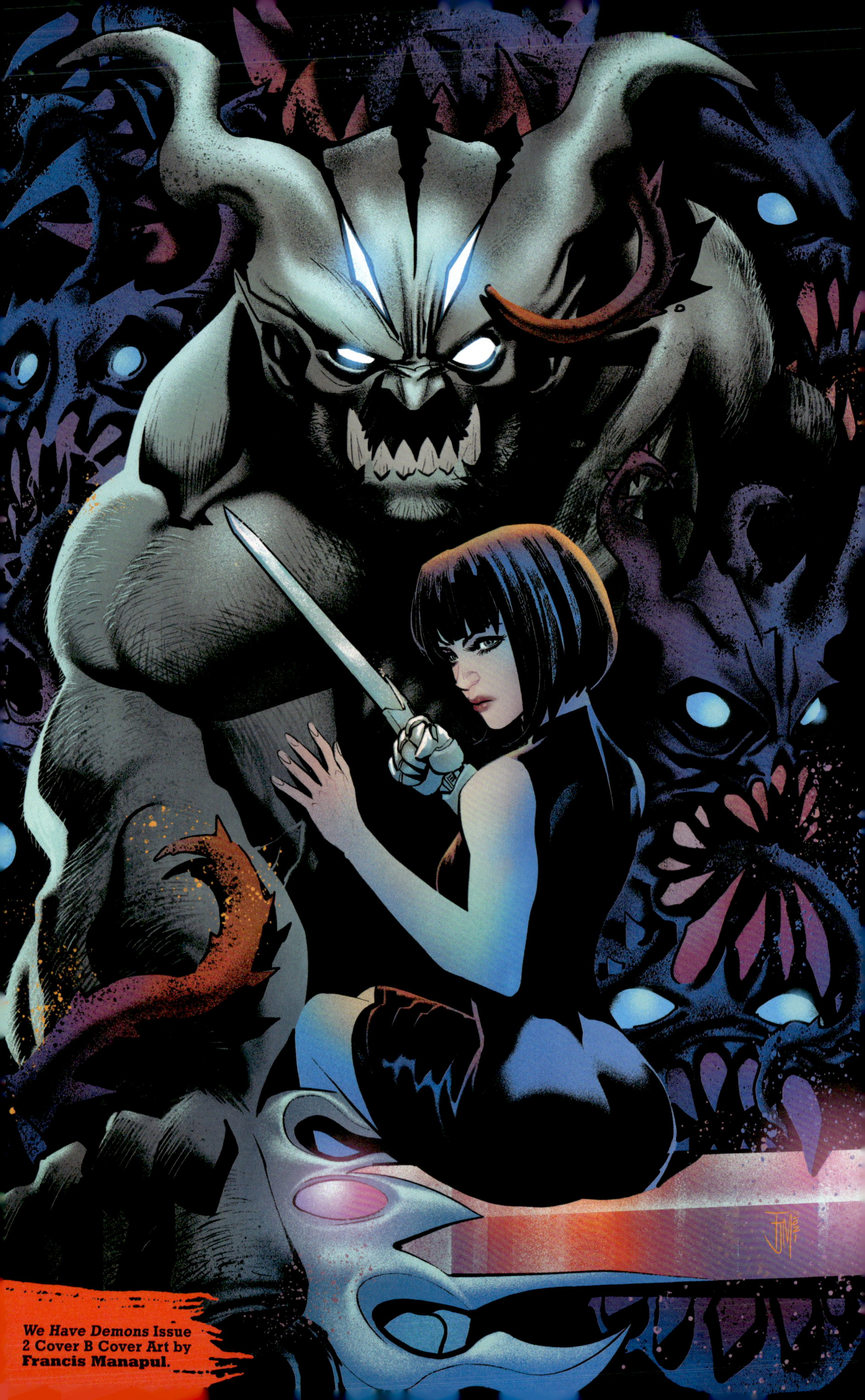

We Have Demons Issue 2 Cover B Cover Art by **Francis Manapul**.

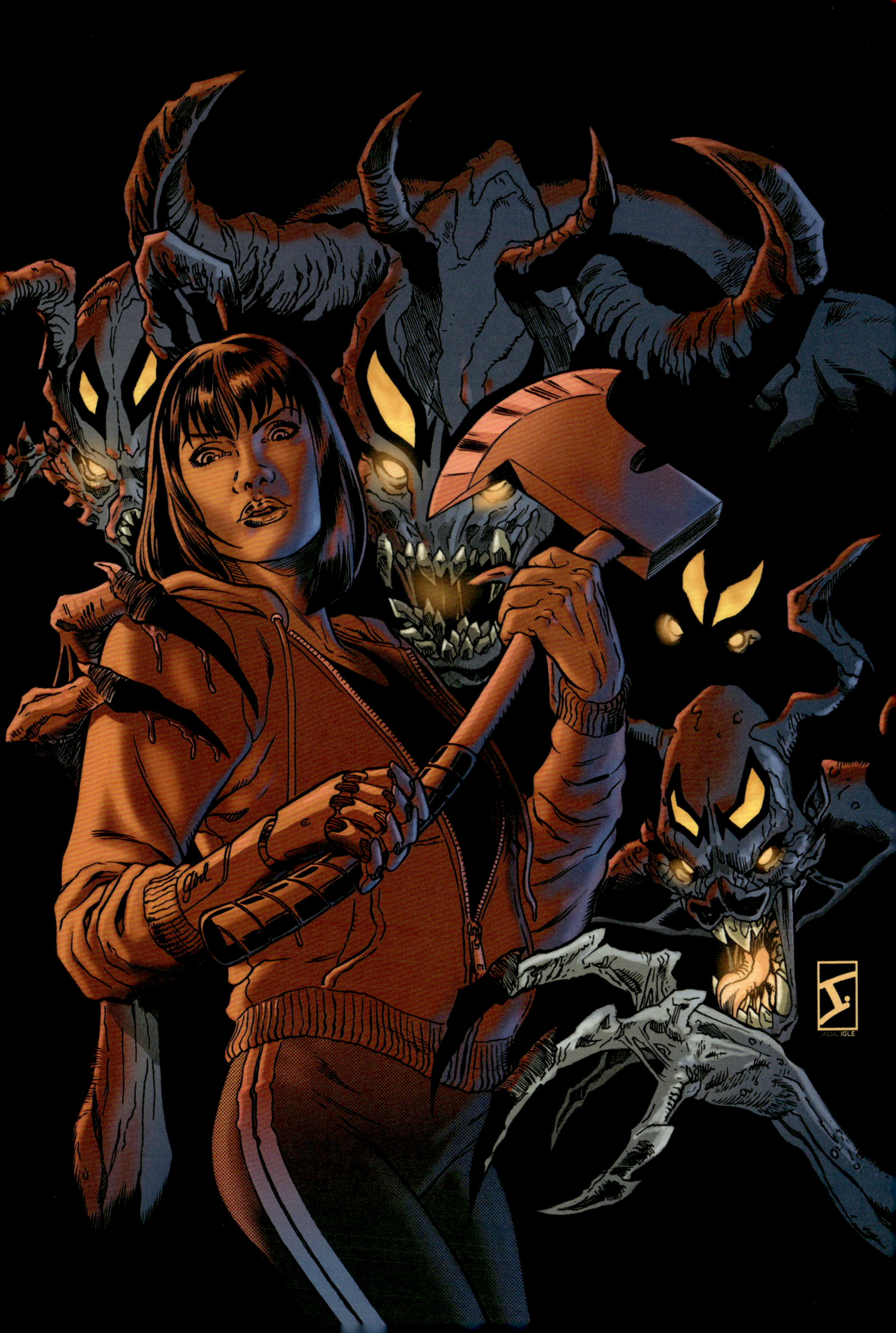

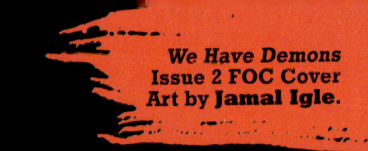

We Have Demons
Issue 2 FOC Cover
Art by **Jamal Igle**.

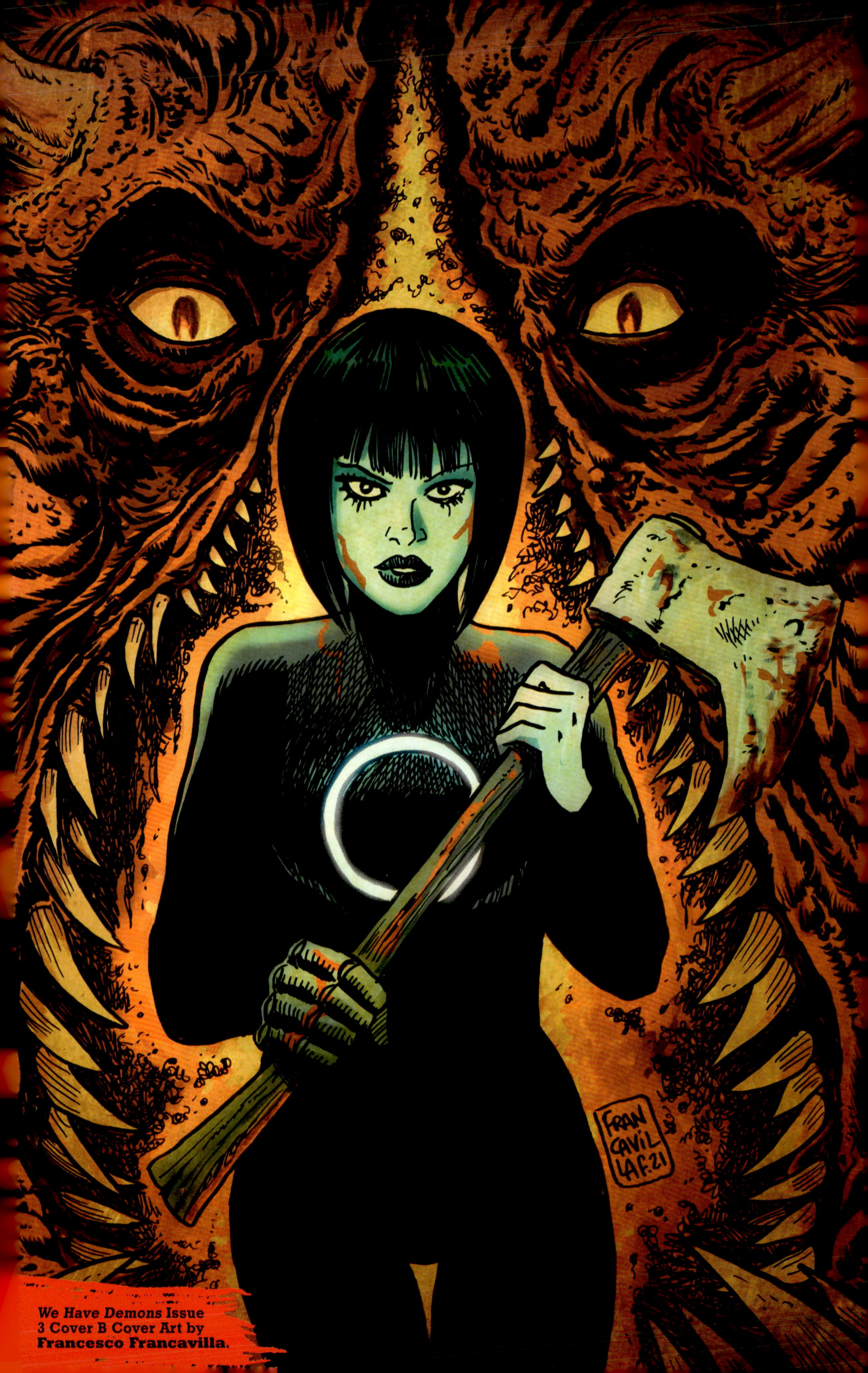
FRAN
CAVIL
LA F.21

We Have Demons Issue 3 Cover B Cover Art by **Francesco Francavilla.**

We Have Demons Issue 3 FOC
Cover Art by **Ariela Kristantina**
with **Sarah Stern**.

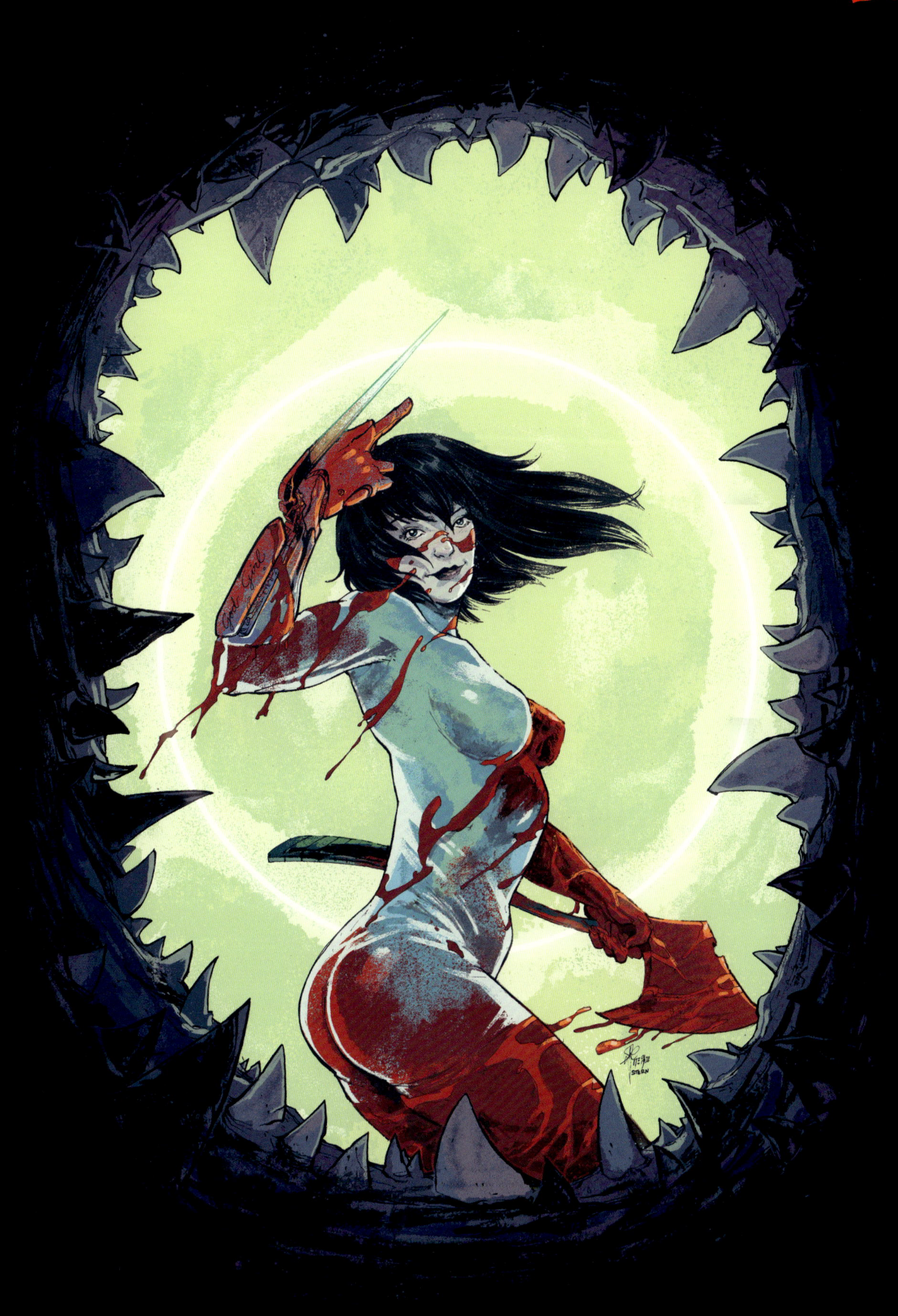

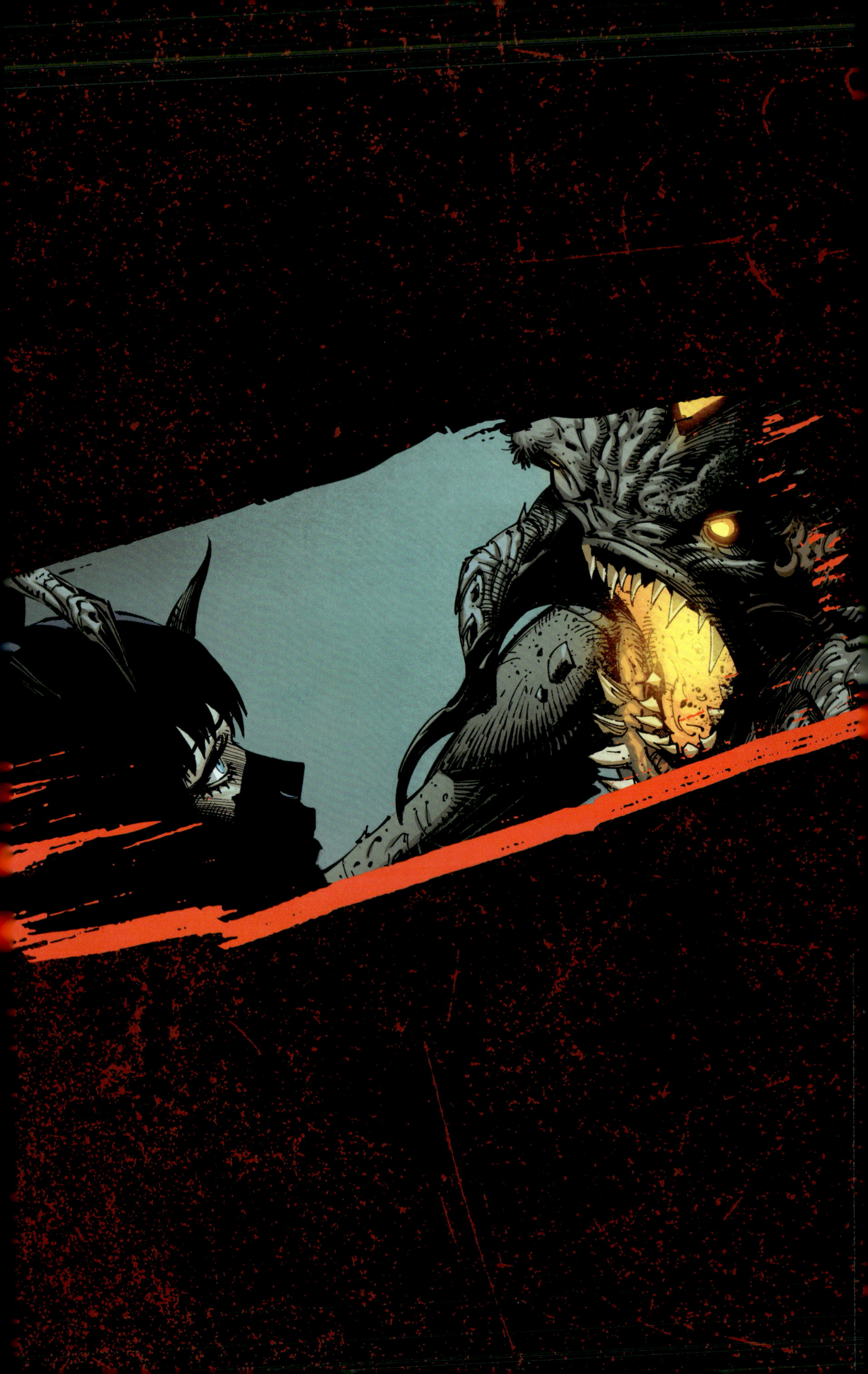

WE HAVE DEMONS
BONUS SECTION

WELCOME, EVERYONE!

I'm so happy and so grateful that you've chosen to join us at Best Jackett Press on this new endeavor with Comixology Originals and Dark Horse Comics!

For anyone still wondering what Best Jackett is—BJP is my own creative studio; it's where I'm going to be working for the foreseeable future. It's an engine for all the creator-owned books and projects, by friends and up-and-coming creators, that I'm helping produce. We have eight books coming with Comixology and Dark Horse over the years—all written by me, and drawn and cocreated by some amazing partners, as you'll read below.

These eight books are about challenging myself on every front—they're my attempt to both embrace the kind of stories I love, and to try wildly new things, all with cocreators who inspire me on every level—folks I feel lucky and grateful to partner with: Greg Capullo, Francis Manapul, Francesco Francavilla, Tula Lotay, Jamal Igle, Dan Panosian, Rafa Albuquerque, and Jock! They range from huge fun blockbusters, like *We Have Demons*, to historical fictions, like *Barnstormers*. They are stories for younger audiences, like *Dudley Datson and the Forever Machine*; tales that explore this moment in dark and piercing ways, like *Clear*; books that play with classic genres, like *Canary*; and books that break from tradition altogether, like *The Book of Evil*—a blend of prose and illustration. There are series with sprawling, robust mythologies, like our 1950s apocalyptic adventure *Duck and Cover*, and claustrophobic thrillers, like *Night of the Ghoul*. BJP is about range—both on the page and off—and I'm thrilled and nervous and excited to be sharing them all with you.

So, why Comixology Originals? When we started Best Jackett around 2019, my cocreators and I had a simple goal: make our books without any creative constraints, on our own terms. We had other work, so we all squirreled away what time we could. Then the pandemic hit. Publishers were shutting down. Stores were closing shop . . . everyone was scared for the future of the industry.

We had a lot of discussions about what we should do—about whether we should put these books aside (even though they were often turning out to be our favorite things to work on) and instead lock down whatever work for hire we could secure. Should we play it safe or should we find a way to commit to these books and take a huge leap? And what would it mean for fans—would they even have access to the comics and be able to afford them in such challenging times? Suddenly, finding a new way of making, publishing, and distributing the books felt like the right choice. How could we work on these projects consistently, retain the rights, and also make sure fans would have easy, affordable access to them, in a way that felt like it pointed ahead, toward a healthier industry?

Now, I'd already been an avid user of Comixology for some time. My older kids are both big huge comic fans and they read all their comics digitally, then go to the store to buy their favorites to hold and put on the shelf. I've started doing the same in recent years, and for a while I've felt that a major factor in strengthening the industry is greater synergy between digital and print. So, on the advice of my editor, Will Dennis, I began looking into the Comixology Originals line and saw that Comixology was already creating original comics with some of the most exciting emergent creators around—folks who, in my opinion, were pushing the industry forward in all kinds of energetic ways. And through a single subscription, fans could read all these new voices AND have access to classics like *The Sandman* or *Swamp Thing*—the books that made me want to write.

Talks began in spring of 2020, and right away we all clicked. Above all, we shared the belief that the industry as a whole would expand and strengthen if digital and print could start working supportively rather than competitively. Comixology had already put in place a deal with Dark Horse Comics that ensured our books wouldn't just be digital but would also come out in print. Dark Horse has published some of the greatest comics of all time, and we're thrilled to be working with them too. It was total kismet!

Brow 1/2
1
2
Below Sternum
3
Crotch
4
Mid Knee
5
Ankle
1/2

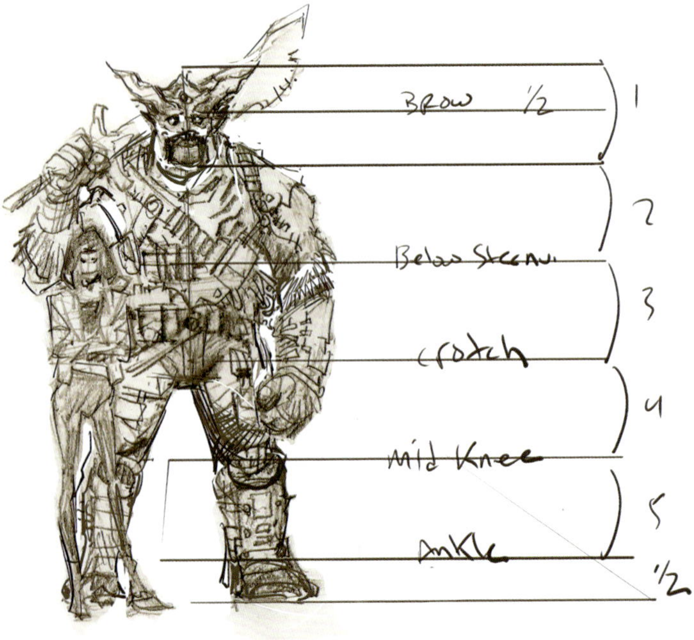

So, here we are. As I hope you'll see, our line is about pushing forward creatively, trying all kinds of new things on the page that we believe will expand the audience and lead to a bigger, stronger, and better comics industry. I couldn't ask for better partners for this first big slate of books than Comixology Originals and Dark Horse Comics, and I couldn't be prouder of these books.

Thanks again!
Scott Snyder

WE HAVE DEMONS

ISSUE 1 - rough outline

Scott Snyder

For Greg Capullo

Jon Glapion

Dave McCaig

Tom Napolitano

and Will Dennis

Guys, I can't even tell you how excited I am for this - to make something NOT under corporate pressures and deadlines, something OURS. THANK YOU for doing this. My hope is that every page is enjoyable to work on, and if not, just say and we'll fix it.

As for the book itself, WE HAVE DEMONS, the goal is to make something personal, but above all, something FUN. Like the Saturday morning cartoons we grew up on . . . but very R rated. Something that marries the ballsiness and bombast of 90's comics to the sensibilities of today. Gruesome demons, badass angel warriors, secret organizations, action and mayhem and cheers. The tone is fast-paced, character-driven, a little bit irreverent, but mostly just sincere big hearted, big fisted, summer blockbuster.

At its core, WE HAVE DEMONS is about a kid struggling to find faith in this moment — trying to believe that people are better than they are bad, that it's all worth the leap, and that together, we WILL make it through these dark times. In many ways, it's written as a letter from a father to his child, so it's a very heartfelt book — but deep fried in a burrito of crazy-ass fun. Okay! To Florida!

PAGE 1

- LAM, 19, sits in a nice living room sitting across a table from a happy young COUPLE. BOB and LAYLA SPOON (early thirties). The woman is very pregnant. These are her neighbors. They're cheerful and kind. In the background or off to the side are amateurish ceramic sculptures of different sizes that look weirdly like angry, anthropomorphic penises (more on this later). They shouldn't draw our attention in this panel though really. The feel should be almost painfully quaint. In fact, if you want to position the sculptures so we don't see them for a panel or two, go for it.

  > Lam is talking to the neighbors, all kind and pleasant. But all we hear is her narrating to us . . . She's like, "My father always told me that some people, you know right away they're good."

  > "Soon as you lay eyes on them, you know they're God folk."

  > "Bob and Layla Spoon are those kinds of people. So good they're hard to look at."

- We see LAM here, smiling, talking to them, sweet.

  > Lam narrates, "That's me, trying to look at them. High school sweethearts. Church-going. Bob is a pediatric nurse and Layla works training support dogs. On the weekends they literally volunteer at a place for kids who're blind . . . or deaf. Maybe both? And Bess? The old lady they bought the house from?

- Detail - we notice the weird, phallic looking ceramic sculptures.

  > She has no one and is going senile so they let her STAY . . . AND they take care of her. She lives upstairs and makes sculptures that are weirdly phallic which THEY DISPLAY all over. God folk."

- All of them, enjoying each other's company.

  > She narrates: They've been my neighbors for years. Since I was a little kid.

  > She narrates that, and in one minute from now, I'm going to murder them both.

- Now, Lam pulls out a massive AXE or hatchet if you prefer (her father's blade). She's still smiling, like a good girl.

  > Lam narrates: "My name is Lam. After Lamassu, an ancient angel."

  > "But I am not a God folk."

SLAM CUT TO a double spread of the TITLE PAGE: WE HAVE DEMONS in massive letters. Grindhouse style. In your face . . .

On this page it'll also say: CHAPTER 1 "God's Finger."

PAGE 2

A page with 3 images.

- The time of BOMBARDMENT 3 billion years ago, when the earth was still raw, being hit by asteroids frequently. Here we see a particularly dark looking ASTEROID headed toward earth. This is the one that's carrying the demon rock called HORN.

    Over this she'll narrate, "So where did it all go wrong for me? How far back should I start? 3 billion years ago? With the SERPENT STONE?"

- The RACE of EARLY HUMANS Hellvis is from. We see them here as an advanced society, but one that uses wood, stone, some metal. Still non-industrial. But we want to create something impressively technological here. That evokes Atlantis, wonders.

    "Or one hundred thousand years ago, with the SECRET SPECIES OF MAN?"

- We see some of the ANCIENT SWORDS — I know a hundred is too many to show, but whatever evokes the cool, glowing mystical power of them is more important than the number we show. So, whatever you think! We could show them in a literal way, like some of them lying on a table in a ring (we could do 9 — the 9 that now remain). Or you could show them in a figurative way, like floating, whatever you think!

    "Or maybe five thousand years ago, with the HUNDRED BLADES?"

PAGE 3

- We see backwoods Florida. A modest house, overgrown yard, nestled near the swamp. Cypress and canopy trees. Sultry.

    LAM narrates, "Or maybe with this story, about the fall of mankind, I should just start where it feels most natural."

    "In Florida."

- We see LAM as a 4-year-old, from the POV of her DAD, staring down. She's staring up at us, smiling. So cute.

    "Sixteen years ago. Pascaloosa County. That's me. Age four."

- Now we reverse shot to see LAM'S FATHER'S FACE from her (baby) POV, smiling down back at us, the sun behind his head, a tender vision. He's gray haired, a tough looking guy, but kind, like Indiana Jones but in professor mode, not adventure mode.

    "That's my dad. Cashel Cullen. My mom died in a hit and run when I was little, which we're not going to discuss here, so it's always been me and him. He's about as God Folk as they come."

    "It's all going to be all right, honey," he says.

    She narrates, "This is my first memory of him . . ."

- And then next panel is the same but he brings the AXE/HATCHET we saw on 1 into the frame . . . What?!

    " . . . It's right before he chops off my arm."

- We see her father chopping off her arm but we can't see DIAMOND BACK RATTLESNAKE (there was none, as it was Hellvis who bit off her arm, but we want to hide this fact). We could show this from behind or whatever keeps it NON-gruesome. We have plenty of gore later.

    "A seven-foot rattler had bit me while I was playing by the swamp. I'd left the PATH, and it just jumped up and got me. Bit me on my middle finger. By the time my dad found me, my whole arm was rotted out."

PAGE 4

- Not long after the "snake bite incident." Her dad lovingly making her a PROSTHETIC ARM that says "god girl" on it. Then fitting her with it.

    Over this she talks about how her dad made her a new arm, carved and inscribed it himself. He made her a new one every year. He was her hero, back then. This paragon of strength. For him, it was always black and white, good and evil. Things distilled down to a war for the soul. Good and bad. But he was kind, too, compassionate.

- Now a scene or 2 of Lam growing up with her dad, ages 7-10. She's a tomboy, fishing with him, hunting, real deep FL culture. This should be endearing. <u>We also catch a glimpse of JUNE here, dad's companion</u>. She could be watching, supportive. She should seem like an extremely kind, bookish mom.

PAGE 5

- Now we see her dad as a pastor. Preaching to his flock. The church is small, rural, but diverse.

    She talks about how she wasn't the only one who looked up to him. He was the town pastor. Everyone loved him. He was the cool pastor, though, if you can get your head around it.
    He was rough and tumble, anecdotal up there. His big catchphrase was . . .

- He and his CONGREGATION (BOB AND LAYLA front and center) are giving the finger to . . .

    Dad saying: GIVE EVIL THE FINGER!

    Lam is like, It's something he came up with after I was snakebit on my middle finger.

- . . . The SNAKE, stuffed, and coiled, head up, menacing, as a trophy in her dad's church. It's high up, where no one would reach it. Above the wood paneled wall. (There's a secret panel doorway under it – for later.)

    She narrates, "he hunted the snake for days, until he found it and killed it himself. Not that the snake was evil. But the temptation to stray from the path."

- Lam and June together, watching him, proud.

    She'll narrate that "sure, he traveled a lot without explanation. And sure, he could be guarded. But he was God folk. Or so I thought . . ."

PAGES 6-7

- One night, she's about 14, gaming in her room . . . headset on, talking to her friend (whose face could be on the screen if you want, an African American girl, same age). This will be dialogue, no narration as they argue about a game detail. Something about a cycloptic monster with plumes on its head or something!

- Suddenly she hears arguing on a monitor hooked up to her phone. She put a RING alarm kind of thing outside in the bushes to hear if her dad was coming home. Don't worry, I'll explain this in her dialogue with her friend.

- She looks out the window and sees across the yard, by the church, hidden in shadow and obscured, her father arguing with a hulking man in the shadows (Hellvis).

    Her father says, no one can know about us, ever. Not what we do together, not any of it. Hellvis's dialogue is too low to hear, but the argument goes on, intriguing and shocking Lam . . .

- Lam is stunned.

- After, she starts snooping more. We see her in his office (which is like a book-lined library inside the church).

    I'll have her explain in narration, after that, she started getting curious. Digging deeper.

- In his drawer, her dad keeps an old leather PLANNER, and in his calendar, he has some dates where he's written "HELL."

    She'll talk about how the trips he took, he always wrote "hell" by them. Whatever he was doing, it must have been tearing him up.

- One time he came back, and she checked the laundry after he went to bed . . . and she found clothes covered in BLOOD. And CHAINS. And weird 90s DANCE RECORDS? "What the fuck was he doing?" she'll ask herself. "Who was he? Some kind of psycho? Maybe a crusader? Maybe just . . . a flawed, human being."

- And if you want, Greg, we can do a kind of imaginary grid of images of her father as the different things she imagines him as: The Punisher. An S and M guy. And then maybe him as himself. Whatever you think though!

PAGES 8-9

Big emotional conversation. Choreograph however feels right for the 2 pages, brother. But the point of the scene is a daughter reaching out to her father, timidly but determinedly, and getting rejected.

- It goes on for a year plus until she confronts him. Now Lam is sixteen. Her father is working on her NEW ARM in the garage of their house (more on this particular arm later . . .).

- She comes in, nervous. She says she needs to talk to him. But he's half there, so into this arm he's making.

- He's talking about the arm, how it's the best one he's made. And it's a special one. That'll help her when she's older. When she's ready to do more of what he does.

- She raises her voice, like DAD. I need to talk to you.

- He turns to her, okay, honey, what is it?

- She tries to get through to him. She says I know about your trips. That they're not for the church. He's like that's ridiculous, honey. But she gets more adamant. Dad, I know you go places you hate yourself for. I know you have some secret life. But her dad continues to protest, smiling, like this is silly.

- She goes on, trying to break through. "I know about your secret partner." And her dad is like, "I don't have any secret partner." He says, come look at this arm.

- And she's like "Listen to me goddammit! I love you. Whatever you're doing, whatever this is . . . we all have demons."

- This comment makes her dad FREEZE. Go cold.

- He goes back to her arm and says, "don't you ever say that again."

- She's like Dad-

    And he says NEVER! There's fucking good and there's fucking evil and that's all there is. When you're older you'll be ready to understand. But . . . not yet.

- She leaves.

Let's do a CHAPTER BREAK here, whether we use a design page (my preference) or a panel.

CHAPTER 2: "Passage"

PAGE 10

- We see Lam away at college, a year later. She has a typical prosthetic. Her look is what we planned. Darker, a bit tougher. Like the whole thing with her dad hardened her to the world. Maybe a hoodie. She's in astrophysics class.

    Over this she'll narrate about after that, things changed. She and her father grew apart. She went away for school and didn't look back.

    The Professor will be talking about the Fermi paradox, what is it?

- Lam raising her hand.

    "He tried calling a couple times but we had little to say. I talked to June instead. She encouraged me to reconnect with my dad, but I wasn't ready."

    She answers the question in dialogue about the Fermi paradox (the mystery as to why there are no signs of life in the universe. – this will tie into our mythos later, b/c the dark material is partly responsible . . .)

- Lam trying to date. I figure we can use that familiar meme as a template for the GUY: the drunk dude yelling into the girl's ear as she stares into the void.

    She'll narrate: "I tried dating." And I'll have the guy saying in a balloon:

    "And then Liam Neeson, he drives the SNOWPLOUGH straight into . . ."

- Maybe the same image but a GIRL – pretty, seductive.

    "And I tried some more," she can say.

    And here I'll have the girl finish the thought, like "And Liam Neeson, he drives the fucking ZAMBONI right into . . ."

- Now she's in the library, in the stacks.

    "Mostly I studied. All the good and evil god folk stuff, it felt like bullshit. She dove into studying astrophysics, the sciences, where nothing was good and evil. No finger of God, just the cosmic billiard ball clacking of cause and effect. Until one day, June called . . ."

- Talking into her phone. She's like, June I don't want to talk to him. And June is like, Lam. He's dead.

- Her face is shocked. "What?"

PAGE 11

- CUT TO: The church, overflowing with MOURNERS, all from the congregation. Bob and Layla could be here. Lam's friend from gaming years ago.

    She'll narrate here about how it didn't feel real.

- Inside, Lam is looking on as June speaks about her father, whose picture is on display.

    "That he was gone. Just . . . poof."

- In the crowd of mourners are a few strange people. These are the ANGELS/GLORIES. Five of them. They're from all over the world, so let's have them be diverse in background and gender (let's hop on the phone to make them up, man! We can do their backgrounds, all of it). But none are younger than 21. I'd like Lam to be the young one on the team. Lots to brainstorm here, but I see one Muslim woman from Pakistan. One man from rural China. One man from Russia, another from Ghana. And a woman maybe from Polynesia. But lots to grow together, here. All of them are just dressed in black.

    "In the crowd there were all these faces I knew. But they all seemed like strangers. And among them, a handful that I'd never seen before. Strange, out of place. All I wanted to know was who he was. Really."

- Lam sitting there, sad, confused, angry . . . Use as a transition to:

PAGES 12-13

- Later: same but now it's night. Like the same shot, but a time lapse where now the church is empty and it's late at night. Lam is still there. But now totally alone. A small figure in a dark church.

- Her father's PICTURE is still up.

- She goes up to it.

- And she talks to him. She's like, I just wanted to know who you were. You didn't have to hide from me.

- She's crying, angry as she goes on. You didn't have to pretend to be some . . . hero!

- The SNAKE staring at her from above the wall.

- In frustration, she throws her prosthetic arm at it!

- The whole thing is knocked back, as though it's a lever . . .

- And what the . . .

- A secret panel sliding DOOR opens in the wall!

PAGES 14-17

14-15

- Quiet, tense . . . Lam enters, looking around. It's a secret office full of occult books and globes. Like the study of an Indiana Jones. Big image. The feel here should be like we just went down the rabbit hole, literally and figuratively . . . thrilling, scary; we have to keep going!

- She sees the innocent objects first. But then . . .

- . . . On his desk the AXE (the one she was holding on page 1). And . . .

- . . . On the wall are pictures of MURDERED PEOPLE. Polaroids.

- Closer on them, they have scribbled beneath, classifications. What the?!

- She's horrified. Behind her, a voice:

    "I'm sure you have a lot of questions . . ."

16-17

- Lam spins around to face June.

    Lam is like, June? And June is like, your father had . . . secrets. But it's time you knew the truth.

- And Lam is like, I think I know it. And June is like, just listen to me. Your father was . . .

- And here let's do a panel with them in profile facing each other so their balloons are concurrent, like they say this at the same time.

    June is like: a demon hunter. And Lam is like: an S&M DJ serial killer.

    Then both of them are like, wait what?

- And now June is trying to calm her down. Like, "your father, and his partner, they hunt demons, Lam. His partner is kept down there, if you'd like to meet him."

- June points to a DOOR we didn't notice before. It's metal. Like a secure door. Ominous as fuck. And above it, the word HELL is visible. Could be a sign on the door too — whatever you think gives the best effect. The idea is — "Dad kept his partner in a DUNGEON?!" If you want it to be covered by a sheet or something that's removed to reveal it, go for it — whatever works!

- Lam is like what do you mean he lives down there? Down where?! And June is like, in the underground.

- June says, look, let me explain. Lam is like, no! I don't want to know, actually.

- But June says, YES, you do.

    And Lam is like, "and then she told me the story I was telling you, but she started at the very beginning.

TITLE PAGE

CHAPTER 3: "The Fall of Man"

PAGES 18-21

Greg, this will be the big info dump but the key is to make it feel like THE secret history of life. Like the biggest secret ever. So to give it the kind of grandeur and majesty it deserves. You do this better than anyone, so rock out!

The images are:

18-19

- The BIG BANG.

    Over this, I'll have Lam narrate what June told her. Like, June began 13 billion years ago. At the start of the universe, when an explosion of matter filled an empty void.

- The early days of the universe, collections of dust and gas . . .

    The universe filled with all kinds of matter — an abundance of gasses and solids, metals and stone. From nothing . . . everything. For every kind of matter, its opposite. Some additive, some subtractive. Some that nourished life, some that prevented it.

- TWO PARTICLES, one light, one dark.

    And at the extreme ends of this spectrum, life giving, and death dealing, came two materials [I still have to name them, but I'm thinking Halo and Horn if you like it!]. Some of the rarest in existence, found only in cosmically minuscule amounts . . . but out there, circulating. One is the FIRST and LIGHTEST element, atomic number ZERO (like a halo), and the other is the LAST and HEAVIEST . . .

- Young EARTH, during the time of bombardment. Asteroids hitting.

    Eventually, young earth formed, and for millions of years was bombarded with material from space. It wasn't until the end of this period . . .

- We see a large ASTEROID of the LIGHT MATERIAL HIT. BOOM!

    . . . That an asteroid containing the light material hit the planet.

- And many years later, smaller, DARK ASTEROIDS are coming . . .

    And then other asteroids, containing DARK particles reached the earth.

- And breaks up over in the atmosphere, releasing small amounts to earth.

    . . . breaking up over the Pangaea and leaving only residual amounts around the globe.

- We see scenes of early animal life. Whatever prehistoric period you want to draw a glimpse or impression of, Greg, Permian, Triassic . . .

    Life evolved unaware of these two substances. Some say the light and dark are themselves sentient. Or move by some secret design.

- We see the LIGHT MATERIAL creating the GARDEN OF EDEN in the desert.

    The light created pockets of vitality wherever it landed, sacred and secret oases to help life along. Granting those who came into contact with it long life, strength . . . It's responsible for many myths, from the Garden of Eden to the Fountain of youth, and so on.

- We see the DARK MATERIAL deep in the veins of water in the earth, or down in a cavern, whatever you think implies it's down there lurking.

    The dark stayed hidden. Only rising when a species worth corrupting appeared on earth . . .

20-21

- Now early man, HOMO ERECTUS.

    Man.

- We see a secret species of man, the one HELLVIS is from. They're advanced, as discussed. They're trading with HOMO SAPIENS (who are not advanced at this time).

    The dark infected the species of man that should have ruled the planet. The Nephilim (as referred to in the bible). They were far more advanced than homo sapiens. Which is why the dark sought them out.

- They're now demons! Tearing each other apart (though we just see this in silhouette so we don't reveal the demons yet.

    Infected, they tore each other apart, brought down the Neander-thals too. Nearly ended Homo Sapiens as well. Would have, if not for small groups finding refuge in the distant pockets where the light particle had taken root.

- Ancient Sumer, blacksmiths forging the BLADES.

    Over time, it was decided that all light found would be used to create weapons to fight back the dark should it rise again. One thousand blades were made. Passed down from bearer to bearer. Often responsible for legends about mystical swords, axes, spears. They glow in the presence of the dark and strike down those infected by it easily.

- Now NINE.

    Over time, light faded from many. Others were destroyed. Now there are nine left. Only nine. And after years of slumber, the dark is rising again. June said it has begun infecting people all over the country, maybe the world.

- The ANGELS/GLORIES (no Hellvis though, obviously).

    Nine blades, entrusted to bearers located around the globe, dedicated to stop the dark from taking down the human race. "Glories."

- And LAM'S FATHER, holding the AXE.

    And according to June, DAD was one of them. He and his partner, they were legends in the group. Like the Indiana Jones of angels. Or John Wick or whatever.

- CLOSE on her dad holding the AXE and use as a transition to . . .

    She said that's why he died. People infected by the dark got to him. Demons.

PAGES 22-23

- CUT TO: The PRESENT: The AXE in Lam's hand as she's standing over Bob and Layla.

    In dialogue to them, Lam is like, "She said you two are the prime suspects. But that's crazy right? Not just that part, but I mean all of it. ALL OF IT."

- Bob and Layla are like, "very crazy". Nervous as any normal person would be.

- Lam holds out the AXE. She's like, I mean, if you were demons, this should glow.

- The axe touching Bob's shoulder menacingly.

- He waits . . . A tense moment . . . .

- But nothing happens.

- And Lam sits down, exhausted, putting the axe on the table beside her.

- She's like, I'm so sorry. I really am. I just . . . I don't know what the hell's going on anymore.

- And they say it's okay. Really.

- But as she apologizes . . . she doesn't notice BOB and LAYLA starting to change behind her . . .

PAGES 24-29

- Huge image! Bob and Layla as DEMONS!!! WTF?! Think the Thing, think Cronenberg, let's indulge our inner teenagers. So whatever body horror you want to do here, faces opening into mouths, veins and sinew, anything, go for it. My only thing is that there should be sharp bone protrusions so horns, claws, these things we associate with demons are vaguely there, at least in some of them, you know? Let's create our own consistent distinctive look for our demons – make our monsters recognizable as ours, so however you want to play with a certain kind of bone protrusion from the head, back, whatever it is, the skull stretched with bone crown points ripping through the skin to wing or umbrella-like bone fingers coming out of the back, go for it!! Let's just make sure our demons have some consistent elements so folks out there will be like that's a Capullo Snyder demon! When they see one. Oh, and our demons curse. A LOT.

- BOB attacks! All mouths and teeth biting.

- Lam grabs for the AXE but knocks it to the floor.

- She reaches for it but SNAP! LAYLA'S demon teeth gnash in front, not so fast . . .

- One of the demons lunges . . .

- . . .but she blocks with her prosthetic arm! Chomp!

- Lam takes a sharp phallic sculpture . . .

- And uses it to stab the demon in the face, or smash the demon on the head. CRASH!

- She runs for the door, leaping over a couch or table, something athletic . . .

- But then Layla's stomach opens and the TRIPLETS POP OUT on long veiny extensions, the most vicious, horrifying little things ever!

- And they block her from the door.

- She's backing away . . . doomed.

- Defiant. Lam gives them the finger, Fuck you.

- They lunge!

- She closes her eyes.

- And SHUNK! Off panel, a massive SWORD fells the demons as . . .

- . . . blood spatters on Lam. Who? What . . .

    It's okay, Lam, says a voice.

- Lam opens her eyes.

- She's shocked. Lam is like . . . who are you?

PAGES 30-31

- SPLASH or huge image: our big reveal of HELLVIS! Looking BADASS.

    My name is difficult to pronounce. The angels call me Hellvis. I was your father's partner. It's good to finally meet you Lam.

- He helps her up. She's stunned.
- He gives her the arm. You might want this, says Hellvis.
- Shaking, she puts on the arm.
- Just then the hiss of a demon coming down the stairs . . .
    The OLD LADY. And as the OLD WOMAN approaches down the stairs . . .
- . . . Hellvis is like, you know what to do.
- Lam, shaking, starts to raise the middle finger. Give evil the fing--

    Over this I'll narrate from her, like and so maybe the best place to start this story wasn't 3 billion years ago or even 19 years ago. But right now. At the moment I realized that no, I wasn't God folk . . .

PAGE 32

SPLASH - SHING! <u>The BLADE pops out.</u> She's like Holy sh—

    " . . . but maybe it was time to try?"

Initially Lam is supposed to discover the blade is in the arm later in the story, at a low point, so I'm a little hesitant to use it here, but it's tempting? An ALTERNATE ending is to just put them in fight mode together,
give a great last portait, like . . .

(end of 31)

- Just then the hiss of a demon coming down the stairs . . .
    The OLD LADY. And as the OLD WOMAN approaches down the stairs . . .
- . . . Hellvis is like, go on.
- Lam picks up the AXE.

    Over this I'll narrate from her, like and so maybe the best place to start this story wasn't 3 billion years ago or even 19 years ago. But right now. At the moment I realized that no, I wasn't God folk . . .

PAGE 32

SPLASH - LAM and HELLVIS, badass, together, rushing the demon creeping into the frame. She has the AXE and he has his sword.

    " . . . but maybe it was time to try?"

WE HAVE DEMONS™

LOGO PROCESS

DESIGN BY EMMA PRICE

comiXology ORIGINALS
WE HAVE
Demons
NO.1
SCOTT SNYDER
GREG CAPULLO
JONATHAN GLAPION
DAVE MCCAIG

We Have
DEMONS
ISSUE 01
comiXology ORIGINALS
Scott SNYDER
Greg CAPULLO
Jonathan GLAPION
Dave MCCAIG

We Have
DEMONS
ISSUE 01
SNYDER
CAPULLO
GLAPION
MCCAIG
comiXology ORIGINALS

WE HAVE
DEMONS
01
SNYDER
CAPULLO
GLAPION
MCCAIG
comiXology ORIGINALS

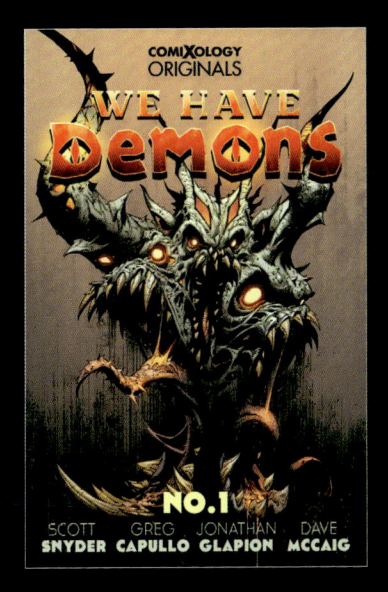

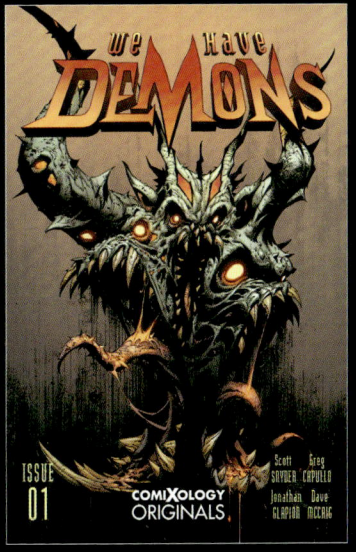

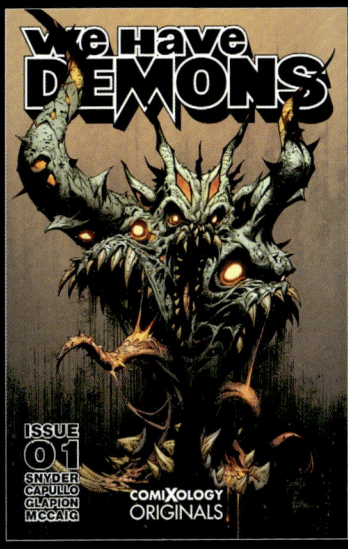

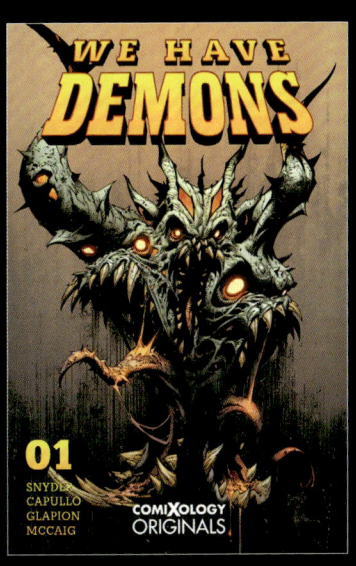

WE HAVE
DEMONS
01
SNYDER
CAPULLO
GLAPION
MCCAIG
comiXology
ORIGINALS

WE HAVE
DEMONS
01
SNYDER
CAPULLO
GLAPION
MCCAIG
comiXology
ORIGINALS

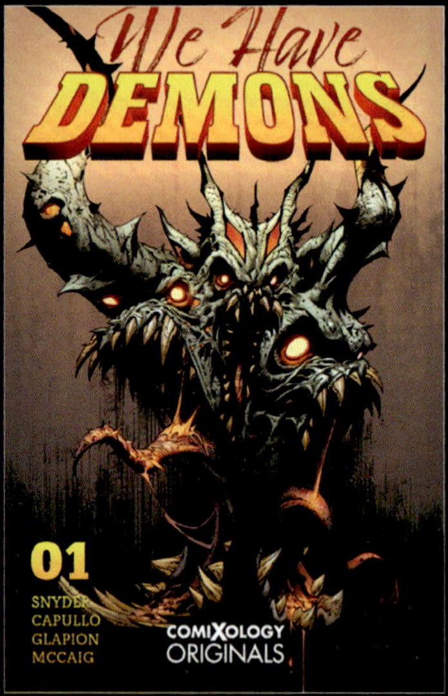
We Have
DEMONS
01
SNYDER
CAPULLO
GLAPION
MCCAIG
comiXology
ORIGINALS

We Have
DEMONS
01
SNYDER
CAPULLO
GLAPION
MCCAIG
comiXology
ORIGINALS

WE HAVE
DEMONS
01
SNYDER
CAPULLO
GLAPION
MCCAIG
comiXology
ORIGINALS

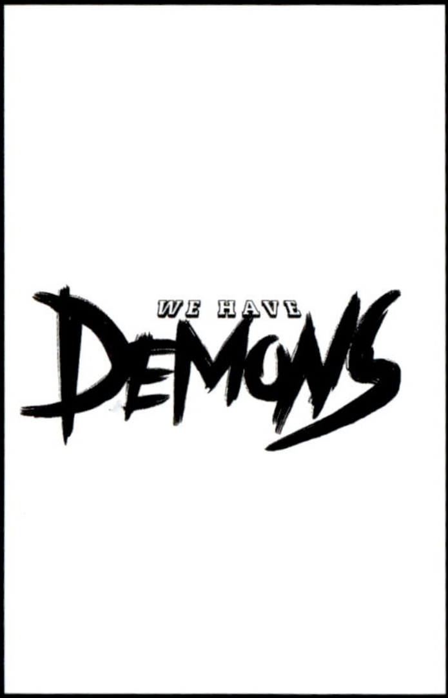
WE HAVE
DEMONS

WE HAVE
DEMONS
01
SNYDER
CAPULLO
GLAPION
MCCAIG
comiXology
ORIGINALS

We Have
DEMONS
ISSUE
01
SNYDER
CAPULLO
GLAPION
MCCAIG
comiXology
ORIGINALS

We Have
DEMONS
ISSUE
01
SNYDER
CAPULLO
GLAPION
MCCAIG
comiXology
ORIGINALS

WE HAVE DEMONS

ART PROCESS

ART BY CAPULLO, GLAPION, AND McCAIG

INTERIORS

GREG CAPULLO
JONATHAN GLAPION
DEMONS
INTERIORS

INTERIORS
DOUBLE PAGE SPREAD: CUT AS SHOWN, ABUT PAGE EDGES, TAPE ON BACK, DO NOT OVERLAP

INTERIORS
DOUBLE PAGE SPREAD: CUT AS SHOWN, ABUT PAGE EDGES, TAPE ON BACK, DO NOT OVERLAP

GREG CAPULLO
DEMONS
JONATHAN GLAPION
2
2
INTERIORS
DOUBLE PAGE SPREAD: CUT AS SHOWN, ABUT PAGE EDGES, TAPE ON BACK, DO NOT OVERLAP

GREG CAPULLO
DEMONS
JONATHAN GLAPION
3
2
INTERIORS
DOUBLE PAGE SPREAD: CUT AS SHOWN, ABUT PAGE EDGES, TAPE ON BACK, DO NOT OVERLAP

INTERIORS
DOUBLE PAGE SPREAD: CUT AS SHOWN, ABUT PAGE EDGES, TAPE ON BACK, DO NOT OVERLAP

INTERIORS
DOUBLE PAGE SPREAD: CUT AS SHOWN, ABUT PAGE EDGES, TAPE ON BACK, DO NOT OVERLAP

PENCILLER GREG CAPULLO
JONATHAN GLAPION
4
TITLE DEMONS
ISSUE # 2
MONTH
INTERIORS
DOUBLE PAGE SPREAD: CUT AS SHOWN, ABUT PAGE EDGES, DO NOT OVERLAP

PENCILLER GREG CAPULLO
INKER JONATHAN GLAPION
PAGE# 5
TITLE DEMONS
ISSUE # 2
MONTH
INTERIORS
DOUBLE PAGE SPREAD: CUT AS SHOWN, ABUT PAGE EDGES, TAPE ON BACK, DO NOT OVERLAP

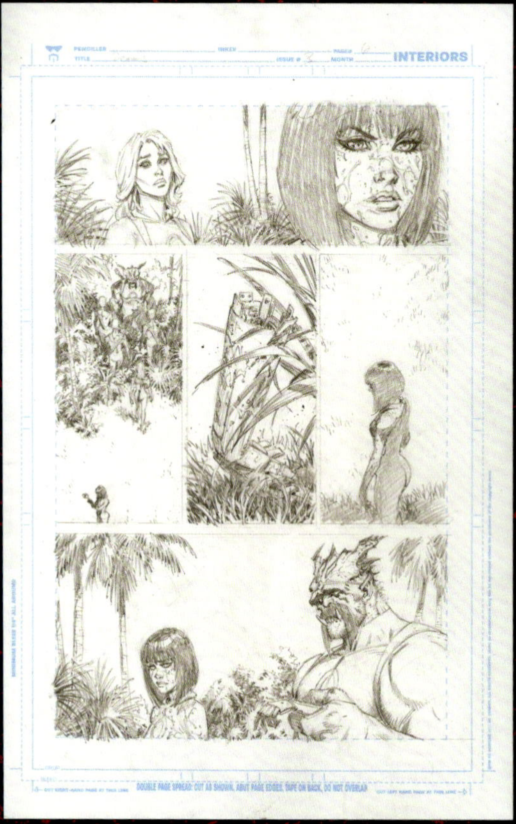

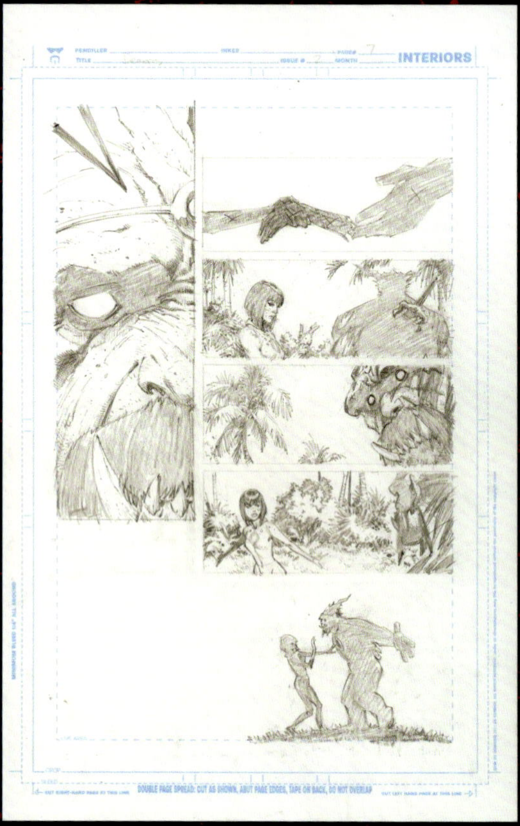

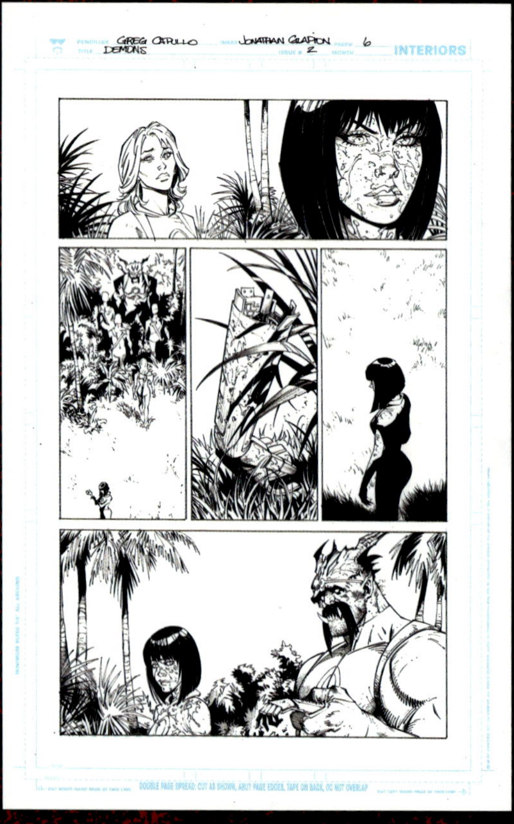

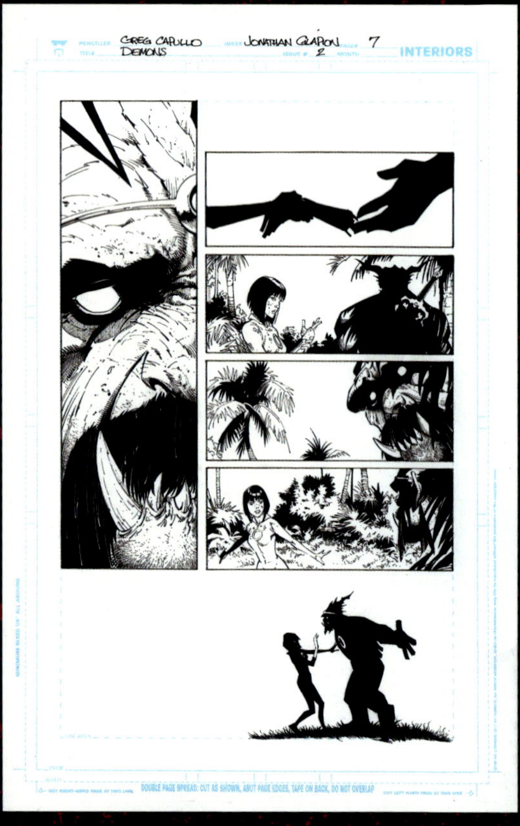

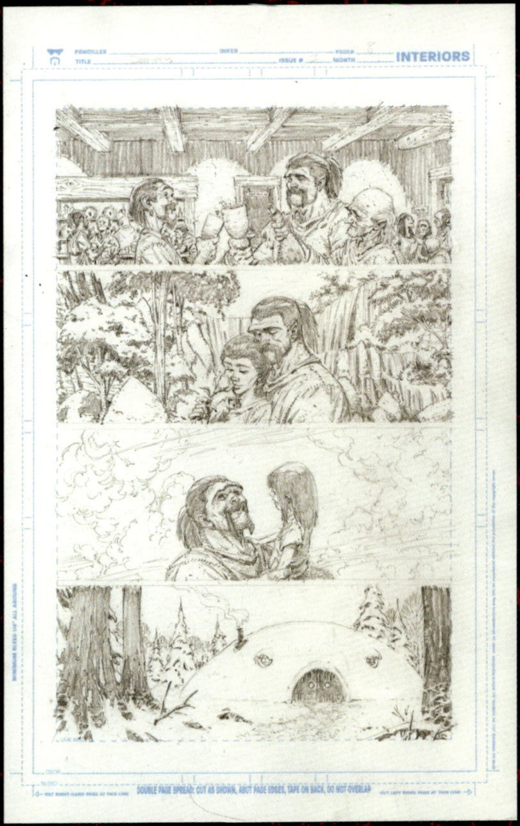

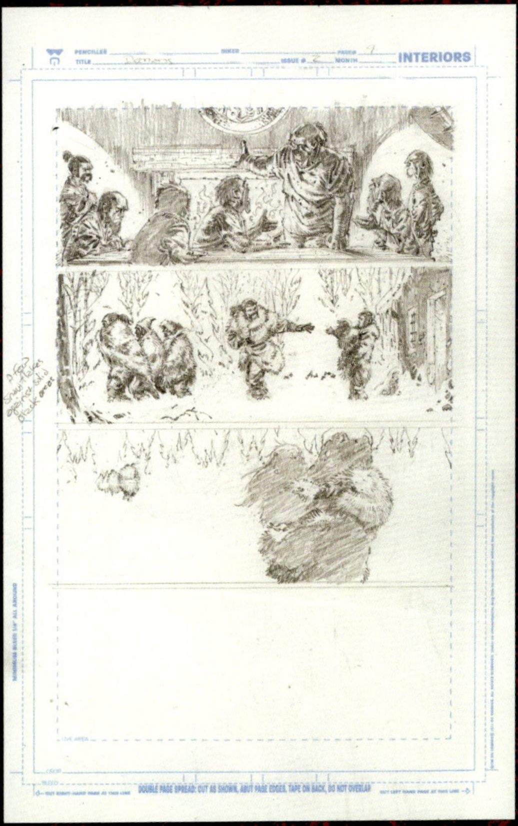

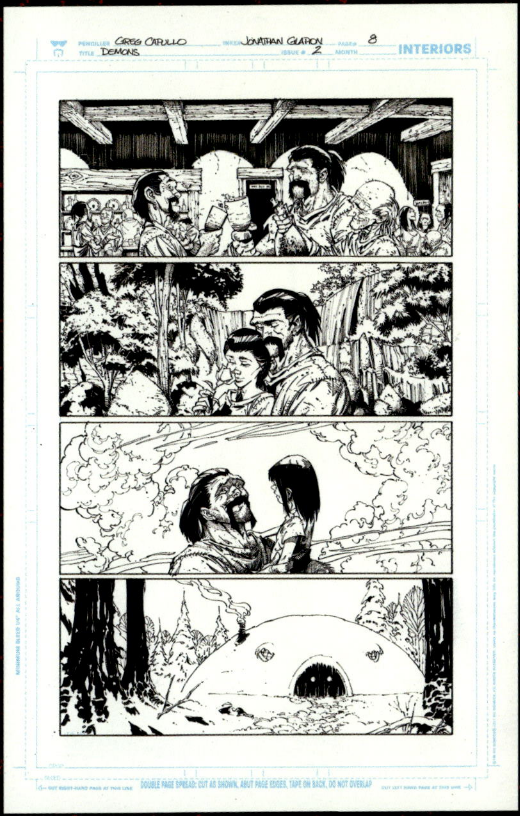

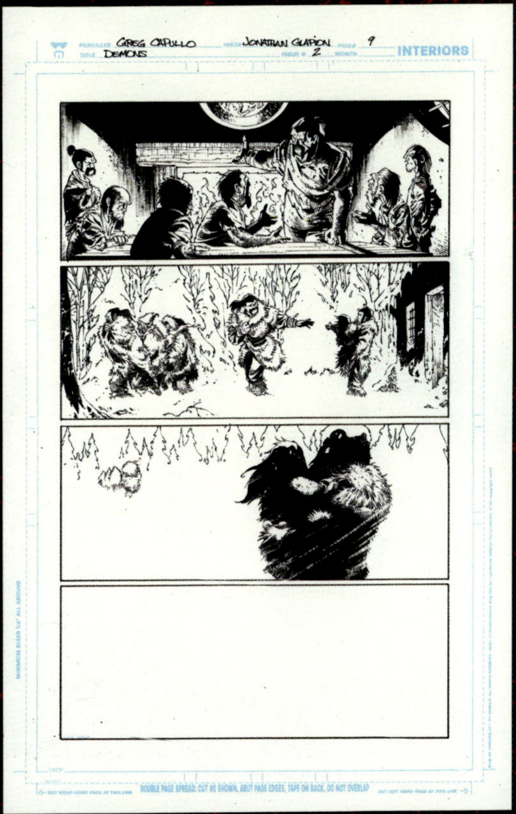

PENCILLER GREG CAPULLO
INKER JONATHAN GLAPION
PAGE# 12
TITLE DEMONS
ISSUE # 2
MONTH
INTERIORS
MINIMUM BLEED 1/4" ALL AROUND
CUT RIGHT-HAND PAGE AT THIS LINE
DOUBLE PAGE SPREAD: CUT AS SHOWN, ABUT PAGE EDGES, TAPE ON BACK, DO NOT OVERLAP
CUT LEFT HAND PAGE AT THIS LINE

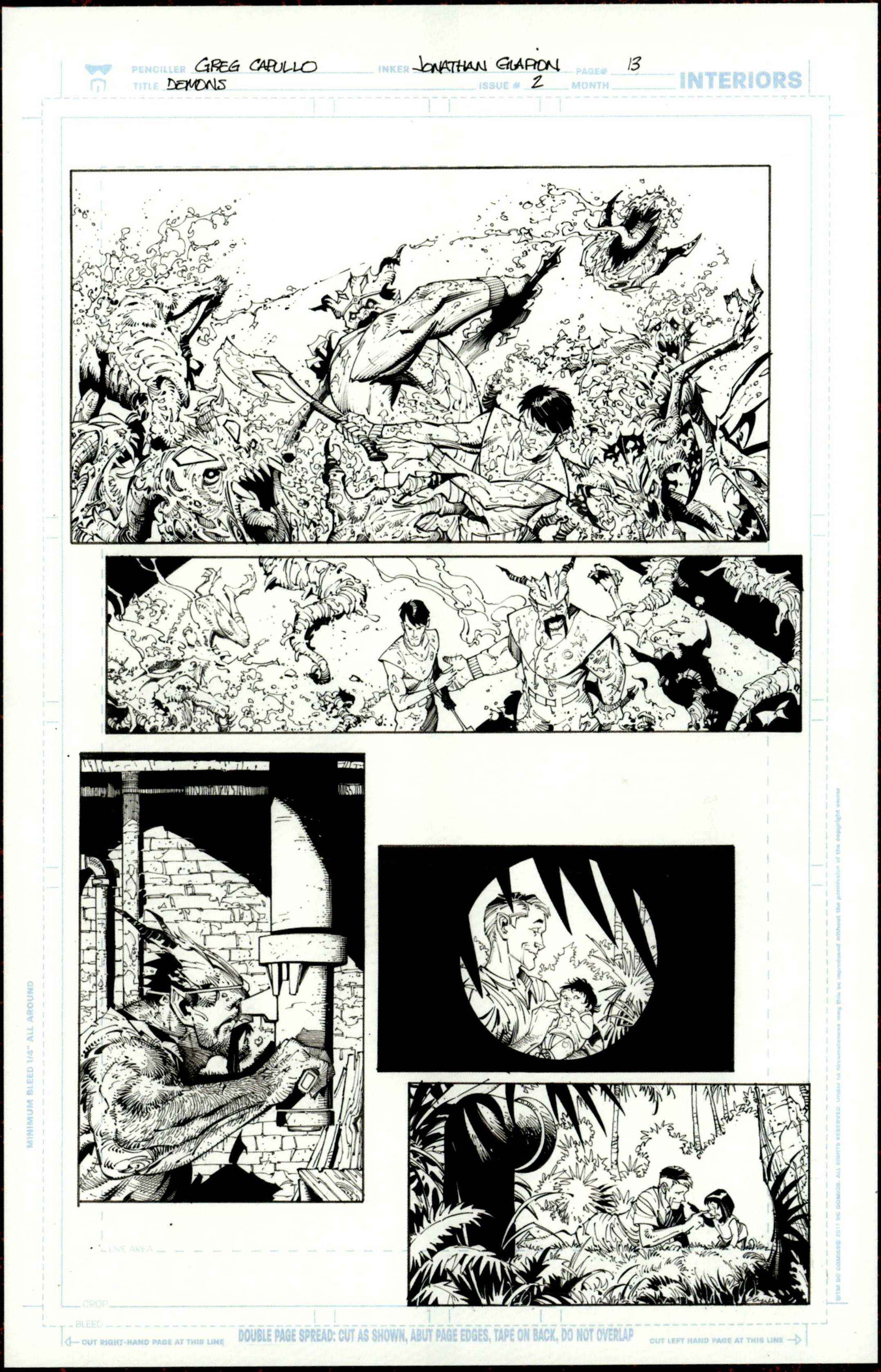

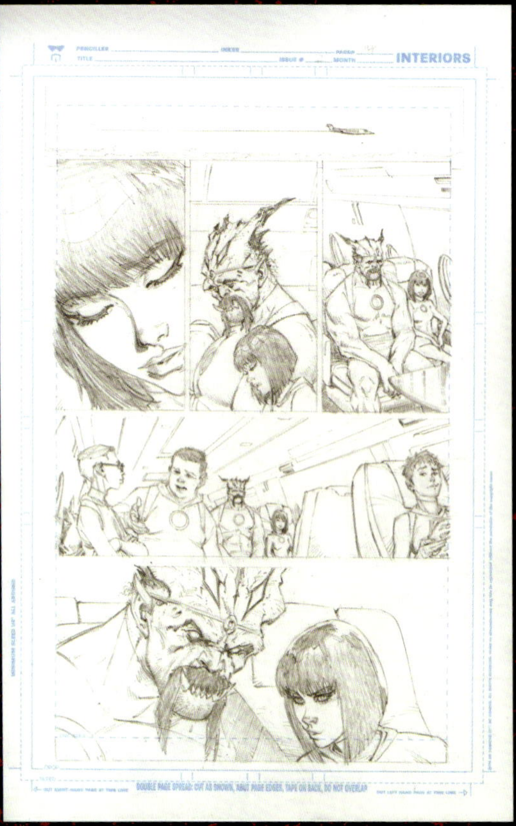

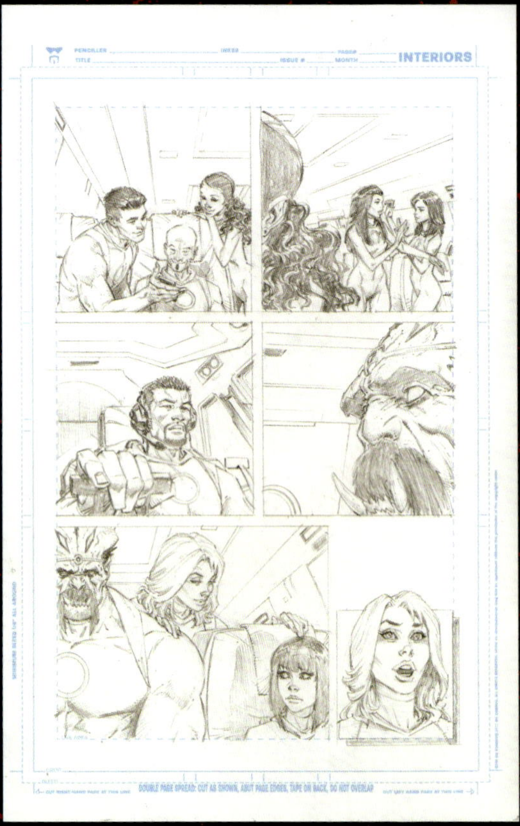

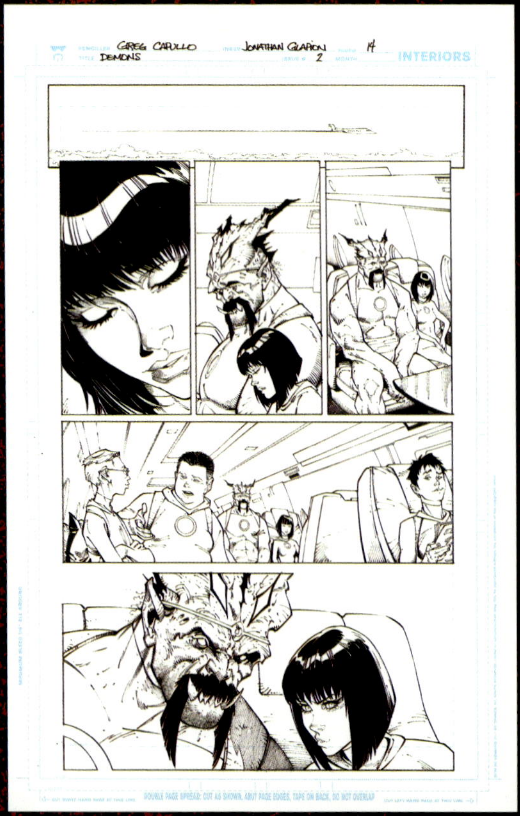

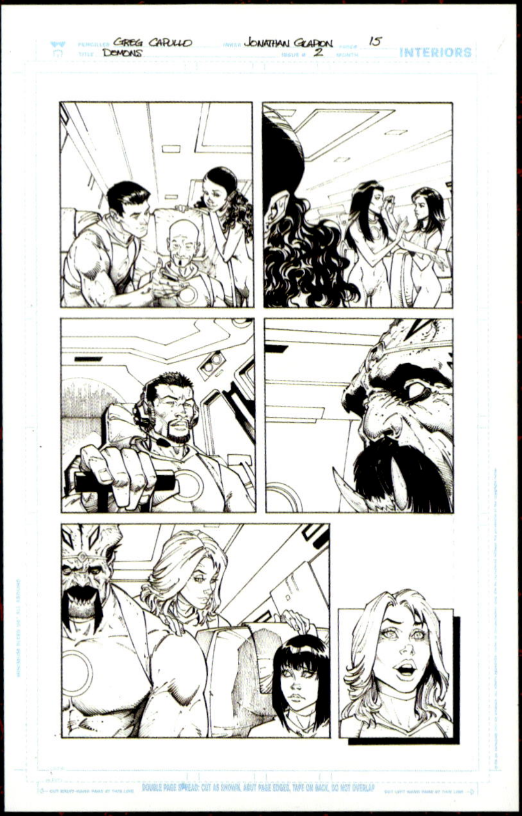

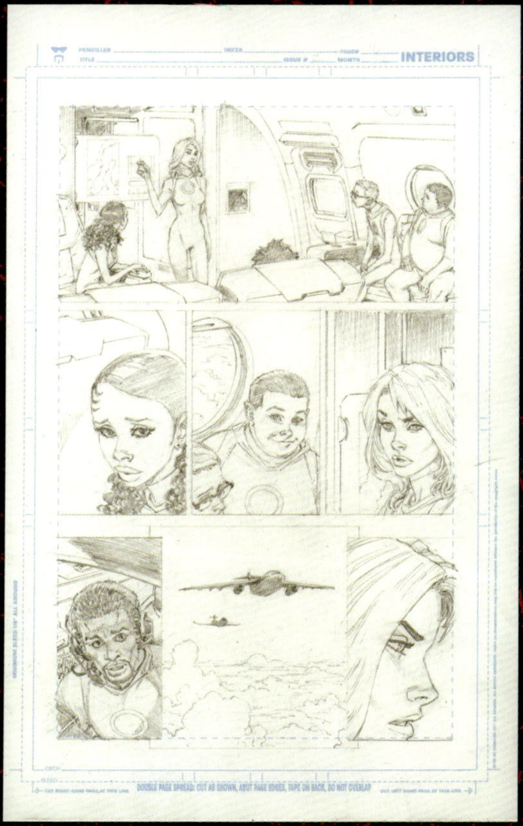

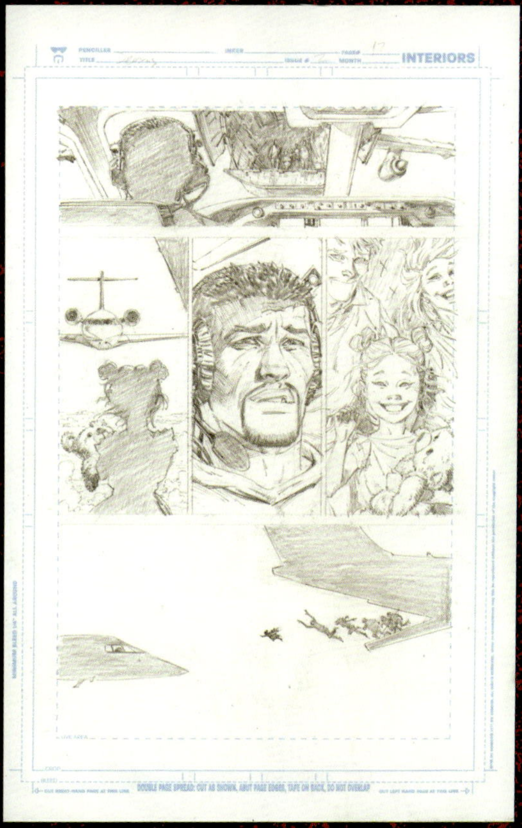

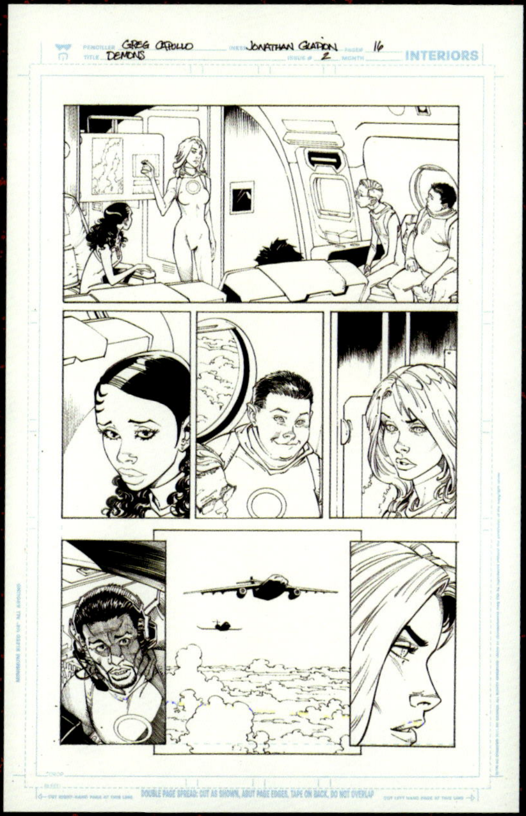

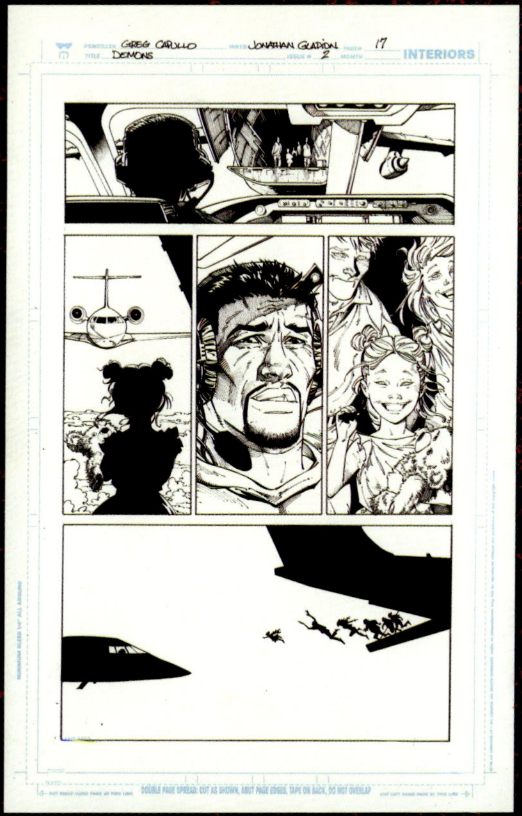

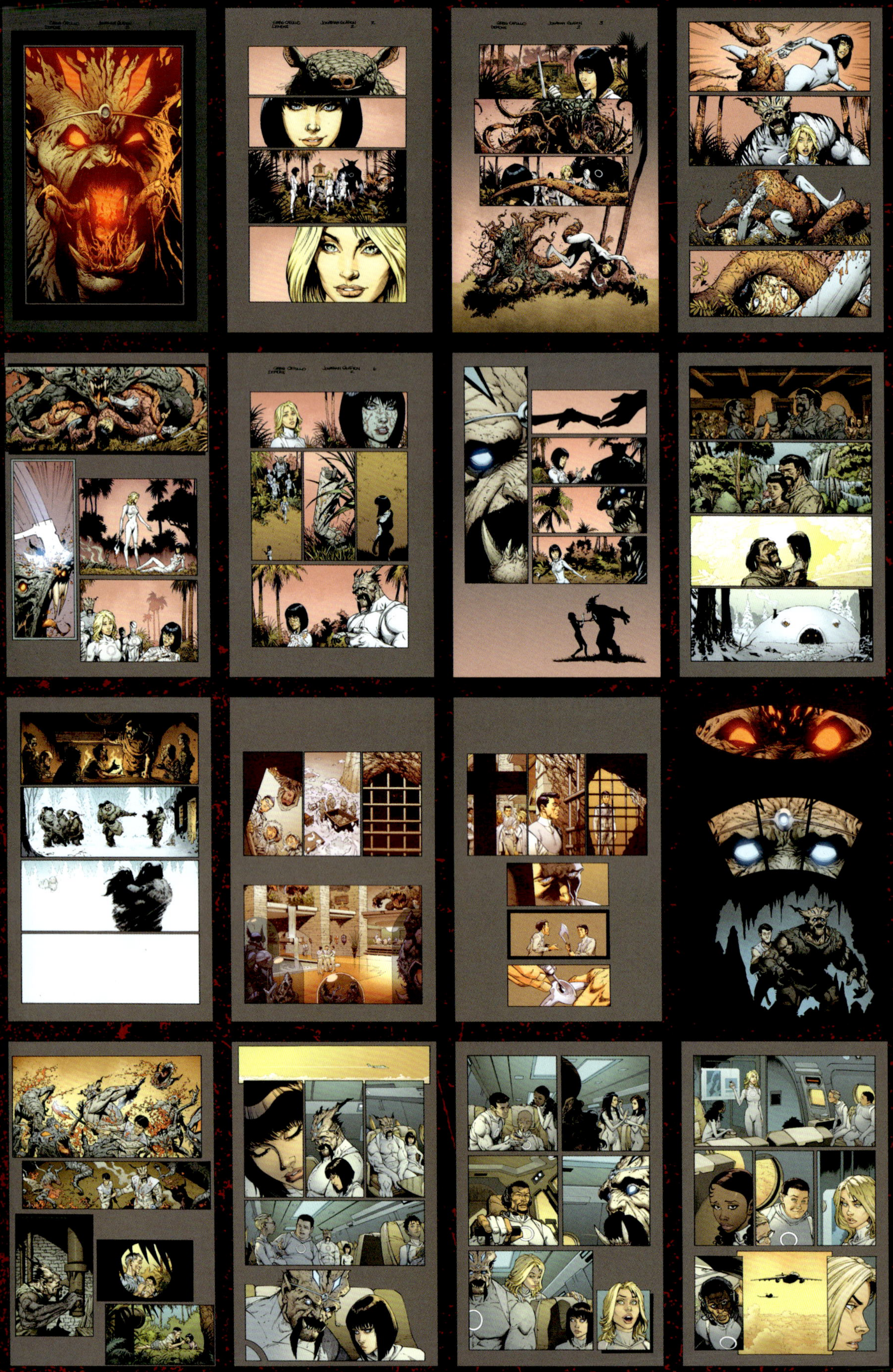

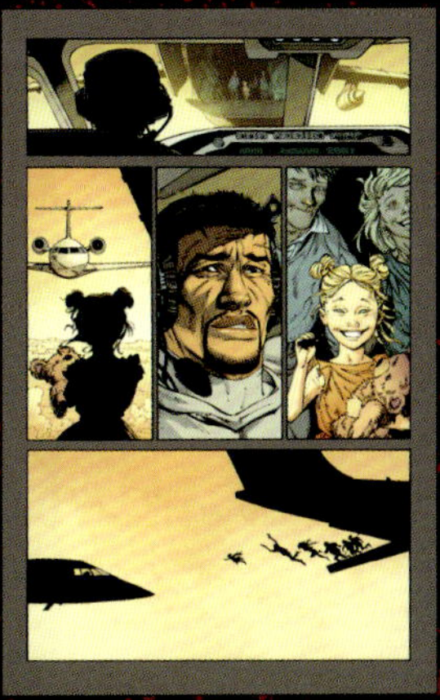
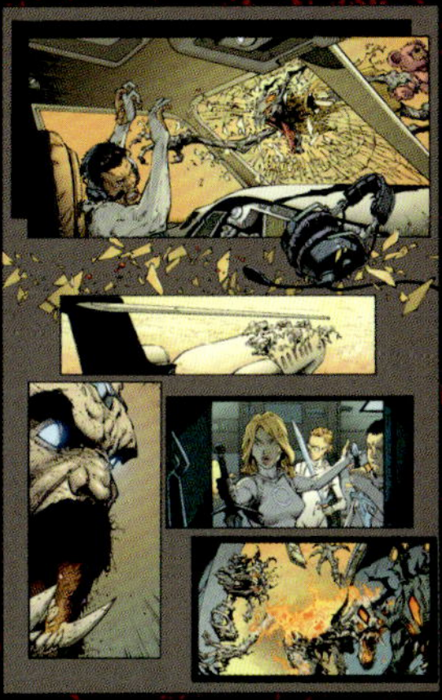
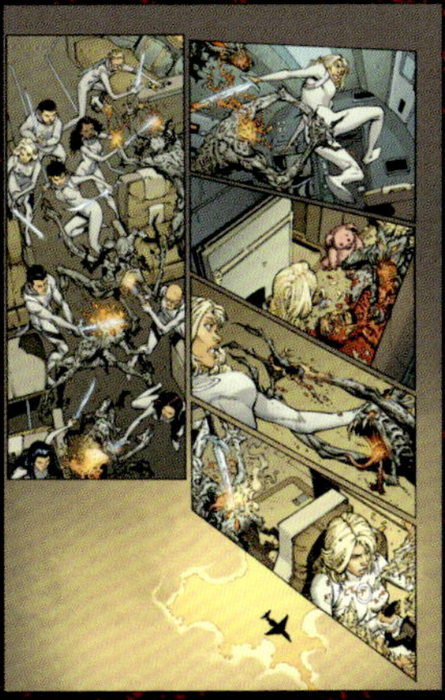
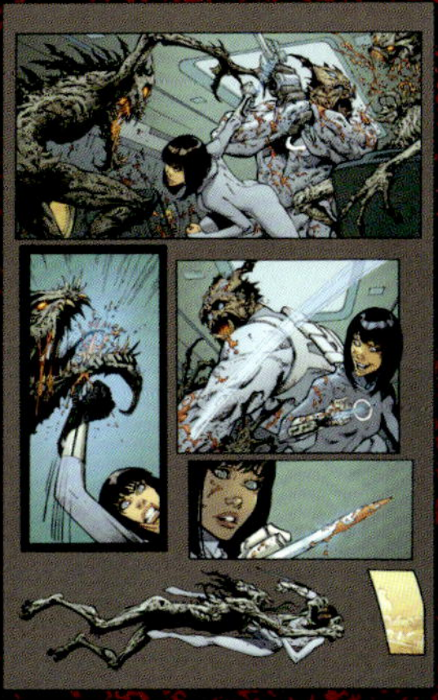
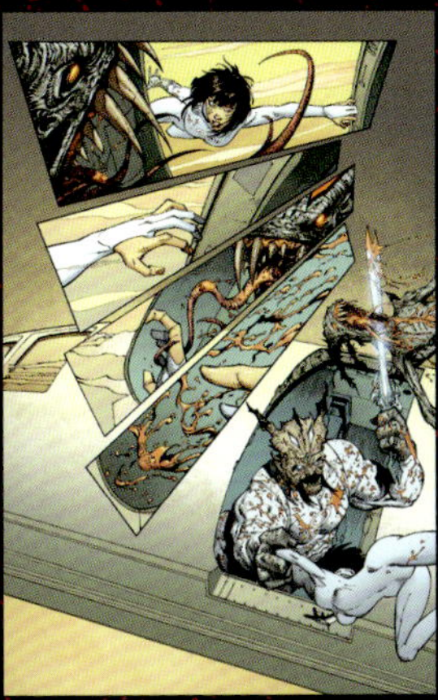
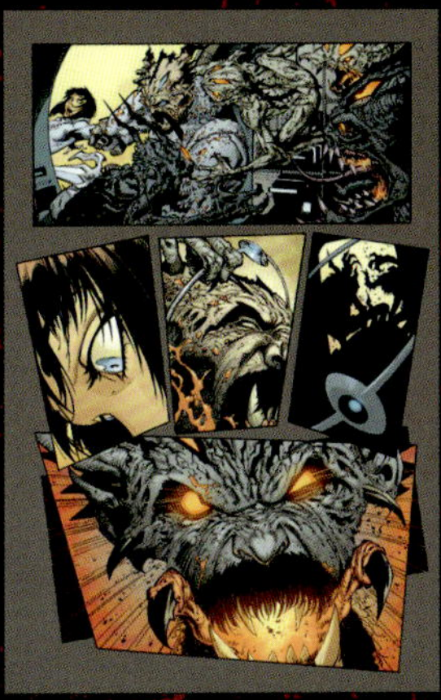
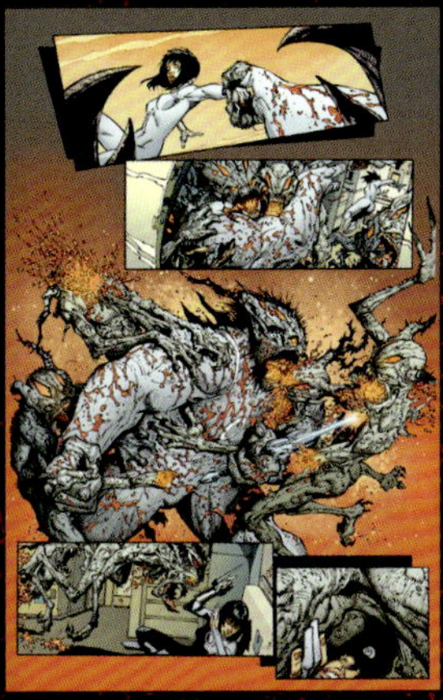
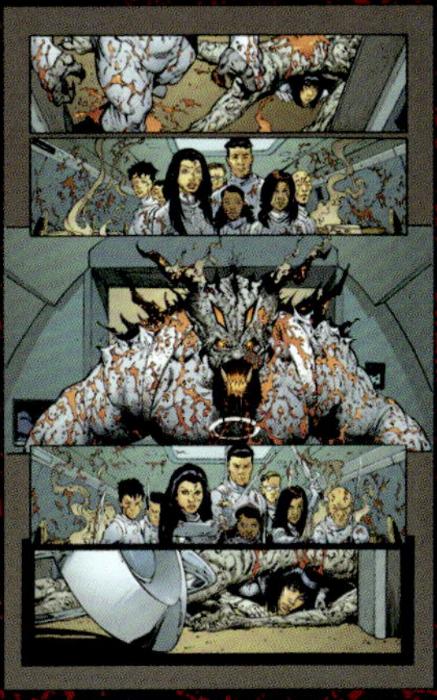
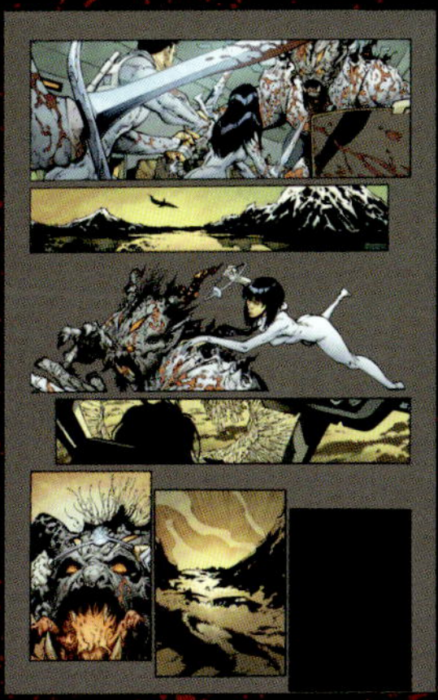
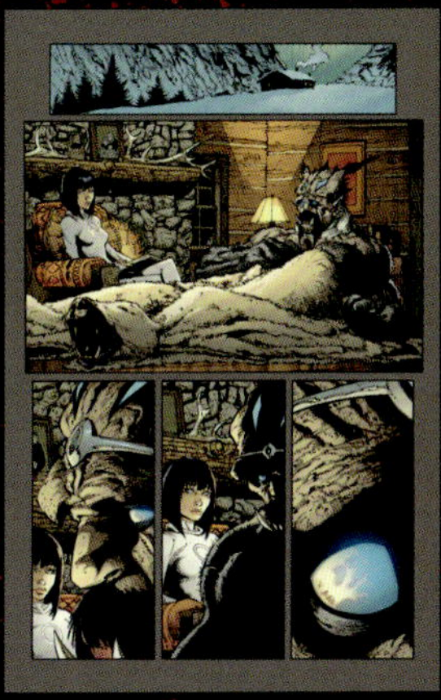
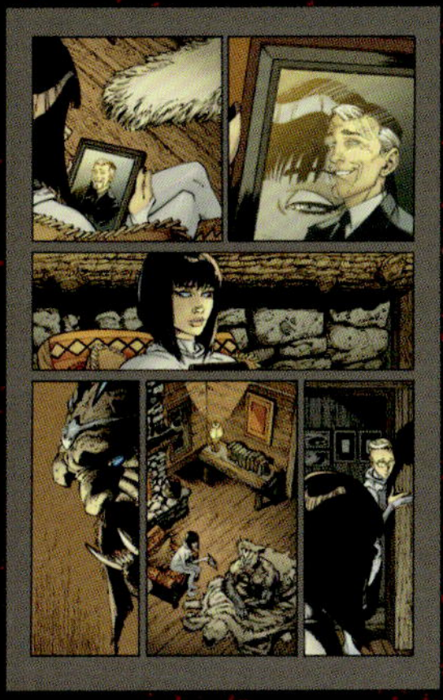
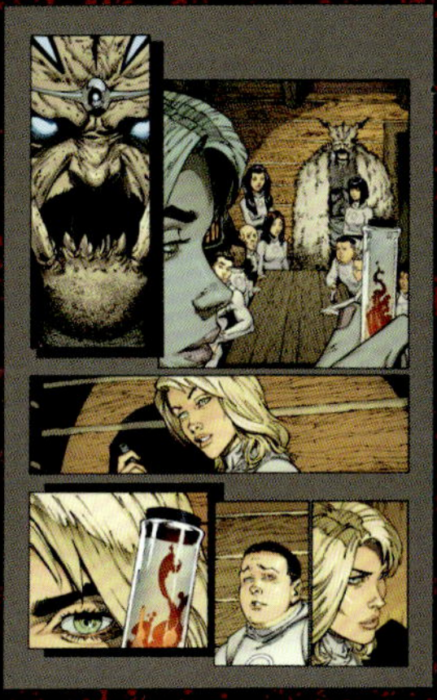
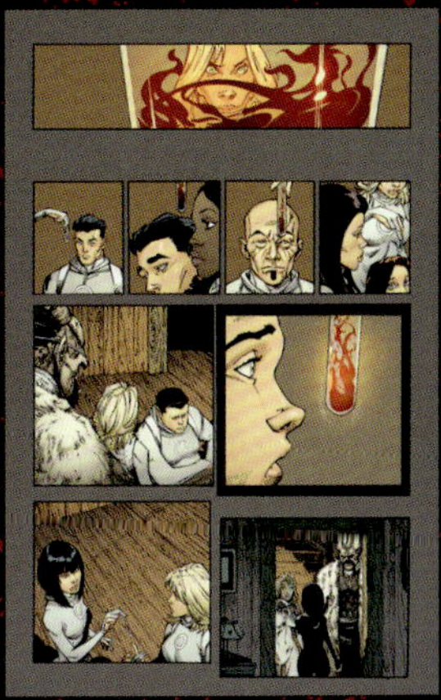
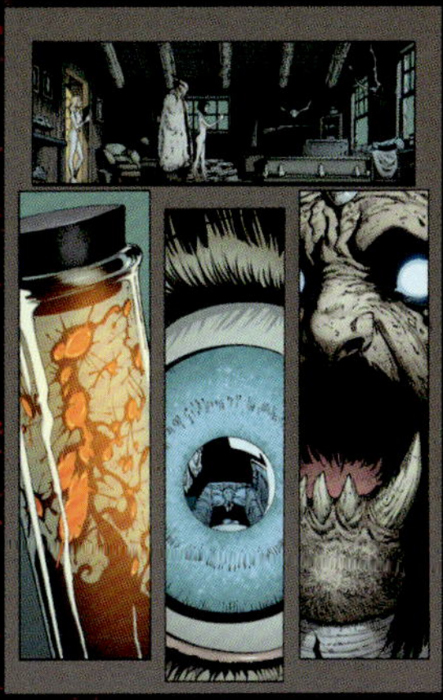
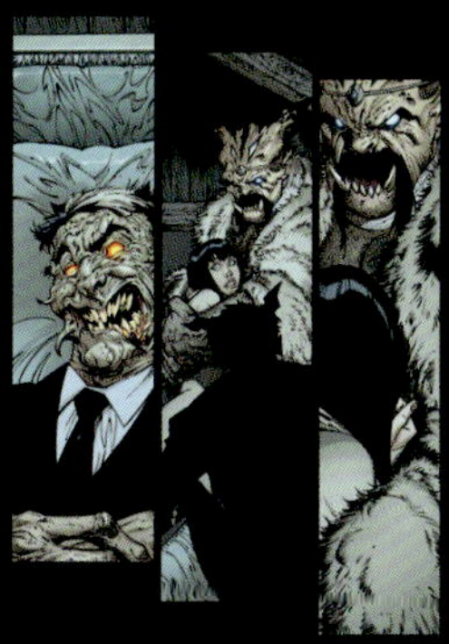
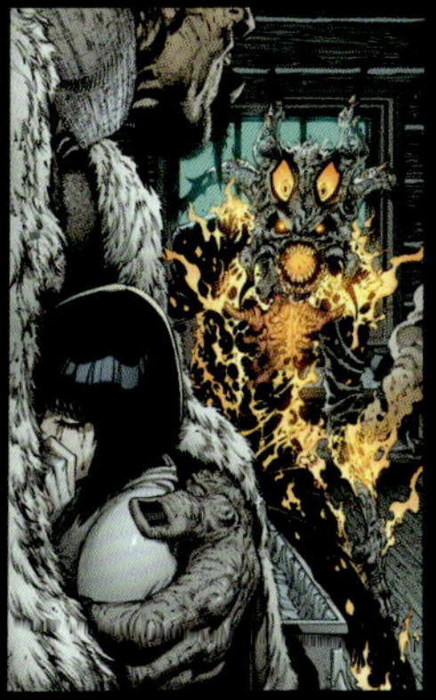

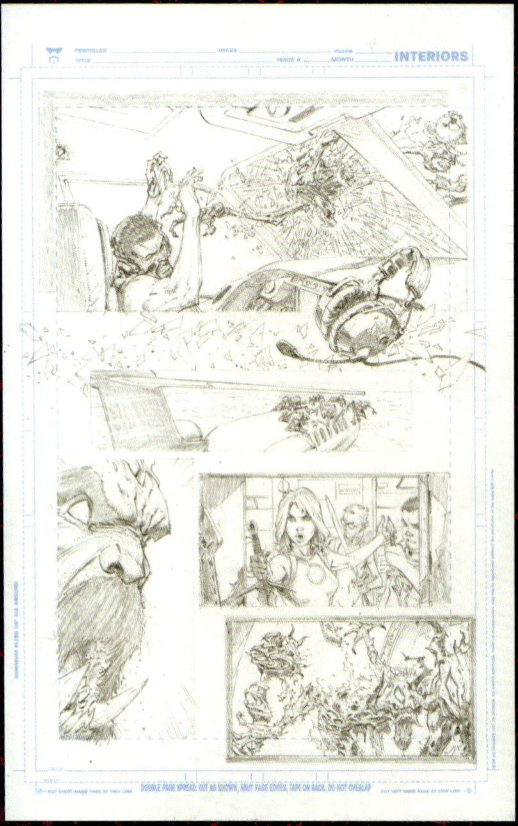

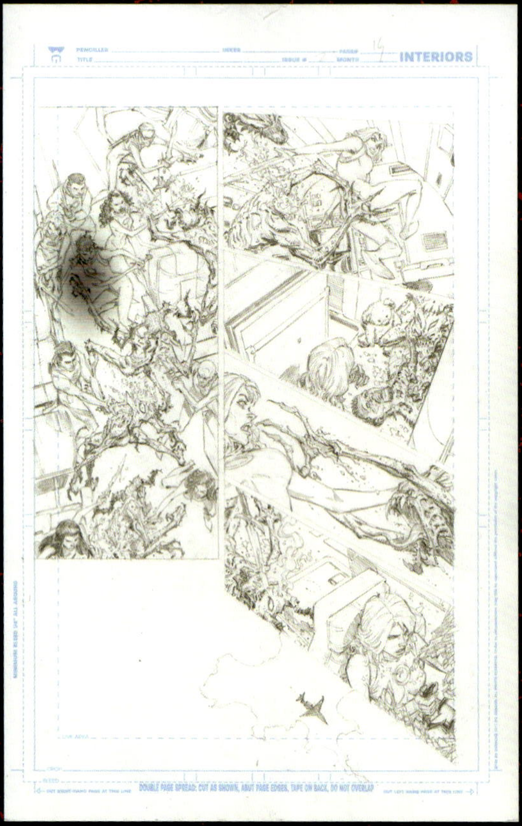

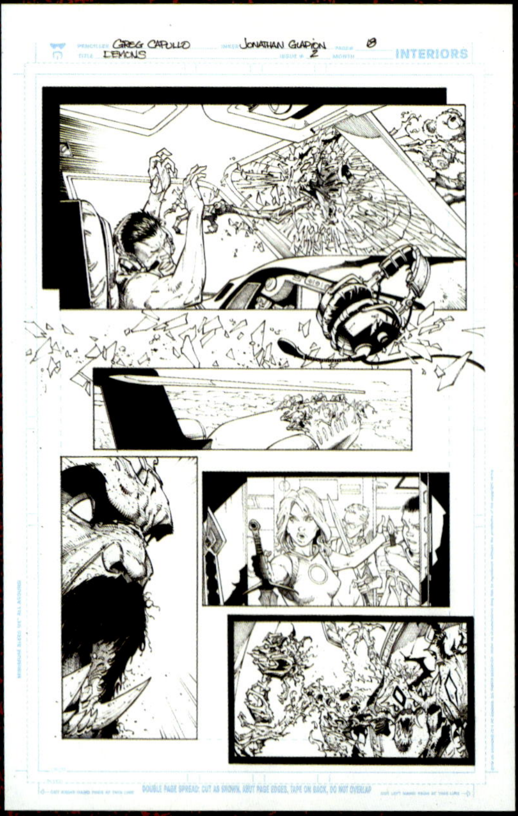

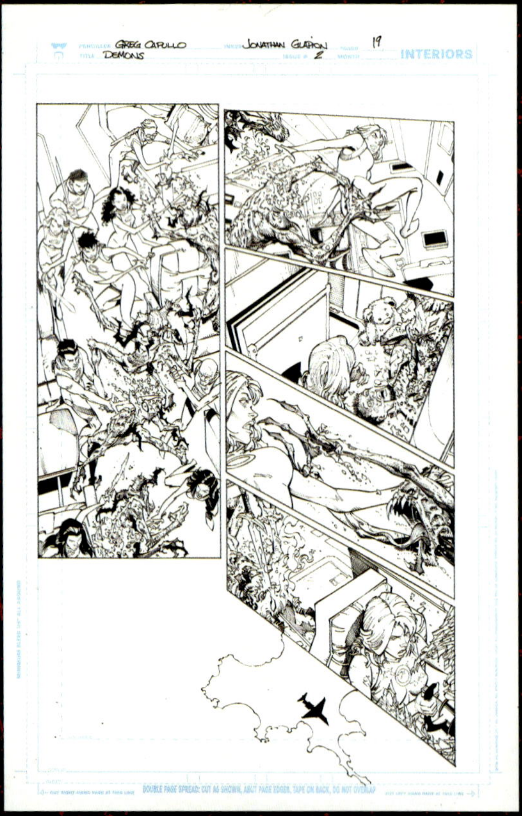

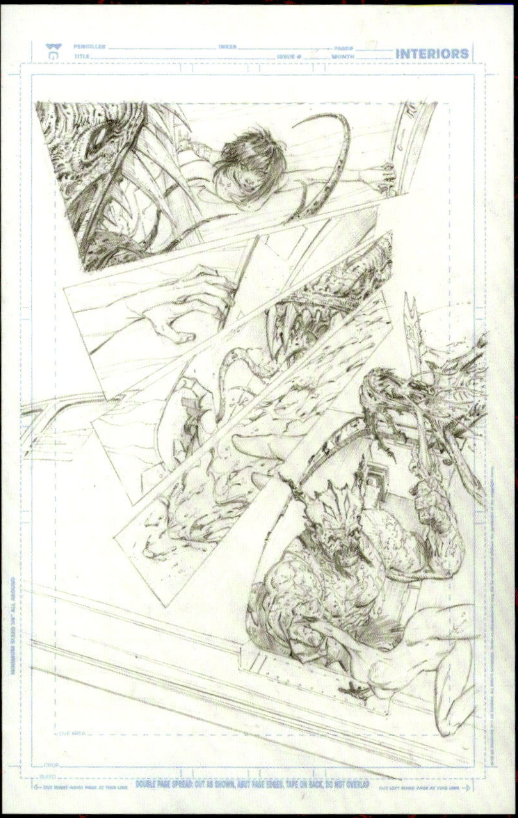

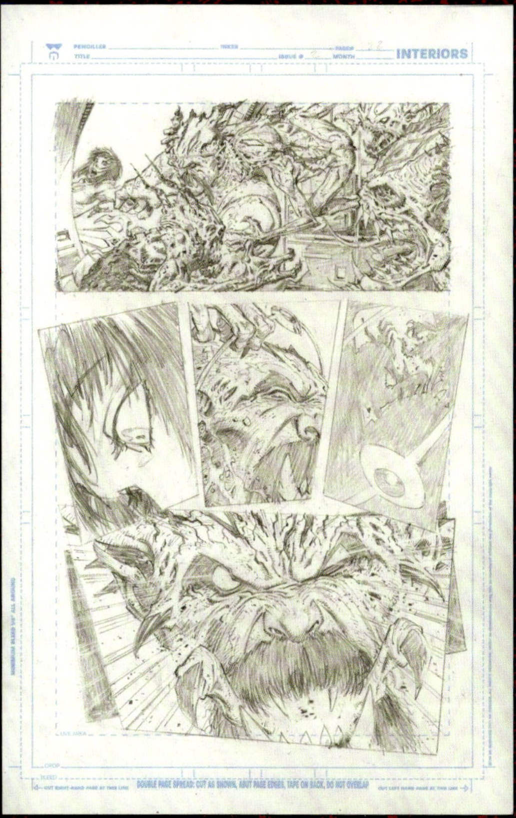

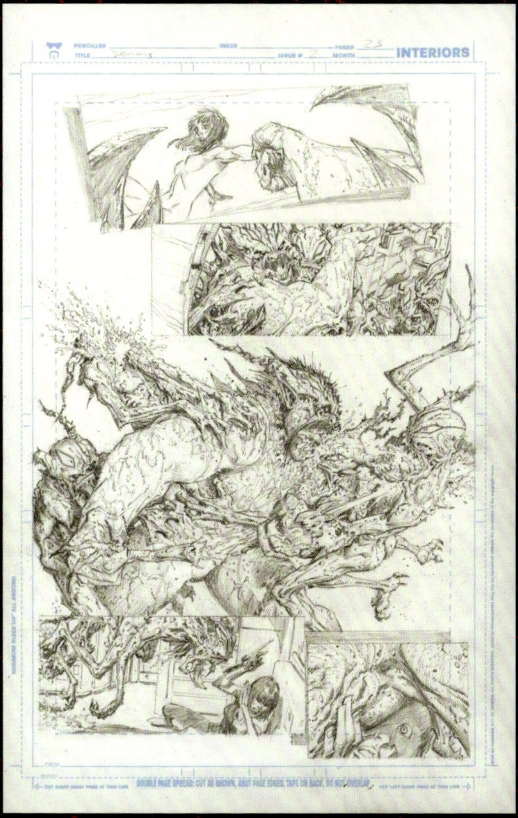

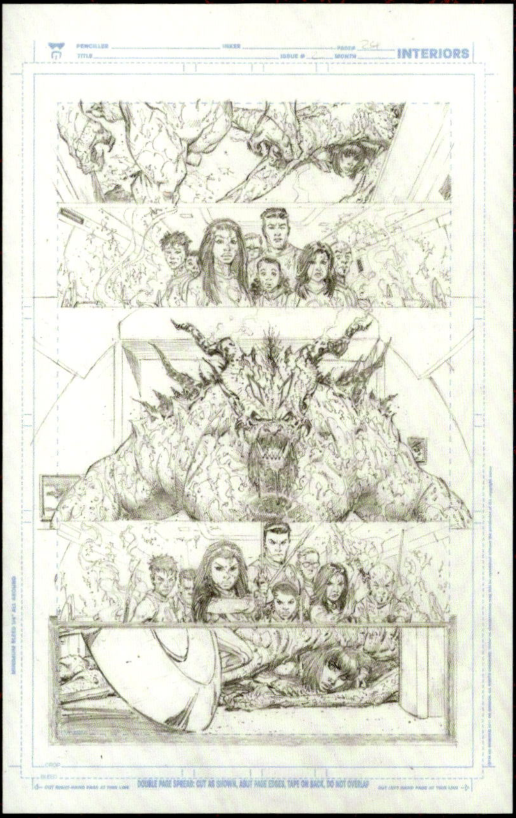

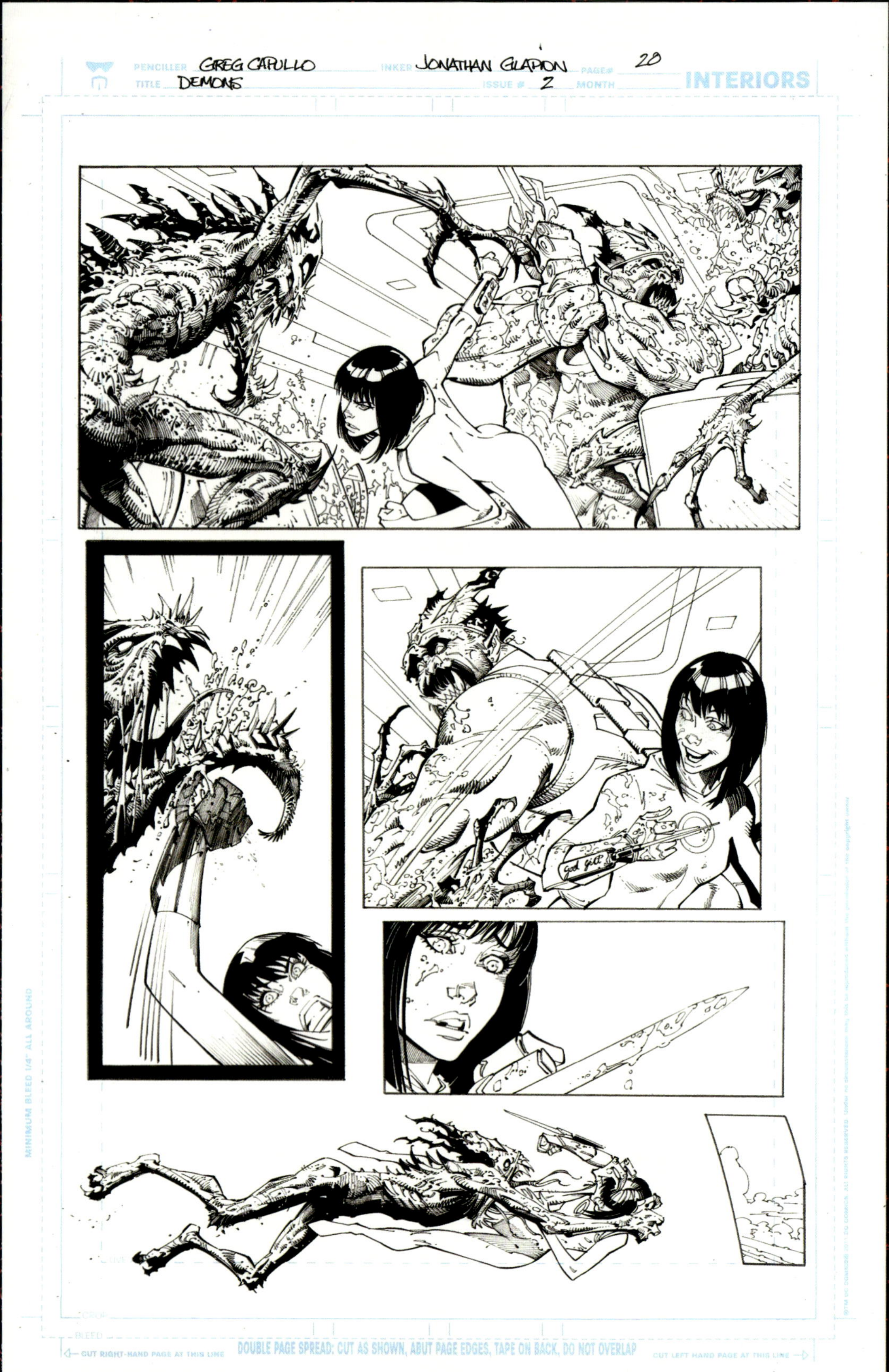

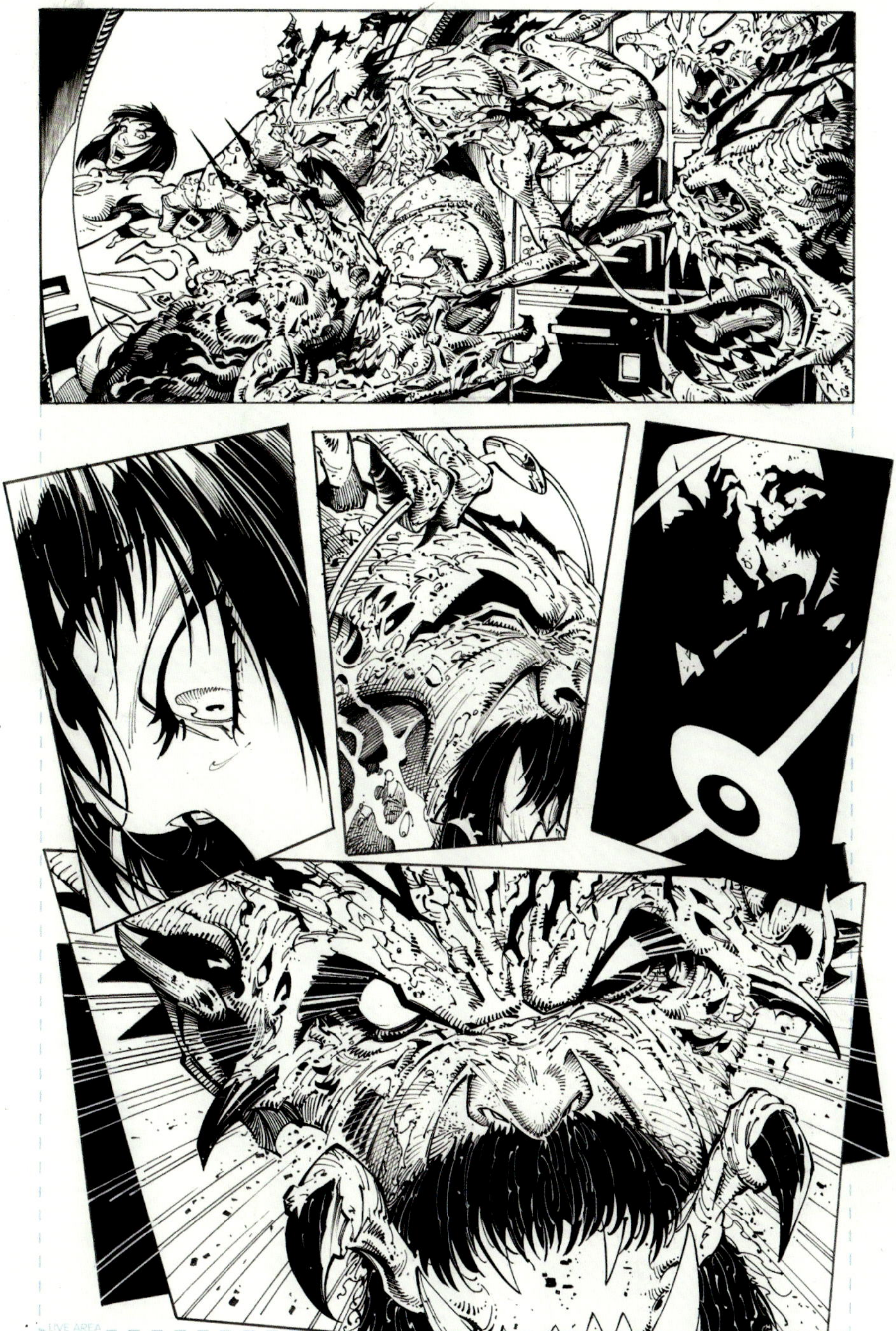

INTERIORS

INTERIORS

GREG CAPULLO
DEMONS
JONATHAN GLAPION
2
25
INTERIORS

GREG CAPULLO
DEMONS
JONATHAN GLAPION
2
27
INTERIORS

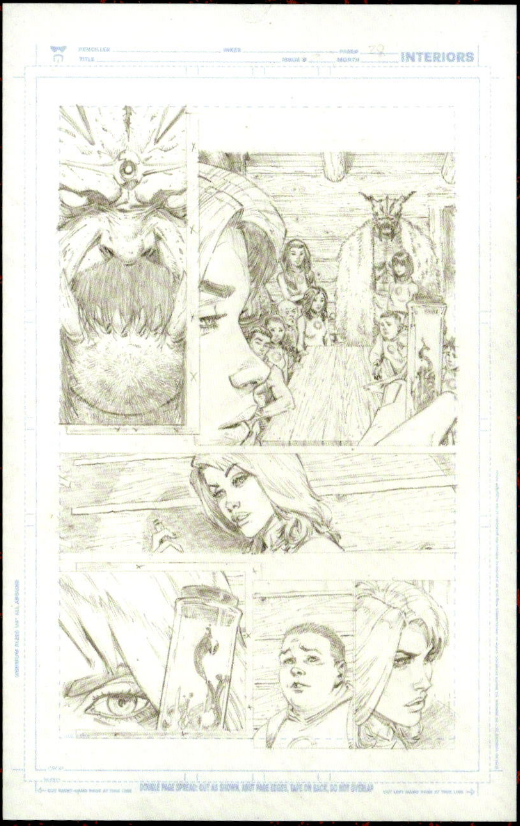

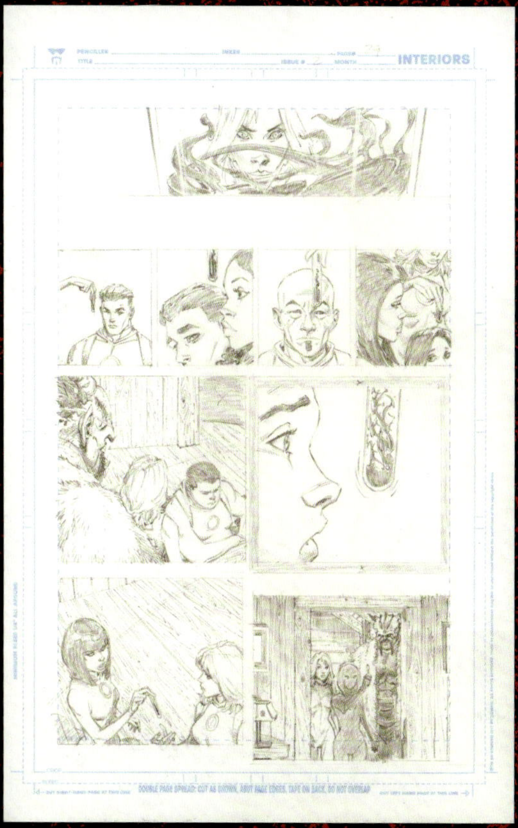

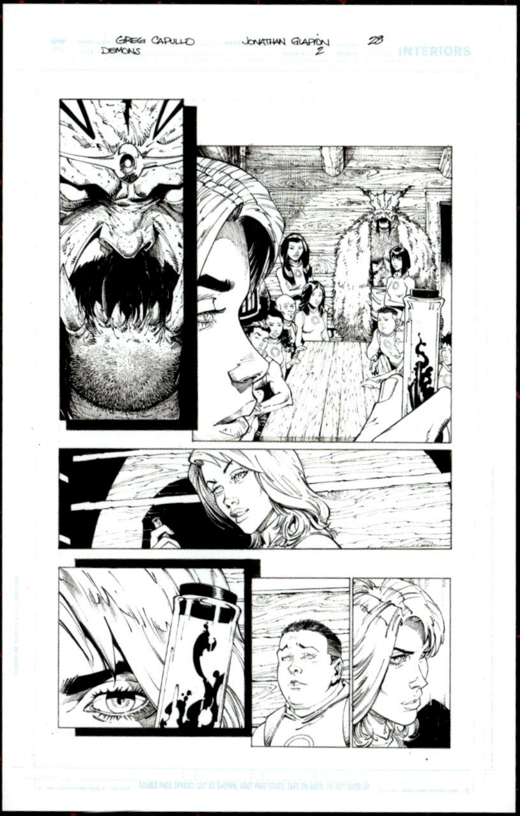

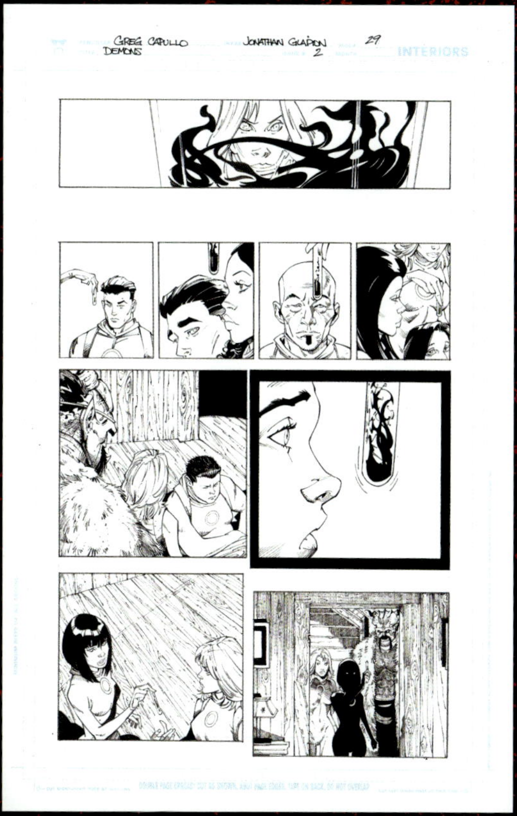

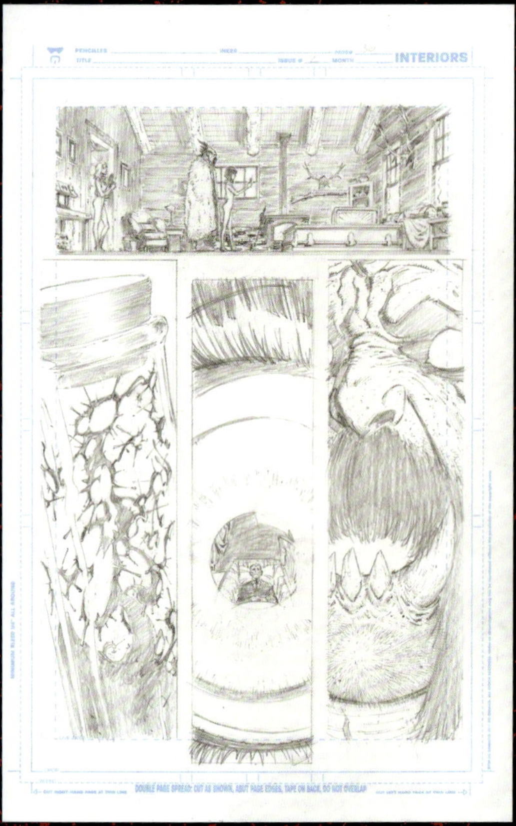

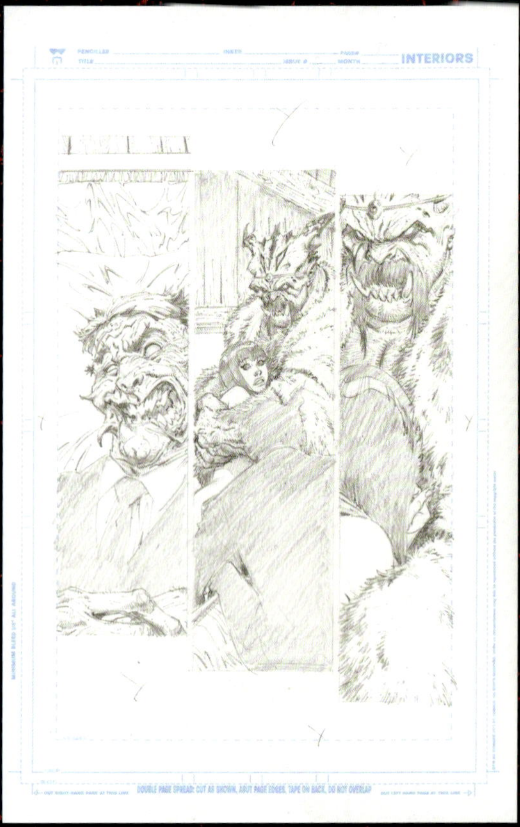

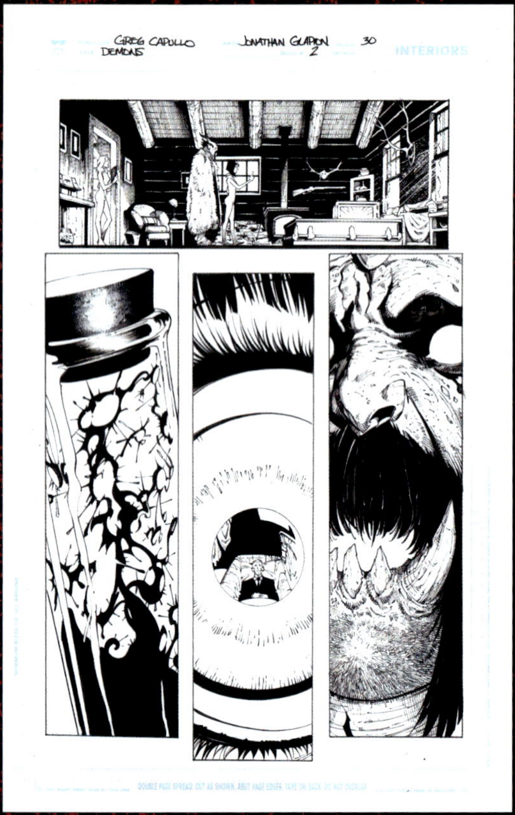

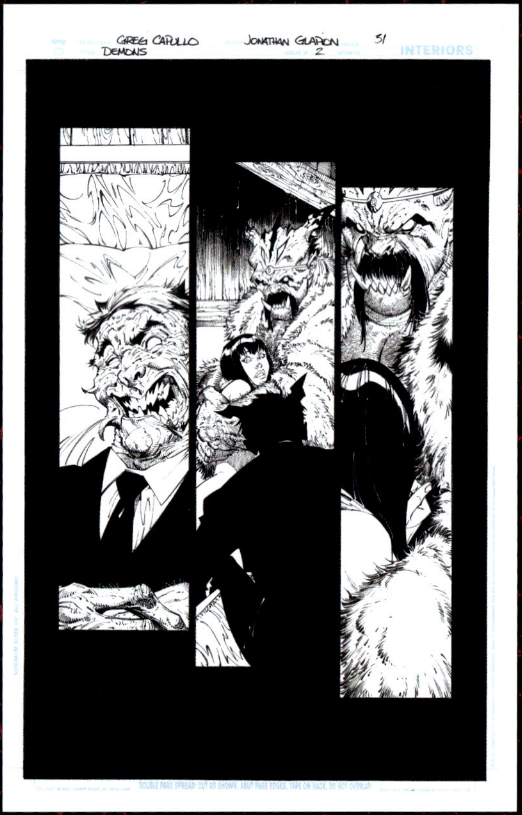

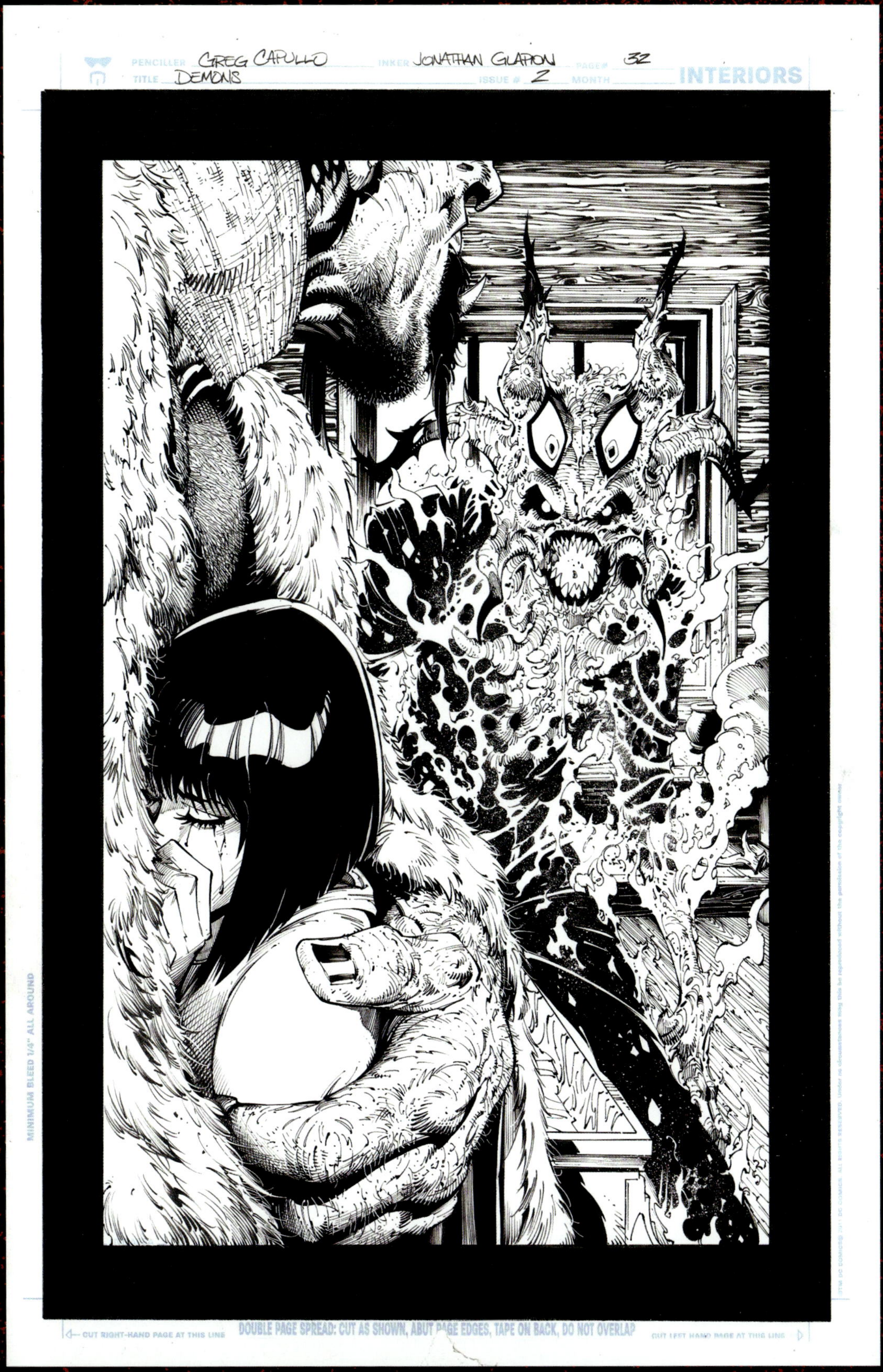

WE HAVE DEMONS

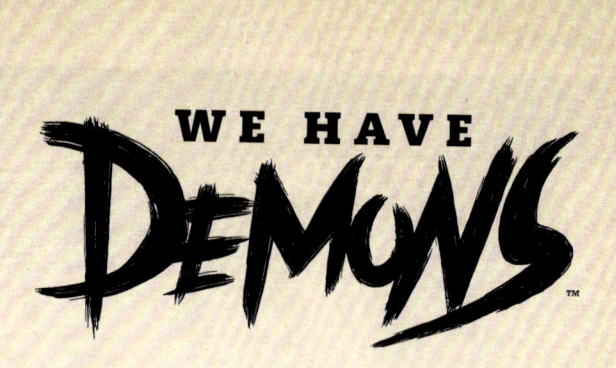

ISSUE 3 Script
By Scott Snyder
For Greg Capullo
Jon Glapion
Dave McCaig
Tom Napolitano
and Will Dennis

BLACK TITLE PAGE

Chapter 7: "Burn It All Down"

PAGES 1-5

Again, take the pagination as pacing for me, nothing more! If you want to do 1 as a splash, or make any other changes, always do it – things are always better for your artistic choices!

All right, for issue 1, LAM narrated about the fall of man from the POV of Godfolk ("This is a story about the fall of man. So where to start? Maybe with Godfolk. My Father says that . . . "). For issue 2, GUS narrated from the POV of demonfolk. Here, we'll narrate about the fall of man from BOTH their POV'S about it all. I think it'll be a fun way to start to really cement them as a team.

1

- We pick up right where we left off, the face-off between CASH/DEMON (Lam's dad) and the ANGELS. The horror of the situation apparent to the team, Gus and Lam especially.

    I might have a couple quick lines of narration from LAM and GUS here that repeat the opening lines of the last couple issues, like,

    LAM CAP: This is a story about the fall of man. So where to start?

    GUS: Maybe right here, Lam? At the end itself.

    CASH (Tom, let's give him a super creepy font): Hello, friendsssss . . . Welcome to my home!

- Lam steps out front, angry, sad, defiant. Behind her, Gus is like, no, don't! June, too.

    She's like, Dad?! No it can't be you!

    Gus is like, Lam . . .

    June says, get back!

- But Lam is like trying to reach him.

    Lam is like, Dad, please . . . look at me! It's me, it's . . . Lam.

- Cash looking evil as can be, straight at her, too.

    Cash is like, I know it's you, Armadillo (his nickname for her as revealed in issue 2). And I'm so glad to sssseee you!

    Cash: I'm proud of you . . . for failing just as I KNEW you would!

2-3

- Large – Cash LASHES out with sharp TENTACLE extensions from his mouth – maybe they have little mouths on them or each one has a little sharp tooth, really whatever gross ass body-horror off-shoot you want to do, go for it!

- Gus KNOCKS Lam out of the way . . .
- . . . and gets SPEARED by CASH'S tentacles.
- The force slams him through the door frame and out of the room.
- The angels go to rush into the room, blades drawn, but . . .
- BOOM. Cash slams the door and holds it closed with a massive claw.
- He's alone with Lam, looming over her. Just the two of them. If you want to make this really creepy, Greg, I think he could start to have Cash's face again, even with the rest of him demoned-out, like a deformed version of Lam's dad, but recognizable, even sweet looking at times to hurt her worse.

    He says, look at you . . . finally you know everything. About me, and about yourself.

- Lam lashes out, slashing him as she lunges with her arm-blade! Angry!

    She's like, you're not my father! You're not him!

- He smiles, the father's face grinning, twisted.

    He's like, I'm your real father, not the mask, the one who lied to you, about who he was, about who YOU were. See, I always knew you'd be the end of the angels, the downfall of it all! From childhood, I knew. You were weak, you had no faith, in me, in yourself, in anything. So I gave up. I let the demon virus infect me, because of you, Lam. Now come, join me. We can kill the rest of them and I'll show you the true God of all things! Join me, Armadillo.

- She lunges at him again, furious. But her blade is NOT glowing . . .

    RAHH!!!!!!

4-5

- And he knocks her back . . .
- Into his coffin.
- He stands over her, grinning.

    He says, I'm just glad your mother never lived to see this. She'd be so . . . ashamed.

- Lam, crying, angry, gives him the finger.

    She's like, fuck you, you're not my father.

- And sticks the blade into him.
- Smiling, he goes to kill her SHRIEK! - bite her face off, anything, when suddenly . . .
- He stops . . . like he's stunned by something . . .
- And he starts to dissolve. Did Lam's blade work?! Did it light up? Did she find some kind of faith?!

PAGE 6

- No, because as Cash falls, disintegrating, we see Gus' sword in his side/back.
- And as he really dissolves, falling, he accidentally knocks the LID closed on the coffin.
- Crouched in the window we see Gus — he threw his sword at Cash. He's crushed, but angry, too.

    Gus is like, Lam, are you hurt?

- He has entered the room, and is standing by the closed coffin, asking again.

    Gus: Lam? Lam are you okay?

- Inside the closed coffin, she's crying.

PAGES 7-11

We're with the angels as they deliberate what to do. They are outside on the porch, the landscape behind them. They have their swords . . . all dramatic . . . Everyone looks upset (obviously) but Lam looks crushed. She's lost in thought, angry, looking at her father's research. Graphs and astronomy charts, trajectories, spread on the old wooden table outside. She could be using the blade of her arm to hold the papers in place. Gus is concerned about her.

7

- Kellan (the heavy Irish guy) is arguing with the two girls (Hedra and Tee) who were practicing fighting technique on the plane. Behind Kellan are Ketch (the nerdy guy) and Effie (the punk girl).

    Kellan is like, we have no choice!

    Tee is like, we do have a choice. We need to make it as a team.

- Kellan angry, with Effie and Ketch backing him up.

    Kellan is like, Cash was turned. We need to go, leave, exit. NOW.

    Effie is like, I hate to admit it, but he's right.

    Ketch says this whole thing is a trap. We already lost Jonesy (the pilot from last issue).

- The older man (Aki) is sympathetic, with the jock (Tucker) beside him — he's talking to June.

    Aki is like, when did Cash first tell you about the Seraphim Stone's impact? When did he say, this was the time it would hit?

    Tucker is like, yeah, when?

- June, clearly deeply broken by this (or is she?). We're trying to make folks really think she's good here.

    June . . .

    Aki (OP): June?

    June: two months ago.

8-9

- Kellan again, being like, see? See?

    Kellan says, There you go. Two months. He got infected by his neighbors, lied to us, told us that the Seraphim Stone was coming to get us all here . . .

    Ketch is like, if it was me, I'd have a horde of demons there, waiting. I mean a horde.

    Effie is like, we need to go.

- Gus, sensitive but stern. Lam still studying the papers.

    Gus: We don't know that he was infected when he mapped the stone's trajectory. It could still be coming.

- Kellan and co.

    Kellan says, a fragment of Seraphim Stone hasn't hit the earth in five thousand years. But Cash discovers one is coming here right around the time his neighbors are revealed to be demons? I'm sorry, but come on. Tee, you had Jonesy's contact. We need to leave. We all loved Cash, but--

- June, angry.

    June is like, yes, we did. We all loved him and maybe we just slow down a moment. Jesus. How about we just . . . this can't be happening.

- Aki, with Tee and Hedra, caring.

    Aki says, the vial, June. Do you have it?

    Tee says, Aki's right. If we have demons down at the clearing, the demon shard in the vial will reach for them.

- June looks at Gus and Lam.
- June pulls out the vial.
- The gunk inside . . .
- Goes crazy straining over the hill toward the valley.
- June looking away. Shit.

10-11

- Aki and Tee and Hedra, all sad but sure of what needs to happen. Tee is looking at her phone.

    Aki is like, we have to leave.

    Tee is like, the boat will be here in an hour.

- Kellan and co, sympathetic, now that the decision has been made.

    Kellan says, the rule is we burn it down.

    Ketch is like, it is. But—

- Here Lam SLAMS her blade down into the table.

    Lam: No one is burning anything.

- Lam, a fire in her eyes.

    She says, the path my father charted for the Stone. He named it after my mother. Look.

- We see the chart, an astronomical path hitting the earth in this spot. And handwritten is the name Isla.

    Lam says, he wouldn't have done that if he was a demon when he charted it. I know it.

- Kellan, Ketch, Effie, really almost all the angels — like they're all on one side, Lam and Gus on the other.

    Kellan is like, Lam, a demon does and says ANYTHING to trick you, to get you to fall for its game. Cash WOULD HAVE named it—

    Lam is like, NO. He wouldn't have. And I have faith in him.

    Ketch is like, your blade hasn't lit up.

- Lam, still angry.

    She says, someone tainted my blade. I know it. Bob and Layla. My blade might not work, but I believe. I do. And I'm staying.

- Gus stands by her.

    He says, I am too.

- The angels, looking at them, impressed but knowing that they need to go.

- Lam and Gus a team.

    Lam says, go on. But I have faith.

BLACK PAGE

TITLE: Chapter 8: "The Clearing"

PAGES 12-13

- The clearing is like one of those tall-grass ancient fields at the bottom of a bowl of rocky slopes – the kind of haunted, windy place where battles took place a thousand years ago. There's a kind of strange STONEHENGE feature in the center, but more spread out. Like broken, ancient stone structures in a ring. The center of the ring is clear.

- Gus and Lam, hiding at the clearing's edge behind some rocks. From where they are they can see the coast.

    They'll be talking to each other over this. Gus and Lam. They'll say, if there are demons, they're hiding down in that clearing.

- Gus checks the vial with the goop and it is going super crazy – uh oh. Ancient, powerful demons.

- Lam talks into a small walkie.

    She tells June that they're going to check it out. And if anything attacks them, she can flank them.

- We see June, hiding at the other side of the field, behind gnarled trees or whatever you want to draw! She's on her walkie.

    June says, I got it.

    Lam says, you could have gone with them you know.

    June says, I know . . .

- In the distance, on the water, the BOAT ostensibly carrying the angels away.

    June says over this: "but we're family. And if this is the path, we take it together."

PAGES 14-17

14-15

- Back to the clearing: They see figures moving behind the stones. Demons . . . Shit. Time to fight.

- Lam is like, okay, Gus, give me the halo. If I wrap it around my arm, it'll strengthen my blade so that even tainted, it should glow. Gus can't bring himself to do it. He says, there has to be another way.

- She's like, come on, I believe in you. Just like my father did. You have enough seraphim in you and beyond that, you're a creature of faith. You can--

- He yells at her, she doesn't know him at all!!!

- A beat, where she refuses to give in, and he caves, sighs.

- Gus, close on him. Emotional. He tells her the story of her arm. How it wasn't a snakebite. It was him. Her father, Cash, thought Gus would have enough seraphim in him to take the halo off. So he took it off, and what happened? Gus bit Lam's arm off. So no, he says, he won't be giving her the halo.

- A light falls on his face . . . a beautiful glow. What?

    Yes, Lam says from off panel. You will give it to me.

- Because we see her blade is glowing so bright. Because she has faith in him.

16-17

- But the blade flickers.
- She takes his hand.
    > She's like, we can do this, together. My father didn't trick us. It was Bob and Layla. The stone will land. We CAN win.
- Scared, but determined, Gus takes off his halo.
- She wraps it around her arm.
- Gus grips his sword . . .
- And they step out. Looking badass.
- Lam says, show yourself, demons!
- Come fight!!!
- Figures step out from behind the stones, the shadows . . .
- Lam is like, oh no.
- Gus is shocked . . .

PAGES 18-19

- And he should be – it is a HUGE shocker: Big image of GUS' TRIBE! Here. Thawed out. Ten or twelve of them, including his wife and daughter.

- Focus on his wife and daughter, evil, grinning. They taunt him. Painful.

- Gus, his blade stops glowing. He's like, no . . . no . . . It WAS Cash. The only person who could have done this was . . . Cash. We were wrong. My God . . .

- Lam is like, it doesn't make sense . . .

- And then she realizes. She says the name. June.

PAGES 20-21

- June is walking out. Revealed. Evil.
- Lam is like, it was you, all along.
- And June is like, oh yes.
- She grins evilly as she explains how she did it. How long she'd been working her way inside, waiting, learning it all. Right now the angels are on a boat rigged to explode. Your father is dead. And the stone, when it comes, will be ours to destroy forever. **[I'm toying with the idea of having her admit SHE'S the one who killed Lam's mother in the hit and run, but I'm not 100% on it yet — dark though, right? ☺]**
- Lam, furious, like, I'm going to kill you so hard.
- June turns into the queen demon! Huge, gross as can be — she's an ancient one, old as the tribe. Her face is still recognizable but all monstrous . . .
- And the tribe turns into terrifying demons. Our heroes are fucked.
- Lam and Gus, together . . . Lam is like, we can do this. We can. And Gus says, we can. We can!!!

PAGES 22-23

- Fight! Lam fighting June, Gus fighting his tribe. Greg, you're a master of this stuff so I feel like choreographing it is silly when you just do it far better than me, but the fight is all blood and guts, gross and horrible, with Lam fighting June and Gus fighting his tribe. B/c they're all ancient, a single stroke from a lit blade won't kill them — it takes a kill blow in earnest. So arms can be chopped off, faces, teeth, they need to be stabbed real bad, cool?

- June, her face twisted, gleeful, Joker-ish but demon. She's taunting Lam . . .

- Lam fights back, badass, chopping.

- Meanwhile, Gus chops down members of his tribe . . .

- But then toward the end of the sequence, his daughter slashes his back!

- He falls, cut in more ways than one. Lam is like, NO!!!

- The tribe is moving in on Gus . . .

- . . . June gloats. This is it. It's over.

PAGES 24-29

- But it's not! Because SURPRISE! The Angels are here! BLADES GLOWING! They didn't get on that boat after all.
- Lam smiles. Now it's a fight!!!
- And it is a fight, all slashing and blood and gore! Aki can die if you want (he's old) . . . Maybe someone gets a leg bitten off.
- But it's a brawl! Lam stays on June, doing all kinds of cool moves. Ducking a slash . . .
- Cutting off a leg.
- Then another.
- At some point, Gus stabs his wife, being like, you are not her!!! Angry more than sad.
- As his wife dissolves, his daughter jumps on him, all demoned out, scary, twisted, biting.
- He knocks her back.
- She's like, Daddy, Daddy it's me.
- He's sad, knowing it's not.
- As he looks down . . .
- She grins and leaps, monstrous.
- And he chops her down.
- She dissolves as she falls . . .
- The angels have taken out most of the demons, and now they're finishing them off.
- Lam has cut June down so that she's all charred and scarred, a hulking monster like an elephant thing with no legs, little faces and claws and such trying to shoot out of her body to get Lam but she's too weak.
- Lam stands over her with Gus.
- June, dying, still mostly monster, but recognizable as her, like the guy mid change in American Werewolf in London or the fly before his human shell falls off. She smiles, leaking blood and goo, smoking, dying. But she still grins.

    She's like, you have no idea what you're up against. You think you can win? You're a fool. You're a—

PAGES 30-31

- Huge- BOOM. The SERAPHIM STONE CRUSHES HER! It's big, like the size of a truck. This should be like a Bambi vs Godzilla moment. If it was a movie, it'd be a shocker!

- The stone is responsible for myths of seraphim angels, the angels that are like blobs with lots of wings and eyes, so let's evoke that here, but divine and beautiful in the way the stone glows and steams and glints. It can look like a seraphim b/c of how it's shaped, how it reflects and bends light . . . it's holy.

- The angels stare at it in the near blinding glow. Shocked. Lam can be like . . . the Seraphim Stone?

- Kellan and them are like, it's . . . real. Cash was right.

- Lam smiles at Gus.

- And goes to give him back his halo . . .

- But he pushes it back.

- Smiles.

- And we pull back . . .

CODA!

BLACK PAGE

Chapter 9: HALO

- Over this, I'm going to return to the JOINT NARRATION, which I won't have used since PAGE 1, do a couple lines like:

    LAM CAP: I DID warn you.

    GUS CAP: She did.

    LAM CAP: I mean I even said HARK. Because this was, is, and always will be a story about the fall of man.

    GUS CAP: The big F.O.M.

    LAM CAP: So the thing is, there can't be a happy ending. Not really.

    GUS CAP: Nope. No way.

    LAM CAP: So how to end it then, Gus?

    GUS CAP: How about right back where it started, kid . . .

PAGE 32

The idea here, Greg, is to just do a quick tour of the place, showing how much more awesome things are now that they have the HALO to make blades. They have more members, more money, more everything. We're seeing this from the POV of a new recruit, coming to meet Lam and Gus but we won't really realize that until the last page. The first couple pages will just be a tour of the place with CUES and HINTS about how much more awesome the glories are now.

- A panel mirroring the opening. We're back at the house and the church, but it all looks nice, spruced up a bit. We see our own shadow, like we're a visitor.

    They both say: "In Florida . . . "

- We're inside the church, all nicely set up, a picture of CASH there. The SNAKE is there, too.

    LOC CAP: One year later.

- The SECRET DOOR opens – <u>feel free to show the snake being tipped if you want but I figure it can be implied? Whatever works best IYO.</u> And we see the ELEVATOR. It says HELL but now it could say + LAM with a middle finger painted on or whatever you think is cool, Greg!

    Lam will say in NARRATION: yeah, this feels right.

    GUS agrees. Full circle.

- Our hand (in ANGEL/GLORIES GEAR and colored in shadow maybe so we can't discern sex or skin color so it could be any reader) pushing the button.

    Lam will say, Because that's the thing, isn't it? It's all circles. This IS a story about the fall of man. Every day more and more Horn hits the earth. It's all speeding up, because we draw it here. It's IN us, and we want more. Of course we do. You feel it, I know you do! We all have demons.

    Gus will say, But we all have Halo in us too. Not as much as Horn, nope, but it's there. And we know you feel THAT, too.

PAGE 33

- Detail - The elevator doors open on . . .

    Lam will be like, now it's easy to give in to your demons.

    Gus will be like, it's hard to find your better angels. But we're asking you to. Because yes, this is a story about the fall of man.

    Lam will say, But it's also a story about our RISE. An R.O.M. story.

- (Almost SPLASH) Our BATCAVE — the base, similar to the one you showed in issue 2, back in the day, when Gus was caged here, but even more sleek and modern. There can even be a frozen demon or a demon in amber that mimics the dinosaur in the Batcave without being too obvious. But all the things you had in that base, but more here. A nicer waterfall, more coats of arms . . .

PAGE 34

- We see details of the place that underscore what Lam and Gus are saying.
    - o   The taxidermized or frozen in amber DEMONS, looking horrible.

        Lam will say, because every day, more and more of us give in, sure.

        Gus will say, but more and more of us are fighting back.

        Lam says, yep. In just one year there are more demons out there, yes, and what we've learned about them . . . what they did to other planets, where they came from, all the species, it could fill a library.

    - o   A glass screen with a global map with LOTS of red spots for Horn/Demons but also same map shows (not nearly as many) but SOME light spots for Halo/Glory bases.

        Gus will say, But how we've evolved too, the glories? We . . . have more members in more countries.

    - o   Punching bags and targets with demons crudely drawn on them. The targets are shredded.

        Lam chimes in, like – hey, and more money, too.

        Gus is like, So the time is now.

        Lam says, It is, because there ARE no happy endings. There's only the circle. The fight. It has gone on forever and will go on forever, but it's all there is. So find something to have faith in. Something bigger than yourself.

    - o   I'd love to show some badass vehicles if you can, if only a his and her motorcycle pair for Gus and Lam with helmets for them and his has holes for his horns. Or if this is too silly then we could do a badass car or monster truck with a license plate that says DMNH8R or something like that ☺.

        And here they'll make some jokey suggestions that call back to the book, like, Beyonce, 90's house music . . . etc.

        But then they get serious and say, but really. This is the moment. We need you. What do you say?

PAGE 35

SPLASH - We're with Lam and Gus, looking awesome, staring straight at us and if it doesn't seem hostile, they could both be giving us (and evil) the finger? ☺ Or if that feels too much they could just be looking badass, smiling, her leaning against him, etc., staring at us, grinning. On the table/desk in front of them, and being presented to us are BLADES! Amazing blades forged from the HALO meteor. All glowing for us! As for the office, it could have pictures of the other angels from the arc on the shelves/desk, and a couple pics of the two of them, Lam and Gus, making faces, being family. And Dad's AXE on the wall. And somewhere, a pic of him and mom Katherine and little Lam.

> Gus is like, Yeah?

> Lam is like, Great. Now pick your blade. And give evil the finger!

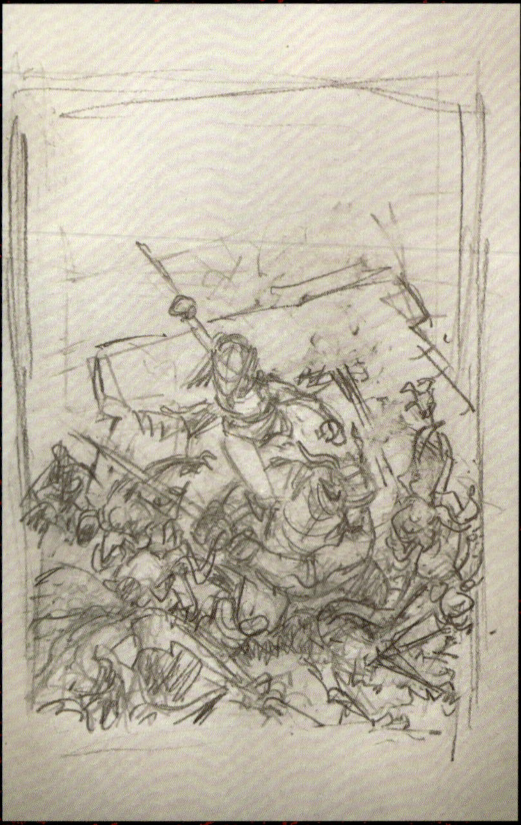

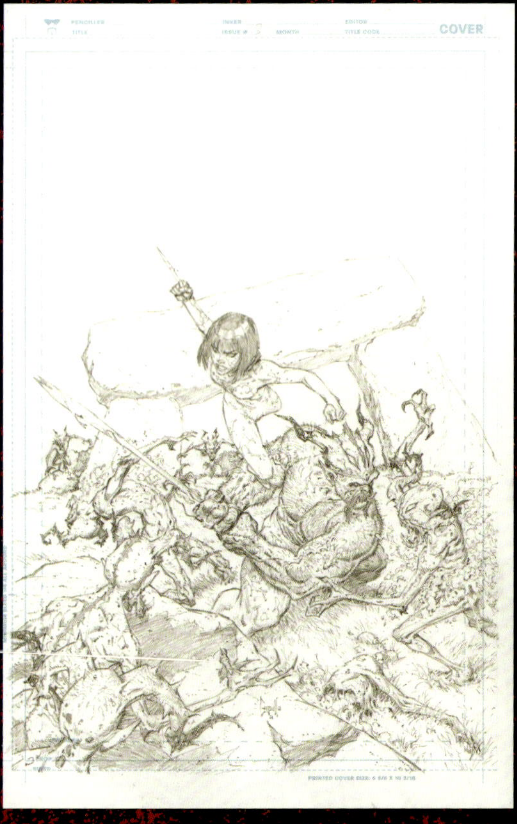
PENCILLER
TITLE
INKER
ISSUE #
MONTH
EDITOR
TITLE CODE
COVER

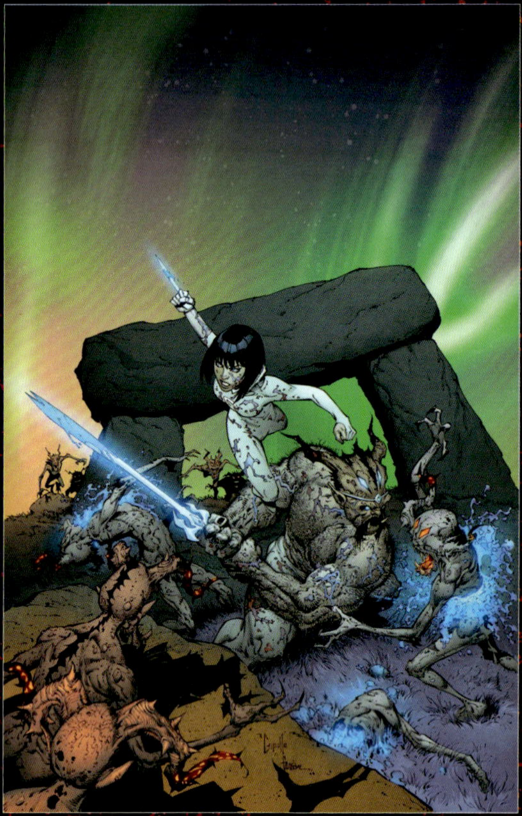

PENCILLER GREG CAPULLO
INKER JONATHAN GLAPION
EDITOR
TITLE WE HAVE DEMONS
ISSUE # 3
MONTH
TITLE CODE
COVER
MINIMUM BLEED 1/4 ALL AROUND
CROP
BLEED
PRINTED COVER SIZE: 6 5/8 X 10 3/16

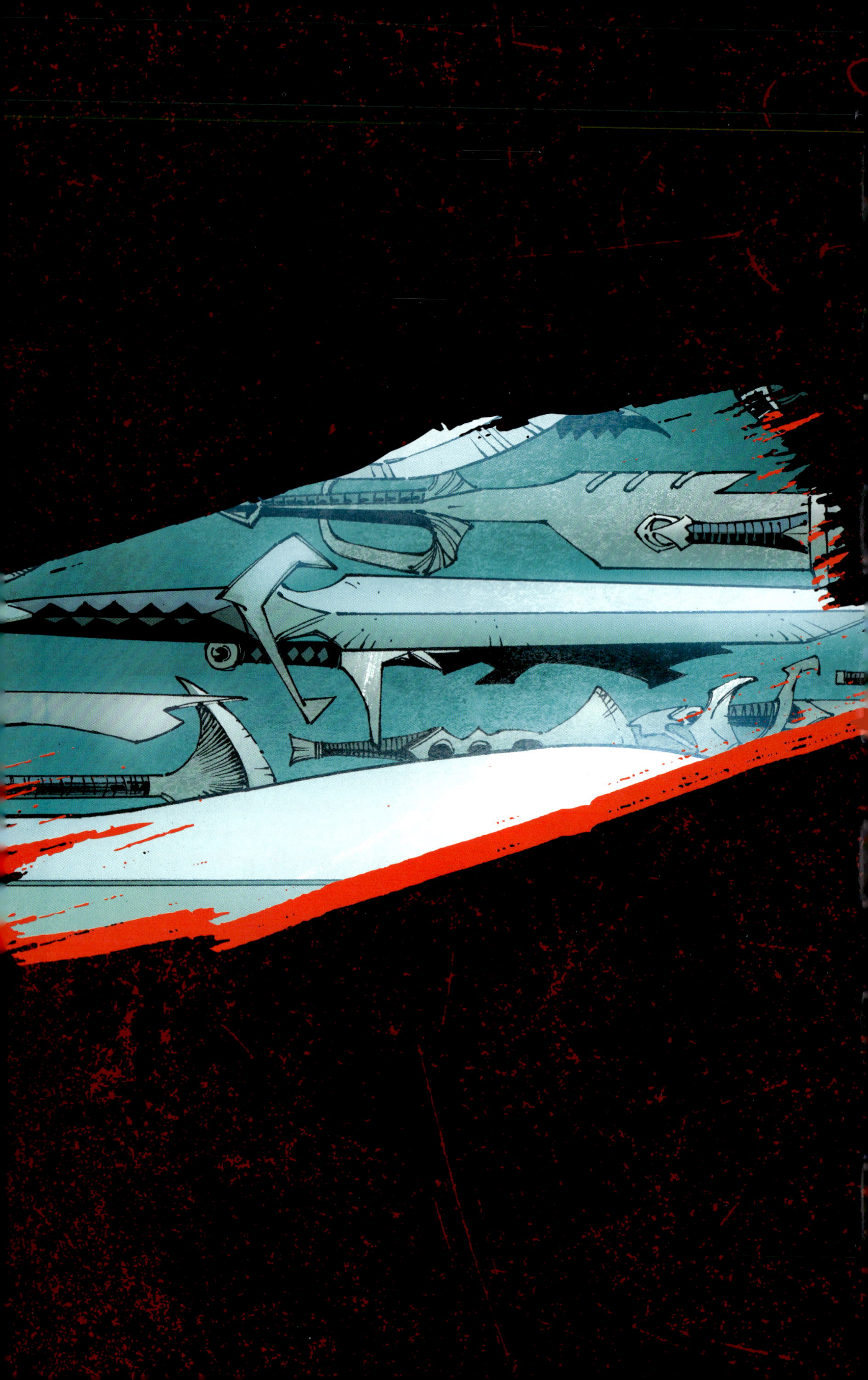

COMIXOLOGY COMES TO DARK HORSE BOOKS!

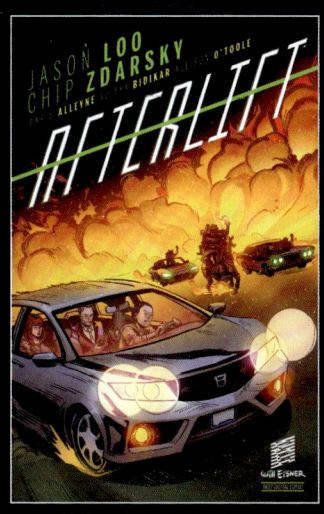

ISBN 978-1-50672-440-9 / $19.99

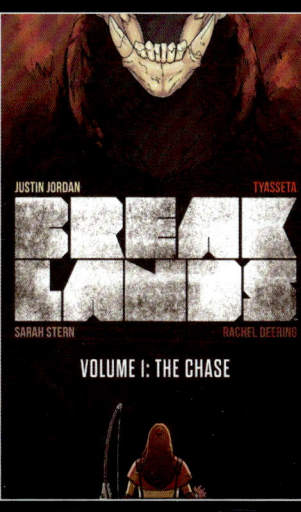

ISBN 978-1-50672-441-6 / $19.99

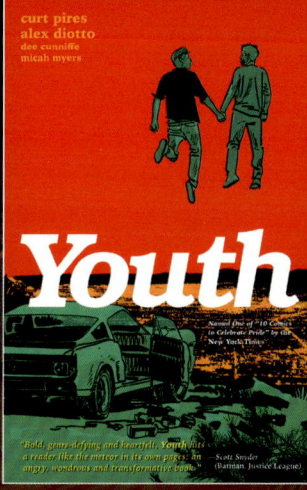

ISBN 978-1-50672-461-4 / $19.99

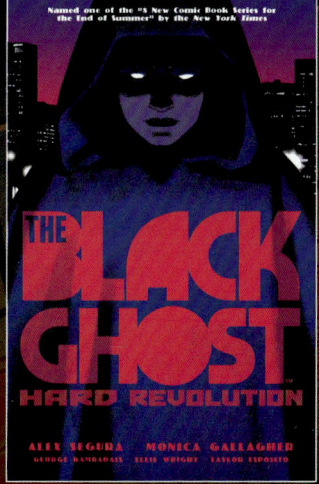

ISBN 978-1-50672-446-1 / $19.99

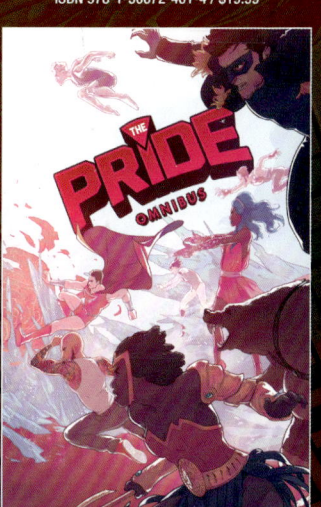

ISBN 978-1-50672-447-8 / $29.99

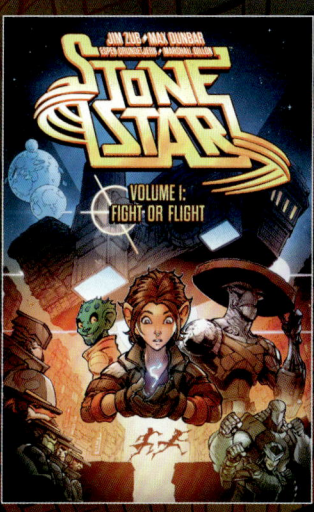

ISBN 978-1-50672-458-4 / $19.99

AFTERLIFT
Written by Chip Zdarsky, art by Jason Loo

This Eisner Award–winning series from Chip Zdarsky (*Sex Criminals*, *Daredevil*) and Jason Loo (*The Pitiful Human-Lizard*) features car chases, demon bounty hunters, and figuring out your place in this world and the next.

BREAKLANDS
Written by Justin Jordan, art by Tyasseta and Sarah Stern

Generations after the end of the civilization, everyone has powers; you need them just to survive in the new age. Everyone except Kasa Fain. Unfortunately, her little brother, who has the potential to reshape the world, is kidnapped by people who intend to do just that. *Mad Max* meets *Akira* in a genre-mashing, expectation-smashing new hit series from Justin Jordan, creator of *Luther Strode*, *Spread*, and *Reaver*!

YOUTH
Written by Curt Pires, art by Alex Diotto and Dee Cunniffe

A coming of age story of two queer teenagers who run away from their lives in a bigoted small town, and attempt to make their way to California. Along the way their car breaks down and they join a group of fellow misfits on the road. travelling the country together in a van, they party and attempt to find themselves. And then . . . something happens. The story combines the violence of coming of age with the violence of the superhero narrative—as well as the beauty.

THE BLACK GHOST SEASON ONE: HARD REVOLUTION
Written by Alex Segura and Monica Gallagher, art by George Kamabdais

Meet Lara Dominguez—a troubled Creighton cops reporter obsessed with the city's debonair vigilante the Black Ghost. With the help of a mysterious cyberinformant named LONE, Lara's inched closer to uncovering the Ghost's identity. But as she searches for the breakthrough story she desperately needs, Lara will have to navigate the corruption of her city, the uncertainties of virtues, and her own personal demons. Will she have the strength to be part of the solution—or will she become the problem?

THE PRIDE OMNIBUS
Joseph Glass, Gavin Mitchell and Cem Iroz

FabMan is sick of being seen as a joke. Tired of the LGBTQ+ community being seen as inferior to straight heroes, he thinks it's about damn time he did something about it. Bringing together some of the world's greatest LGBTQ+ superheroes, the Pride is born to protect the world and fight prejudice, misrepresentation and injustice—not to mention a pesky supervillain or two.

STONE STAR
Jim Zub and Max Zunbar

The brand-new space-fantasy saga that takes flight on comiXology Originals from fan-favorite creators Jim Zub (*Avengers*, *Samurai Jack*) and Max Dunbar (*Champions*, *Dungeons & Dragons*)! The nomadic space station called Stone Star brings gladiatorial entertainment to ports across the galaxy. Inside this gargantuan vessel of tournaments and temptations, foragers and fighters struggle to survive. A young thief named Dail discovers a dark secret in the depths of Stone Star and must decide his destiny—staying hidden in the shadows or standing tall in the searing spotlight of the arena. Either way, his life, and the cosmos itself, will never be the same!

AVAILABLE AT YOUR LOCAL COMICS SHOP OR BOOKSTORE / To find a comics shop near you, visit comicshoplocator.com / For more information or to order direct, visit darkhorse.com

COMIXOLOGY ORIGINALS

Afterlift™ © Zdarsco, Inc. & Jason Loo. The Black Ghost © Alex Segura, Monica Gallagher, and George Kambadais. Breaklands™ © Justin Jordan and Albertus Tyasseta. The Pride™ Joseph Glass, Gavin Mitchell and Cem Iroz. Stone Star™ © Jim Zub and Max Zunbar. Youth™ © Curt Pires, Alex Diotto, Dee Cunniffe. "ComiXology" and the ComiXology logos are registered trademarks of ComiXology. Dark Horse Books® and the Dark Horse logo are registered trademarks of Dark Horse Comics LLC. All rights reserved. (BL5108)

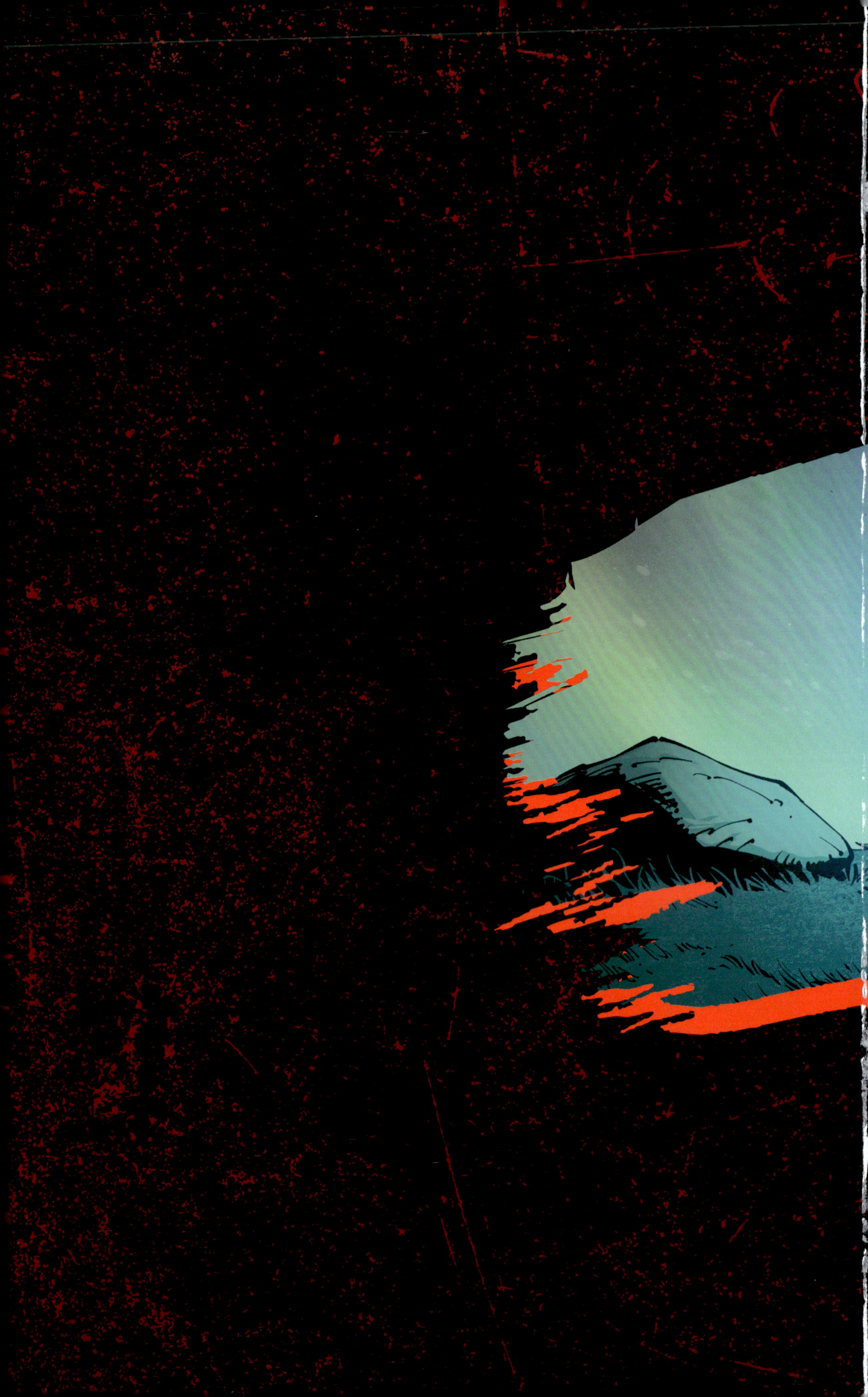

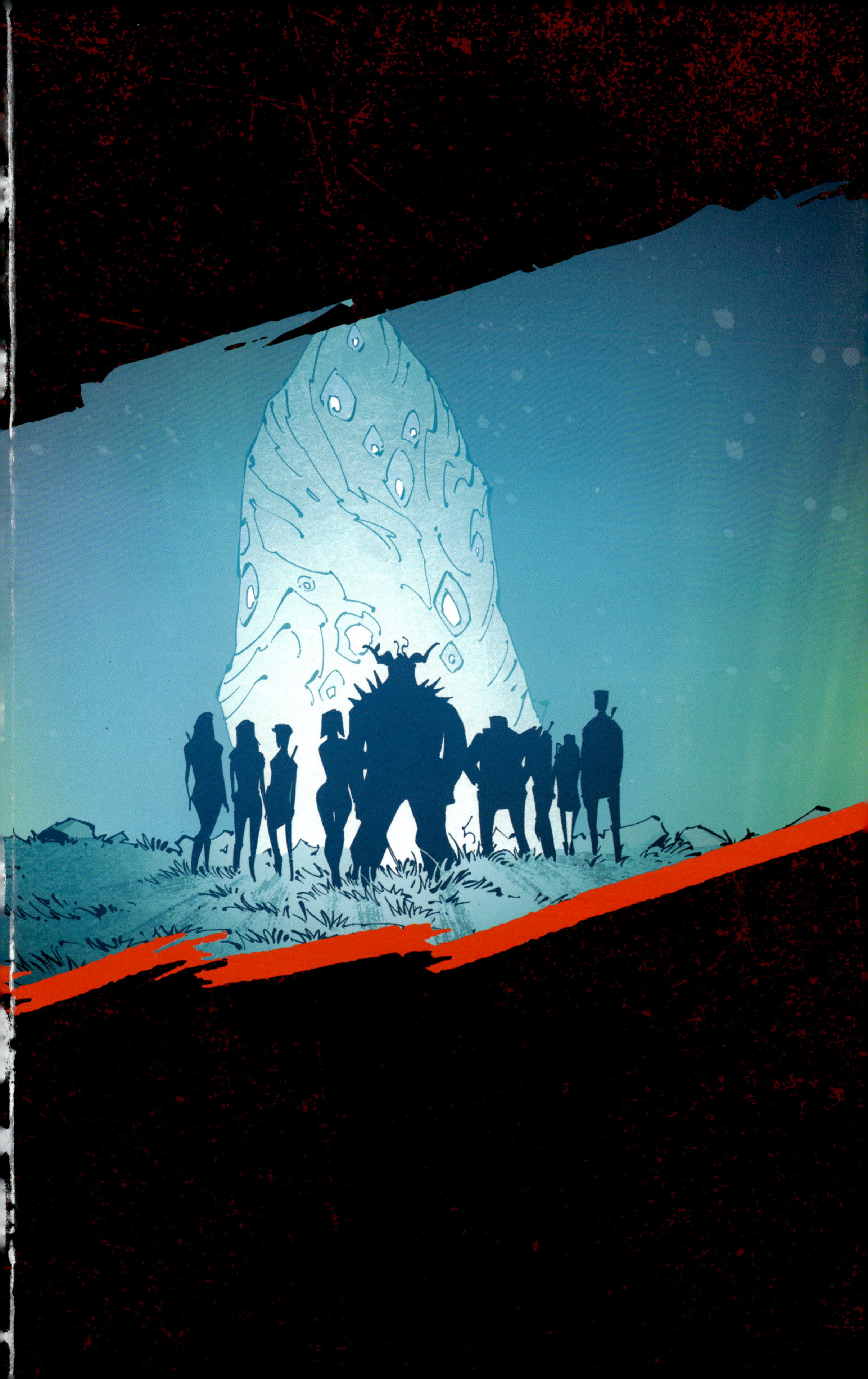

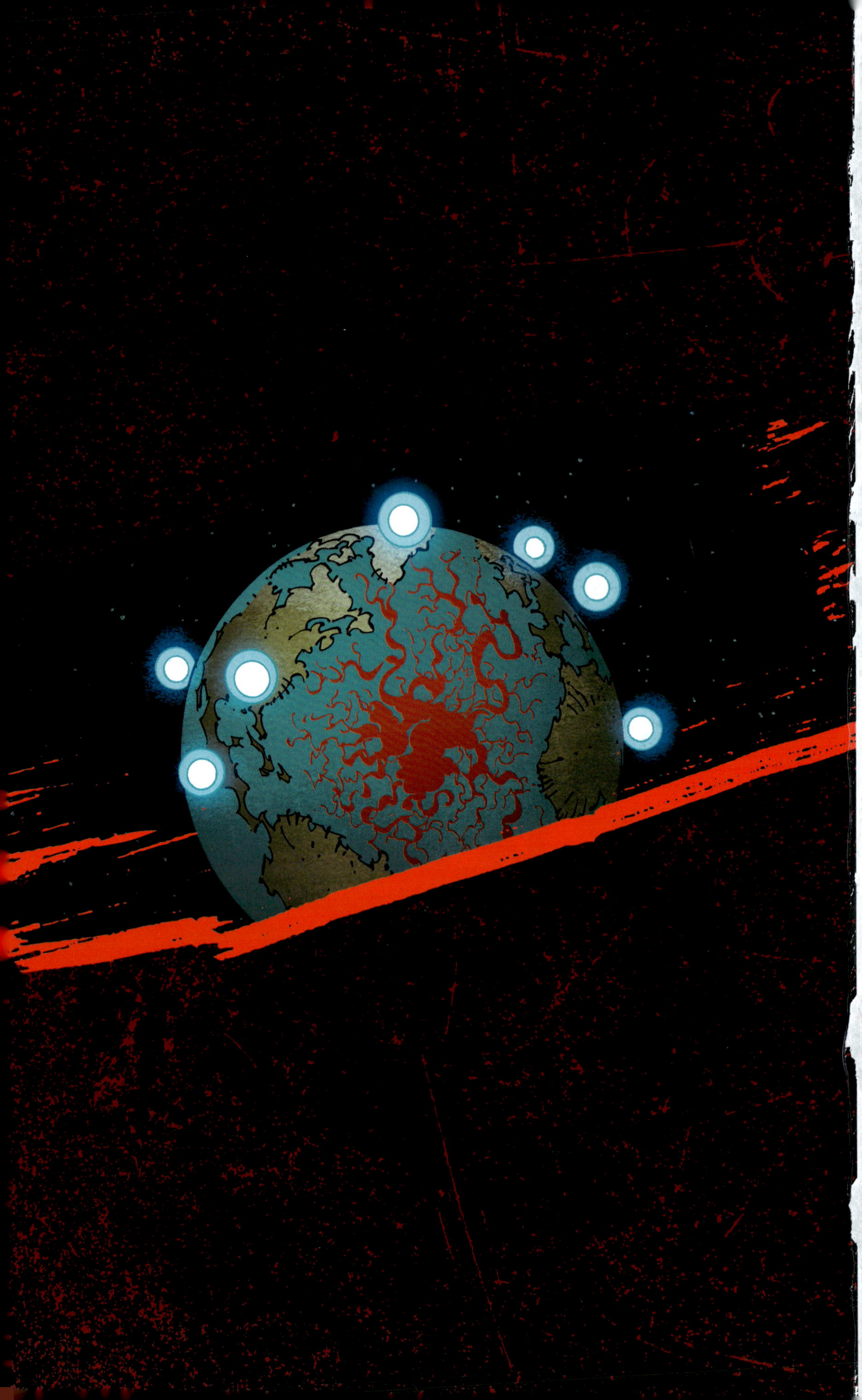